ADELAIDE T(

The first wagon wheels into the interior, shod in heavy bands of iron, a pair of their axles as tall as a man and more than five men could lift, changed forever the land over which they travelled.

Between the deepening wheel ruts, the hooves of the straining beasts trod a highway along which the wagons, loaded with wire and heavy gum saplings, groaned, lurching over dry creeks and gullies, skirting the ranges and salt pans. Walking beside the sweat and dust-streaked teams, the drivers cracked their great lengths of greenhide, crying out curses and encouragement. Outriders wheeled away to locate the springs reported by the explorers.

It was a journey of many months and difficulties. As the caravans increased in number at the Peake, John Ross and his explorers repaired their equipment, packing supplies and breaking in fresh horses. The unknown, this time, would begin for them where they had last time turned back.

The Longest Wire

HUGH ATKINSON

SPHERE BOOKS LIMITED
London and Sydney

First published in Great Britain by
Angus & Robertson Publishers 1982

Published by Sphere Books Ltd 1986
30-32 Gray's Inn Road, London WC1X 8JL

To Charlie, a longtime friend, and to Colleen, a new one.

TRADE
MARK

Set in 10/11 Plantin

Printed and bound in Great Britain by
Cox & Wyman Ltd, Reading

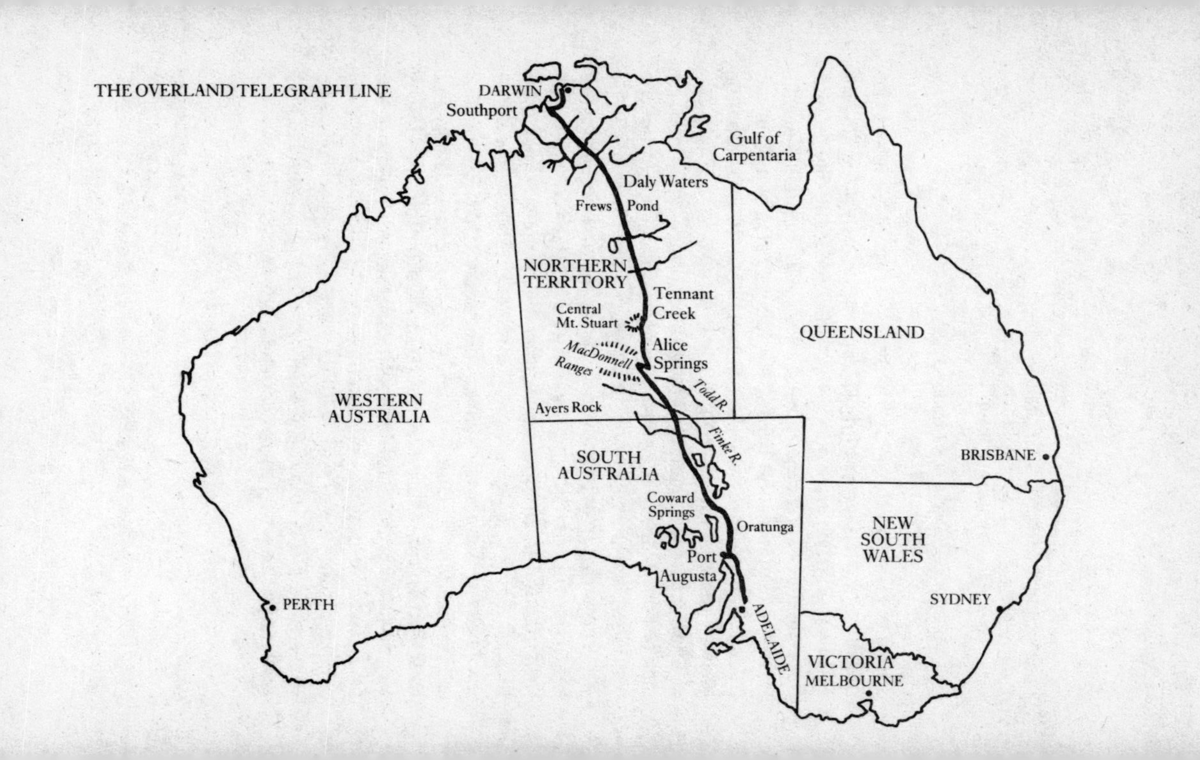
THE OVERLAND TELEGRAPH LINE
DARWIN
Southport
Gulf of
Carpentaria
Daly Waters
Frews
Pond
NORTHERN
TERRITORY
Tennant
Creek
Central
Mt. Stuart
Alice
Springs
MacDonnell
Ranges
Todd R.
QUEENSLAND
WESTERN
AUSTRALIA
Ayers Rock
Finke R.
SOUTH
AUSTRALIA
Coward
Springs
Oratunga
Port
Augusta
ADELAIDE
BRISBANE
NEW
SOUTH
WALES
SYDNEY
PERTH
VICTORIA
MELBOURNE

Author's Note

This novel, set in the early 1870s, has as its background the building of the Overland Telegraph Line between Adelaide and Darwin (then known as Palmerson), under the direction of Superintendent of Telegraphs Charles Todd. For much of that time, the explorer John Ross was leading a party of men in the tracks of his predecessor John McDouall Stuart, in an attempt to chart the best route for the longest wire.

The venture was hampered by water shortages and flood, by lack of knowledge of the terrain and by political opposition. It was aided by the bravery of such men as the Milner brothers, who succeeded in overlanding sheep for the first time from the south to the north, and by Charles Patterson, who was instrumental in completing the disaster-prone section of the line.

Charlotte Waters was named after Lady Charlotte Bacon, who resided in Adelaide for a few years in the early 1860s, and to whom Byron addressed the poem 'To Ianthe'. Sir James Fergusson was Governor of South Australia at the time of the Overland Telegraph's construction.

Apart from these historical facts, the main characters and events in *THE LONGEST WIRE* are fictional, and bear no relation to the actual history of its building.

One

It was Hannibal Harper's habit, after morning service on Sundays, to walk beside the Torrens in the company of his eldest son, young Hannibal, the one mentioned alongside his father on the sign above the coachshop.

The naming of Hannibal for his father had been almost unnaturally apt. He had favoured his father from birth and each year grew more in his image, being given to gravity, stability and utterances of impeccable common sense. When the two walked together, both bearded, their black ties folded identically into boiled white collars, dressed in the same good broadcloth, the one could be seen in the other, as alike as two different-sized peas in a pod. Even their shining pates reflected their similarities; old Hannibal's tall black hat covered a dome which had gone quite bald, and under young Hannibal's hat this inheritance had already wreaked havoc at the age of twenty-four.

The charming vista of the Torrens, grassed to the lips of its banks, with ducks paddling and showing their bottoms, pleased old Hannibal with the memories it evoked of rivers he had known at home in England. Modest, kempt rivers with gentle bends and tranquil reaches; not barbarous in behaviour like some Australian rivers he could mention.

On these Sunday strolls the elder Hannibal usually indulged himself with gratifying reflections both on his own prosperity and that of the growing young city which Colonel Light had founded little more than three decades earlier. Business sometimes required him to take ship for Melbourne and Sydney, and he found both cities inferior; the one second-rate, the other an offence to his sensibilities.

'Couldn't take my leave soon enough,' he would expostulate to his family on his return from Sydney. But what would you expect from a convict settlement which had 'just grow'd', as he put it, 'any old how, in misery and corruption'?

Old Hannibal was as contemptuous of Sydney as he was proud of Adelaide, the free settlement to which men of good, even aristocratic, family (like himself) had been drawn in the spirit of enterprise. Hannibal's hints about the nobility of his ancestors had become broader with his increasing wealth; the late Sir Henry Harper, who had commanded a corps under Wellington and who had been awarded a bronze medal in 1821, was now claimed as an uncle, although the distinguished warrior had been rather more distant in lineage than that.

After morning service, during which old Hannibal fervently thanked the Almighty for the financial gains of the past week, it had been his habit to discuss business with his son while the rest of the family returned home in the carriage. But this morning his attention faltered. His mind was on his twin sons, Matthew and Martin, whose birth nineteen years ago had almost cost him his wife, and whose behaviour ever since had caused him no little amount of anxiety and exasperation. Matthew, robust and fearless, was almost a man at nineteen and the very devil for trouble. Martin was his pale imitation, frail, a prey to every childhood illness, who nevertheless followed his brother unquestioningly into every bit of mischief that Matthew's febrile imagination could devise. Except at birth, when Martin, with Matthew already lusty and squalling in the midwife's hands, had shown no great hurry to follow his brother into the waiting world. And a scrap of a thing he was when he did appear, all black and blue from the doctor's forceps.

In their early years, old Hannibal had often scratched his head about the twins. Although identical, temperamentally they were only alike in their devotion to each other. And similarly they bore no likeness to either parent, nor anybody old Hannibal and his wife could conjure up on either side of the family. Although, to be sure, Matthew might have had something of Sir Henry Harper in him; he was adventurous enough and would undoubtedly have gone off to war, had there been a war to go to. Instead, there he was, away in the barbarous inland of Australia with the explorer John Ross, scouting in the tracks of John McDouall Stuart for a suitable route along which to string, of all things, an overland telegraph wire.

The mere thought of that outrageous scheme brought a flush of irritation to Hannibal's face. Why, the whole idea – building a telegraph line between Adelaide and Port Darwin, nearly two thousand miles long, through terrain that had taken the lives of Burke and Wills, and Leichhardt, and tried Stuart to the limit three times before he'd been lucky enough to struggle back from the northern sea – the whole idea was preposterous. Tens of thousands of poles to be erected across gibber plains and desert and swamps and jungle – it was lunacy, sheer lunacy, and the staggering sum of money involved in its construction would undoubtedly bring the colony to its knees.

Thus old Hannibal had fulminated at any number of Sunday dinners since the scheme had been proposed. Hadn't he himself travelled around Spencer Gulf to Port Lincoln from Adelaide as a young man? And hadn't that arduous journey been a mere picnic compared to this 'egregious piece of insanity', as one Member of Parliament had expressed it, and whose words old Hannibal had often quoted with relish? And he cut out of a Queensland newspaper, snorting loudly with appreciation, a cartoon showing little Charles Todd, the Government Astronomer and Superintendent of Telegraphs in Adelaide, riding in a chariot drawn by two white elephants, carrying a trident of three insulators on a telegraph post, followed by some blacks, a group of skeletal navvies, a giggling goanna, and the ghost of Leichhardt in the distance, waving his hand.

No one knew where the bones of Leichhardt and his party lay, nor how their deaths had come. Perhaps in the terrible torments of thirst, their flesh dehydrated to jerky by the inland sun. In his years at Port Lincoln old Hannibal had once come upon a prospector dying of thirst, dried away almost to the bone, with his tongue swollen to a purple mass that prised his jaws apart. Now he shivered at the memory.

Young Hannibal, cheroot firmly clamped between his teeth and oblivious to his father's preoccupations, turned and pointed with his cane. 'More residences being built, I see.'

'The finest houses in the finest city in all the colonies,' returned old Hannibal automatically.

But young Hannibal, his head back and his hand on his hip, frowned.

'I don't care much for the area. Eventually it will receive all the traffic to the port.'

The comment pleased old Hannibal.

'A most sensible observation. I once considered buying a block for investment, but decided against it for that very reason.'

He paused.

'Incidentally, I had occasion to speak with Mr Todd yesterday. He has, of course, had no dispatch from Mr Ross's party so soon, but I took the opportunity of telling your mother that he had said that the explorers were well and advancing steadily. It was like a tonic to her.'

'Martin's pining for Matthew, you know, Father. He's put up a map of the continent in their room, tracing Matthew's course north.'

Old Hannibal sighed.

'There's an unnatural bond between those two. If only Matthew had shown an inclination to join us in the business.'

'Matthew was born headstrong. Let us hope that this expedition will knock the nonsense out of him.'

'I pray for it,' said old Hannibal. 'Come, let us see if the carriage has arrived.'

Lucinda Harper had been excused church service on the grounds of a headache. She had been late to bed, having attended a performance of *Othello* at the Theatre Royal, and rashly accepting champagne afterwards. The *South Australian Advertiser* had devoted half a column to the visiting performance.

'Mr Bandmann's elocution,' the *Advertiser* advised, 'was exceedingly correct and effective, whether when pleading his cause before the senate, addressing his officers in command or reproof, lavishing expressions of affection upon his wife, bewailing in despairing and agonising accents his cruel and calamitous error, or making his dying appeal against any misconstruction of his conduct.'

Lucinda had been most interested to read the notice.

'Mr and Mrs Bandmann,' the *Advertiser* went on, 'were rapturously applauded and appeared several times before the curtain.'

Lucinda had also applauded, but if the truth were told, she had enjoyed much more the recent farce *Poor Pillicoddy,* which had been acted by a troupe led by a handsome Englishman from Drury Lane.

Lucinda sat in her teagown and waited on her headache, slighter than she had given her mother to believe, to ease. Even so, it was an inconvenience to be even slightly discomfited on this of all days, when her new friend Lady Charlotte Bacon was calling.

In looks, Lucinda favoured her mother. Her hair was almost blonde, with a natural wave that heaped becomingly under the brush. Her eyebrows were attractively arched, her cheekbones almost a distinction, and she had two fetching dimples.

Old Hannibal was a little unsure of Lucinda. Still unmarried at twenty-two, with a will of her own, she was always dashing about on horseback, getting herself involved, quite unnecessarily in old Hannibal's view, with other people's problems. The Old Bushmen's Home was one charity she favoured. That would have been acceptable enough, her father considered, if she had confined herself to raising funds, but Lucinda had taken to going there and spending hours with the rough old men who made it their final retreat.

'I'll not have that,' old Hannibal had told her.

'But you should hear some of their stories,' his daughter had replied.

Old Hannibal could well imagine some of their stories. He had known a number of old bushmen in his time. He knew of their fondness for the bottle, and of their habit of taking the wild Aboriginal women into their camps, and had stumped off to see his wife about it, who had taken to her bed again as a result.

Lucinda was tall, generously built, with fine swelling breasts and skin like her mother's, which gave off a translucent glow in certain lights. Now she fastened her pantaloons and arranged the corseted bodice before the cheval mirror, twitching her shoulders and bottom to get the cumbrous undergarments settled.

She had fitted the crinolette and adjusted the hoops when she heard the carriage and opened the casement window in time to see Mrs Harper being handed down. Catching sight of her daughter's naked shoulders leaning out in public view, Mrs Harper flushed, then quickly looked away lest the driver's attention be caught. But certainly she would have something to say when she got inside the house.

Lucinda retreated from the window and slipped on a new dress, made on a sewing machine, and trimmed with the ribbons, paste spangles and tinsel that were the very latest fashion in London, according to Lady Charlotte, who was only very recently from that city. Lady Charlotte was an earl's daughter, and not only that, had the distinction of being the very child to whom Lord Byron himself had addressed his lines 'To Ianthe'. What a sensation that had caused when Governor Fergusson, never discreet at the best of times, had let it be known at a reception! No one among Lucinda's acquaintances had failed to be impressed by this glimpse into the sophistication of aristocratic London society. What a fuss among the women, in the hunt for copies of Lord Byron's verse!

On the banks of the Torrens old Hannibal extracted the gold Hunter from his vest, frowning at what it told him.

'He was instructed to be early this morning,' he said of his coachman, replacing the watch and rearranging the heavy gold chain.

Old Hannibal had bought the watch and chain at the auction of a deceased estate in Sydney, and although that event was two years since, he was still not accustomed to the pomp of his timepiece. His head was buzzing a little today, what with his plan to buy up an undertaking business, his fretting about Matthew, and now Lady Charlotte coming, who was the born daughter of an earl.

'I'm told she has brought her three children with her on this visit.' he said to the horizon.

Young Hannibal blinked. He, who tended to keep one thought in his head at a time, had been reflecting on the subject of undertaking.

'Father?'

'Lady Charlotte Bacon. I wouldn't be surprised if her late husband left her a little short of money.'

He was finding that thought more than a little reassuring when the carriage came into sight.

In the Residency, the Right Honourable Sir James Fergusson, Bart., K.C.M.G., served himself China tea and waited on the arrival of Charles Todd. The Governor was still uncomfortable with his vice-regal duties, which irked his soldier's tongue and circumscribed his soldier's manner. Criticism had already been made of the Governor's outspokenness, particularly in the matter of this telegraph line which he had so strongly embraced.

But if male voices grumbled at him, there was little complaint from the females. Governor Fergusson was remarkably well favoured, with side-whiskers and handsome moustaches. A fine figure of a man, they considered, and well fitted to represent his sovereign in the colony.

Of course, the men could not help but be impressed with the Governor's military reputation. He had gone from Rugby and Oxford into the Grenadier Guards and had been in the Crimea in 1854. At the battle of Inkerman he had been wounded while repelling a Russian attack, and had subsequently led a charge, in fine disregard of his wounds.

Sir James put down his teacup and decided upon a brandy. His support of Charles Todd's telegraph line, while based partly on his soldier's love of adventure, also owed something to a deeper and more subtle vision. Almost everywhere the map was coloured red, Englishmen were at work laying marine cables and operating booster stations by which the politics and trade of the Empire were expedited in London. Every form of intelligence could be relayed to Westminster by the evocative clicking of Morse keys. The colonies, united by communication and linked directly with England, would stand firm in the face of the future.

Charles Todd, the diffident but capable Government Astronomer and Superintendent of Telegraphs, was motivated more by his love of science, Fergusson considered.

When the British-Australian Telegraph Company had been formed earlier that year, Charles Todd's vision of building a line across the continent seemed as if it was to become a reality. Now a firm date had been set by the company for the Overland Telegraph Line to meet the submarine cable being laid from Batavia in the East Indies. Failing completion on that date, a substantial forfeit would have to be paid. The line had not only to succeed, but it had to succeed within a time that had been estimated by guesswork, against who knew what unknown factors. All told, Sir James believed he could do with a brandy.

Everything now depended on Todd, whose slim shoulders had assumed a far greater responsibility at the age of twenty-nine than many men would know in a lifetime. Arriving with his seventeen-year-old bride at the colony in 1855 to take up his government appointment, Todd had since witnessed the linking of Sydney, Melbourne and Adelaide by telegraph. Indeed, he had supervised the Melbourne-Adelaide link himself. Now, of less importance to the Governor himself, but no doubt highly important to the people in question, the political careers of a number of men depended on Mr Todd's ability to complete his next project. And even at this early date, the building of the line was behind schedule.

'Enter,' Sir James called to a firm knock.

The double doors were opened to announce the subject of Fergusson's deliberations. Charles Todd came forward eagerly. There was little ceremony between the two men.

'The Premier is being much harassed by his Opposition, Sir James,' said Todd without preamble.

'And by certain members of his own Cabinet,' the Governor added dryly. 'Not everyone stands fast, Charles, when the shells begin to fall. But let us be seated.'

Todd polished his rimless glasses with quick movements that might have been evidence of nerves, but which were characteristic of the energy of all his gestures.

'I propose to make a trip north myself at the earliest opportunity, to review the realities of the situation at first hand.'

Sir James poured Todd a brandy.

'Ah yes,' he said. 'The realities of the situation.'

'We do have some guidance in the diaries of Stuart's crossing of the continent eight years ago,' said Todd quickly. 'And John Ross and his party are scouting ahead to map a route for the line. We must forget the lobbyists, Sir James, and concentrate on construction.'

Fergusson, perhaps a little more aware of the destructive possibilities of political infighting than Todd, nevertheless smiled.

'You can be sure, Charles, that any influence I can wield will be at the service of the Overland Telegraph.'

Todd picked up his glass.

'I thank you for that,' he said.

The house built by Hannibal Harper had become a valuable property as the city of Adelaide had grown and prospered. The local stone was excellent for construction, and, mottled in grain, lent a decorative appearance. A deep verandah, roofed in slate, ran around two sides, and roses and bougainvillea climbed the wrought-iron footing of its pillars. Old Hannibal took a deep satisfaction in the home he had created, and often reflected on the tent he and his young wife had first inhabited when they took up land at Port Lincoln.

The evening had chilled and logs flamed and spat in the fireplace. Reflections glinted in the gilt-framed, cupid-embellished mirrors, rivalling the glow of the polish on the fashionable heavy furniture.

The midday dinner had been a great success. Lady Charlotte had not put on the slightest side. Rather, she had chosen to flatter old Hannibal with her attention whenever he made one of his pronouncements.

Now he and young Hannibal drank their evening sherry and read their newspapers with some satisfaction.

Old Hannibal broke the silence suddenly. 'Those rascals of the 18th Regiment have staged a drunken brawl at Goodwood

Park. The sooner that lot is packed home to England the better.'

The remark appeared to be delivered to the air.

Hannibal's commentaries on the news of the day were a trial to the family although Mrs Harper had hardly heard a word in twenty years. Immediately old Hannibal launched himself into a pronouncement, two little trapdoors in her ears banged shut in a perfect seal.

'There are blackfellows camping behind the zoo. Don't understand why the council tolerates it. Useless creatures. They erect nothing permanent, know nothing of cultivation or the domestication of animals, or even how to wear clothes. Devoid of religion, of conscience, or any sense of responsibility. The council should drive them off.'

Young Hannibal frowned. He had something on his mind, and it had nothing to do with blackfellows. He didn't usually attend to gossip, but something had been troubling him for weeks, and it involved a conflict of duty and loyalty. But when jokes were made to your face, and about your own sister . . .

Old Hannibal said, 'The Attorney-General has proposed the second reading of the bill to amend the law of insolvency . . .'

'Father,' young Hannibal interposed, colouring at his sudden compulsion.

The old man was startled at the unaccustomed interruption, and showed his displeasure over his reading glasses.

'I must tell you that there's been some talk. About Lucinda. Not to put too fine a point on it, I should say, gossip.'

'What's that you say?'

Young Hannibal plunged ahead.

'She's been seeing a lot of Steven Woodrush. It appears they've been meeting secretly.'

'What's that?' old Hannibal repeated, half-rising in his chair.

'You know who Woodrush is, Father?'

'Of course I know who he is,' said old Hannibal impatiently. 'He's that protégé of the Bishop's. Been serving at St Paul's for years. Church orphan. What do you mean, Lucinda's been seeing a fellow like that?'

'That's the gossip, Father.'

Old Hannibal struck his newspaper a blow.

'Damned rot. Isn't the fellow about to be ordained?'

'I believe so, Father. But I repeat – that is the gossip.'

'Get me another sherry,' old Hannibal demanded. 'Where did you hear such a thing?'

'From friends. And from others at the club.'

'I've a piece of my mind to give to your friends, then.'

Old Hannibal lapsed into thought.

'Altogether too free in her ways, that miss, the way she gallivants about.'

He restored himself to composure with the sherry.

'Damned rot. Wagging tongues, with nothing better to do.'

Then another thought occurred to him. 'If your mother gets wind of this, she'll take to her bed for a month.'

Old Hannibal made a great display of returning to his newspaper, but the effort was unavailing.

'Steven Woodrush. Stuff and nonsense. That namby-pamby without a penny . . . your sister's on the Church Women's Fellowship. They've probably been discussing that between them.'

Young Hannibal raised an eyebrow. 'At the zoo?' he pressed. 'In the conservatory behind the cathedral? Out on horseback, Father?'

'What's that?' old Hannibal wailed, this time coming completely out of his chair, spilling the pages of the *Advertiser* about his boots.

'It's what I was told, Father.'

Old Hannibal put his head back and bawled for Lucinda.

'She went to her room to change,' said young Hannibal, searching nervously for a cheroot.

'I'll give her something to change.' Old Hannibal's dome had turned a most extraordinary colour. 'Instruct your sister to present herself, this instant.'

Two

It was a battered-looking exploring party, its horses no longer high-tailed, which found itself six weeks into the interior, and well north of the Peake. The Peake, South Australia's furthest outpost, was to become the supply depot from which the central section of the Overland Telegraph would be built. The wagons which were lumbering up from Adelaide now would consolidate the camp.

John Ross, chosen to lead the explorers because of his reputation as a bushman and because he had once before ventured north of the Peake, stood six feet tall. He was as rugged as a post of ironbark and, above a bushy beard, as bald as old Hannibal Harper. He had taken up quarters in the York Hotel in Adelaide while the expedition was being recruited, and had interviewed applicants there. Quite a number of Adelaide men had aspired to the honour of scouting out a suitable route for the Overland Telegraph Line, which had so caught at the imagination of the little colony. After Ross had decided on his man he'd ask a last question, looking down from his height, squinting from his sun-furrowed eyes.

'Are you sound in mind and limb? Can you live on bandicoot and goanna?'

His men had signed on for twenty shillings a week and the supply of three pairs of moleskin trousers, the same of boots, two hats, and a ration of belts, pouches, knives, pipes, tobacco and firearms.

The second-in-command, and the expedition's surveyor, was William Harvey from Glasgow, another Scot. The others were cattlemen from distant stations, or wanderers who had been out on other expeditions, probing for grass and water where holdings might be settled. These were Tom Crispe, Billy Hearne and Alfred Giles, bushmen all. Matthew Harper, barely a man, was the greenskin, and, in the beginning, Ross had been chary of him. He had told the others he would keep an eye on Matthew's style in the weeks before the Peake was reached. If he didn't measure up, he would be packed off home. But Matthew had been accepted by the bushmen, and was proud of that, and of the feeling of comradeship which had developed between them.

Now he rode easily in the long stockman's stirrups, very aware of the long-barrelled colt in his belt and the carbine at his knee in its bucket. Little Billy Hearne, riding beside Matthew, his weathered face looking as if it had been sculpted from saddle-leather, pointed to the horizon with his pipe stem.

'You see that there smoke, Matt? Now, what would an old hand, such as yerself, reckon on that being?'

Matthew thought it might be a bushfire in the porcupine grass.

Bill put his pipe back decisively between his teeth.

'That there's wild blacks, making talk. How they can tell about us at that distance, I'm dratted if I know. But them's smoke signals, what we call making yabber, so ter speak.'

Matthew felt a sudden thrill to his stomach. Would they meet wild blacks, the true myall blacks, who had never met a white man?

Billy Hearne reined his mount in closer, and his stirrup iron rang on Matthew's.

'The thing is, Matt,' he leaned towards him confidentially, 'did yer ever learn to catch a spear?'

Matthew felt it wiser not to answer. He was becoming familiar with Billy's sense of humour.

'What yer do is shape up like this.' Billy thrust an arm out, open-palmed.

'Then yer stare into the wild man's eyes. When they open up, somethin' 'orrid, yer go like this.' Billy dashed his arm across his chest and closed his fist, then leaned back in his saddle.

'Yer've caught that spear in full flight, right before it goes through yer gizzards.'

They rode on in silence, while Billy put a match to his pipe.

'The thing is,' he mused, 'there's them that never learn the trick.'

Matthew kept his eye on the little bushman and carefully maintained a neutral expression. Billy relented.

'Nay, boy,' he said. 'I've seen them wild men scamper at the first sight of horses. I've seen painted warriors project theirselves up trees with astonishing velocity. I'm only pulling yer leg.'

All the party except Ross carried Westy-Richards breech-loading carbines and the uncertain ammunition of skin cartridges, which had to be capped. Ross had rejected the carbine in favour of a pair of double-barrelled shotguns, one in the saddle bucket, the other wrapped in his swag.

Earlier that day, the leader had signalled a halt at a glisten of water, dismounting and going silently ahead to shoot wild duck, two of whose plump bodies now dangled behind his saddle. Later in the evening, coated in mud, buried in hot ashes, the birds would be deliciously cooked in their own juices, the feathers coming off together with the baked casing of clay.

The expedition had ridden due north all day, and the country, mostly well-grassed sandhills, had not varied until mid-afternoon, when they got into rough going. Ross stopped to deliberate on the wisdom of taking another tack. Tom Crispe and Alfred Giles voted to go on. In Tom Crispe's opinion, a straight line was still the shortest distance between two points, and, he further remarked, you could cut that up any way you liked.

John Ross leaned on the pommel of his saddle, deliberating. All that could be seen ahead, until the land dipped, was an arid plain of red flinty stones, some of them as alive in the sun as burning coals and as flat as if their Maker had hammered them. Ross looked at the sun, judging the time, and decided to go forward.

The country became rougher as the party advanced over the plain, until it seemed that all the stones in creation were spread as far as the eye could see, crowded so close together that they obliterated the earth. The riding horses laboured, the pack horses jibbed and bucked, and the men became absorbed in keeping them alert, lest they should go down on the stones and injure their knees.

'Yer can stick yer shortest distance,' Billy Hearne told Tom Crispe, who had begun to sweat, and wonder, like the others, when the gibber plain would end.

Showers of sparks were struck as the curved iron of the horseshoes came down on the flints. There was not a tree or a bush in sight, although a few blades of grass struggled up wherever the gibbers made room. The party toiled on while the day lengthened into late afternoon. Harvey, now leading, with no landmarks to take a bearing, repeatedly checked his compass.

Ross was beginning to worry. He regretted his decision. It would be a rough camp if they had to make it on the gibber plains, with a plague of stones under their backs to sleep on, and no wood for a fire or grass for the horses.

The men were quiet now, and Matthew watched their faces for some sign that would still his own apprehension. He felt the grip of the wilderness upon him as he had not done before, and began to fill with forebodings of what might lie before them. It struck him now, with a sudden jolt, that he was involved in something more than an adventure. Burke and Wills, experienced explorers, had died somewhere ahead. Leichhardt and all his party had been swallowed up and never heard of again. Matthew swallowed as his horse's hooves slipped and slid on the gibbers, and tried to contain his fear.

They came off the stones at last, with only a sliver of sun left and that fast sinking in a blaze of red. The stones had come to a sudden end in dry country which nevertheless was a welcome sight to the band of men. They dismounted and eased the smalls of their backs with their hands, stretching out the stiffness of the long haul, grunting at each other and smiling now at the prospect of a reasonable camp and some cropping for the horses, however meagre. In the last light John Ross discovered a dry creek bed, where, digging in the sand, he found water. It was dark by the time enough wood was found for a fire and the ducks put in the hot ashes.

'Shortest bloody distance,' snorted Billy Hearne at Tom

Crispe again. 'Next time we come on country like that, we bloody ride around it.'

'We got across,' Tom Crispe answered. 'You never know what we might of struck going around.'

'Poppycock,' Billy said. But his heart was not in the argument. 'How are them ducks progressing? Me belly's beginning to think me throat's cut.'

Later, long after the others had begun to snore, Matthew lay staring up at the navy blue dome above him, almost as crowded with stars as the plain had been with stones. He'd never before seen such a sky, and he wondered at it. There was only one sky to cover all beneath. The stars in it were fixed in their numbers. How then could this sky be so different? How was it that this sky could sparkle and gleam with stars from horizon to horizon, when there had never before seemed so many?

It was almost as though the stars had come to breed in this savage isolation. Matthew had been afraid, out on the gibber plain, and now he felt ashamed for it, but all the same he was glad that the men snored around him and that there were still embers alight in the fire. He thought of home and his family, and particularly of Martin, and a sudden pang of loss was magnified by the overwhelming loneliness of the tiny camp under the stars.

He had first been reminded of home the day before, when Ross had made a stop to boil the billy. As they drank their tea, Alfred Giles had got out his diary and licked at the pencil.

'Sunday dinner,' he announced. 'We ate salt beef and damper. Tom Crispe has a lizard up his trousers and doesn't know it.'

Tom had jumped up, knocking over his pannikin, shaking out his trouser legs, swearing hard at Giles. There was no lizard.

The men guffawed. But Matthew had been reminded of Sunday dinners at home, which had always been an occasion, with huge roasts of beef on silver serving dishes and wine on the sideboard for his father to pour for the guests. His father would make a great ceremony of the carving, and Matthew and Martin, sitting by tradition opposite each other at the bottom of the table, would wink at each other as he made pronouncements on the quality of the meat and the wine.

While humouring his father in his opinions, Matthew had always gone entirely his own way. Old Hannibal had wanted him to enter the business as bookkeeper, because of his head for figures, but Matthew had perversely chosen to work in the forge after leaving school. He was glad of that now, he reflected. It was there that he had built up his muscles.

He wondered if Martin was thinking of him now, if Martin could imagine such a night in the wilderness. Martin had always been strangely perceptive, a phenomenon that Matthew had often pondered upon. Once when Matthew was sick at home with fever, Martin had come back early from a visit to school friends in the country, although no word had been sent to him. Somehow he had known. Mathew had recovered, but he realised then that Martin had always seemed to know his every thought and feeling.

A star fell, spattering down the sky and burning out suddenly. Matthew shifted into a more comfortable position. He closed his eyes. He'd be willing to bet that Martin knew he'd been thinking of him.

The camp was up shortly before dawn, to breakfast on tea and cold damper. Sitting on their haunches around the fire, they were a subdued group. Six weeks into the interior, they had all, with the exception of John Ross, grown thinner. Ross, already whip-cord lean, had remained the same. The men's eyes had also altered, the expression in them changed as though the mute landscape had imposed its own timelessness on their vision. And their voices were softer and more patient than they had been among the competing sounds of civilisation.

Matthew, now bearded like the others, had taken in several notches on his belt. Sun-blisters roughened his lips and the blade of his nose was mottled with sun-spots. His arms were darkened to a deep tan to the rolled-up sleeves.

Getting up from the fire, Tom Crispe, still heavy with sleep, went to prepare the pack horses to move on. Speaking quietly to the animals, he suddenly stopped still, puzzled. Then he cursed loudly. Old Paddy, a cob of great cunning, was gone, despite his hobbles.

Ross called Matthew to him. The boy was to look lively and find the beggar, before he went too far and the heat of the day was upon them again.

Two miles out from the camp, Matthew could find no trace of the cob, nor for that matter any living thing. He stared about him in wonder. Nearby a great sand dune was humped against the sky, with thorn bushes struggling to raise their growth above its folds. It was coloured a startling red, striated with pink scars of erosion, and it formed a line as sharp as if drawn by a fine-nibbed pen against the horizon.

Unaccountably, an uneasiness began to swell in him, becoming so nearly panic that he had to rein in his horse to compose himself. He stared at the sand dune. It burned fiery red against the blue. Even the flat, stolid leaves of the saltbush and the wriggling tendrils of thorn seemed to pulsate with colour in the clear air. His ears began to pound, and the heart that he'd never consciously heard before beat loudly. He held tightly on to the saddle.

Then it came to him.

It was the silence. The immemorial silence of this empty, unlived-in space. The realisation flooded his mind. A silence so intense, almost a vacuum of sound, that he was able to hear his own heartbeat. He shouted aloud in his relief, and his voice seemed to go out into the air like something hunted, reverberating among the dunes.

A short time later, he found old Paddy cropping saltbush in massive meditation. The party was ready to travel when Matthew got back to the welcome sounds of the camp, the voices and the creak of the saddles and the packs.

All that day they rode among sandhills, some so immense that the party had to skirt around them. Towards evening they came upon sandflats, well covered with mulga and herbage, where a small, astonished group of blacks fled in alarm at their approach. Ross instructed the party to dismount. The blacks could still be seen, hiding in the bushes, popping up their heads. Approaching them quietly, Ross returned with a trembling boy to whom he gave a little sugar. The boy inspected the grains on the palm of his hand as though they might be alive. Taking some sugar in his own hand, Ross licked it, indicating that the boy should do the same. With some suspicion the boy followed suit, until his dark eyes flashed with pleasure and he heaped the remainder of the crystals into his mouth.

Then the boy called something unintelligible into the bushes, and a well-built youth strode out, perfectly naked, his hair in long ringlets tied behind his head. He too was offered the sugar. Before long, the lubras came shyly forward as well. The young ones were well formed, but there was one old woman of such surpassing ugliness that Billy Hearne appeared transfixed.

'Saw a hoorang-hootang once,' Billy commented, 'in an entertainment at the port. That monkey were a raving beauty, fit ter turn any man's head, compared to whatever this 'n is, standing here bold as brass.'

Going to his saddle Billy took out a looking-glass and showed the old lady her reflection. With a grunt of alarm, she started back at this first sight of herself. But then, gaining courage, she looked again, her eyes popping in amazement.

It was an excitement to Matthew to see his first 'wild' blacks, and a comfort that they appeared so docile.

'Gawd knows what they think of us,' Billy said. 'We must look like something fell outer the sky.'

The expedition pushed on, and three more camps were made. But the going was hard and the horses were starting to knock up. Yet the party still ate well: kangaroo steaks one day, a big bush turkey the next, felled by Ross from the saddle with his shotgun. After the third camp had been struck the tracks of wild blacks began to appear as thick as a sheepwalk. In the hope of finding a native well, Ross followed the tracks and came upon two wurleys which had been built on a dry creek bed. The blacks had evidently taken to their heels, leaving their fires smouldering and an assortment of wooden vessels behind them, some containing berries, others a kind of yam. Near the wurleys, there was a seepage dug in the creek bed. Tom Crispe deepened it with a short spade, and as the hole filled with water, the horses drank until their bellies expanded.

But now Ross was becoming concerned at the scarcity of trees. Without trees it was obvious there could be no telegraph poles. Ross and William Harvey sat long over the camp fire, plotting a new course to the east in the hope of finding timber.

The next day, low ranges appeared up ahead and Ross rode directly towards them, finding the trees he sought, a species of oak with straight trunks running twenty feet up before breaking into the lower branches. Harvey took the bearings which would be recorded in dispatches to guide the Overlanders who would follow. He and Ross climbed a low peak and, glimpsing a glittering in the distance, instructed Tom Crispe to ride out and put up a smoke if it proved to be water.

Before long a welcome curl of smoke went up in the sky and the men smiled and nodded to each other. But it proved to be more than water. It was an oasis. A fine lagoon, filled by recent storms, sheltering ducks and cranes on its water and flocks of pigeons in its surrounding trees. Getting the smell of water, the pack horses tried to bolt. The men, touched by the same excitement, splashed into the lagoon as they arrived, laughing, filling up their hats and emptying them over their heads. No more short water rations, at least for a while.

Later, refreshed, Tom Crispe and Matthew went hunting with the shotguns, bagging a number of plump pigeons and a couple of cockatoos. That night Alfred Giles cooked cart-wheel dampers for the next stage, and John Ross declared a rest-up the next day in celebration.

Then Billy Hearne, who had gone off wandering, came back to the camp with a piece of a blue shirt which he had found hooked on a tree in an old Aboriginal camp. The blacks had sewn it in places with twisted human hair, but one of its tears was mended with thread. The men passed the piece of cloth about and became quiet with speculation. A leaving of the dead Burke and Wills, passed from tribe to tribe? The only known trace of Leichhardt and his party? The men fingered this ragged testimony to the unknown, each given pause by his own thoughts.

'Drat the thing,' said Billy Hearne at last. He rolled it into a ball and hurled it into the bushes.

During the rest at the lagoon the men's voices rose again in timbre, and some of the haunted look went from their eyes. Ross got out a hitherto carefully-concealed bottle of rum. Alfred Giles, the educated one, noted the finding of the bit of blue shirt in his diary.

Harvey, the surveyor, didn't have much campfire talk, but even he seemed to find some inspiration in the lagoon.

'I canna' say I've seen the flooers I've heard talked about. Lilies as big as dinner plates, I've been told, and a profusion o' wee ones, too, in every colour o' the rainbow, they say.'

Tom Crispe said, 'It's right enough. I've seen them myself. But now, that might be in a season of a few weeks, and then over, and never the same again.'

'The seeds bide their time, Will,' said Ross. 'They're like the seeds found in the tombs of the Pharaohs. Tomb seeds have sprouted after a thousand years in the blackness. They might surprise you yet.'

Because of the number of human tracks around the lagoon, Ross declared two-hour watches, in case of unfriendly blacks. The blacks could be hostile, unpredictable, if encountered in big enough groups, in the Scot's experience. Tom Crispe, the first watch, a carbine cradled in his arms, spoke to Matt in the darkness.

'Enjoy it, Matt. Only the good Lord knows what might lie ahead.'

In the days following the rest-up, their time at the lagoon began to seem like a mirage. The country again became rough and arid. The horses suffered in the waterless spells, and although there was some grazing, the flesh began to fall off their bones. A continuous torment of swarming black flies stretched the men's tempers. They had to ride in fly-veils, and their horses could hardly see through the clusters around their eyes, or breathe through those seemingly glued around their nostrils. There were clouds of them at each animal's head, crawling inside their lips as they panted in the heat.

Each man's back was black with a swarm of them, and eating and drinking became a tortuous operation. Drinking, they lifted the fly-veils for only an instant; eating, they coughed and choked on the flies that flew into their mouths.

Night brought no relief. When the bushflies had settled, the mosquitoes came out, and the smoke of smudge fires built around each bedroll barely affected the ferocity of their attack. The men's skins became blistered with tiny, suppurating sores; under their veils their faces puffed up in a distemper of itching bites.

There was little to eat now and nothing to drink. The men rode hunched and bent, with few words passing between them, sucking at pebbles to keep some saliva on their tongues. The horses stumbled repeatedly, as did the men when they clumsily got down from the saddles. They did not share their thoughts. Matthew's heart hammered as he recalled some of Tom Crispe's stories. One story deeply etched on his mind was that of the stockman at the Peake who had found the bodies of two gold prospectors, horseless, but with saddle-bags filled with congealed blood. Finding themselves without water the two had cut their horses' throats and filled their saddle-bags with blood, forgetting in their delirium that the blood would solidify. And then Tom's other story about a skeleton, discovered a few hundred yards from a lake, with a last message for the dead man's wife in a notebook. The letter said that all the water tried for had turned out to be a mirage, and now he was dying with a last mirage in front of his eyes.

Tom rode alongside Matthew.

'There'll be water soon, Matt,' he encouraged. 'Just stick it out.'

But he had to work at his tongue to say it.

Blacks had started to appear, big fellows and apparently hostile, waving spears at the party and making much noise among themselves. Reluctantly, John Ross fired his shotgun in the air, and they ran off. But, stopping at a distance, they raised their spears in token gestures of threat, and made a warlike clacking of them against their throwing woomeras.

It was Billy Hearne who found the water that saved them. In the approach to a gorge, he came upon a native well, sunk in the sand, full of cold, clear water that replenished itself as it was used. Alfred Giles, with a quart-pot in his hand, recovered a little and pointed to the cliff face.

'See that up there? If that were solid gold I wouldn't change it for this quart of water.'

The horses had been without water seventy-two hours. The men had not wet their lips in two days, in an oven of merciless heat. Now both men and horses drank greedily. That night a pack mare foaled, aborting out of weakness. John Ross shot both mare and foal with his revolver, leaving the bodies where they lay.

The expedition was five hundred miles north of the Peake, by William Harvey's reckoning. Ross now decided that when the men were rested and had regained some strength, it was time to attempt their return. With their meagre supplies it was impossible to go further inland. He had mapped a route, and he had found some stands of good timber. It was enough, for this time anyway.

Matthew had many thoughts running through his head that first night after the finding of the water. The privation had hardened him. But the bonds of comradeship among the men had become doubly dear to him. He hardly recognised himself as the stripling he had been in Adelaide. He whispered, 'We got through, Martin,' before he fell finally asleep.

The long ride back had its share of hardship. Before the Peake was reached the explorers were out of meat, tea, sugar and tobacco. Damper and water were all that remained. The first evidence of civilisation as the exhausted party rode in was a deserted collection of stockyards. Those disordered timbers, shaped by white hands, appeared to them as significant as a cathedral.

Three

In Adelaide, while Matthew was returning to the Peake, old Hannibal had found it prudent to alter his attitude to the Overland Telegraph Line, and no longer held forth about it to guests at dinner. The cause for this new-found reticence lay in the recent securing, by young Hannibal, of a contract for the rebuilding of all the shaky wheels and axles on the overland transport vehicles. New hands were hard at it in the wheelwright and forge, and old Hannibal fairly strode on his Sunday walks by the Torrens.

J.A. Holden Esq., of Holden's Saddlery, Gawler Place, had his own cause for satisfaction. He had long been an enthusiastic supporter of the Overland, as it had come to be known, being distinctly more far-sighted in his self-interest than old Hannibal, and had recently gained the contract for the making of hundreds of sets of harness, headstalls, reins, saddle girths, canteens, collars, straps, satchels, revolver holsters and rifle buckets. Now, when the two men met, and J.A. Holden slapped old Hannibal's back and asked him what he thought of the Overland these days, it was hard for old Hannibal to stomach his rival's evident satisfaction.

'Yes, siree. It's going to be the making of this colony,' he would say, twitching his dense eyebrows, where more hair grew than did on the whole of old Hannibal's scalp. 'Of course, there were those who didn't think so. There were those who wouldn't recognise a gift-horse if it kicked them up the backside.'

Unable to invent any useful reply, old Hannibal would stamp away, his dome suffusing with colour and his mind with even more colourful thoughts.

At night, in the big attic room he had shared with Matthew since childhood, Martin often started awake in a sweat of fear for his twin out in the wilderness. But his cry would die away on his lips as he stared wildly around the room, the neatly drawn counterpane on his brother's bed seemingly mocking the disorder of his thoughts.

If Martin had never been able to rival his brother's personal appeal, nor assume the easy command that he exercised over his fellows, he possessed a quiet inner strength that Matthew lacked. In the many scrapes that Matthew had got himself into at school (and indeed out of it, with that sorry business of the girl at the Port), it was always Martin to whom he ran for counsel. On these occasions a calm would come over Martin and he would probe at Matthew's blusters, evasions and rationalisations, more like a father than a brother, while Matthew would twist and turn like a hounded rabbit rather than admit to error.

All the same, Martin sorely missed the lively company of his twin.

In his father's business, Martin was responsible for the purchase of all materials for the forge, and for the presentation of a situation report each week to Hannibal the younger. Martin's methodical brain coped easily with the tasks, and his visits to the forge, where communications were shouted over the dinning of metal and the fierce red heat, provided a welcome distraction from the tedium of his daily routine.

Recently, he had begun to observe with interest a new striker, a man much spoken about amongst the others. His face, neck and arms were pitted with the scars of smallpox, and Martin had been compelled to shift his attention elsewhere the first time he saw him, his face seemingly ablaze, the scars livid, in the blast of the furnace.

'A Yankee whaler, name of Solomon,' he had been told. 'A harpooner, they say, before he threw in his lot with the Yankee sealers on Kangaroo Island.'

Martin had never met a Yankee, particularly a Yankee harpooner. Kangaroo Island, south of Adelaide, had been a base for American whalers and sealers even before the free colony had been settled, but they were more talked about than seen in Adelaide. Martin was curious about the stranger from his first day in the forge.

Now, as the Yankee swung the shaping hammer, bending the hot metal across the anvil, knotted cords of muscle writhed across his neck and shoulders. Martin could imagine him balanced in the bow of a whale chaser, the stocky body poised to hurl the bolt of the harpoon. As he watched furtively, marvelling at the accuracy of the striker's blows, the American unexpectedly caught his eye. The pitted face smiled and winked, but with such warmth and generosity that Martin flushed, startled, before he smiled in return. For the remainder of the day the smile stayed in Martin's thoughts, warming him.

Late that afternoon Martin, having delivered his report, lingered in his elder brother's office. Young Hannibal was smoking a cheroot and obviously feeling on good terms with himself. He was wearing celluloid cuffs over his white shirt sleeves.

'Is there something else, Martin?' he asked amiably.

'I was just wondering about that American in the forge. The one the men call Solomon.'

'What is there to wonder about?'

Martin began to feel a bit of a fool.

'I just wondered what you might know about him.'

'The foreman speaks well of the man. Have you heard something to the contrary?'

'No,' Martin hesitated. 'I suppose it was just curiosity.'

'Curiosity killed the cat,' Hannibal told him. 'Now be off with you, I'm trying to finish up.'

In the mid-afternoons the apprentice brewed tea, heavily sweetened with condensed milk and sugar, and handed out rock cakes which the workers bought for a penny. All the next day Martin waited for this break.

Solomon was sitting on a bench, wiping his face with a sweat rag, when Martin entered with his stock sheets clipped to a board, and busied himself checking equipment and stores. He could feel the American observing him, and eventually felt compelled to steal a glance at the man.

His face crinkling again into that rare and marvellous smile, the striker patted the bench beside him invitingly. Martin felt uncertain; after all he was 'Master Martin' to the workmen, and not encouraged to patronise them by his father.

Hesitantly he crossed the forge and sat down on the bench. He tried to appear at ease.

'When the forge battens down,' Solomon said, touching an ear, 'it takes a man time to get his hearing back. I heard on the wind that you used to have a brother working here.'

'That was Matthew.'

'And you'd be Martin, in the articles, as you might say. I'm known as Solomon.'

'Is it Mister Solomon?' Martin asked.

'As to that now, would it increase the understanding? Solomon is name enough, and a weighty one to bear. If I had a lay of Solomon's wisdom, I wouldn't be striking at a forge at the bottom of all the world.'

The boy forgot his shyness, and Solomon's damaged face.

'Is it true that you harpooned with the whalers?'

'Aye, lad, a harpooner I was. And a forger of harpoons, fit to split the leviathan. And a boatsteersman before that, when first we came into the southern oceans.'

Martin was fascinated by the strangeness of the other's accent and speech.

'What was it like on the southern seas? Have you not been home again since?'

'Taking first things first,' Solomon said, knocking out his pannikin, 'there's good and bad in the southern seas, which is the way God made men and the world. I've seen cannibal islands and I've shipped with crews no better than savages.'

Solomon touched at the pits in his face.

'I got these in the Sundra Straits, on a whale ship stricken by the pox. And well it might have been God's judgement.'

Solomon looked into the glare of the furnace and his mouth tightened for an instant at the memory.

'As for home, now,' he said, his expression changing again as he turned to Martin. 'I've seen home since, although before that it was four years at sea hunting the sperm.'

He touched Martin's knee.

'I prate on, lad. It's a habit of Solomon's. Now I must be up and bear a hand. But not without a thank'ee for your company.'

After that, Martin was drawn frequently to the forge to hear

Solomon recount his tales. In his bedside drawer he kept a whale's tooth, hung from a necklet, which Solomon had presented to him. The outline of a New Bedford whale ship was scrimshawed on the tooth, and the necklet, Solomon said, had been plaited from human hair.

At the Peake, John Ross camped for some weeks, resting his men and refitting his equipment after the trials of the first exploration. In that time more wagons came up from the south, some loaded with general stores, some with extensions on them for the telegraph poles that were to be carried into the treeless country, some loaded with wire. A caravan of a hundred camels arrived, treading the baked earth with their soft, splayed footfalls, belching and grumbling as they slowly folded themselves on to the ground in response to the guttural cries of their Afghan masters. As the new wagons arrived and the bullock teams were unyoked, the camp spread far over the plain.

John Ross found Matthew with the camels, putting out a hand to pat a supercilious muzzle. The tall Scot squinted at the boy and, from habit, pulled at his beard.

'Do you know how the beasties are called, Matthew?'

Matthew didn't know.

'The ships of the desert.' Ross got out his pipe. 'You've seen a wee bit of desert yourself, laddie. How think you now about ganging awa' exploring?'

Matthew said that it had been a great – a wonderful – experience.

'Aye, there is a wonder abiding in it. Are you for getting home then, to your ain folk?'

Shifting about a little, while his leader waited, Matthew swallowed at this reference to what was uppermost in his mind. He had deliberated long about it on the journey back to the Peake.

'I'd like to go out again, Mr Ross. If you will have me.'

'I'm proud to have you.' Ross's big hand touched lightly on Matthew's shoulder. 'You've proved yourself, laddie.'

He paused.

'I'm sending back a mail tomorrow, with one of Mr Todd's stockmen. You'll be wanting to write to your Da, then, and inform him of your intention.'

* * *

The family received Matthew's letter, delivered by messenger, as they sat down to their evening meal.

Martin, with an immediate instinct, jumped up to answer the door.

'Well,' old Hannibal asked, wiping his lips with a napkin, 'what the blazes is it at this hour?'

Martin was pale.

'It's a letter from Matthew, Father.'

'Dear God,' Mrs Harper cried, putting a hand to her throat.

'Don't stand there gawking,' old Hannibal demanded, 'let me have it.'

Old Hannibal fumbled with the envelope while the family remained poised on the edge of their chairs.

'Something has happened,' Mrs Harper wailed. 'I can feel it in my bones.'

Old Hannibal had got out his spectacles and was busy with the sheets of paper.

'For goodness' sake, Father,' Lucinda said, 'can't you read it aloud?'

'I'll be damned,' was her father's response. And then again, 'Well I'll be damned.'

Mrs Harper clutched at her throat.

'For goodness' sake, Father,' young Hannibal pleaded, echoing his sister.

'The boy is writing from the Peake,' old Hannibal announced. 'Ross got out five hundred miles north of the Peake.'

Young Hannibal found himself a cheroot.

'They have crossed sandy deserts and gibber plains . . . they have come across wild blacks.'

'Is he well? Is he well?' Mrs Harper asked, getting back her colour.

'As fit as a fiddle,' old Hannibal told her, reading on. Then he half-rose in his chair. 'What's this?' he bellowed. Mrs Harper sagged.

'Damn the boy,' old Hannibal shouted. 'He's going out again with Ross. They're going out again, all the way to the centre!'

Mrs Harper seriously sagged at this, and young Hannibal

leapt up to support her. Lucinda hurried for the smelling salts.

'Brandy!' old Hannibal ordered.

And to his wife, 'Will you behave, Madam? Nothing has happened to him yet.'

Lucinda seized on the news from the Peake as an excuse to pay a visit to Steven Woodrush at St Paul's.

She had almost grown up with Steven Woodrush, not as a social intimate, but through the family's association with the church. An instinct for kindness, a further puzzling division of her nature, had led her to regard this ward of the church with a mixture of sympathy and patronage. When she joined the Church Women's Fellowship, mainly to appease her mother, Lucinda had been brought into closer company with the dark-eyed young man, and she was impressed that he was in Orders and soon to be ordained.

Lucinda's Christianity was as much an inheritance as the opalescent skin she had got from her mother, and went about as deep. But lately she had taken an active interest, faithfully attending her Bible studies and often holding the floor in discussions.

Marriage was a prospect not yet seriously considered by Lucinda. Despite the advertisements of her rich figure and her manner with men, she had kept her sensuality well checked. Yet she had been aroused once, by a soldier who had been posted to the colony from service in India to become a lieutenant in the 18th Regiment stationed in Adelaide. In the course of that arousal, Lucinda had discovered a thrilling power.

Now when she marked out a suitor to entertain her, it was more in a spirit of conquest than in the innocent guiles of femininity, and by the time her lieutenant was posted to Ireland, he had already become a shadow, without the smallest understanding of the wayward will that had used him. Lucinda was in new company, galloping recklessly on one of her father's hacks while the young soldier was still in port, yearning over the ship's rail.

Now she debated the fine cuts of theology with Steven Woodrush, who was at first surprised and then flattered that Lucinda Harper should discuss with him the well-being of her soul. In fact, it was not her soul that concerned Lucinda.

Eventually, according to her planning, Woodrush would be drawn into untheological discussion and intimate revelations. That would be the first step.

Steven, an orphan adopted by the church, had been led into Holy Orders in much the same way that young Hannibal had gone into his father's business. Encouraged by the Bishop, of course, who had no other businesses to offer.

A series of apparently accidental meetings between them, the frequency of which surprised Steven, continued for a long time before they began meeting by appointment. Considering these sessions to be good practice for him in counselling, Steven attended the appointments in a spirit of some gravity. It wasn't until he and Lucinda were walking in the zoo one day, discussing the Church Council, that Lucinda, her eyelashes fluttering, drew Steven's attention to the affinity that had developed between them, and made him understand how fond of him she was.

Steven returned to his quarters that evening and sat on his cot in some confusion. Forgotten chance meetings and snatches of conversation crowded into his mind until he felt himself compelled to go to the chapel and pray. But the image of Lucinda's flushed cheeks and flashing eyes was not easily dispelled.

Now, having told Steven about Matthew's letter, Lucinda confided in him how much she had come to depend on his company and counsel and suggested another meeting at the zoo. She wanted to ask his opinion about the risks of Matthew's excursion further inland and how she should best comfort her mother and father. Woodrush knew little about the Overland Telegraph, except that a ceremony of blessing on the undertaking had been conducted in the church. But he readily agreed to the meeting, although he already had a suspicion that Lucinda's interest in his opinion might have rather a different motive from sisterly concern.

In the days following the receipt of Matthew's letter, there had been much discussion in the family, and the pencilled pages were beginning to smudge with the constant handling.

In King William Street, old Hannibal buttonholed J.A. Holden and gave him such an account of Matthew's exploits, followed by such earnest inquiries as to how Holden's son was progressing as an articled clerk, that the master saddler had gone home with indigestion.

Martin, in turn, couldn't wait to tell his friend Solomon, who grew thoughtful as he listened, sitting on his bench and wiping his brow with his sweat rag.

'Whistle it up again, lad. About the great lagoon in the wilderness, and the reef of stones where all hands near went to the bottom.'

Martin retold it for Solomon, adding certain embroideries of his own.

'I've seen wondrous things in the watery world,' Solomon said, 'across the bosoms of the oceans and in the regions of ice, where a man's very breath freezes.'

He rubbed at his black, tight curls.

'You see what those strange sights caused? They made Solomon's hair curl like a nigger's.'

He fell silent, and when he spoke again it was as though to himself.

'A man like Solomon, now, who can forge an anchor or a belt buckle. Won't they be needing such a man in the far places? With them moving on iron wheels, with chain traces and horseshoes?'

Solomon's face changed again, dreaming and impassive.

'You're not thinking of going on the Overland?' Martin began.

'It has come to me,' Solomon said slowly. 'I sometimes get visited, lad. When it comes over Solomon, as it's coming over him now, there's nothing for it but to sign on, though it be with the devil in hell.'

'But Solomon . . .' Martin had to stop and swallow at the protest in his voice. Something had begun to bump inside him.

But Solomon's eyes were unseeing. 'There is much that Solomon has seen and learned in the years on the heaving waters. But what does Solomon know of voyaging on land, born and brought up as he was on the coast at New Bedford? Solomon was fated for the watery world and in truth that's all he knows. All the same, it comes to him that voyaging on the land might complete the log, as it were.'

'But Solomon . . .' Martin began again, and had to stop.

Solomon made no answer, his curly head and pockmarked face hunched into his shoulders. It seemed to Martin that his spirit had already gone wandering off.

The boy grasped Solomon's arm with both hands.

'Is that what you intend, Solomon? Is that what you're going to do?'

Solomon remained distracted.

'You see, lad, there are demons inside this scarred body. Sometimes they sleep for years. But when they awake, they take Solomon by the hand, and there's never been anything for Solomon but to follow.'

Martin felt that he would burst with a feeling he had never known before.

'If you are going, Solomon, will you take me with you? Will you, Solomon? We would be bound to meet Matthew. I am sure of it.'

Solomon seemed to come awake then, and the rare smile again beamed from his face.

'You'd sign on with Solomon, would you?'

'I could work with you. Fetch and carry for your forging.'

'And what of your family, lad?'

'They let Matthew go with Ross. They never – nobody could ever resist Matthew. There's nothing I've ever done by myself. I've always followed Matthew. I'll take some things and just go, Solomon, leaving a letter behind.'

Martin's voice became more intense.

'If you go, you must take me with you.'

But Solomon had withdrawn again.

'What are you thinking?' Martin persisted.

'I'm consulting my demons, lad.'

'What do they say?'

'Do you know Ma Ryan's crib, on the way to the port?'

'No, but I can find it.'

'Solomon has a room there. Ask for him at Ma Ryan's crib, two days from now.'

Solomon took off his leather apron and draped it over the bench. In his singlet, he walked out of the Harper forge for the last time.

Four

Martin had little talent for dissembling. Some irrevocable honesty had got into his genes, an honesty which at times had been a trial to him in his school days when he had to submit to the cane on the ready admission of his misdemeanours.

After Solomon had walked out of the Harper forge, the ferment in Martin's mind over the next two days might have been easily observed had his family not been so self-absorbed. The two Hannibals had little attention for anything outside the expansion of the business, and the fact that Matthew was going out again with Ross, Mrs Harper had embraced as a martyrdom, as other women took up whist or tonic wine. She had taken to her bed, unable to eat except when unobserved.

Lucinda's growing preoccupation with Steven Woodrush left her with little awareness of others. Tasks required of her by her mother were forever being left undone, postponed, or half-managed, and her elegant arched eyebrows were losing their charm in frowns and moody meditation.

Thus there was no one in the family to remark on Martin's odd nervousness and elation, and on the day appointed, Martin found Solomon at Ma Ryan's crib, a rough boarding house in which the American had a room on the warped verandah.

'Are you still determined, lad?'

'Yes,' Martin answered.

Solomon was drinking rum and water at a small table. The other furniture in the room consisted of a bed and a wall mirror, the latter suspended on a rusted chain and spike. The American narrowed his eyes at Martin.

'A man can get an impulse, a man being an impulsive creature,' he said. 'He might get an impulse about this, or that, or the other. He might get an impulse to out-yell a typhoon and get that yell blown back down his throat until his belly blows up and bursts.'

Solomon squeezed his eyes tight and the pits on his face seemed to flicker in the light of the kerosene lamp.

Martin looked at Solomon apprehensively.

'Have you changed your mind about the Overland, Solomon?'

'As to that, when it comes over Solomon to sign on, there's no other tack. It's you I've in mind, sitting there like a new cabin boy. And all on impulse, as you might say.'

Martin spoke with determination.

'I've thought hard about it. It's what I want to do.'

'And you've discussed it fore and aft, to be sure. You've been into the matter with all hands and here you sit with their blessing?'

'I've not discussed it with anyone, nor can I,' Martin said. 'There's worry enough already about Matthew.'

The American poured rum and scratched in his curls.

'So it all comes back to Solomon. Hell's flames! To Solomon in his wisdom.'

He tilted his head and stared about as though seeking an answer from the bare walls. Then he drank the rum at a draught and banged the pannikin down on the table.

'Then bless my soul. Let us waste no more words. I've been into the problem of recruiting. We sail for Port Darwin, Saturday afternoon, on the vessel *Omeo.*'

Martin concealed the sudden lurch in his stomach.

'Where shall we meet?'

'At ten in the morning, at the tram for the port, in King William Street.'

'Until Saturday,' said Martin. 'Goodbye, Solomon.'

On Friday he wrote a short letter to each member of his family, distracted by tears he could not hold back, and, after Harper and Son had emptied for the weekend, left the envelopes on his father's roll-top desk.

The dispatch to the north of the barque-rigged steamer *Omeo,* loaded with men, provisions, equipment and livestock, coincided by the most lively good fortune as far as Martin was concerned, with the posting home to England of the 18th Regiment. In the disorder of that departure, there was little chance that he would be noticed.

King William Street was riotous with drunken soldiers when

Martin arrived for his meeting with Solomon, and by the time he had pushed through the crowd of military and found the other man, the Overland transports had already left for the port. The only alternative was one of the Irish jaunting carts that stood for hire. The carts were packed with soldiers of the 18th, bootless and some only partly dressed, who were passing bottles and shouting ditties, and generally attempting to prolong their last celebrations in the whorehouses and grog shops of the Adelaide slums. Solomon, tolerant at first, became offended when he and Martin were jostled, first shouting 'Avast!' and then putting three of the rankers at temporary peace with a blow to the tops of their heads.

Martin's heart beat hard, and he feared disclosure at the port, if he were seen by one of his father's friends. But in the confusion of the regiment's embarkation, increased by the crowd of colonists come to wish the Overlanders bon voyage, there was little cause for anxiety.

At the port a Member of Parliament addressed the intending Overlanders, emphasising the importance of the telegraph line as a national undertaking and claiming that the men would have little complaint in the matter of food. But his assurances were barely heard in the fret and uproar of the *Omeo*'s departure, with bullocks still being chiacked aboard and slings of netted cases hanging perilously overhead.

On board at last, Solomon and Martin hastened to examine the vessel. The saloon of the barque-rigged steamer was amidships, and most of the Overlanders were to be installed in the forecabin in reasonable, if crowded, comfort. The afterpart of the deck was loaded with drays and wagons lashed to bolts; the hurricane deck was stacked high with hay bales, and, below, bullocks bellowed and horses stamped. Bundles of telegraph wire, with insulators and pins by the thousand, were heaped in every space.

Solomon inspected it all, shaking his curly head in wonder.

'Hell's flames and Mother Carey's chickens,' he exclaimed to Martin, who was quivering with excitement. 'I've put to sea in this, and I've put to sea in that, and I've pulled oar in the other. But in all Solomon's born days in the watery world, he's never seen the like of this. It might have risen up and berthed alongside out of a fevered imagination.'

The *Omeo* was scheduled to catch the tide that would clear

the inner bar, and the mooring ropes had to be slipped in time, despite the disorder. At last, the vessel moved off from its hold on the land, in a great hurrahing from the wharf and the ship's rail, to steam downriver, shake hands with the tide, and point out the gulf to the southern ocean.

Solomon soon established billets for himself and Martin, making himself comfortable before the crossing of the bar. A small wooden bucket was stowed beside his sea-bag. He pointed it out to Martin.

'As for that, it came into Solomon's hands by way of the greatest deliberation.'

Martin tried to take an interest in the bucket.

'By and large, the Pacific isn't an ocean given to tantrums,' he continued. 'You might say it can be serene in its undulations. But you might also say that certain hands, who've never been to sea, can come over queer-like, and most unexpected, with a mutiny in the guts.'

He stared hard at Martin.

'If that should happen to a certain shipmate, whose name I won't mention, he'd better quickly get his head into that very same bucket.'

The *Omeo* had barely cleared the gulf into blue water when signals were given in the forecabin as to the usefulness of Solomon's bucket. These were evidenced by a sudden quietness in men who had been previously noisy, and by noticeable changes in their colour. A brandishing of handkerchiefs and neckcloths followed, with much dashing to get on deck and stumbling over gear. Solomon rolled his eyes at those who failed to clear quarters before succumbing.

Soon a crewman poked his head through the entrance and announced that the captain had given permission for all parties to go on deck, now that the cargo had been stowed and secured.

It was a marvel to Martin to witness the endless leagues of blue, dimpling and dipping to the curved horizon. Climbing the bales on the portside hurricane deck, he stared in disbelief at the promontories and inlets of a coast as wild as it had been since time's beginning.

The voyage continued in peaceful seas, with no more contention than rain squalls, and all sails were run aloft. Smoke belched from the short stack aft of the middle mast.

The Overlanders settled down for the duration, gambling at cards and yarning.

Each evening, as Martin watched in wonder the sun burning into the water, he tried not to think about the uproar that would have broken out at home after his father found the letters on his desk. Despite the reassurances of his letters – that he would be safe in the company of the line-builders, that he was playing his part in a most worthy venture, that he was bound to meet up with Matthew – Martin knew that his mother would be prostrated, and his father, after his initial outrage, would feel betrayed by this quiet son of his.

Only one other disquieting note marred his contentment.

One evening, as he stood in admiration of the sunset, he overheard a fragment of conversation between a crewman and a stockman. The Yankee with the poxed face answered the description of a sealer who had near killed a man on Kangaroo Island, said the sailor. He'd heard the story when the *Omeo* had laid over at American River on a charter last time out. There couldn't be too many Yankees who answered that particular description around the colonies.

Martin was much disturbed and wanted to report what he had heard to Solomon, but could find no easy approach. The Yankee sometimes became testy when Martin urged him to elaborate on his past experiences. In any case, the story was fantastic; reminding himself of the gentleness and warmth of his friend, Martin dismissed it from his mind.

All the same, there was a part of Solomon that was unfathomable, hidden from him. There was the mysterious matter of his friendship with one of the Overlanders quartered in the afterpart, a stocky, greying man whom Solomon had obviously known before they came on board. When the two conversed, it was always apart from the others, their heads close together, and when on one occasion Martin tried to join them, the stranger broke away without a word. In surprise, Martin turned to Solomon, but the Yankee's face was expressionless as he leaned on the rail and stared down at the water.

'Who is that man, Solomon?' asked Martin in consternation.

'An axeman, from the afterpart.'

'Where does he come from? Why does he always keep to

himself? You're the only person I've seen him talk to.'

'There are some things it's better not to inquire into, lad. Let this be an end to your question.'

But Martin persisted.

'What's his name?'

Solomon deliberated.

'You might say his name is legion. Aye, you might say that.' Then, with a finality that Martin dared not argue with, he jabbed a finger at a promontory they were passing.

'There lies the extremity of the colony of Victoria. We're in Bass Strait, lad. Tasmania and Hobart Town lie due south. It's many a time that Solomon has sailed into Hobart Town on a whaling ship, with as many others lying at anchor there as the gulls crying in our wake.'

But Solomon's strange and private friendship so intrigued Martin that he felt compelled to enquire about the stranger of the others quartered in the afterpart. All he found out was that the man's name was Stubbs, and that he kept as much to himself as was possible in the cramped quarters. Nothing more about him was known to his shipmates. For the moment, the boy had to contain his curiosity.

The *Omeo* put in for coal on the east coast at Newcastle, the space for fuel having been much reduced by the bulk of the Overland cargo and the stock. Captain Calder chose the outer route to the Torres Straits, and was favoured with a fine run through the great coral reefs of the north-eastern coast. North of the reef, into the tropics, the men in the forecabin were tormented at night by the heat, and, sweating and sleepless, were driven to search out crannies on the deck. On sounding the water tanks, Captain Calder found the supply of fresh water greatly reduced by the extra needs of the animals tethered in the oven-like holds. A condenser was improvised by the chief engineer, an ingenious device which, with elbow connections fixed to the tubes of the donkey boiler, allowed steam from the boiler to condense in a deck hose put overboard for that purpose. This invention watered the animals sufficiently to make them manageable until further north into the Arafura Sea.

Then the ship, having rounded the pinnacle of the

continent, entered a storm which set everything pitching and rolling. A wagon broke its lashings and smashed into the carts. The maddened bullocks broke free and the horses, kicking out in panic, smashed some stalls to kindling, causing so much damage to themselves that three of them had to be shot. After the storm, mercifully brief, had abated, the *Omeo* found itself grounded on a soft coral reef not mentioned in the charts, and was left high by a fast-falling tide, tipped dangerously to one side. When the vessel refloated itself and was again upright with the turning of the tide, the stockmen who had had the job of calming the animals below came up on deck ill and shaken at the havoc.

'It's many a time that Solomon has gone aground,' the older man told Martin, 'with all hands to the oars, and all the boats out, roped to the stricken ship to pull her free.'

He scratched at his scars.

'But I've never seen the ship, now, piled high on the decks with the clutter of this and that we're carrying to the north. Nor the ship packed with beasts below, in an imitation of Noah's Ark.'

The crew and passengers had barely recovered when a big Malay proa was sighted, making as if to give chase. Aware of the risk of pirate attack, Captain Calder gave orders that a small cannon be loaded with broken bottles and scraps of iron. All the available firearms were readied at the rails.

Solomon smiled at Martin.

'It's grey to the gills you are, lad. Those Malays, now, they'd cut your throat for a penny, or perhaps for the entertainment. But one broadside from us and they'll yap and yell for their distant islands. There's nothing to fear, lad. It's just in the nature of things.'

After nosing about a little, approaching and withdrawing, the big wooden boat sheered off, with not a shot fired by the *Omeo*.

In tranquil seas to the north of Port Darwin, with calm restored aboard, the *Omeo* anchored off Melville Island, the melancholy outpost abandoned some years before by a contingent of British soldiers whose attempt at settlement had utterly failed due to both fever and the attacks of fierce local Aborigines.

Solomon became talkative, 'prating on', as he put it, about the romantic islands he himself had come upon in his years as a young whaler. Encouraged by the men, who smoked their pipes and nudged each other, unsure whether the muscular Yankee was pulling their legs, he spun endless yarns in the forecastle.

Finally, early one morning, the *Omeo* moved from its anchorage off Melville Island for the last leg of the voyage. Most of the men were astir at first light, excited at the approach of the journey's end and their voices rose with jokes and speculations about the new territory that lay before them. One of the stockmen, clad in a suit more appropriate to Adelaide society than to the already sweltering morning, gave as his opinion that the settlement at Port Darwin would have to be considerable, because didn't it have a resident to represent the government? And wasn't that the equivalent of a governor of some kind? There would have to be at least one important building, he insisted, even if the government resident had only arrived the year before.

Entering the harbour, the *Omeo* anchored close to the shore. The government resident's quarters were revealed in all their glory. Three or four log huts and a tent with a flagstaff through the centre comprised the establishment. The settlement, with some modest homesteads scattered about, was a primitive hamlet. Sweating in his suit, the stockman fell silent, and fingered his lapels reflectively.

Coming aboard, the government resident closeted himself in the saloon with Captain Calder and the officers of the Overland. The Overlanders stared silently over the rail at the reality of the settlement before them. Among them, Solomon was cheerful, keen to get ashore, already identifying trees and plants he thought he remembered from other tropical islands.

'Don't cock a snook, lad,' he instructed Martin. 'We're here to go voyaging on land. To see the far places, as you might say. Why, this is an elegant city compared to the whaling camps on some wild coasts where Solomon has made his billet.'

The consultation in the saloon was lengthy, for the landing operation had to be planned in meticulous detail. First, the horses and bullocks were lowered over the side, and encouraged by the men in the ship's boats to swim ashore.

Next, the drays and wagons were floated to the beach, their wheels being taken to shore in the boats, which then began to convey the rest of the ship's cargo. There was no jetty, and all cargo had to be carried two hundred yards up the beach so that it was clear of high water. It was a long and wearisome job.

As further supply vessels arrived, the *Antipodes* and the *Himalaya*, the settlement began to take on the appearance of a tent city.

Many of the bullocks landed from the *Omeo* did not survive, as did not the water-starved beasts brought up by the *Antipodes*, down to half a day's water in the tanks. The *Himalaya* suffered such extreme difficulties in landing its stock that the crew mutinied the morning after its arrival, taking with them one of the ship's boats. Considering the inhospitality of the coast, the chief constable remarked, the mutineers must be as mad as the bullocks. Time was lost chasing the runaways, who came to their senses and made a grumbling return.

After ten days all the supply ships had anchored, and the wells ashore had run dry. It was necessary to drive the surviving animals to a lagoon, well away in the bush. Some, unable to complete the journey, left their bones on the route. The head stockman furnished the government resident with a summary. The loss to the expedition was a hundred and forty-four bullocks out of five hundred shipped.

There were also deaths among the horses. As well, many were found too light for the work and others were found to be unbroken. Those too wild to be handled had to be roped and thrown for breaking-in by the stockmen and accustomed to harness and saddle.

Solomon had set up a forge among the tents, with Martin fetching wood for him, and he hammered the dray and wagon wheels which had been damaged when their lashings had snapped in the storm.

The silent man, Eli Stubbs, had been chosen by Solomon as one of his axemen. Martin's attempts to converse with him continued to be futile, achieving no more response than a grunt or a nod. But he still sometimes went aside to converse with Solomon, as they had done on the *Omeo*.

Everything that Martin saw at Port Darwin was like something out of a romance, unrelated to anything he had known. He wandered the wide white beaches where soldier crabs marched and drilled at low tide, seemingly acres of the small creatures, parading and wheeling with a military order and precision difficult to believe. The harbour seemed immense, a refuge of tractable water that sparkled and shimmered in the uninterrupted sun. An amiable young constable, important in his smart uniform and superior knowledge, informed Martin that all the might of the British Fleet might be safely at anchor in a shelter of this size.

The harbour shores were massed with vegetation as green and dazzling in the sunshine as the sea was blue. Palms in great profusion spread upon the cliffs, mingling with ironbark trees, casuarinas and the shriller colours of the milkwoods.

There were black tribesmen in the area who gaped at all this new activity, coming each day to a hill nearby, bringing their families, leaning on tall bundles of spears to survey the newcomers. The chattering of the women was as loud as the screeching of cockatoos, and their children cut capers, laughing and pointing and pushing at each other.

'Black they be,' Solomon said, 'blacker than a yard up a chimney, and blacker than the blackest Solomon ever saw in the islands. A fine entertainment it is that we're making for the heathen.'

Martin had seen blacks before, in their camp near the zoo and in other places near Adelaide. But these blacks were different. They were taller and better made, with something proud and independent in their gestures, and he felt a sudden qualm for Matthew, so far out in the wilderness.

Solomon became impatient in the weeks it took to organise the men, equipment and animals for the assault on the northern line.

'It's voyaging on land that Solomon came for. Not to be beached on top of its head. I'll be glad when we set sail, lad.'

But in the listing of the parties to proceed to the different starting points, Martin and Solomon found themselves separated. Martin's wagon was miles into the bush before he realised what had happened. When he voiced an alarmed objection, he was curtly told to shut up. Solomon was in a party that was to go directly down the route of the line. Martin's group was bound on a journey south-east, to the supply depot being set up on the far reaches of the Roper River.

A feeling akin to panic filled Martin and wild thoughts of jumping down and running back raced through his mind as the wagon jolted inexorably onwards. But he knew there was no going back.

He felt a tiny thread of comfort when he glimpsed Eli Stubbs at the first overnight camp. Stubbs at least was some connection with Solomon. But when he tried to speak with him, hoping for some commiseration, the man only nodded and went away to eat his food alone. Amidst the noise of the men around him, Martin yearned to be back at home in the attic room he had shared with Matthew.

One of the stockmen, drinking his tea from his pannikin, noticed his downcast expression.

'Weren't you working with the Yankee, boy?'

'Yes. They've made a mistake sending me here. I was recruited to work with Solomon.'

The stockman was understanding.

'There'll be many worse mistakes before we're through. You'll just have to make the best of it.'

There was indeed no going back. Only the man who had come up from the Roper to lead the party to the depot knew the way, and what awaited them there. Matthew had never heard of the Roper River, and neither had most of his companions. But in the next few days it got about among the men that it was a tidal river, that it was navigable from the sea at its mouth by vessels of supply, and that a supply camp had already been established on its headwaters as a short cut from the coast to the building line.

Martin grieved that night in his bed. But the stockman was right. There was nothing to do but make the best of it.

Five

In his sudden compulsion to go on the Overland with Solomon, Martin had underestimated the shock and hurt his sudden departure would cause his father and mother, and indeed, the other members of his family as well. Young Hannibal was especially displeased, burdened as he was now with his parents' fixed belief that both twins had disappeared forever into the wilds of the Great South Land. And Lucinda, too, had been extremely upset, though her pain had been alleviated a little by her preoccupation with Steven Woodrush, to whom she again hurried with this family news, drawing him still further into her net.

'It's madness,' old Hannibal had moaned weakly, waving Martin's letter from his swivel chair on Monday morning. 'A madness come down on everyone. Who would believe such a thing of Martin? As responsible a boy as ever lived. I'm in mortal fear of having to tell your mother.' He took a large gulp of the brandy he had poured himself. 'When did the wretched vessel sail?'

'The *Omeo* sailed on Saturday's tide, at the same time as the ship bound for England with the 18th Regiment aboard.'

'Who in the world is this Solomon the boy says he's gone with?'

'The American, Father, who was striking in the forge.'

'What's that?' old Hannibal shouted. 'The one with pox scars all over his face?' He paused, now finding ground from which to accuse young Hannibal. 'The striker that you hired?'

'I'm afraid so, Father,' young Hannibal answered, with misgiving.

'A viper, nurtured in the bosom of my own business!'

'Don't blame the American, Father. In both Martin's letters, he makes it clear that his reason for going is to meet up with Matthew.'

Old Hannibal got up and paced the floor, his hands clasped under his coat tails.

'There's an unnatural bond between those two,' he muttered. 'Pour me another brandy. I'm going to need it to face your mother. Port Darwin! Sweet Mother of Mercy!'

He gulped his newly-replenished brandy.

'A curse on Todd and his hare-brained scheme! A curse on the hare-brained government, a curse on our hare-brained Governor who backed it!'

'Remember that Martin will be in the safety of a large party, Father.'

'That's well enough for you to say. It's not you who will be breaking the news to your mother. I'd rather be out in the wilderness myself than face up to that duty.'

'It must be done, Father. Shall I come home with you now?'

Old Hannibal knuckled his dome.

'No,' he decided. He topped up his glass. 'There's going to be hysterics. You can take your turn later.'

Mrs Harper could not believe it. Martin, her little one who had never been strong, to sneak away from the bosom of his family, like a thief in the night, to disappear, probably forever, into the savage jungles where no white man had ever set foot. Old Hannibal had to send for Doctor Thornhill, who gave Mrs Harper a strong medicine of sedation.

Some days later, the Harper household had regained an appearance of calm. Old Hannibal, sitting by the fire, was reading aloud to young Hannibal from the *Advertiser*. Mrs Harper, recovered sufficiently to make an appearance in her teagown, had opened the trapdoors in her ears at the sight of her husband's bald head, which was slowly going purple.

It appeared, from Old Hannibal's perusal, that the South Australian government had advertised a reward for the first thousand head of sheep, or hundred cattle, to be delivered to Port Darwin overland. Not only was this idea preposterous, in old Hannibal's opinion, but someone had actually taken the matter up.

Mr Ralph Milner, with his brother John and seven stockmen, three black stockboys and a gin, had decided to make the attempt. He had abandoned his own property and intended driving all he owned before them: seven thousand head of sheep, three hundred horses and all their cattle, as well as ten sheep dogs, fifteen hunting dogs, and a year's supplies in the wagons.

'They'll be swallowed up and never heard of again,' old Hannibal fumed. 'Why, we had the deuce of enough trouble getting stock over to Port Lincoln. They're going into the never-never, that's where they're going.'

He sank back into his chair and young Hannibal went automatically for the brandy. His father had turned up his eyes, as he did when responding 'Amen' at St Paul's.

'Am I the only sane man left in the colony? Is there a contagion of madness going about, driving everyone out of their wits? Was Charles Todd treated for it in England? Did he bring it to the colony to infect everyone from the Governor downwards?'

Young Hannibal brought the brandy, and old Hannibal took a swallow.

'Is that what happened to Matthew? Did Martin catch the disease? Did Matthew give it to Martin?'

Young Hannibal tried to light a cheroot. His father seemed to be getting worse in his upsets of late, with even less to set them off.

Afterwards, young Hannibal spoke to his mother in the pantry.

'I've never seen Father blow up quite like that before.'

To his surprise, Mrs Harper became dreamy.

'It reminds me of when your father was young. Oh, how he used to carry on then! He set fire to a new wagon at Port Lincoln once, because the wheel kept coming off.'

Young Hannibal was astounded.

'Father did a thing like that?'

But Mrs Harper changed the subject.

'This business has been a great strain for him. He worries more about the twins than you think. And he does upset himself about Lucinda – goodness alone knows why.'

Mrs Harper, with not the least understanding of her

daughter, held the view that Lucinda could do no wrong, despite the overwhelming evidence that existed to the contrary. Old Hannibal had by tradition ruled his roost and Mrs Harper had by tradition been an obedient wife. But in any discussion concerning Lucinda, Mrs Harper was fierce in taking her daughter's side. Lucinda was not unaware of this trump card, and exploited it to the utmost.

Hannibal remembered how his father had chastised his difficult daughter, after he himself had recounted the gossip he had heard about her to the old man. It had had little effect.

'I know how it might appear,' Lucinda had said, 'but there's really nothing in it.'

'There's been enough in it to set people talking, miss. Where there's smoke there's fire, in the opinion of most people.'

'I don't care about people talking.'

'What's that?' old Hannibal had rumbled. 'You don't care about your reputation? You don't care about the reputation of your family?'

Lucinda's resolve hardened.

'If I want to see Steven, I shall, and a few old cats aren't going to stop me.'

She had run from the room, and old Hannibal had sat for a long time in silence. His daughter had always been something of an unknown quantity to him, perfectly happy one day, difficult and defiant the next. After one of those days, old Hannibal always knew that his daughter had been thwarted in some intention or other.

But Woodrush? And Lucinda? Recalling the pale, slight young man, without family or material prospects, old Hannibal felt a little reassured.

But Steven Woodrush was not altogether the milksop that old Hannibal had judged him. He had fought lonely battles within himself, growing up as a ward of the church, and had learned to be devious in his self-protection. He could be shrewd and calculating, and was clever enough not to let it show. After his first surprise at Lucinda's frank interest in him, Woodrush found it expedient to make himself less available, out of both curiosity and a desire to test her determination.

This had the effect of doubling Lucinda's interest, making her frown with purpose. An accomplished pianist, she indulged her moods at the piano, now dreaming over the keys with something light and romantic, now waxing rebellious, crushing all opposition, *fortissimo.* When Lucinda realised that Woodrush was avoiding her, she almost fled to the piano. But her father's lecture and Steven's retreat had only hardened her will. Today there was nothing light and romantic in her repertoire.

In a gossip with Lady Charlotte Bacon, deliciously enjoyable in its frank exchange of female secrets, Lady Charlotte had remarked lightly on this steely streak in Lucinda. Intended as a mild reproof, Lucinda had accepted it as a compliment.

'Oh, yes,' she said, in a tone of pure satisfaction, 'I always get what I want, one way or another.'

Lady Charlotte nodded and smiled thinly. Originally perceiving Lucinda as a kind of vivid, colonial rose, refreshing after London society, the earl's daughter began, belatedly, to recognise a type she was more familiar with. Her husband had not been immune to the charms of predatory females.

Although competent at most practical things, Lucinda was unable to accommodate many thoughts at once in her head. Now she had narrowed them still further to a single focus. She would make Woodrush hers, body and soul, whether he wanted it or not.

Having studied all the procedures at St Paul's and the priest's school, she knew his movements at any appointed hour. She would not waste any more time.

Getting up from the piano, she found the family in the morning room.

'I shall be out this evening, attending Lady Charlotte's musical soirée,' she announced.

'You'll be wanting the carriage then,' said old Hannibal agreeably, from the depths of his newspaper.

But Lucinda had provided for that. Tom, the Harpers' driver, who was also the gardener, was hardly appropriate for this evening's proposed entertainment. She would take a carriage for hire, from a stand in King William Street.

'No need, Father, Lady Charlotte is sending her carriage.'

She marvelled – really, it was ridiculously easy.

Old Hannibal sighed. At that moment Lucinda's jaunts were of little moment to him. He put his newspaper on the side table, and cautiously beckoned his eldest son.

'The northern line is still in trouble,' he muttered, 'but they don't go into detail. I pray we get some news of Martin before your mother worries herself sick again.'

'There's talk in the club about a depot being set up on the Roper River,' said young Hannibal. 'Martin might have been sent there.'

'Where in the blazes is the Roper River?'

'What are you two whispering about?' Mrs Harper asked, over her knitting.

'Just a matter of business, dear,' old Hannibal replied.

'I will not have whispering in my own home. We must have no secrets from each other. How much longer will it be, do you think, before we hear from Martin?'

'It shouldn't be long now, Mother,' young Hannibal said. 'You must remember that it takes time for the mail to travel by ship from the north.'

Dressed for the evening, Lucinda inspected herself with satisfaction. She had made her prominent cheekbones even more so by the use of a little rouge. Her arched brows were darkened, the curve of her lips outlined. The expression on her face softened in response to her tumbling thoughts.

'How pretty you look,' Mrs Harper said, remembering herself at Lucinda's age and taking a vicarious pleasure in her daughter's comeliness. 'Aren't you taking your music, dear?'

'I almost forgot. How silly of me. Ah, I think I hear the carriage. I'll meet it at the gate. Goodnight, all,' said Lucinda, with less composure than she might have wished.

Near the cathedral, on a close and convenient corner, Lucinda had the hired carriage stop, tipped the driver, and asked him to wait. She was unsure of how long she would be.

An old staircase provided a back entrance to Steven's living quarters. Picking up her skirts, Lucinda hurried up the warped wooden steps. She had begun to pant a little with excitement. She knew the number of Steven's room, and taking a deep breath, she knocked.

There was no response, and her courage failed a little at the possibility of somebody coming upon her in the passage. Quickly she tried the door knob. The door opened easily and she slipped inside. For a moment she stood leaning against the closed door, wondering at the sparseness of the furnishings. There were but two wooden chairs. She sat down to wait.

Then she heard steps and voices, aware too late that Steven might bring company to his room. Her breath quivered on her parted lips as she saw the doorknob turn.

'Lucinda! My God! What are you doing here?'

Woodrush was alone, his face turned ash-grey. He leaned back as though something had struck him. His hand shook as he ran it through his hair.

'Lucinda . . . why are you . . . how did you get in here?'

She studied his confusion, and felt herself instantly steady.

'I came up the back steps. I wanted to see you, Steven.'

'But . . . but . . .' he spluttered. 'Here in quarters? Don't you know what this could do to me? Have you gone out of your mind?'

He hurriedly turned the key in the door, his hands shaking.

'This . . . this is impossible.'

'It needn't be,' Lucinda said. 'Here I am, Steven.'

Woodrush pulled the other chair back, to maintain a distance, continuing to shake.

'Don't speak too loudly,' he hissed. 'Someone might hear.'

'You have been avoiding me, Steven.'

'Avoiding?'

'You know that you have. Is it because of the gossip? Has anything been said by Father?'

Woodrush was helpless. He had no idea of what Lucinda meant.

He shook his head.

'I don't know what you're talking about.'

That satisfied Lucinda. She leaned forward a little.

'I told you I felt an affinity between us. I told you I was fond of you, Steven.'

'Yes,' he said, looking back at the door. 'You have told me that.'

'Do you not feel that way, too?'

Woodrush's instinct for survival now came belatedly to his aid. His pulses raced to be so enclosed with Lucinda Harper. Her perfume embraced him in the airless room.

'Yes,' he said, his mouth tightening.

'Say it.'

'I feel an affinity.'

The predator in Lucinda straight away took command.

'I want you, Steven. I want you any way I can have you.'

He recoiled, amazed.

'I don't understand.'

'It's quite simple. I want you.'

'In what way, Lucinda?'

'In any way it takes.'

Woodrush had little experience of the world, but he was far from stupid. Steps were heard in the corridor. Woodrush put up a warning hand. The steps passed, retreating. Woodrush felt an unexpected start of power. After all, this was Lucinda Harper. From one of the best-known and wealthiest families in the city.

'Do you mean . . . in that way?'

Lucinda's eyes became luminous. Two hard lines led away from the corners of her mouth.

'In that way . . . if it is necessary.'

He marvelled at her, as though a mote had been removed from his eyes. It was suddenly clear to him that there were two Lucinda Harpers. The one that other people knew, and this one, the secret Lucinda, who would stop at nothing to satisfy her desires. Calmer now, he wanted to know more about this second Lucinda.

'Have you ever done this . . . before?'

'Not altogether. There was an officer in the 18th Regiment. I allowed him some liberties.'

Woodrush marvelled again. Even her tone had coarsened, as the opalescent skin of her cheeks darkened.

'Well?' she demanded.

Woodrush shook his head, as though to arrange the disorder in it.

'I don't know what to say. It has been a shock, opening the door and finding you here.'

'You won't continue to avoid me?'

'No. Not within the bounds of discretion. But if there has already been gossip . . .'

He needed time to himself, to ponder upon the meaning and possible advantages of having Lucinda Harper throw herself at him.

'I've a class soon,' he lied. 'I must get you out discreetly, Lucinda. How did you come?'

'I have a carriage waiting, around the corner.'

Woodrush unlocked the door and peered cautiously into the corridor. Lucinda prepared herself for the next step. Some physical token between them was necessary, something of herself to leave behind as a mark on Steven Woodrush. She left the chair and crossed to the doorway. With her elegant shoe, she shut the door and placed a hand on his arm.

'You're still shaking,' she said, coming closer, until her breasts pressed softly against his chest. Woodrush shut his eyes and swallowed, feeling her body flow over his. Putting her hand behind his head, Lucinda drew him down to her lips.

'Kiss me.'

In that kiss, Lucinda used the experience of many flirtations. She could feel the leaping of his heart, the trembling of discovery in his body. Then, after what seemed a long time, Lucinda looked up at his agonised face and was content. She had marked him.

'You are mine, Steven,' she said. 'Don't forget it.'

Woodrush took a handkerchief from his pocket and wiped at his forehead.

'I can't risk being seen with you in the corridor. You'll have to leave by yourself, Lucinda. For heaven's sake be careful. A scandal would ruin me.'

'Don't worry,' Lucinda said, 'it's not far to the back stairs.'

She took a last look at the small, spartan room.

'You don't own much, do you?'

In the carriage, Lucinda sank back on the cushions, every cell in her body glowing. It was much too early to return home. She gave the driver a friend's address, where she could spend some time. On the way, she began to make a mental list of others who would have attended Lady Charlotte's musical evening. Her mother would be sure to ask.

The first wagon wheels into the interior, shod in heavy bands of iron, a pair of their axles as tall as a man and more than five men could lift, changed forever the land over which they travelled.

Between the deepening wheel ruts, the hooves of the straining beasts trod a highway along which the wagons, loaded with wire and heavy gum saplings, groaned, lurching over dry creeks and gullies, skirting the ranges and salt pans. Walking beside the sweat and dust-streaked teams, the drivers cracked their great lengths of greenhide, crying out curses and encouragement. Outriders wheeled away to locate the springs reported by the explorers.

It was a journey of many months and difficulties. As the caravans increased in number at the Peake, John Ross and his explorers repaired their equipment, packing supplies and breaking in fresh horses. The unknown, this time, would begin for them where they had last turned back.

Six

The reports, maps and surveys that John Ross had dispatched from the Peake greatly cheered the little visionary, Todd. Wagons and buggies and camel trains were continuing, it seemed, to push up from the south, erecting poles, wire, insulators and relay stations on the southern sections as planned.

The group of men for the central section, which was to proceed from the projected end of the southern wire, had been divided by Todd into five working parties. Overseeing the axemen, stockmen and linesmen were trained surveyors, each with an assistant and a cadet surveyor.

Todd's planning had to be meticulous. Word had reached Adelaide that the cable ship *Hibernia* was well out of Java, laying submarine cable on its route from Batavia to Port Darwin. The news jolted Todd, ever mindful of the urgency of the task. He needed no reminding that if the Overland Telegraph were not completed by the contracted date of January 1, 1872, the British-Australian Telegraph Company's penalty clause would come into effect, something that the little colony could ill-afford.

He announced that a new depot would be set up in the centre, at a place with good natural water in the foothills of the ranges. It had been named Alice Springs, after Charles Todd's young wife.

When old Hannibal read of this in the *Advertiser,* he slammed his hat on his head and left for the club. There were many others to shake their heads in old Hannibal's company.

'He's too cocky, by half,' a clubman commented about the Superintendent of Telegraphs. 'If he thinks he's building a line across gentle England, he's very much mistaken. There could be dragons in the centre. There could be sabre-toothed tigers, for all Charles Todd knows.'

' "If the going proves good",' old Hannibal quoted from the *Advertiser*. 'What "going", I'd like to be told. Men on horses have been turned back by it. How in the blue blazes does Todd expect to get through with caravans of wagons and drays?'

'There could be dragons in the centre,' his companion repeated.

Old Hannibal took no notice. 'Mad as a hatter,' he murmured to himself. 'Stark, raving mad.'

At the bar's far end, a middle-aged man in naval uniform was at the centre of an eager group.

'Who's that?' old Hannibal asked. 'Why is that dimwit J.A. Holden hanging on his every word?'

'An officer off the *Gulnare*, the government schooner commissioned under Captain Sweet to locate the mouth of the Roper River in the Gulf of Carpentaria,' the other informed him. 'You remember that Todd has also set up a depot on the Roper.'

'Certainly I do. That's where my lad might be. You'll have to excuse me. I want to hear about this.'

'He's been telling the story all day,' his companion said. 'I've already heard it. A reporter from the *Advertiser* was in the club earlier to interview the man.'

Old Hannibal took his brandy to where the group was gathered, avoiding J.A. Holden. What he heard, as the officer began his story yet again, caused the dome of his head to take on an almost magenta hue, and a weakness to settle on the pit of his stomach.

Captain Sweet had located the river's mouth in the Gulf of Carpentaria, and had entered the river to make his first soundings. After some days of careful progress, the chief mate and a party in two of the ship's boats were lowered over the side to investigate ahead.

On the evening of the first night out, the mate and the crew had rigged up their mosquito nets in the boats. They had eaten wild duck for dinner, strung others in the rigging for the next day, and had smoked their pipes and gone to bed, weary from the oars. The mate was sleeping on a seat with his feet propped on the gunwale. Suddenly a scream set the whole party jumping up, struggling in their nets. Or rather, the echo of a scream. The mate was gone, and his pillow and net were floating on the water.

Shouting for the mate as they stumbled for the oars, the crew squinted into the dark for a sight of they-knew-not-what. The mate's bedding had begun to move on the current, slowly being engulfed as it soaked through. But the night was eerie with silence, the crew said, and they started pulling in terror for the *Gulnare.*

Then something broke the surface of the water a short distance away, a body lifted upwards almost to the thighs. It screamed as it was shaken, only its outline visible in the dark. Then it was gone, pulled under, and the brief disturbance was erased by the calmly flowing river.

In the long pull back to the schooner, the officer reported, other crocodiles had accompanied the boats, their snouts and backs breaking surface beside them.

Old Hannibal felt he needed another brandy, but could not risk missing the rest of the officer's story.

By the time the other vessels of supply entered the river, Captain Sweet had mapped a landing place for the depot ninety-six miles upriver.

The first horses to be swum ashore at the depot clambered up the banks and shouldered their way into the thick jungle, avid for the fresh green cropping. Then, as more horses splashed into the river, the crocodiles struck. The agonised screams of the horses sent the men running for their rifles, and they loaded and fired until the barrels were hot, setting the cockatoos and parrots in screeching flight. But to no avail. Torn to pieces in a carnage of flesh and entrails, the horses lost at the Roper River landing christened the depot with their blood.

In the next few days still more horses were lost to the crocodiles before they could be found and rounded up in the tangled timber. The Overlanders could hear them being taken at night as the animals went to the river to drink, and they cursed helplessly and bitterly around the camp fires.

When old Hannibal had heard enough he took his brandy and sat down heavily on a chair. He had never seen a crocodile, but he knew well enough how they looked. There was the skeleton of one, over twenty feet long, its great jaws of snaggled teeth open, in a room at the zoo. When he thought that Martin, skinny young Martin, always a dreamer, might be on the Roper River, old Hannibal sagged with despair. It had all been brought about by this Overland Telegraph madness. If his wife were to hear what he had heard tonight, she'd have an attack of the vapours on the spot.

Old Hannibal had something of an attack himself when he eventually got to sleep that night. A nightmare of monstrous crocodiles, with Martin's pale young face somehow mixed up in it all.

In the long trek to the Roper River depot, Martin's anxiety at being separated from Solomon dulled his eyes to much of the new terrain the wagons were passing over. His curiosity was awakened only when the great river itself came into sight, the Overlanders standing up in the wagons to see it. Martin had only known the gentle Torrens, in which he had swum and played as a child. This great green monster, writhing between its banks, took his breath away.

The depot was set back from the river, beyond the tangled mangroves and the mud banks on which the bubble-nostrilled, sleepy-eyed crocodiles sunned themselves.

When he had an opportunity, Martin explained to the depot boss that he had been recruited as a blacksmith's help and should have been sent inland on the line to work at Solomon's forge. Grunting unsympathetically and noting Martin's lack of muscle, the depot boss put him to work as cook's help and general jobsman.

'Make the best of it,' Martin told himself again, and tried to settle into the camp.

Still just as wary of the others as before, Eli Stubbs made his own camp away from the tents, rigging up a low shelter of tarpaulin, with a waterproof sheet under his bedroll and a mosquito net over it. There he retreated, when not at work, to read a book which Martin believed to be a Bible. He continued to reject Martin's attempts to get to know him, but the boy had made friends among the others, who were kind to the youngster in their rough fashion. Stubbs was welcome to his privacy, as far as the Overlanders were concerned. If he thought himself too good for colonial company, he knew where he could stick his English accent.

The single crossing of the continent by John McDouall Stuart in 1862 had been made during the northern dry season. Little was known of the wet, of the tumult of the monsoon, the great unburdening of rain clouds pressing in from the Timor Sea.

Storms, regular almost to the hour, now arrived in the mornings and mid-afternoons, gathering almost black in the sky, with lurid outbursts of lightning stalking the camp and thunder growling as the deluge approached. The Overlanders in the depot quickly learnt the ritual signs. The sudden agitation of leaf and branch, the silencing of bird cry, the darkening light, and then deafening explosions overhead and the fall of water like something solid.

In time, the tents, spotted with patches of mould, began to rot, as did the men's beds of canvas and hessian, their clothing and their leather boots. Some of the men contracted the rot in their groins and armpits, and their feet puffed into such deformities that they could not walk. Sitting in their disintegrating tents, the flaps propped open on forked sticks to take advantage of any breath of air, the men watched dully as the Roper River became violent, its swelling, turgid waters swirling ever closer to the camp.

Further inland, the spilling-over of unknown rivers, the flooding of ancient chasms, had turned the north into an inland sea. The men at the depot were marooned, and soon rationed to a few strings of jerky each day.

One night in the mud and darkness, the starving horses got out of their yard to seek their own survival. The depot boss cursed long and loud. Although reduced to skin and bone, the horses, in the last resort, could have made a banquet for the hungry men.

To everyone's surprise, Eli Stubbs volunteered to look for the missing animals. Martin immediately offered to go with him; here at last, he thought, was a chance to break through the unshakable reserve of Solomon's friend. In the firm belief that they wouldn't get more than a mile, the depot boss let them go. The misery in the camp had bred an indifference to almost everything.

But Stubbs and Martin had got out more than a mile, sloshing through the mud, when another deluge left them isolated on a palm-covered knoll. The silent determination of his companion had, until now, stilled Martin's feelings of disquiet, but now, as he gazed around at the vile-smelling, inexorably rising waters, he felt the first stirrings of fear.

Without preamble, Stubbs took out his knife and began to hack at the young fibrous stems of the pandanus palms.

'Mr Stubbs . . .' began Martin, suddenly alarmed that the man had taken leave of his senses.

The impassive countenance of Stubbs was unexpectedly lightened by a smile.

'Racks, lad, that's what I'm going to build, to elevate us above the water.'

A few hours later, the knoll had disappeared. All round was water, as still as soup in a plate and reeking with muddy malevolence.

For Martin, the next two days passed as in a dream. Suspended on the rack, seemingly floating above the water, his mind flooded with images of his home and family as he gazed up through the parasols of pandanus at the muddy sky. Father, Mother, the house, the forge, his bedroom, Sunday dinners – had those phantoms really been the substance of his life?

Gradually, despite the low, foreboding sky, the rain ceased. Now Stubbs took up the notched measuring stick he had made when he built the racks, and held it beside his outstretched legs, wiping off the slime on his trousers. He dipped the stick into the water and then held it up, squinting at what it showed him. Not trusting himself yet to encourage the boy, he prodded the stick into the water again, feeling for resistance, then held it up dripping and again counted off the notches. This time he was clear in his mind. There was no mistake. He lay back and smiled. Fever had whitened his lips, and the black and broken teeth in the pale gums appeared to be embedded in perished rubber.

He turned towards the other rack and suddenly grimaced with pain, putting a hand almost furtively to his back. The body across from his lay perfectly still, the torn shirt fallen away from the rib-cage. Martin's matted fair hair and fair down of beard were turned away from Stubbs.

'You sleeping, boy? You're uncommon good at it, and I'd say so before a jury. You hear me? The water is going down. It's going down faster than a hole in a bucket.'

His companion still did not move, but a voice came from the averted face.

'I was just daydreaming, Mr Stubbs.'

'It's an uncommon time to be wandering in your wits.'

Martin sat up and pulled the tatters of his shirt across him. 'You're right about the water. Look at those rocks. Yesterday you couldn't see them.'

'Aye,' Stubbs agreed. 'Tell me, boy – have you any jerky left? I've a powerful ache where my belly used to be.'

Martin passed him his last half-strip, and Eli chewed tenderly on the dried meat, touching a fingertip to his gums.

'And what might you have been daydreaming about?'

'Oh, just about Sundays at home. Mother and Father always had guests to dinner on Sundays.' He stretched himself out on the rack again.

Stubbs poked again with his measuring stick.

'Harper,' he said ruminatively, 'there's something familiar about the name.'

'Hannibal Harper and Son, the coachbuilders in Norris Street,' said Martin dreamily.

Stubbs had become unusually talkative, now.

'I recollect,' he said, 'Harper and Son, by appointment to his Excellency, the Governor. With a fine stone house, like a squire's, on the corner.'

He eased himself up again on the slats and stared through the dripping pandanus.

'Now why would a young Harper want to leave all that comfort?'

'I hope to meet my twin brother. He's out exploring with Ross.'

'Twin brother, is it? He's young to be out exploring.' The tone of the man's voice changed. 'I've a brother. Perhaps I will also meet with him again one day, if there's any mercy left in Providence.'

Martin sat up. There had been something heavy, doomed, in the man's voice.

'You're not a colonial, are you, Mr Stubbs? I mean you weren't born in Australia like me.'

'No, lad.'

'My father came out from England on the *Moffat*, in 1839. He settled in Port Lincoln, but the great drought ruined him there. Did you come out to settle, Mr Stubbs?'

The question hung on the heavy air.

Stubbs swung his legs off the rack and stood in the shallow water, which came halfway up the calves of his legs. A break appeared in the clouds, through which the sun beamed in golden shafts like a biblical illustration. He pushed at his greying hair.

'If the horses did find high ground, they're gone forever,' he said. 'My first name's Elijah, called Eli. It's been sink or swim together. We'll not stand on further ceremony. Give me your hand on it, and we'll turn our faces for the camp.'

On the trek back to the camp through the mud and shallows, Martin realised that Stubbs was not going to answer his question.

Back in the depot, the plight of the men had worsened. They hardly spoke of their fear of what might have happened to the axeman and the young 'un, gone now the best part of three days.

When Stubbs and Martin limped painfully back into the camp, each supporting the other, those men still able rushed to meet them.

'What was it like? What was it like?' a stockman kept asking.

'It were uncommon wet,' Stubbs answered, the vestige of a grin flickering over his face.

Soon on their beds, deep in a slumber as luxurious as though they lay on feather mattresses, the pair did not hear the unfamiliar sounds that began to echo through the jungle a little while later. As the sounds became louder, the Overlanders stared at each other, speechless, hardly daring to believe their ears. The sounds had miraculously become the cries of human voices, hallooing through the timber.

In a short while, a party of five, with pack horses, rode into the camp. Led by Robert Patterson, the man appointed by Charles Todd to oversee the failing northern line, the group had come to see how the Roper River depot was faring in the floods.

Patterson sat on a box in the depot chief's tented wagon. Flecks of dried mud streaked the soft leather of the riding boots that came above his knee and clung to the thighs of the moleskins, reaching even to his shirt and vest. Mud streaked the full black beard that almost obliterated the man's face.

'I never thought to see so much mud and water,' he told them. 'All transport down the line has been bogged over the axles. Eighteen and twenty bullocks in a team and it has taken three weeks and all the efforts of the drivers to move the wagons five miles.'

Patterson drew on his pipe as the depot boss drew on his, the tobacco cut from Patterson's plug filling the deprived man with a delicious sensation of faintness that made it hard for him to concentrate.

Patterson continued, 'We passed other teams, fifty miles north. Most of them were bogged and the drivers in like predicaments.'

The depot boss drew again on his pipe, and arranged his face in an expression of concern. The man in front of him seemed to be floating in the air.

'But what worries me most is that the *Bengal,* which I dispatched from Darwin to come along the coast and up the river to relieve this depot, has failed to arrive. We left Darwin on the thirtieth of November and the station master was instructed to superintend the loading of the vessel immediately. You should have been relieved weeks ago.'

Patterson fiddled with the stained pith helmet on his knees, and stopped to examine the other man.

'Have you been having a touch of the fever?' he inquired curiously.

The depot boss puffed once more at the almost-spent pipe and looked at it regretfully. Then he pulled himself together, appearing to remember something.

'Mr Patterson,' he said, ignoring the other's question, 'do you by any chance have anything spare to eat on those pack horses of yours?'

That evening there was a ration for each man of a slice of tinned bully beef, a slice of damper and a pannikin of strong tea. Eli and Martin had to be woken to eat and drink. All afternoon the other men's craving for tea and sugar, their need for flour and baking soda for damper, had troubled their guts as they stared at the pack horses. Patterson's party now shared out tobacco and gave the others what news they could.

At their separate fire, Patterson spoke with the depot boss.

'The *Bengal* must have gone aground. It is the only explanation. If we take no action the camp will starve – there is little left in the packs. I propose to improvise a boat, perhaps out of one of the bullock wagons, and search for the vessel.'

'She'd sink like a stone,' the startled depot boss stated, almost aggrieved at such a suggestion. He wondered if the tobacco was still affecting him.

'I don't think so. I don't see why we couldn't shore up a wagon, waterproofing it with tenting . . .'

The depot boss, his belly appeased for the first time in weeks, considered for a moment the alternative prospect.

'Perhaps it would work,' he said doubtfully.

'It will work,' the other man said. 'It must.'

Martin and Stubbs, having tried their legs again and found them as strong as they would ever be, sat together inside the tent. Martin was content, considering now that he had made a companion of Solomon's mysterious friend. Together they discussed the proposition that was being bandied about the camp.

'Do you think the wagon will float?' Martin asked.

'Mr Patterson strikes me as a man who knows what he's doing. But how well it will float, to what destination, and when, would be uncommon hard to estimate.'

'Solomon would have known if the wagon would float. I wonder where he is, Eli?'

'Solomon will be in his element, wherever he may be. The floods would be no more than a mouthful of spit to Solomon.'

Martin took his chance.

'Solomon's the one human being I've seen you take up with, Eli, since we first went aboard the *Omeo*.'

Eli Stubbs, picking at a patch of rot on his trousers, was silent.

Martin continued to press the subject.

'I heard words spoken about Solomon, on the *Omeo*.'

'Words?' Eli asked, suddenly alert.

'I heard a sailor say that Solomon looked like a Yankee who had done something bad on Kangaroo Island.'

'Have you heard words about me, boy? Any words at all?' Martin shifted in sudden discomfort.

'No, Eli.'

Stubbs was leaning forward, a strange expression on his face.

'Are you sure? Think well, now. Any words at all?'

'Nothing, Eli. Only that you always kept to yourself.'

'Is anything strange found in that? My keeping to myself?'

Martin was puzzled .

'Why does it matter, Eli? What does it matter what the men say?'

'My keeping to myself has been remarked on. Is that what you're telling me?'

'That's all, Eli. And not any longer – the men are used to you.'

Stubbs had begun to shake a little, a nerve ticking in his cheek.

'Have you a touch of the fever, Eli?' asked Martin with concern.

'Aye,' Stubbs answered, 'that's what it must be. A touch of the fever, come with the cold of night.'

Seven

There was no rain that night, and in the morning the northern sun poured fiercely through the clouds that wandered overhead. Steam as palpable as fog rose above the coarse grass, and the men who were set to work on the wagon found themselves soaked with sweat almost instantly.

Patterson smoked his pipe and directed the work. The great wheels and axles were removed and a long crack in the wagon tray sealed with new timber. The biggest and best tent was dismantled and the canvas was tacked to the wagon's bottom, then pulled up and over the sides, and folded in for nailing.

The Overland axemen, who could fell a tree and shape it into a telegraph post as easily as others chopped kindling, prepared poles for punting. Everything was done at speed in an attempt to catch the ebb of the tidal river. Traces were attached to the wagon and two horses hitched up, a man to lead at each head. Patterson made a final inspection and gave the order to proceed. Resisting at first, the horses pulling and straining, the heavy wagon, with a loud plopping noise, suddenly lurched forward. Someone waved his rotting hat and cheered.

Eventually the unlikely craft was poised above the water. A few provisions were loaded together with rifles against the possible nuisance of blacks or crocodiles. The possibility that the craft might founder was carefully not remarked upon.

When all was ready, Patterson and two of his stockmen climbed aboard. The clamour of the men hushed into silence.

'Push!' Patterson shouted. Then, 'Put your backs into it!'

A dozen men bent their shoulders to the tail-gate. Sliding over the bank and splashing mightily into the river, the wagon immediately began to whirl and spin on the murky current. The two stockmen strove to steady the wagon with their punting poles.

All the camp, except those too sick to walk, had gathered to watch Patterson's departure, forgetting, in the business of the launching, how important this desperate effort was to each of them. In a gesture of uncharacteristic humour, Patterson turned his bearded face to the cheering men and lifted his stained pith helmet in salute.

As the stockmen pushed their poles at the river's bank, the craft put on speed and in a few minutes it had disappeared from sight behind the mangroves. Again a hush overcame the watching men. Then one spoke for all, his voice not much above a whisper.

'It ain't no picnic, here. But sooner them than me there.'

Another said, 'Suppose the *Bengal*'s not in the river? Suppose the pesky thing's out at sea?'

No one answered. The men avoided each other's eyes.

All that day, while the last of the tea and sugar in Patterson's packs was shared by the Overlanders, Patterson's craft rode far out on the river. Water began to slop into the tray, and the stockmen fell silent, bailing, until an eddy swung them towards the bank, where they almost ran aground.

Patterson remained unperturbed, poised at the front of the wagon, his pith helmet pitched low on his forehead. He looked back at the stockmen, displaying no apparent concern at what might lie before them. One of the men cleared his throat, as the massive walls of mangrove continued to sweep past.

'The *Bengal*, Mr Patterson? Let us say, for argument's sake, that the *Bengal* is not in the river?'

Patterson got out his pipe, tobacco and matches, waterproofed in a pouch. 'That would be no argument. No argument at all,' he said.

There was light rain in the late afternoon, and when the day began to dwindle, Patterson began to open ration tins.

'Since we will be sleeping aboard tonight, and since we appear to be making water, there might be some advantage in sleeping on the punting poles,' he said. 'Those who are not on watch.'

The next day, sometimes poling, sometimes riding with the current, sometimes bailing, Robert Patterson, like the men back at the depot, could only hope and wait. He well knew the risks. If the *Bengal* had been diverted, had not gone aground in the river, then he and his stockmen would be swept out into the Gulf of Carpentaria to die at sea in the wagon. There would be no way of getting ashore, with only poles to help, in the wide and rushing mouth of the great river. The Overlanders at the depot would starve to death in a matter of weeks. Patterson smoked his pipe and kept his thoughts to himself.

He was aware of the gaze of the stockmen upon him, their watching as heavy as hands. In the afternoon of the second day they took to whispering amongst themselves, their fear clear on their faces. Patterson remained inscrutable behind the screen of his beard and pipe smoke.

'We should sight the vessel soon,' he said, to cheer them. 'By my calculations we've made more than thirty miles.'

But Patterson had made another calculation, which he did not mention. If he failed to find the *Bengal* before the next change of tide, they would be helpless before it. If it did not sweep them out to sea, but bore them back into the mangroves where the crocodiles lay in the mud, their deaths would not be easy.

The rain came again, and the river teemed with the deluge. The drenched crew took turns at bailing out the wagon, cursing the unrelenting sky. Patterson's hopes began to fail as the river widened and they moved towards its mouth.

It was he who first saw the vessel, its looming bulk dimmed by the sheeting rain. Shutting his eyes and opening them to make sure that he wasn't deceiving himself, he gave up a prayer of thanks, mumbling between his bearded lips. He shook out his pith helmet with which he had been bailing, and settled it firmly on his head. When he was fully prepared, he spoke casually to the backs of the bending men who scooped at the deepening water.

'We will have to try and use the poles as oars. That's the *Bengal*, up ahead, to the right.'

* * *

On the third day after Patterson's departure on the river, the men at the Roper depot were rationed to a single strip of jerky a day. The cook had been taken with a cramping fever that caused him such agony that he begged the others to shoot him. The others had fallen into silence, abandoning all speculation. Some wrote last letters, and searched for empty tins and bottles to keep them safe.

Martin wondered at himself, because still he felt no fear. He had not felt fear on the pandanus racks, and now felt no compulsion to write letters of farewell to his family.

The quinine had long run out, and now malaria struck at the tormented men. Their mates tended the worst of the fever cases but there was little they could do, except sponge the sick faces and bodies and give the comfort of their presence.

Martin's curiosity about Eli Stubbs returned to him in this time of waiting. He felt he could speak more directly now.

'Eli, where did you first meet Solomon?'

Stubbs stared out of the tent in a strained silence.

'Why do you want to know?'

'I'm not sure,' Martin said, creasing his smooth forehead.

'You set great store by Solomon, don't you, boy?' said Stubbs.

'I wouldn't be here, if it wasn't for Solomon. He got me recruited as his help.'

Stubbs scratched his ear and almost smiled.

'So Solomon did you a service. And here you are, as like as not to perish.'

'Oh, we're not going to perish,' Martin announced firmly. 'We might starve a bit, that's all.'

Stubbs looked at the young face, fair hair tumbled on the forehead, so tranquil despite their circumstances.

'May I be given to know,' he inquired, 'the source of your information?'

'It's a feeling. Sometimes I know things without having to be told.'

'And these things come true, usually, do they?'

'They have done,' Martin said. 'But you've not answered my question.'

'You want to know where I first met Solomon?'

'Was it on the whale ships? Was it on Kangaroo Island?'

Stubbs bent his head.

'No, lad. I met Solomon in another colony. He did me a service.'

For a moment, Stubbs was quiet and when he spoke again, his voice shook a little.

'Whatever happens to me here, however bad things might get, Solomon did me a service. There are worse things than to die by starvation. And worse ways than this to live, for that matter.'

Martin was puzzled.

'When I asked Solomon about you, on the *Omeo*, he said that your name was legion. What did he mean by that?'

The doom was in Eli's voice again.

'My name *is* legion, lad. I have been one of a legion.'

Martin waited. But Stubbs suddenly stirred himself.

'Let's be done with questions. The rain has stopped. I think I'll go and wash the remains of this shirt.'

Martin jumped up.

'I'll wash it for you. I was going to wash my own.'

Stubbs clutched at his shirt with both hands, backing away.

'No!' he almost shouted.

Martin was astonished.

'What is it, Eli? I only offered to wash your shirt.'

Stubbs rubbed at his face, his expression relaxing but as if with conscious effort.

'Pay no attention, lad. I'll wash my own shirt.'

When Stubbs had gone it suddenly occurred to Martin that he had never seen the other man washing clothing at the camp tub, or even using the hot water from the copper to wash himself. And, in the good weather when he and the other men went about shirtless, Eli always remained clad in his tattered shirt. In fact, Martin realised, he had never seen Eli without his shirt. He must have been going out of the camp to wash his clothing or bathe. Why would he do that?

Patterson and the two stockmen halloed long and loud to the *Bengal*, desperately working the poles to bring the wagon closer. An amazed crewman came to the rails with a loudhailer.

'Who are you?'

'Robert Patterson, from the Roper River depot. Get us aboard, while you can.'

With relative ease, a ship's boat took Patterson and the two stockmen off the bullock wagon. In silence the men watched the craft until it disappeared from sight on its journey into the Gulf.

'Did you put out from the depot in that thing, sir?' the steersman asked with disbelief.

'There was nothing else for it,' Patterson replied, putting a match to his pipe.

Aboard the *Bengal*, after they had eaten, and warmed themselves with tea and rum, Patterson conferred with the captain.

'The men at the depot are starving,' he told him. 'There's no quinine or other medicines. They must be relieved at once.'

Almost immediately two boats loaded with provisions and medical kits were lowered and set off against the current for the Roper River depot. The first boat returned the ninth day after setting out, the second on the eleventh day. Both crews told the same story. The river had risen by twenty feet. In the struggle to reach the depot, against the flood, the boats had to be rowed close to the banks, at times from tree to tree. Ultimately, they were forced to turn back.

Now the phlegmatic Patterson was truly alarmed. He knew that the men at the depot would be in the last stages of survival. Jamming on his pith helmet, he had the captain of the *Bengal* immediately organise the ship's cutter for another attempt. He himself would captain the cutter.

But even with a good wind following and five strong men at the oars, the water pouring downriver from the flooded inland eventually drove them back to the ship. Again Patterson tried, in the ship's pinnace this time.

When he finally got through, he unloaded supplies the Overlanders were too weak to handle.

'You see, Eli,' Martin said, 'I told you we'd only starve a bit.'

Stubbs shook his head.

'You're a strange lad, to be sure.' Then a sudden emotion appeared to shake him. 'Ah, for just one sight of home,' he said. His eyes were filled with tears.

Martin turned away and pretended interest in the loading of a buggy. He couldn't understand Solomon's friend.

Over the next few days, the malaria cases were dosed with the necessary quinine and all were nourished on rich soups. Robert Patterson, the hero of the Roper relief, saddled up for the ride back to Darwin. His farewells were heartfelt. Each man owed Patterson his life.

Meanwhile, in Adelaide, the first bad news from the north had been much augmented by the imaginations of the crew of one of the supply vessels, just returned from Port Darwin.

Rumours and exaggerations sped through the city. Men had been drowned in the floods, others had died of starvation, others had been eaten by crocodiles. A wagon train had been slaughtered by cannibal blacks. The Overland was about to be abandoned. The Treasury would be bankrupted. The Premier was going to Governor Fergusson to tender his resignation.

In the Harper household, old Hannibal was, for once, rendered speechless. Mrs Harper took to her bed in genuine prostration. Lucinda, through habit, hurried off to Steven Woodrush. Young Hannibal smoked cheroots by the box, moved in his emotions as he had never been before.

Martin, they knew, was somewhere in that northern section. They felt they had never properly appreciated him, until now, when it might be too late. Old Hannibal appeared to shrink, the weight falling off him by the day. He drank brandy in his office, tippling there and presenting an unapproachable front.

In the Residency, Sir James Fergusson paced in front of Todd, his hands clasped behind his back.

'These rumours must be refuted, Charles. Why, they are even being repeated in Parliament.'

Charles Todd was staring through the window into the Governor's garden.

'The Queenslanders are crowing,' the Governor continued angrily. 'I have an extract here from a Brisbane newspaper. They refer to the Overland as Todd's Folly and remind everyone that the Queensland government warned the British-Australian Telegraph Company, and even Westminster, that this would happen. You must prepare a statement for the newspapers. A strong and truthful statement. Confidence must be restored, at all costs.'

'The Premier intends to address Parliament about these rumours,' said Todd quietly. 'After all, the truth is bad enough.'

Governor Fergusson ceased his pacing.

'Dammit, Charles, I mean a statement of faith from you to the people. To the citizens of this city and colony.'

'If that is what you wish, sir.'

'It is, indeed, what I wish. I propose to call my secretary. We will prepare such a statement, over your signature, and issue it on Government House stationery.'

Todd became brisk. He had been a little absent before, his head running with new plans for the north.

'I would first like to make a draft.'

'Then sit down,' Sir James ordered. 'I will call for pen and paper.'

Eight

Sometimes it seemed that there was so much good sense in young Hannibal that it threatened to become an ailment. He had trodden sensibly in his father's footsteps as long as could be remembered. Young Hannibal had been the only child when his father had arrived at Port Lincoln. He had fleeting memories of the old homestead, but these were as insubstantial as the fragments of dreams that glisten in the mind for an instant, in the limbo between sleeping and waking. Since then, the stability of the family, his father's prosperous and respected place in the community, had enveloped young Hannibal like an invisible cocoon.

Young Hannibal had been surprised to hear that his father had once set fire to a wagon out of irritation with a wheel. He had heard other brief mentions of Port Lincoln days, even including that of a dispute about the price of stock, which his father had settled with his fists. But young Hannibal found it difficult to connect such stories to the father he knew. They appeared to him impossibly remote, as whimsical as the story of Jack and the bean stalk.

Yet there was more of his father in him than young Hannibal knew. Little had touched him during his schooling, or afterwards in the business, but he knew that he had a temper.

Amongst in the young set at the club, Hannibal was popular, although the wilder members were somewhat patronising about his conservative nature. On mixed picnics, efforts had been made to get Hannibal drunk, and to push him in the direction of the more willing girls.

Tubby Baker was usually the ringleader of these plots.

Tubby had inherited a sheep station on which he kept a manager, so that on occasion he could be in Adelaide for weeks at a time, spending up and generally enjoying the good life. Tubby had an amused liking for young Hannibal. Once he organised a party in a whorehouse, for what he defined as Hannibal's enlightenment, in conspiracy with a sporting group of friends. That had been years ago, and young Hannibal's behaviour had surpassed even their wildest expectations.

He had supposed himself to be in a private house for a birthday celebration, in accordance with the invitation card which Tubby had had printed for him, and had addressed the giggling girls with an alarmed mixture of courtesy and mounting confusion as the others dispensed with coats and ties, took their companions on their laps, and drank and sang around the piano.

When young Hannibal realised that he was the butt of a joke, he had sat down quietly and waited for Tubby Baker to return from a sally upstairs. When he did, young Hannibal stood, pulled his waistcoat down firmly, and marched through the rioting party.

'Now, now Han,' Tubby said warily, at the sight of young Hannibal's face.

'Put up your fists,' young Hannibal told him.

'Come on, Han. It was only a bit of fun. Why don't you enjoy yourself?'

Young Hannibal stretched Tubby Baker out on his back with a single punch, leaving the girls screeching and the young bloods at a loss. He was a little differently regarded after that, and Tubby Baker became a good friend. But perhaps the experience had worked a change in young Hannibal. In the next year he arrived at a mutually satisfactory understanding with a widow, and settled down to that as solidly as he had to his business concerns.

On the evening that Lucinda Harper had made her assault on Steven Woodrush, retiring with the satisfaction of a general after a successful campaign, she congratulated herself on the ease of the deception. But her congratulations proved to be premature. Young Hannibal, returning from a visit to his widow, glimpsed a familiar female form, unaccountably leaving the rear of the seminary to hurry towards a carriage waiting at the corner. It caused him some consternation.

Young Hannibal tried to disbelieve it, as the image repeated itself in his mind. It was, and it was not, Lucinda. The idea was preposterous. Yet there had definitely been something familiar about the young woman's carriage, something he knew in her walk. Young Hannibal fumed on his cheroot.

Returning immediately to the house, he asked after Lucinda. Mrs Harper was reading, old Hannibal was taking a late stroll in the garden.

'Lucinda?' Mrs Harper said. 'She's gone to a musical evening at Lady Charlotte's.'

'Did she take the carriage?'

'Sorry, dear?' Mrs Harper was absorbed in her magazine.

'I asked if Lucinda took the carriage.'

'I believe Lady Charlotte sent her carriage.'

Young Hannibal pulled at his moustache. The carriage he had seen on the corner had been a hired vehicle.

'When did she leave, Mother?'

Mrs Harper removed her spectacles.

'Perhaps an hour ago. But why this sudden interest in your sister?'

'Nothing, really,' young Hannibal answered. 'I just thought we might have played cards this evening.'

'If you've nothing to do, go and talk to your father. He's out in the garden. That man has no idea of the terrible burdens I bear.'

Young Hannibal was far from uncharitable. His own feelings about his adventuring brothers were deeper than he let show, but Mrs Harper's terrible burdens had become a desolate refrain. He escaped to the garden, with half an ear for his father's conversation, edgy and restless as he waited for Lucinda's return.

Later, upstairs, in his room where he had gone for its view of the road, young Hannibal heard the approach of a carriage. He felt ridiculous in his furtive stance at the curtains, but paled in recognition of the vehicle which halted a distance from the house. He lit a cheroot and went down to join the family.

Lucinda hurried in. Mrs Harper immediately put down her hot cocoa.

'Did you have a nice time, dear?'

Lucinda gave a little practised whirl, holding her music.

'It was lots of fun.'

'Who else was there?'

Lucinda rattled off names, adding amusing comments on the imaginary guests.

'Take your hat off,' old Hannibal grumbled, and went back to playing patience.

'I though the Sandersons had gone to the country,' remarked young Hannibal quietly.

Lucinda's eyes flickered.

'Did you? Then they must have returned.' She paused. 'I'm going upstairs to change.'

Young Hannibal lay staring at the ceiling for a long time before he slept. Decisions about how he should act petered out in confusion. Then he remembered that Tubby Baker was in town to attend a sale of blood horses at the John Bull yards. Tubby would be able to advise him.

At the club the next evening, the two carried their drinks to the privacy of the reading room, pulling the leather chairs close. Young Hannibal presented Tubby with a hypothetical problem. Tubby's glistening red face took on a serious expression.

'Do you have an interest in the woman concerned?'

'Just an acquaintance,' young Hannibal said.

'Is the man she goes to a friend?'

'Damned if he is,' young Hannibal answered, with heat.

Tubby stared at his glass.

'Look here, Han. Let's not beat about the bush. You're talking about Lucinda, aren't you?'

Young Hannibal squirmed as if his chair had suddenly got hot.

'Why do you say that?'

'We've all heard the gossip, old boy,' said Tubby sympathetically.

Hannibal tried to be angry, but his confused emotions failed him.

'I didn't mention Lucinda.'

'No, you didn't. If you want it straight, Han, you don't know your sister very well.'

'Now, look here,' young Hannibal began to protest.

'You look here,' Tubby said, patting Hannibal's knee. 'If you want the truth, Lucinda's making quite a name for herself. There was an officer in the 18th Regiment, a while back – the word was he was just about to become engaged to a girl. Lucinda had a tiff with her and set her cap at the officer for spite. She led the poor beggar on until he didn't know what he was doing, so they say. When he shipped out, Lucinda didn't even say goodbye.'

Hannibal gulped his drink.

'I've given it to you straight,' Tubby said. 'If you want to hit me again, go ahead.'

Hannibal shook his head, miserable at this appraisal of his sister.

'If it should ever get back to Father and Mother . . .'

Tubby, the expert, shrugged. 'It's bound to. These things always do.'

'What should I do?'

'I ain't got a sister,' Tubby said, 'but I know a bit about Lucinda. Try warning her off. If that doesn't work, you can always shake the stuffing out of Woodrush. He's on to a good thing. He could be seeing money in it.'

Tubby stood up and put a hand on young Hannibal's shoulder.

'Let's have another drink. I'll tell you about the thoroughbred stallion I bought at the auction.'

For weeks young Hannibal took no action. But he did establish, firstly, that the Sandersons had not returned from the country, and, secondly, that there had been no musical evening.

During that time, Lucinda joined the church choir to be with Steven on Tuesdays and Thursdays. The gossip increased proportionately, with scalding comments being made behind Lucinda's back, although, in the usual fashion, most of her friends and acquaintances were as amiable as ever to her face.

The few open signs of disapproval were ignored by the girl. She simply marked those who made them as the enemy, and cut them ostentatiously when they met.

At church on Sundays, Lucinda pressed Woodrush on her

mother. At home she made frequent observations on his wit, his character and his charm. Mrs Harper hurriedly adopted a new interest in Woodrush, putting herself out to be friendly at service. She thought it was sweet of Lucinda to take such an interest in a ward of the church.

Meanwhile, Steven Woodrush had been pondering the question of Lucinda. Apart from her obvious attractions, the fact that both Lucinda Harper and her mother were so publicly interested in him had already elevated his social standing. For the moment, he would play for time, not discouraging the girl exactly, but neither laying himself open to any possible criticism. Lucinda was playing her game and he could play his. He allowed himself to speculate a little further, his head spinning with dizzying possibilities. Marriage with Lucinda – was the thought so far-fetched? I, Steven Woodrush, insignificant, patronised, an object of charity since my obscure beginnings, do take thee, Lucinda Harper . . .

Young Hannibal might have had a good head for business, but it had never been much good for anything else. Business was simple and orderly, emotions were the reverse. With Martin missing in the northern floods and Matthew out with Ross, young Hannibal had already been shaken out of pattern. He tried to file the scandal of his sister away in a dusty recess of his mind, but the vision of her stealing to the carriage from the rear of the seminary continued to haunt him.

Family reputation was as dear to young Hannibal as even the smallest family conflict was not. Reluctantly he steeled himself for the confrontation.

Lucinda was at the piano, absorbed in romantic fantasies. Old Hannibal read his newspaper while Mrs Harper knitted.

Young Hannibal coughed.

'I want to talk to you, Lucinda.'

'Talk away, then,' she answered.

'Privately,' young Hannibal said, 'in my room, after cocoa.' A little later, he retired to his room to await her.

Lucinda knocked once and entered, flouncing into a chair. 'What's all the mystery?'

Young Hannibal was pacing like his father when about to deliver a lecture.

'I'll make it short, Lucinda. It concerns you and Steven Woodrush.'

Lucinda hardened in the instant, her thoughts immediately mobilised.

'I've had enough of that from Father.'

'Apparently not.'

Lucinda glared.

'Say what you have to say.'

'It has to stop. If Mother and Father ever learned what you've been doing . . .'

'Stuff and nonsense,' Lucinda said. 'Mother is very fond of Steven.'

'Mother would be fond of anyone that you paid attention to. How can you be so selfish? And so reckless?'

Lucinda's pretty face was scowling.

'I don't have to listen to this.'

'Indeed you do, miss. I won't have this family talked about, do you hear?'

'Hear yourself,' Lucinda scoffed. 'You're an echo of Father.'

Young Hannibal felt his temper rising.

'How could you lie like that, about Lady Charlotte's musical evening?'

Lucinda was shaken. The set of her mouth weakened, but she continued to bluff.

'What on earth do you mean?'

'Don't try to brazen it out. I know where you were.'

Unsure now, Lucinda watched for clues in her brother's expression.

'If you're so smart, then, where was I?'

'I saw you, Lucinda. I saw you leave in the hired carriage from St Paul's corner.'

Lucinda stood and turned her back, her feelings a mixture of fear and uncertainty. Young Hannibal was satisfied with the effect of his words. Perhaps that small thunderbolt would bring his wayward sister to her senses. But she turned suddenly, with an expression in her eyes that made young Hannibal falter.

'Spying on me, were you?'

'I passed quite fortuitously. And quite fortunately, I would venture to suggest.'

'And what do you propose to do about it?'

Hannibal waved his cheroot and considered.

'I propose that you give me certain guarantees.'

He paused at the immediate rage in her eyes.

'You can go to hell,' Lucinda said. 'And the world can go to hell with you.'

Young Hannibal paled, disbelieving, as Lucinda jabbed a finger at him.

'Don't try to tell me what to do,' she hissed. 'If you go to Mother she won't believe you. Mother will believe anything I tell her. Father has enough to worry about, with the twins on the Overland. He's not been well, you know that. If you go to Father, I'll simply deny everything.'

Young Hannibal could not believe his ears.

'Deny it? Deny it to your own father? Deny my word, in his presence?'

Lucinda smiled. 'Exactly. Anyway, I know you, Hannibal. You wouldn't have the stomach for it. You've had your head in a ledger too long.'

'You expect me to stand by, while you . . .'

Lucinda cut in.

'I expect you to mind your own business, or I'll make it equally uncomfortable for you. I know about your merry widow. How do you think that would go down with Mother and Father?'

Hannibal stood blinking, as Lucinda banged the door in her departure.

'Good Lord,' he exclaimed, spilling ash on the floor.

He went to the window, jingling coins in his pocket, his head reeling. He had never been close to his sister. As a boy he had been jealous of his mother's endless indulgence of her. That had been at least one of the causes of his drawing so close to his father.

Not having been close to his sister was one thing. But it was a shock to find that he knew nothing of her at all. He relit the cheroot, but got no comfort from it. Lucinda had faced him down like a harpy, as if he might have been an impertinent stranger. Her reference to his merry widow burnt his cheeks. How could she possibly have known that?

The renewed optimism which had slowly spread through the colony after the news that the marooned men had been delivered from the floods was soon deflated by the news ridden back from the central section. Waters discovered and charted by Ross had mysteriously disappeared from sight. Further maps and instructions buried under trees marked *Dig* had been uprooted by blacks, who had left behind only their footprints.

Men and animals had been desperate for water. Work on the line had ceased in the urgency of well-sinking. Tanker wagons, accompanied by relief teams of horses, were being driven hard towards the centre.

Old Hannibal rattled the pages of the *Advertiser*.

'Floods in the north, fit to sink a ship. Drier than a bleached bone in the centre. I tell you, the Todd disease has contaminated Mother Nature herself.'

He rolled his eyes towards heaven.

'The Premier has said in Parliament that the line is six months behind. How many more months will be lost on the central section? Do you have any idea of how much this will come to in penalties?'

Old Hannibal glared over his glasses, waiting for some response.

'No, dear,' Mrs Harper answered patiently.

'No, dear,' old Hannibal mimicked. 'This colony will be bankrupt, that's all. Nothing at all to carry on about. We will all of us be shipped out, penniless, starving, ruined. Everything will go back to the benighted savages. They'll be camping in this very room, I tell you, toasting goannas and witchetty grubs in my marble fireplace. They'll be busy in my kitchen, making sandwiches of snakes. The damned cannibals will be holding corroborees in the ballroom at Government House.'

Old Hannibal's concern, though loudly voiced, was not a great exaggeration of the concern being felt everywhere. One government project at the port had already been indefinitely halted, to conserve Treasury funds for the emergency.

The proud, free settlement of South Australia had temporarily lost its swagger.

* * *

At Daly Waters, almost two thousand miles to the north, Solomon had his own troubles.

His help in the forge was a dark, hulking man named Ben Barton, difficult and sullen. The crew working with Solomon had often urged him to get rid of the troublemaker. Solomon had refused.

'As to that,' he said, 'there are storms enough in this life, without setting sail for one.'

Now Charles Patterson sent a message to the area administrator, listing the men to be posted from the Roper River depot to the Daly Waters staging camp, with classifications of their jobs. The overseer at Daly Waters posted it outside his quarters.

When Ben Barton read the notice he set his own sails for a storm. Carrying an axe, he strode into the forge, his heavy shoulders humped, his expression thunderous. Solomon's workers were sitting down to their morning tea break. Barton spat on the ground.

'There a Harper and a Stubbs, from the Roper, to be posted here as blacksmith's help.'

'To be sure,' Solomon answered calmly. 'That's on the notice as plain as a pikestaff.'

Barton's breathing quickened, seeing the men grinning.

'I've already done me time on the line,' he stated. 'I'll break the back of any bush rat thinkin' ter take me place in the forge.'

'Well, now,' Solomon answered, taking sips from his pannikin, 'that would be calamitous wrong on two scores. First, the shipmates posted to come aboard were specially requested by Solomon, and should never have set sail for the Roper at all. Neither do they have hide nor hair nor any passing resemblance to bush rats. Second, as you might say, Solomon would be strongly prejudiced in the matter of the breaking of their backs.'

The enjoyment of the others in the forge, and their evident dislike of him, shown naked now, drove Ben Barton to further fury.

'Tell me straight. Do yer mean ter get rid of me?'

Solomon considered.

'Let's say that when the new hands arrive, we'll be overcrewed, so to speak.'

A nerve in Barton's cheek had begun to twitch uncontrollably. He made a sudden run at Solomon, the axe held in both hands, its sharpened edge pointing forward. Solomon, still seated, wrenched the axe from Barton's grasp, turning the blade away from his face.

'Anything to oblige, my sweet and courteous fellow. Here Solomon stands. What do you have in mind?'

Barton made a sobbing sound and swung from his superior height. Solomon intercepted the blow on a knotted forearm. His fist went into Barton's face once, with a sound like the crack of a whip. The big man's fall was heavy. Blood shot from his mouth and nose.

Solomon took a few steps forward.

'In the matter of explanation, now, as to how you came by that face, you came by it out of an ill-directed kick from a horse. There's not a man in this forge who'll say different.'

Barton backed away. The furnaceman handed him a sweat rag to put to his bleeding face.

'I'll get yer,' he snarled, spitting blood. 'I'll get yer yet, yer poxed Yankee bastard.'

'Out,' Solomon shouted.

When Barton had gone, Solomon picked up his hammer.

'In the matter of the posting,' Solomon told his men, 'there's a bit of a boy coming to help in the forge, who shipped out with Solomon on the *Omeo*. The other is a quiet man, who keeps to himself. It will be a good ship and a happy crew when they get here from the Roper.'

'A kick from an 'orse,' the furnaceman said, shaking his head. 'I've suffered many of them in me time. But I ain't ever seen an 'orse kick like Solomon.'

Solomon knew that he had made an enemy, and a dangerous one. But Martin and Eli would soon be with him. Solomon cast out his darker thoughts, beaming his luminous smile as he swung the hammer.

Nine

In the period before the monsoon had made a sea and a quagmire of the northern section, poling down from Port Darwin had advanced a hundred miles. But the effort had strained man and beast to the limit. The axemen, who had both to clear a track for the wagons and fell and strip poles, had wasted to sinew and gristle.

Behind them in the sucking mud, the carcasses of bullocks and horses rotted, bloated and bursting in the sun as it burned through breaks in the murky cloud. Great coils of wire and cases of insulators lay where they had been abandoned. Wagons and drays, embalmed to their axles in mud, littered the track.

The Overlanders had persevered in the first rains, sinking four-foot holes with spades and crowbars, the cavities filling with muddy water as they were dug. The iron-footed poles had to be splashed in and fastened with stones and dry earth brought from quarries.

As the poles advanced the linesmen followed, their moleskin trousers and flannel singlets soaked and heavy on their bodies, climbing the poles in spiked boots to hammer the insulators home and connect the shining wire forked aloft from the pole before, straining on their perches to gather in the slack.

After the monsoon had spent its burden, men, beasts and landscape continued to fester in a steaming torment while the earth slowly turned to cracked, swollen blocks of hardened mud.

Plagues of blowflies, glutted on the rotting carcasses, appeared; great swarms that laid their eggs even in the sweated flannels on the Overlanders' backs. And the blacks also became a plague, shinning the poles for the porcelain insulators which they chipped into sharp spearheads. Pillaging the bogged transports for metal, they somehow contrived to remove even the iron wheel sheaths from their rims. In the slab telegraph station at Darwin, the great batteries that were to galvanise the wire between relay stations were brought hurriedly into use. Massive charges of current were applied at intervals to the line, and the raiding blacks at the insulators were felled to the ground. The vandalism ceased.

Then a new cause for despair disrupted the line. The great termite mounds of the north, sometimes twice the height of a man and in communities that covered dozens of square miles, awoke to the feast of dry wood being slowly marched across their territory. After the wet, as work began anew, the poles of gum, stringybark and bloodwood were being invisibly reduced at their hearts. The myriad tiny jaws converted the solid timber into soft-centred shells.

It was easy to detect the sections being cannibalised by the termites, though little of their depredations could be seen. It was enough to put an ear to the timber: the uninterrupted gnawing could be heard as a clamour.

When this news reached Charles Todd, it tried even his resolution. Everything in nature seemed to be conspiring against the Overland Telegraph. Thousands of iron poles would have to be ordered from England. Those poles destroyed would have to be temporarily replaced with new timber. When the iron was shipped in, the northern section, advanced by such bitter hardship, would have to be repoled.

A new gloom settled on the South Australian government. Sir James Fergusson, the hero of Inkerman, felt himself enlisted in a war in which there was no tangible adversary. The enemy was the unknown centre and north of the most isolated land mass on earth, a continent which rejected, with an unexpected violence, every footfall of civilisation. The dream of being joined to the outside world had turned into a nightmare.

Yet the small colony rallied itself again. Todd prepared to sail north to aid Patterson's endeavours to keep the northern line moving. New ships were fitted with supplies, new men recruited. With so much achieved in the south and the centre, the little Superintendent of Telegraphs was not about to admit defeat.

* * *

After the floods had receded, all hands were kept busy at the Roper River depot. Scrub was cleared, new tents replaced the rotted ones and solid store huts were built. New horses were landed from the supply vessels by way of a railed barge. There would be no more massacres by the crocodiles.

Martin could scarcely conceal his impatience to be gone from the Roper. On his urgent petitioning, Mr Patterson himself had agreed that, when the new shifts arrived at the Roper, Martin would join his blacksmith friend on the line.

Eli Stubbs, just returned from an expedition to take supplies from the depot to the men on the line, had hardly dismounted before Martin rushed up to him, breathless and beaming.

'Did you hear anything, Eli? Did you ask about Solomon?'

Stubbs had not altered his ways with the relieving of the camp. He had taken no quarters in the new tents, with their sound flooring and bedding, and had made a new camp for himself at a little distance. Now he smiled gently at the boy.

'Did I hear anything, boy? Well, I do believe I did hear something about a pox-scarred Yankee who half shook to death the official that sent young Martin Harper to the Roper.'

'Did Solomon do that?'

'That's the hearsay, lad. He's at a place they call Daly Waters. That's where we'll be going.'

Solomon had made spirited attempts to find Martin, according to Eli, after the first camp was made out of Darwin. He had walked back to the port the next day, in defiance of the overseer, and had shaken the clerk who had posted Martin to the Roper with such vehemence that he afterwards remarked to his mates that it had been an astonishment to find the teeth still in his head.

For the rest of the day, Martin smiled at his tasks.

The new horses brought to the Roper landing were urgently needed on the line, and little time was wasted in mustering a mob to go inland to Daly Waters, a hundred and eighty-five miles away. Dick Mitchell, a drover from Queensland, with his offsiders Bill Johnson and the Irishman Mick Ryan who was to drive the supply dray, was to lead the mob. Leaving early one morning, the forty horses were sleek and fresh and the men exhilarated at the prospect of the journey ahead.

Six days later, a bloody dray hurtled into the camp at Daly Waters. Johnson was dead, stiff under a tarpaulin on the floor. Mitchell, the remains of a spear protruding from his back, was horribly burnt. Ryan, the driver, could not speak through the barb that had pierced the bridge of his nose and lodged itself into the roof of his mouth.

As riders galloped to Darwin for a doctor, Ryan died, his mouth still agape on the spear settled in his head forever. The doctor, racing down the line in a sulky, reached the camp in time to save only Dick Mitchell.

When Mitchell could speak, his words coming out in great rasps, he told of what had happened.

About eighty miles away from Daly Waters, the draught horses were knocking up and some of the mob needed reshoeing. Mitchell decided that when they came upon the next good water, they would spell for a while.

The lagoon they came upon was a veritable Eden in the wilderness. Waterlilies flourished on its surface, which stretched out of sight, the trees on its periphery blazed trails of purple convolvulus, and great flocks of duck, crane and jabirus arose flapping as the horses went to the water to drink.

Bill Johnson decided on a swim. Mick Ryan determined on a stroll. Mitchell stayed behind to set up the camp. An hour passed peacefully.

Then it happened. A big, naked black, with tufts of parrot feathers in his headband, a bone knife in his belt of human hair and a bundle of spears in one hand, stepped out of the scrub near the tent. In that frozen instant, as the black hurled one of his spears, Mitchell caught sight of Ryan emerging from the trees. Pitching forward, Mitchell fell into the flames of the fire he had lately got going.

Ryan, unarmed, ran back to the lagoon to warn Bill Johnson. He found him sprawled in the shallows, the water around him an oily red. Trying to speak as Ryan dragged him up on the verge, he pointed to his belt and holstered revolver that hung from a bush. Ryan had reached the revolver and was turning when the spear took him in the face, smashing through the bridge of his nose and the roof of his mouth until the barbed tip rasped against his tongue. The shaft quivering across his vision, he took aim. The warrior screeched, dropped his arsenal of spears and fled into the scrub.

Ryan lifted Johnson and supported him back to the camp. Mitchell had crawled out of the fire, managing to extinguish the flames, with six feet of throwing spear stuck in his back.

Holding up the shaft buried in his face, Ryan staggered towards the dray. There was a small butcher's saw there, and half a case of rum. He sawed off the spear an inch from his face, then sawed the shaft in Mitchell's back. It was impossible to remove the spearheads. The men slobbered at the rum, getting down as much of it as they could.

Ryan made himself harness a cart horse to the dray, string two more horses behind it, and lift his mates over the tailboard. Mitchell handed Ryan his compass before he lapsed into a coma.

All that night Ryan steered by the compass, striking matches to take bearings and holding pannikins of rum to the lips of the stricken men. In the blackness, while he swooned on the dray seat, Bill Johnson died.

The burial of Johnson and Ryan was attended by Overlanders from far up the line, and the Irish among them held a wake for Mick Ryan.

Ben Barton, now the camp horse-handler, glowered at the mourners as he repeatedly lifted the rum bottle to his lips. Finally he spat out the words that had been forming in his sodden brain.

'If there's a man among you gutless blatherers, he'll ride out with me and leave a few bullets in them stinking blacks.' His words were slurred, his eyes heavy and bloodshot. 'Them black bastards that murdered my mother and father and sisters back in New South Wales. If there's a man among you lily-livered lot –'

The Irish thought about it and made great threats, and then returned to their drinking and sentimental songs.

'Yer call yourselves men,' sneered Barton, swaying and waving the bottle about. He spat noisily on the ground. 'There's more guts in that there gob than there is in the lot of you.'

'Would that be the truth, now?' One of the drinkers dashed his coat to the ground. 'And would ye be likin' to try Paddy O'Casey's guts, ye big ugly baboon?'

Barton tossed aside his bottle.

'Them pole cutters that came in yesterday said they'd seen blacks west of the camp.' He staggered to his feet. 'I'll leave a black carcass to stink in the bush this day. And I'll bring yer back a pair of black balls to celebrate yer gutless bloody wake.'

A weedy little fellow, holding a bottle, followed Ben Barton from the wake.

'I'll be no lavin' yer alone in this. Mick Ryan was a boyo. Jist saddle a dacent cratur fer Dan O'Halloran too.'

Kicking his horse to a gallop on the flat, Barton headed for the area where the pole cutters had been working. O'Halloran followed at a canter, stoking himself with rum.

The group of blacks digging for yams near the swamp were ill-fated that day. The men leapt up, chattering and grabbing for their spears as the horsemen bore down on them. Barton fired once from the saddle, the impact of the bullet hurling a young boy on to his back, while the other men and two lubras raced for the deeper parts of the swamp, knowing there could be no pursuit in the tangle of mud and reeds. Barton fired again, wounding a black who floundered in the reeds before disappearing from sight.

The single figure of a girl remained transfixed at the yam patch, her dilated eyes fixed on the dead body. She was young, perhaps thirteen.

As Barton reined in and turned to look, the girl broke out of her frozen trance and started to run for the swamp. Barton wheeled his mount to course her. He raised his rifle, then thrust it back into its bucket. As man and horse caught up with the black girl, Barton slipped his right stirrup from its hook and swung it by the strap. The circling stirrup iron took the girl at the base of the skull.

She fell on her back, stunned by the heavy blow. Barton dismounted and stood over her. The girl, well formed, already had the raised weals, the tribal decorations of puberty, across her body.

O'Halloran cantered up, ashen-faced with the realisation of what was about to happen. Barton took the bottle that the Irishman had been holding so tightly that the knuckles showed white on his sun-blackened hands. He tipped back his head and drank.

'But it's just a wee girl,' O'Halloran gasped, taking back the bottle.

Barton was unbuckling his trousers.

'It's as choice a bit o' black velvet as I've ever see'd in the north,' he said.

O'Halloran's voice shook with protest.

'Och, man, you can no be thinkin' on that. It's jist a wee slip o' a girl.'

'If yer don't like it, yer don't have to watch.'

O'Halloran leaned over and vomited.

'Git back ter camp,' Barton ordered. 'And mind yer keep yer trap shut, you hear? Yer in this as much as me.'

The black girl came out of her stupor as Barton grunted on her body. Her big eyes widened in unspeakable terror, became luminous and rolled under lids that had been touched with ochre. The man over her was crazed, shouting obscenities at the slight body crushed under his weight, calling incoherently on a dead mother and sister. Virgin blood seeped out and spread on his loins.

Making a fist, she thrust it in the face of the white man. Her head lolled sideways as he punched her.

When he was spent, he rolled off the unmoving body and grunted. He reached for the bottle the Irishman had dropped. Mumbling, watching the girl, he tore a strip off his shirt to wipe at the hymen stain on him. Past his horse, he could see the body of the dead youth. He heaved himself up and walked back to kick at it.

The young male was decorated in red ochre, now run and mingled with darker red from the big, black-rimmed hole in his chest. Stooping to grasp his ankles, Barton dragged the body towards the swamp, wading with it through the scummy water and reeds until he cast it from him with an oath.

The spread-eagled black girl had still not moved, and now there was blood at the corner of her mouth. Barton mounted his horse, drank again from the bottle, and let the animal turn for the camp. For a long while he let the horse walk, shaking his head and conversing with himself. Then he dropped the bottle, gathered up the reins, and began to canter over the flat.

Ten

As Lucinda had cut those friends and acquaintances who had made even the smallest criticism of her association with Steven Woodrush, so she now ignored young Hannibal with a frankness that jarred his mild soul. To be cut by his own sister, at table, in the drawing room, wherever they were brought together, was really quite intolerable. But to Lucinda, the matter was simple. By speaking out, brother or not, Hannibal had numbered himself among the enemy.

His attempts to heal the breach merely signified his contemptible weakness to his sister, and compliments upon her dress and small affectionate overtures fell on stony ground. In Lucinda's mind, Hannibal's attempts at reconciliation demonstrated her mastery of the situation. She could truly do as she pleased. Her brother could jump in the Torrens, along with anyone else who tried to cross her.

Mrs Harper could not but observe her daughter's blatant hostility towards her elder brother, and she reacted to it with her habitual shortsightedness, chiding young Hannibal.

'Whatever have you done to upset Lucinda? Really, Han, it's too bad of you. After all, you are the elder brother. Disharmony between you only adds to my burdens. At Lucinda's age, I was out in the wilds of Port Lincoln with your father. One of the few pleasures I now have is to see Lucinda happy and enjoying herself.'

She put down her knitting. 'In any case, whatever you have done to upset your sister, I wish you'd apologise.'

'Godamighty!' said Hannibal.

'Hannibal, you will not blaspheme in this house,' said his mother. 'You will make your peace with Lucinda. Now where are you going?'

'Out,' young Hannibal announced. 'Out, out, and out.'

Tubby Baker visited Adelaide in the next week for the races, with high hopes for a horse he had bred on his property.

In the club, the Overland Telegraph was again the subject under discussion, news having been ridden back to the city once more from the central section. The story most often repeated in the club concerned a scouting party which had been attacked at sundown by a group of blacks armed with spears, waddies and nulla-nullas. The scouting party took cover behind the wagon, and in the subsequent exchange one of the scouts was wounded. Pulling out the spear, he took refuge inside an empty hogshead and waited out the rest of the attack, holding off his assailants by firing his revolver through the bunghole.

'Just as well it wasn't Tubby,' one of his friends laughed at the end of the tale. 'Tubby would have stuck in the rim of that barrel like a cork in a bottle!'

Tubby became serious.

'You can laugh all you want about the Overland. If I wasn't such a selfish bastard, I'd be out there helping make history. Say what you like, the Overland beats everything else attempted in the Empire till now.'

The latest dispatches from the centre also contained news about the discovery of subterranean deposits of water, which had greatly helped the central section. Wells had been sunk for a hundred miles up the surveyed line. This meant faster progress north with the wire.

Tubby Baker took young Hannibal aside from the crowd.

'Did you get anywhere with Lucinda?'

'Damned if I did. She flew at me. I tell you, Tubby, until recently I just didn't know my own sister.'

Tubby nodded.

'How about Woodrush? Have you had a go at him?'

Hannibal felt inadequate.

'Didn't know how to approach it.'

'For Pete's sake, Han. Frighten the hell out of him. Tell him you'll go to the Bishop.'

'To the Bishop?'

'Why not? That would put ants in Woodrush's breeches.'

'I couldn't do that. I couldn't tattle on Lucinda to the Bishop.'

'You're bloody well hopeless,' Tubby said. 'Look here, Han – I've been told that they're seeing more of each other than ever.'

'Not at the seminary?' Hannibal asked.

'I'm damned if I know where. You were going on about your parents, when we last spoke. Isn't it time you did something to stop it?'

Hannibal nodded. Something would have to be done. The image of Lucinda hurrying secretly to the hired carriage still disturbed him. Tubby hammered a little harder at the nail of anxiety.

'Do you want to wait until he gets into her skirts?'

'Look here . . .' Hannibal was appalled.

'Wake up to yourself,' Tubby advised. 'Oh, hang on, my trainer has just come in. See you later, Han.'

After the next Sunday service, when Lucinda and Mrs Harper had finished fussing over Steven Woodrush, young Hannibal waited behind.

'I want to talk with you, Woodrush.'

'Now?' Woodrush asked.

'I walk with my father after service. I suggest this afternoon, at five o'clock.'

Woodrush looked uneasy.

'What do you want to talk about?'

'The subject can wait,' Hannibal said curtly. 'Where can we meet?'

'Would the church be suitable? I'll be preparing for the evening service then.'

'At five o'clock then,' young Hannibal repeated.

Old Hannibal leaned on his cane and gazed unseeingly at the Torrens. He had thinned considerably in the past months, and his gold watch chain drooped noticeably across his stomach.

'You seem to have given up the idea of buying Smythe's

undertaking business, Father,' remarked young Hannibal, welcoming the opportunity to set aside, if only temporarily, the wretched business of his sister.

'I've lost interest in it,' old Hannibal admitted. 'I've come to dislike the idea of undertaking.'

'But you intended to put in a manager.'

'No,' old Hannibal was firm. 'It's a sordid way to make money. I've enough on my mind, without preying on other people's miseries.'

Young Hannibal understood, now.

'The news from the north and the centre has been encouraging,' he said, without conviction.

'Encouraging?' Old Hannibal studied the ducks on the river. 'Cannibals attacking the scouting party, that's encouraging? No news from Martin is encouraging? Ross out to blazes somewhere, Matthew gone with him, I suppose that's encouraging, too?'

Hannibal tried again.

'Business has never been better.'

'Overland business. I'd rather be without a jot of it and have the twins safely home.'

Old Hannibal made half-hearted whacks at the seeding grass with his cane.

'Have you heard any more of that rot about your sister? Why your mother has now taken Woodrush up is more than I can understand.'

'It's only a church relationship, Father.'

'It had better be.' Old Hannibal frowned. 'Sometimes I wonder how well I know my own daughter.'

He sighed and paused to ponder.

'Everything seems to be turned upside-down. Nothing can be relied upon for tuppence.'

In his room, Woodrush waited anxiously on the appointed time. He had made many conjectures as to why Hannibal Harper wanted to talk to him. If Hannibal intended warning him off Lucinda, he would have to be careful. In the future that he sometimes allowed himself to imagine, he could not afford an enemy in the family.

The silence of the empty church overwhelmed young Hannibal when he entered. In the sanctuary, the three tall windows of stained glass, capped by a stone arch with three roundels in it, whitened by the outside light, seemed to hallow the altar as he had never felt it hallowed in congregation.

He seated himself uncomfortably in a back pew. Always sincere in his devotions, he shifted about uneasily, feeling that the church was no place for the discussion he intended.

Woodrush entered the sanctuary from a panelled side door, carrying a pile of books which he put down when young Hannibal arose. Woodrush bowed to the altar and walked up the carpet between the pews.

'Shall we be seated?' he asked.

Hannibal pointed to the pew across the aisle, and the two young men faced each other. Hannibal came straight to the point.

'You know why I'm here?'

'You said you wanted to talk.'

'I want you to stop seeing Lucinda.'

'Your sister is a friend of the church,' Woodrush said. 'I can hardly avoid seeing her.'

'Your meetings have become damnable gossip.'

Woodrush appraised this man, whom he had known by sight for years.

'We have met, it is true, in order to discuss religion and church affairs. If there is a certain affinity between us, I can't see how that would cause offence.'

'Can't you? Then you'd better think again. You're studying for the priesthood, Woodrush.'

Woodrush decided that he could handle Hannibal Harper.

'Perhaps you shouldn't listen to gossip. I've the greatest respect for your sister, as indeed, I have for your mother.'

Hannibal reddened.

'Leave my mother out of this. If Lucinda burned the church down, Mother would find good reason. What are you after, Woodrush?'

'After? I'm afraid I don't understand you.'

'Are you telling me there's nothing between you and Lucinda?'

'We are friends,' Woodrush said. 'That's all.'

Somehow Woodrush seemed to be taking control of the interview. He was damnably cocksure.

'I've spoken about this to my sister.'

'Oh? And what did Lucinda say?'

'She told me to mind my own business, that's what she said. She made it clear where she's got her sights set.'

'You're surely exaggerating,' Woodrush said. 'I don't want any ill-feeling between us, Hannibal.'

This was too much.

'Don't Hannibal me,' young Hannibal shouted, and then shrank at the echo flung back like a reproof from the nave.

Woodrush flushed, reminded of his social inferiority.

'I'm sorry you feel that way.'

Hannibal said, 'You're sure of yourself, aren't you?'

'My conscience is clear,' Woodrush answered.

The moment was ripe for young Hannibal to take the initiative.

'Then you have a very convenient conscience.'

Woodrush faltered for a moment. Then, concealing a twinge of alarm, he stared coolly at young Hannibal.

'Would you care to explain that remark?'

The words were jerked out of Hannibal.

'I'm talking about seduction.'

Still Woodrush was cool.

'I am astonished to hear you suggest such a thing about your own sister,' he said.

'I'm just getting to know my sister.'

He put everything into a shot in the dark.

'What was she doing with you last month, that she had to hide in a hired carriage around the corner from the seminary, at night?'

Woodrush gaped. Young Hannibal, seeing that his barb had gone home, was as helpless as Woodrush.

'How . . . how did you know?'

'Because I followed her,' Hannibal lied.

'You followed her?'

'I followed her all the way home.'

Woodrush searched desperately for a rejoinder.

'Well?' young Hannibal demanded.

'You've got to believe me. I didn't know she was coming. I just opened my door and there she was, waiting.'

'What?' Hannibal shouted again, half-rising in the manner of his father. 'Lucinda . . .?'

'I swear it,' Woodrush pleaded. 'I was shocked. Had Lucinda been seen in quarters . . .'

Hannibal sank back into the pew, unable to speak. Woodrush was pale now.

'You must believe me. You know my position here.'

Hannibal rubbed his balding head and felt for his hat, needing something to hold. He had never imagined anything like this. His family loyalty rose in a tide.

'Have you seduced my sister?'

'No, no,' Woodrush almost whimpered. 'You must believe me.'

Hannibal remembered Tubby, the expert.

'Has Lucinda tried to seduce you?'

'I wouldn't say that . . .' Woodrush began uncertainly, the words petering out on his lips.

Young Hannibal dashed down his hat and clenched a fist. Woodrush slid hurriedly back along the pew.

'I have told and told Lucinda. I have told her that all my feelings are, and must be, centred on the church.'

Hannibal stared at Woodrush, speechless. So Lucinda had been thwarted in her approaches, if Woodrush were telling the truth. Now Hannibal understood his sister's blazing defiance, her conduct towards him, the precariousness of her moods. To have pursued and connived for Woodrush, careless of everything and everyone, and then to have been unsuccessful – Hannibal suddenly had an insight into his sister, into the way she had been in smaller things all her life. Thwarted, she would pull the roof down on someone. In his musings, young Hannibal almost forgot Steven Woodrush.

'It has to stop,' he said finally. 'If it came out, it would be too much for my father. I will have to take it to the Bishop.'

'You must not, I beg of you,' Woodrush cried aghast. 'I'll do anything you want. I promise not to see her again, unless at the church. If she comes looking for me, I'll give the verger instruction that I'm not to be found.'

'So she comes looking for you?'

'I . . . I'll tell the verger I'm not to be found.'

Woodrush had become a supplicant now, all his earlier, almost patronising assurance departed.

'You had better keep your word,' Hannibal said. 'There could be worse things than the Bishop. It would give me great pleasure to thrash the life out of you.'

Each day old Hannibal fretted on the arrival of the mail and each day he swallowed his disappointment and bit back his fears. Mrs Harper made a conscious effort now not to talk of her own anxiety, aware at last of how her husband suffered in the absence of the twins.

Old Hannibal continued to read aloud any news of the Overland.

'It says here that the Milner brothers are still making ready to drive their flocks north. Waiting on the season, it says. What season, may I ask, might be the appropriate one for such foolhardiness?'

'You are worrying yourself unnecessarily,' the transformed Mrs Harper told him. 'I'm concerned about you, Hannibal. You're a shadow of yourself. You must try to eat, my dear.'

It comforted old Hannibal to be thus cosseted. He was grateful to his wife, who had ceased taking to bed with her burdens. They grew closer in this mutual consideration. Old Hannibal sometimes spent only a half-day at the business, so as to take his wife on carriage excursions into the country, something he had not done in years.

Steven Woodrush had been more alarmed by young Hannibal than his adversary had known. The threat to go to the Bishop was only a little less terrible than a threat to go to God.

But he had blundered, blundered badly, he felt, in the critical admission that Lucinda had been in his room. Had her brother known that for certain, he would have acted sooner. He would not have delayed all these weeks.

He had let Hannibal Harper fool him, and the error gnawed at him.

Lucinda recognised a change in Woodrush at the first sight of his face. For a week he tried to avoid her at choir. On Sunday he left the church immediately after service, not stopping to talk. Lucinda wrote Woodrush a note. She would expect him in the vestry, after the next choral practice. If he didn't appear, Lucinda said, she would come again to his room. Woodrush appeared at the vestry at the appointed time.

Lucinda kept her distance, forgoing the embraces to which they had become accustomed.

'Why have you changed?'

'I've not changed,' Woodrush answered. 'I just can't take these risks, Lucinda.'

But he had already begun to melt. He had few resources with which to arm himself against Lucinda.

'Something has happened. There's no use pretending.'

It was indeed no use pretending. There had been too much intimacy between them, too much probing, too many admissions. Lucinda knew him too well, had learned too much in her stalking of him.

'Your brother came to see me,' he said.

Lucinda's brow darkened.

'What did he say?'

'He knew about you having been in my room. He threatened to go to the Bishop.'

Lucinda's breathing became quicker.

'You admitted that, to Hannibal?'

'He knew, Lucinda. He knew.'

She shook her head.

'What a fool you are. How could he have known? He only saw me leaving in the carriage.'

Woodrush trapped inside his own error, continued.

'He followed you home. He told me. He knows everything.'

'What rot,' Lucinda said, scornfully. 'I didn't go directly home. If Hannibal had known, do you dream he would have let me get away with it?'

Woodrush made a helpless gesture. Now Lucinda nibbled at her beautiful underlip, thinking.

'Hannibal would never go to the Bishop. I've been through all that with him. The Bishop would go to Father. You know he's a family friend. Hannibal would never upset Father. Father would have a fit, if he knew I'd been in your room.'

'He insisted that we stop seeing each other, Lucinda.'

So woebegone did Woodrush appear that an unaccustomed tenderness changed Lucinda's face, softening it into beauty. He looked so helpless. She knew him to be unworldly, she knew that she alone was the strength between them. She went to him, kissing his face, drawing his head to her bosom.

'Don't be afraid. I know Hannibal. There's nothing to be afraid of.'

'I don't know what to do,' Woodrush confessed.

'I'll tell you what we'll do.'

Lucinda was staring past his bent head, stroking his cheek.

'Tomorrow evening at six, I'll have a carriage at the corner. We will ride out to a village and be together.'

Woodrush said, 'The driver would recognise us.'

'Don't worry about the driver, I know one who keeps his counsel. We will send him off for a drink, and just be together.'

Lucinda did indeed know such a driver and carriage. She and the officer from the 18th Regiment had used him often.

'Don't be afraid, Steven,' she repeated. 'Everything will be all right.'

That night Lucinda suggested a game of draughts with young Hannibal, kissing him when he won, lighting his cheroot. Blossoming under his sister's attentions, he almost forgot how savagely unforgiving she had been. He decided that his sister had come to her senses. Woodrush had been frightened off, either that or he would surely have told Lucinda of his warning.

'One more game, for luck,' Lucinda said. 'My turn for white,'

Mrs Harper smiled with approval on her son. Whatever he had done to upset Lucinda must have been repaired. Young Hannibal puffed on his cheroot with contentment, until an unpleasant thought began to nag at him. His own sister had tried to seduce a man. Lucinda had tried with Woodrush. The wretched fellow had as much as admitted it. Studying his animated sister, young Hannibal tried to recollect the exact words they had had on the subject. Might there not have been a misunderstanding?

Then old Hannibal distracted him with an announcement.

'They're having to put up lightning conductors on the poles, against damage from electrical storms. Now the Todd disease has corrupted the heavens. The Overland is being attacked by thunderbolts and lightning. The wire is going up in fire and brimstone.'

The carriage hired by Lucinda was fully enclosed, with a small hatch behind the driver through which he would take orders. He specialised in courting couples.

At St Paul's corner, Lucinda knocked on the hatch and settled back to wait for Woodrush. She had Hannibal eating out of her hand, she thought. That danger at least had been disarmed. After cocoa, on the previous night, Lucinda had whispered an apology for her previous behaviour. Hannibal had kissed her cheek affectionately and called her 'Cindy'. She had been hard put not to laugh out loud.

Woodrush turned the corner, glancing behind him, stopping to examine the street. Lucinda opened the carriage door. As Woodrush climbed in, the driver shook the reins and nipped his whip at the horse's back. The carriage moved off smartly, clacking on the cobbles. Taking Woodrush by the hand, Lucinda pulled him close beside her in the darkened carriage. His palm was sweating.

'Did your brother say anything?'

'Not a word. Don't worry about Hannibal. I've pulled the wool over his eyes.'

'You don't think he'll go to the Bishop?'

Lucinda spoke a little tartly.

'Will you get that out of your head? I've told you. There's absolutely nothing to worry about.'

'He had his temper up.'

Lucinda put a finger over his lips.

'Not another word. Hold me, Steven, Kiss me.'

The cobbles clacked into silence and were left behind. The sun began to set in the hills beyond the city. The driver made himself comfortable on his seat and lit his pipe. He had his instructions. Lucinda re-pinned her hair, its order disturbed by her recent embrace.

'Isn't it wonderful, Steven? We can do this whenever we like.' She fondled him. 'Why are you shaking?'

Woodrush pulled away a little.

'I can't think straight, when I'm with you. How did all this happen?'

'Does it matter?' Lucinda whispered. 'Just let us enjoy it.'

The carriage turned off the road, into tall trees and heaped runs of blackberry bushes. The driver knocked on the hatch and pushed it partly open.

'I'll take a walk into the village, miss. The old grey might crop about a bit.'

Lucinda was familiar with the old grey's habits.

'Now we are truly alone,' she told Woodrush. 'You do love me, don't you, Steven?'

He paled at the word.

'I think I do, Lucinda. I don't really know much about love. I've lived so different.'

Lucinda had no intention of conducting a philosophical debate. She pulled at the neck of her dress, exposing her ripe, strong breasts.

'Kiss me,' she said fiercely, while Woodrush stared, mesmerised. 'Kiss me here. I am all yours, Steven.'

Her tone changed to impatience, as she placed her hand behind his neck. Steven Woodrush was awakened to passion, to an intimacy he hadn't dared imagine, compelled to obey. The touch and the scent of the soft, swelling flesh both terrified and overwhelmed him. His mind began to spin. He thought he could actually feel it spinning.

'Again,' Lucinda demanded. 'Kiss me again.'

They were lost in themselves, mindless of everything else. Woodrush was helpless, kissing Lucinda's slim body, burying his head in the unbelievable heaven of her breasts. She whimpered as she drew him to her, lifted his head to kiss his mouth, took him to her breast again. Her wide grey eyes had grown heavy with passion, as though a fine mantle had covered the pupils. She arched herself back on the long leather seat, pulling at her skirts, pulling at Woodrush.

'Touch me, Steven. Touch me.'

'No!' Woodrush cried out. 'I must not.'

Lucinda clenched her small white teeth.

'You must. Come over me, Steven. Let me help you, Steven.'

He groaned as she fumbled at him, feeling an agonising rise in his genitals. Lucinda wore nothing beneath the long skirt and petticoat. He attempted a last resistance and then succumbed, almost choked by his heartbeats, no trace of his own will remaining. Then something seemed to burst in his brain.

Lucinda held on to the leather strap, trembling violently. Woodrush pressed himself into the corner.

'God forgive me,' he groaned. 'What have I done?'

Lucinda steadied herself, rearranging her clothes. Woodrush had barely entered her, as had been her intention, yet she felt it as a consummation. She looked almost coldly at her conquest.

'Are you sorry?'

'Yes, I am sorry.' His voice was small and thin. 'Forgive me, Lucinda.'

'Don't be silly,' she said. 'There's nothing to forgive.'

Woodrush reached for the door handle.

'What are you doing?'

'I've got to get out in the air.'

'Do you want me to come with you?'

'No,' he protested. 'I have to be alone.'

When Lucinda had waited long enough, she looked for Steven, calling his name into the night. He returned, white and silent, only when the driver was climbing to his perch, whistling noisily.

Lucinda was balanced between tears and rage.

'Why did you abandon me like that?'

'I had to get away. I had to think.'

The carriage began to move, quickening as the driver snapped his whip.

'Hold me,' Lucinda said. 'I'm truly yours, now.'

Woodrush sat stiffly beside her, his profile patched with shadows.

'I can't. It's too soon, Lucinda.'

She asked, smiling, 'Whatever are you talking about? Don't you know what we've done?'

'I can't explain.'

Lucinda's smile faded.

'What can't you explain?'

'I don't know,' he said miserably. 'It's all somehow . . . somehow . . . I don't know. It's somehow bound up with my ordination.'

'You are to be a Protestant priest.' Lucinda was sharp. 'There's no chastity in your vows.'

'I haven't taken my vows,' Woodrush said. 'I don't know now if I'm worthy.'

Lucinda's hand went to her throat, in unknowing imitation of her mother. For the first time in her life, she felt a prickling of fear.

'You were prepared for me, Lucinda,' Woodrush said softly, wonderingly. 'You had even even dressed for it.'

Lucinda's lips trembled.

'Are you blaming me? Are you blaming me for letting you take me?'

'Letting me?' Woodrush stopped, biting off the words that rose to his lips. 'Be patient with me. I need time to think.'

Lucinda hunched over in childish tears. She saw she had made a terrible miscalculation. She had sought to make Steven hers, irrevocably hers, and had succeeded only in alienating him from her, perhaps forever. They rode back to St Paul's in silence.

She raised herself as the carriage stopped, a touch of hysteria in her voice.

'Tomorrow night? Tomorrow night, in the vestry?'

'I don't know,' Woodrush said. 'You will have to be patient with me, Lucinda.'

'I will be, I will be,' she promised. 'Whatever you say, Steven.'

The next night Woodrush was not in the vestry. Earlier he had not appeared for choir practice. Lucinda's voice quavered as she tried to sing her parts. The choir master told her that Woodrush was confined to his room, feeling ill. All the next week, he remained confined to his quarters, and was absent from the Sunday service.

'I wonder why Steven wasn't serving?' Mrs Harper said idly to Lucinda, as they walked to the carriage. 'Are you well, dear? You have quite a pallor.'

'It's only a passing faintness, Mother.'

'Is anything troubling you?'' Mrs Harper wanted to know. 'You've been so quiet these last few days.'

Lucinda said, 'Just let me be.'

But Mrs Harper couldn't, or wouldn't, let her daughter be.

'I'll send for the doctor, when we get home. There are some nasty illnesses going about, I believe.'

Lucinda stopped, her lips trembling.

'Mother, will you just let me be?'

Mrs Harper halted, surprised by her daughter's manner and appearance, but said nothing. Perhaps she would just have a quiet word with the doctor.

Returning home from the quarterly meeting of the church board, old Hannibal was sunk in his by now habitual gloom. He stirred mechanically the cocoa his wife had set down in front of him.

'It was the usual routine, my dear. The collections have been short for months. People are closing their purses. It's all this Overland Telegraph trouble, if you want my opinion. Todd and the government are out to bankrupt the colony.'

'Do drink your cocoa while it's hot, dearest,' said Mrs Harper soothingly.

'One bit of gossip surprised me,' old Hannibal mused. 'I'd taken the fellow for a milksop.'

'Who is that, dear?'

'That fellow you and Lucinda always fuss over on Sundays.'

Lucinda pressed herself back in her chair, the colour drained from her face.

'Steven?' Mrs Harper said. 'What about him?'

'He went to the Bishop, asked for a year's leave of absence. Said he didn't know enough about the world. He'll damned well get more than he bargains for. The Milner brothers have taken him on, as a volunteer on the stock drive north.'

Lucinda's small cry startled her parents. She was slumped down in her chair, a bluish tinge around her mouth and eyes.

'She's fainted,' Mrs Harper shrieked. 'Quick, the smelling salts.'

When Lucinda had recovered, and had been helped to bed by her mother, the family conferred.

'I knew she was coming down with something,' Mrs Harper said. 'I wanted to get the doctor to her last Sunday.'

'Has Woodrush gone?' Hannibal asked his father.

'The Milners began their drive on Monday last, I believe. But the subject of our concern is your sister, Hannibal. Should I send for the doctor?'

'Lucinda insists not,' Mrs Harper said. 'I think we should wait and see how she is in the morning.'

'She has been a bit strange lately,' old Hannibal remarked. 'It's not like Lucinda to have a fainting spell. She's always been as strong as a horse.'

Young Hannibal was shaken. He had not intended to frighten Woodrush out of the colony and he began to feel a bit of a brute. But it was a comfort at least that Lucinda did not know he had challenged Woodrush. He would have to be especially kind to her now. It was a queer business altogether. If the man had really been frightened of a thrashing, he'd hardly have the courage to volunteer with the Milner brothers.

It was all too much for young Hannibal. In fact, it was beginning to give him a headache.

Eleven

The track from the Roper River supply depot to the line poling south from Darwin was now worn smooth and hard by many hooves and the wheels of many wagons. Martin, sitting on his kit-bag, jolting along the track, thought he had never before felt so happy. The gaunt and miserable Roper River scrub, with its stretches of mangroves tangling in the slimy mud, was already forgotten in the excitement of rediscovering the extravagance of the tropical rainforest that had so bewitched him at Port Darwin.

As the wagon bumped its way past a lagoon, he stood up to see more clearly the giant waterlilies with their enormous blossoms erect on spreading pads, which he thought so large that a man might easily walk on them. The banks of the lagoon were clothed with ferns and shrubs of copper, silver and gold. Creepers as thick as ropes, with broad, fleshy leaves, climbed the trees beside the track, twisting into a mantle overhead. Staghorn ferns nested in the forks of the big gums, dropping green antlers down on to the papery white bark. Small orchids, their colours as subtle as their blooms were convoluted, seemingly sprouted from dead boughs.

Stubbs smiled wryly. 'It's homesick you are, for sure, for the mud and the stink of the Roper. If I were you, I'd be walking back to declare it too hard to leave.'

Martin stretched out his arms and laughed joyously, his youthfulness shining out of him like an aura.

'It's strange, you know, but when we were starving, it was only for food. I didn't know then that there could be another kind of starving.'

'And what would that be?' Stubbs asked, contending with

his pipe and tobacco plug on the lurching seat.

'A hunger you can have and not know. A hunger for beauty, perhaps. Does that sound so strange?'

Stubbs shook his head, a sadness in his eyes.

'There are many kinds of hunger, lad. I've one in me now, sorer than any starving.'

'I know you have,' Martin said.

Stubb's voice sharpened.

'What is it you know?'

'I just know that there's a soreness, a pain inside you. I don't know what it is.' He paused. 'What is it, Eli?'

Stubbs said, 'Something that goes to the marrow of the bones.'

Martin's voice softened.

'Whatever it is, I have a feeling that one day it will be mended.'

Stubbs scrubbed at his grey hair and smiled at Martin.

'You and your famous feelings. I'm coming to believe in them. So you think that one day I will be mended?'

Martin said, 'Yes, I do. But you will have to believe it too, Eli.'

Stubbs shook his head.

'It's a strange lad, you are. But I'll try to believe it.'

'You believe it and I will believe it with you. When will we make camp, do you think? I want to walk in the bush.'

'You'll stay in the camp,' Eli said. 'There's more than beauty in the bush. You'll stay in camp, my lad, under my eye.'

After an overnight stop, Stubbs and Martin were dispatched in another dray, with two stockmen and provisions, to make their own way to the staging camp at Daly Waters.

Solomon had been waiting impatiently for their arrival. He had arranged a small tent, in which he and Martin and Stubbs could be private, and the three exchanged experiences late into the night.

'It was a cabin boy I last set eyes on,' Solomon declared to Stubbs, the smile like a beacon on his pitted face. 'Now it's Mister Harper, sir, to be sure. Fit to sail before the mast or give command in any chaser. Mister Harper, sir, delivered of the whale's belly, like Jonah.'

Eli Stubbs was transformed that night, his eyes shining in the pleasure of being reunited with his old friend. Yet, in the early hours of the morning, when conversation began to be slower and more subdued, he stood up, his gear under his arm, as if making ready to leave the tent.

'Where is it that you are going, Eli?' Solomon asked.

'Eli makes his own camp,' Martin said. 'He made his own camps on the Roper.'

'As to that,' Solomon said, 'the angry river is far away, and not likely to move from its bed. As for making his own camp, Eli's camp is made for him.'

'I'll make my own camp, all the same,' Eli said, softly.

Solomon scratched irritably in his knotted curls and spoke to Martin.

'An upstanding seaman, such as yourself, with a beard on his face, or leastways something of a resemblance to one, and who was marooned with Eli when the world was submerged, would such a shipmate take kindly to what he's just heard?'

'But you well know that Eli likes to keep to himself, Solomon,' said Martin.

'As to that,' Solomon pronounced, 'there's two sides to such a question. When a man has reason to keep to himself, give him room, I say. When he has no reason, not as much as Solomon could spy through a glass under the bluest sky, such a man could be accused of both offhand conduct and an abuse of hospitality.'

Stubbs stood still, his face hidden in the darkness.

'It's safe harbour, Eli,' said Solomon. 'Mark that and think on it. It's safe harbour, I say.'

Martin was puzzled at Solomon's tone, at the set of his face and the emphasis he had put on his words. At last Stubbs nodded.

'Safe harbour,' he almost whispered. 'Then I'll be accepting your offer, Solomon.'

Martin settled happily into Solomon's team. The men were a good-humoured lot, easily spurred on by Solomon's constant and colourful haranguing.

'There's a cargo of broken wheels coming in from down the line,' he might say. 'I'm betwixt the devil and the deep blue sea to know whether or not to work on tonight. A wheel-less wagon is no better than a dismasted ship. And a sore trial it must be, to the crews so becalmed by it.'

And so the men would work late, under hurricane lamps, while Solomon cheered them on with a sea shanty, punctuating the rhythm with blows from his hammer.

Martin attended the bellows and the furnace, fetched for Solomon and became proficient with the long pincers with which he removed the livid metal from the anvil, quenching it in fierce hissings at the water trough.

A few days after his arrival, he found his path to the forge obstructed by a big, dark man.

'So you be Harper, then? And a squirt of a thing, I must say.'

'That's my name,' said Martin stiffly. 'I came from the Roper to work in the forge.'

The dark man nodded.

'And yer camp with the English bastard, in the poxed Yankee's tent.'

Martin's eyes widened in surprise at the man's hostile tone.

'I camp with Mister Stubbs and Solomon.'

'Me name's Ben Barton,' the other said, 'and I spit on the lot o'yer. Remember me, girlie.'

'Don't call me that,' Martin said.

'Don't call yer girlie? Yer look like one, don't yer? Don't yer know about sailors, girlie? Any port in a storm, they reckon.'

Martin understood the man's meaning, and flushing to his hairline, made to push past the burly figure. Barton thrust out a leg, tripping him.

'That there were an accident,' Barton laughed, 'so just watch yerself aroun' me. Tell that ter the Yankee, too.'

That night, at the fire, Martin had little to say. Solomon remarked on it, in his oblique fashion.

'As to barometers,' he observed casually to Stubbs, 'they can be a friend to poor mariners, in the matter of weather. A man's barometer, now, is a different contrivance. It lacks a needle, you might say, so it's harder to tell how the wind might be blowing. Being that as it may, there's surely something wrong with our shipmate's weather.'

Solomon put a burning stick to his pipe and waited. Martin sat hunched, his arms encircling his knees.

'Who is Ben Barton, Solomon?'

'So,' Solomon answered, 'that's how it blows, is it? Barton was at work in the forge, before you and Eli hove to.'

'He doesn't like you,' Martin said. 'He's a bad man, Solomon – something's gone wrong inside him. You can smell how bad he is.'

Solomon nodded.

'What passed between you?'

Martin paused.

'He just stopped me and told me to be careful. He wanted you to know.'

'It's true,' Solomon said, 'that there was a matter of a small debate between us. But that's nothing for you to worry your head about. Just keep clear of the pleasant and courteous fellow.'

Next day Martin enquired about Ben Barton at the forge and learned how he and Eli had been the reason for Barton's dismissal. From now on, Martin decided, he would avoid the horse yards, where Barton now worked.

Travelling far into the bush with a horse and dray, Eli Stubbs brought in two loads of timber a day for the woodpile. On this day he had brought nothing. The heat was bleeding from the furnace and Solomon sent Martin to find Eli and hurry him up.

It was a pleasant walk, and the tracks of the dray were easy to follow. In the short grass were quail and snipe; cockatoos, sulphur-crested, screeched in the trees; and overhead, hawks in long, gliding patrols searched for game.

Martin saw the dray first. Then he saw Stubbs, lying awkwardly over a log he had been working, the axehead still fast in it. The boy ran towards him.

'Eli, what's the matter? Eli, are you all right?'

'I can't move, lad. The cramp has struck me down.'

Taking Stubbs under the arms, Martin tried to get him seated on the log. The Englishman's face was grey and twisted.

'Where are you cramped?'

'It's in the back. It's the back, again.'

Putting his hands on Eli's back, Martin began gently to knead the knotted muscles.

'No!' Stubbs cried out. 'Don't touch my back.'

Martin whipped his hands away, as though he had touched something red-hot. His fingertips flamed with the shock of the secret that lay under Eli's shirt. The man's back was horribly deformed, corded in crooked and welted scar tissue, set as hard as bone.

'Help me walk,' Stubbs said, holding his side. 'The cramp will ease, if only I can get walking.' His face contorted into a grimace of pain.

'It was the axe,' he groaned. 'I cut the wrong way with the axe. Help me, lad. Help me walk.'

So the boy and the man walked slowly in the woodchip-splattered clearing, until Eli Stubbs could finally stand on his own. Moving stiffly back to the log in which the axehead was buried, he sat down, his head in his hands. Martin, staring silently at him for a moment, cleared the axe and began to use it on the smaller timbers, which he loaded on to the dray. Stubbs remained seated on the log, his head still buried in his hands.

'I've got to get this load back to the furnace, Eli. Are you able to travel?'

'Aye, lad.'

Climbing with difficulty on to the seat of the dray, Stubbs began to speak, not looking at Martin. His voice shook with urgency.

'You must say nothing of this. Do you understand? If you tell anyone of this, I am a dead man. Dead or worse.' He paused. 'A man can pray for death and be denied it. You must promise.'

Tears stung Martin's eyes as the horse jogged back to camp. The tears were for Eli Stubbs and everything about him that Martin would never understand.

'I promise,' Martin said.

Although he avoided the horse yards and the harness tent. Martin was unable to avoid Ben Barton. Waiting for a consignment of firebricks to be unloaded from a supply wagon just arrived from Darwin, Martin spied Barton's surly face amongst the crowd of onlookers.

The tired team was still in its traces, lather on the horses' flanks, rank-smelling sweat steaming off their hides as the roped load was feverishly searched by the Overlanders for flour and salted beef, axes and shovels, insulators and iron footings. Martin pushed through the crowd to ask about the firebricks.

'Firebricks . . . firebricks . . .' The overseer drew his finger down the consignment list. 'Firebricks, cases two. That should keep Solomon quiet.'

The firebricks were at the back of the wagon, and as Martin heaved a case towards the edge of the tray, Barton slouched across, spitting into the powdery dust.

'Need an 'and, girlie?'

He bared his stained teeth at Martin and hauled at the case until it was balanced on the rim of the tray.

'There y' are, whippersnapper. Now let's see yer lift it.'

As Martin jumped down from the wagon, Barton tipped the case and let it drop to the ground. Shaving Martin's leg as it fell, the wire binding ripped the calico from his knee in a graze that beaded his bared leg with blood.

'Coulda bin worse,' Barton said, still smiling. 'That case coulda taken yer foot orf.'

Martin changed his torn trousers before going back to the forge. Barton's act had been deliberate, he knew that. The man had tried to maim him. It left him with a feeling of something hard and jagged inside him, as though he had swallowed a chip of cold iron.

For the past two evenings, ever since Martin had brought Eli back in the dray from the bush, Stubbs and Solomon had gone off together into the night, leaving Martin alone by the fire. But he had thoughts enough to occupy him. He knew now why Eli Stubbs had never washed with the others at the Roper, why he had been the only man there who stayed shirted in the heat. He began to understand the doom that got into Eli's voice, hearing and rehearing his words about death, and how a man could pray for it and be denied.

But what was Solomon's part in all this? Stubbs had said to him once that Solomon had done him a service in some other colony. No matter what their fate might be, Solomon had done him a service. But what was that service?

It was Martin's job to light the fire as the evenings darkened and the first stars began to crowd, like tiny gems sewn on black velvet, into the sky. He filled the blackened billy can with water for tea, fetching a green stick to top the billy and keep the smoke from tainting the water.

Solomon and Stubbs had stayed late in the forge and now came quietly to sit on their boxes. Martin got ready to speak; however ugly the secret between his two friends, he was determined now to share it with them.

Solomon, unexpectedly, spoke first.

'In the matter of Eli, here, a matter discussed fore and aft and not without trepidation,' Solomon paused, glancing at Eli's immobile face, 'a decision has been reached, as you might say.'

'I'm glad of that. I had questions to ask tonight,' said Martin.

'It is a confidence,' Solomon said, 'and by way of being a burden on a young shipmate, brought up genteel. To get to the heart of the matter, Eli has a price on his head. If the truth about Eli should get out, he's bound back for the pits of hell.'

Stubbs did not move, although the small muscles in his face tremored. Instinctively Martin reached out and took his hand, which Stubbs gripped until it hurt.

'It's a long story,' Solomon said, 'and will try the understanding of a shipmate brought up in fair weather. You've got the imagination in you, and if you are a bit short on muscle, there's muscle enough in your feelings. It will take two of us to tell it, though.'

Twelve

The War of Independence, in 1776, which lost the addle-brained George the Third his American colonies, gained him a new one, as miserable as it was, on a wild continent at the bottom of the world.

Prior to this, thousands of petty felons had been shipped each year from Britain into Virginia and the Carolinas, where southern gentlemen bought them into indentured labour. When that dumping ground blew up, in bloody revolution, the prisons at home in England spilled over.

The Great South Land, so long a myth, had already been partially mapped by Captain Cook. There, authority decided, at Botany Bay, was the place for a penal colony. There, into the wilderness, the scourings of Britain's courts could be transported and forgotten.

The last escort of convicts shipped to New South Wales was refused by the emancipists and free settlers. There were now wealth and pretensions to respectability in the colony built on convict pain. Instead the wretches on the transports were dispatched to Western Australia, where there were settlers still eager to exploit convict labour.

Young Eli Stubbs, said Solomon, had been a convict on one of those transports. He had been sentenced to twenty years' penal servitude for assaulting a landlord who had arbitrarily and summarily served notice on his father to quit the acres he had share-farmed for thirty years.

Eli, then twenty-one years old, had worked the land with his father since he was just a slip of a boy. He watched while the landlord's bailiffs piled up the family's possessions outside the cottage, while the important man looked on from his horse. As

Eli pleaded, pulling at his leg, the gentleman slashed his face with a riding crop. Then Eli would have killed him, had the bailiffs not wrestled him to the ground and kicked him unconscious.

The story that followed was partly told by Eli, partly by Solomon, the one taking up where the other left off.

'Then what happened, Eli? What happened to your parents?'

'My brother was at sea. He tracked me down after five years and sent me a letter. He wrote that my parents were dead. I don't know the manner of their passing.'

The penal settlement to which Eli Stubbs was sent was on the water at Bunbury, south of the hamlet of Perth. After the west coast of the Great South Land had been blundered upon by Dutch vessels, blown off course on their trade to the East Indies, most ships shunned those shores as barbarous. But the American whale ships touched there, and on the islands further south, taking on fresh water and boiling the sperm.

'Those whale ships were the mothers of this mighty continent,' Solomon said. 'In the old days, there were many saved from starvation by the biscuits of the whale ships – Solomon has heard tell of it from ancients who were as sappy and springy as young Martin, when they took their first sight of these shores.'

Eli Stubbs had laboured with his fellow convicts, half a world from home, on a continent as strange as the far side of the moon. They had quarried and split stone in their chains and leg irons, built bridges and roads, been assigned as agricultural labourers. There was nothing to hope or strive for, save the continuation of existence, the chance of a scrap of meat in their soup, or a butt of unweevilled bread.

Eli's mother had brought him up on the Bible, and he had stolen one since, keeping it hidden for the next ten years. The comfort and promise in that battered book had kept him alive when others could no longer endure their torment, and found ways to end it; hanging themselves, or slashing their throats and wrists in the dark.

Solomon told it and Eli Stubbs told it, their voices low against the faint sounds of the Overlanders calling to each other, the bullocks lowing and the hobbled horses snorting.

The unboiled billy stood beside the embers of the fire. As Stubbs faltered, Solomon helped him on. Martin scarcely breathed, trying to take it all in. He had thought Eli Stubbs to be in his fifties, lined, bent and grey-haired as he was. But if Eli had been transported at twenty-one, and had gone to Bunbury in 1859, he couldn't be more than eight years older than Martin's brother, Hannibal.

A new transport, mostly of Irish convicts, landed at Bunbury. Eli Stubbs worked on a chain gang with one of these, an educated man called Seamus O'Connor. O'Connor had been a revolutionary, and a respected writer, back in Ireland.

Enlisting in the 19th Hussars with the intent of urging Irish soldiers to the revolutionary cause, he had formed cells among its dissidents, and distributed revolutionary propaganda. An informer betrayed him and he was arrested. Court-martialled in Dublin and sentenced to death, on appeal this was commuted to transportation into penal servitude for the term of his natural life.

The cause of O'Connor's freedom, along with that of another revolutionary sentenced with him, was taken up by a secret society, the Clan-na-Gael. Helped by Irish sympathisers in the American states, a rescue attempt was organised from Ireland.

The clan members knew the American whale ships were familiar with the southern seas and the coasts of Australia. If a whale ship were to be commissioned to drop anchor near the penal colony, a sally party could go ashore and rescue both Seamus O'Connor and his compatriot, Patrick Cullen.

Meanwhile, at Bunbury, the convict Eli Stubbs had escaped from a working party and taken to the bush in the forlorn hope of reaching the free colony of South Australia. While the whale ship was still a few days off the coast, Eli was hunted down by mounted troopers and dragged back to the colony in an iron collar and chain.

Stubbs had proved intractable before. Once, after resisting a guard, he had been left in the open sun in a box in which he could neither lie down or stand up, and fed on rotten bread and water for twenty days. The commandant considered Stubbs had obviously not learnt his lesson on that occasion.

He was sentenced to three hundred lashes.

The triangle was erected on the baked earth outside the administration block. Leather straps bound Eli's wrists and ankles; the flat of his cheek was pressed against the wood. Two convict floggers, one right-handed, the other left-handed, removed their shirts to lay on the lash. Both men were lifers: sadists, or men made so by the privileges they received for this service.

The convicts working in quarters were paraded to witness the spectacle for their edification. The commandant meanwhile stood with the guard who would cry out the count, his sword raised to signal the floggers, who were trying their legs for balance and measuring the tips of the lashes in touches to Eli's naked back. Each stroke must cross the other, working down from the shoulders to the base of the spine.

The commandant had dressed in his parade uniform for the occasion, with frogged buttons on the jacket and badges on the epaulettes, shining all blue and yellow and gold in the glittering sunshine. When the floggers nodded their readiness, the commandant dropped his sword.

The right-handed flogger was the first to strike, both hands on the weathered stock of the lash, bringing the leather whistling from over his shoulder. The pink skin of the Englishman's back rose immediately into a long, purple weal.

'One,' the counter cried.

The left-handed flogger went up on his toes, whistling the cat in a cross-cut.

'Two.'

On his shoulders, Eli Stubbs now wore a cross, bitten into the flesh.

'Three. Four. Five. Six.'

The floggers worked in rhythm, experts in their profession. Stubbs was pressed against the triangle, his body bound so tightly to it that only the tortured flesh could jerk, as the salt-pickled lash sliced into his back.

'Forty,' the counter cried. And then, 'Fifty.'

The day was windy, and, standing fifteen yards to the

leeward of the suffering man, the convicts rubbed at the tiny fragments of bloody flesh which, carried by the wind, lodged in their eyes.

At the count of one hundred, the doctor called a pause. Eli was still conscious, his eyes open and seeing. Not a whimper had escaped him. One of the watching convicts sank to his knees to sob. A guard prodded him with a rifle barrel and set him facing the triangle.

'One hundred and one,' the counter called.

The floggers ran with perspiration now, shaking it from their brows. The commandant pulled down the peak of his cap, troubled by the bright sun.

At the count of two hundred, the doctor stopped the floggers again, taking Eli's pulse and avoiding his awful eyes. The flesh between Eli's shoulder blades had been sliced away to the bone of the vertebrae.

'He's cut away,' the doctor announced. 'The punishment will have to be completed on the buttocks.'

A guard removed the bayonet from his rifle, and edged it inside Eli's belt, slicing it through and down the seat of the trousers until the material could be torn apart. Eli's buttocks, reduced to a pathetically stringy cleavage, were bared to the lash. The floggers went to work again, starting from the small of the torn, flayed back. Blood welled about the legs of the triangle.

'Two hundred and fifty,' the counter called at last.

The guards began to cuff the convicts in order to keep their attention on the triangle. One of the guards turned away to vomit, hoping that his superiors wouldn't notice.

'Two hundred and eighty.'

Not much could be seen of Eli's back, on which the blood had congealed in clumps about the lacerated flesh. His buttocks had been flogged into a formless jelly.

'Three hundred lashes. Punishment completed, sir.'

'Cut him down and attend him,' the commandant ordered shortly. 'The parade is dismissed.'

During Stubbs's and Solomon's account of the flogging, Martin shook uncontrollably, and tears which he could not check coursed down his cheeks. There had been nothing in his life to afford him comprehension of such routine inhumanity.

Eli seemed somehow strengthened by the telling.

'It's a cruel burden to put on you, lad, as Solomon says. But I had my reasons for secrecy. There's a reward for my capture, as you know. Any slip of the tongue about my back could awaken curiosity.'

Martin's voice was strangled with emotion.

'I would never have spoken, Eli.'

'A slip in a lad like yourself would be nothing to wonder at. But I'm glad now that it's out. There's an uncommon closeness that's grown up between the three of us. It's a precious thing to me, and a long time since I've had the joy of any caring or friendship.'

Martin said, 'And Solomon knew? He's known all this time?'

'Aye, Solomon was my angel of deliverance, as the Good Book promised. It was Solomon who rescued me, lad.'

'As to that, now,' Solomon said, 'I'm prejudiced in the matter of flogging. Solomon can put up with this, or that, and you might say he has had to. But there are things in this world, which are no more than Old Nick's doing and not to be abided.'

Eli Stubbs was smiling, as Martin had never seen him.

'He's making light of it. That's Solomon's way. Now that the worst has been told, I'll put the billy on. There's more to come in the story, lad.'

The conspiracy to break Seamus O'Connor and Patrick Cullen out of the penal colony had led to the charter of an American whale ship, out of New Bedford, secretly bound for Geographe Bay, Western Australia, a deep-water haven south of Bunbury.

Preparations were made as though for a normal voyage. The crew was deliberately mixed, with Kanakas, Malays and Negroes in the majority, in order to limit discussion. But Captain Anthony had also needed a man who had touched on the Australian coasts. Solomon had shipped with him years before, in the South Pacific islands. The captain knew

Solomon's history, and knew that he was spelling in New Bedford, after a three-quarter voyage in Australian waters and southwards into the ice. Captain Anthony offered Solomon articles as a mate.

The *Catalpa* lowered chasers for whales on its course to Western Australia, taking two small sperm in mid-Atlantic, and a big one off Tenerife. When Tenerife had been left behind, the captain summoned Solomon to his cabin. Solomon had whaled in Geographe Bay, even before Bunbury had been settled, and the captain needed Solomon's knowledge of soundings in the bay, of how close-hauled the *Catalpa* must be to get the landing party ashore. If Solomon should object to playing his part in the rescue of the Irish convicts, it would go hard with the expedition.

Captain Anthony offered Solomon a generous measure of rum, conversing of whales and storms they had shared together. Solomon listened expressionlessly. He had his suspicions about the crew. There were men articled who could only pretend at their trades.

'Shipmates we've been, Captain,' Solomon agreed, 'which being the fact that it is, hardly needs rum and reminding.'

'We've taken whales on this voyage,' Captain Anthony said, 'but the truth is, Solomon, I'm commissioned to take other fish.'

'The whale not being a fish,' Solomon remarked, 'but by way of being a mammal, there's no other finny thing that comes to mind, worth the charter of a whale ship.'

'It's human fish I'm after,' Captain Anthony told him. 'Suffering Irish convicts, Solomon, in the penal colony of West Australia. You've been into those waters. You've whaled in the very bay where I must fetch up. There's a measure of humanity in it, Solomon. These men were fighting for independence, as were the founders of the proud flag this ship sails under today.'

'It's shanghai'd Solomon's been, for the first time in his days upon the sea,' the whaler remarked wryly. 'And what exactly is to be the nature of Solomon's part in this fishing in the southern waters?'

Some time later, Captain Anthony and Solomon shook

hands on the agreement they had made. For an hour after that, they plotted over maps on the chart table.

Another whale was taken, south of Tenerife, but after that the *Catalpa* made no further pretence of hunting. Captain Anthony was anxious for the south-west and he had the wind in his fist. Day by day they bore down on the continent, trimming for the long run.

Solomon was standing alongside Captain Anthony when the *Catalpa* made Geographe Bay. They had slipped past Bunbury earlier in the night, making out the lights of the settlement through the spy glass. Solomon gave the captain instructions as the *Catalpa* glided towards a cove, the linesman for'ard swinging the lead, singing out his soundings. When Solomon had judged the position, he told the captain. The jib sheet came down, the salted canvas crackling; the chain rattled and rumbled its links as the anchor plumped into the sandy shallows.

The man who had shipped as assistant carpenter, Michael Maloney, and two American Irish sailmakers, Sean O'Donohue and Joseph Flannagan, were to make the attempt on the convict buildings, with Solomon as master of the whale boat and pilot. The attack was planned for just before dawn, when the garrison could be expected to be most soundly asleep. Maloney, an old soldier, was to be armed with a rifle, the other two with pistols. Pitched battle was not intended as part of the plan. Surprise was the object.

Long before dawn, the whale boat was put overboard, the oar-rowlocks muffled in canvas. Solomon took the tiller. The matter had been so deftly managed that not a member of the ship's crew were disturbed in their hammocks.

It was a long haul for so few men in a heavy boat, but they were counting on two more oarsmen for the return. As the raiders strained their backs, Solomon squinted into the dark, trying to locate a beaching on the rocky foreshore where the whale boat could be laid up. There was no moon to assist him. Captain Anthony had also planned on that.

'Ship starboard oars.'

Solomon had found a glint of sand, a thin strip between the black rocks on which the sea-swell sighed. The whale boat was paddled inshore, and the men went over, up to their thighs, grunting as they beached the boat. Solomon secured it with a hawser.

It was summer in the south-west, and the night was sticky with humidity. Maloney took command at the landing, going in front, the rifle slung on his shoulder. After a half-hour's scramble over the rocky terrain, the convict barracks were reached and the men moved swiftly to identify the buildings, keeping well covered behind the walls. Trusted local Irish sympathisers had provided the Clan-na-Gael with detailed maps.

No sentries were posted. The door of the guard room was opened wide, no doubt to catch any passing breeze. Maloney simply walked inside. The duty guard was snoring on a bench, boots off, rifle propped on the wall. A bunch of keys hung from a wall board above him. Maloney put up a hand to halt the others, moving quickly towards the guard. Reversing the rifle, he stood for an instant over the open-mouthed sleeper, then thudded the rifle butt against his head. The man's body twitched, then slipped off the narrow form to the ground.

Pointing to the key board, Maloney lifted the guard and dragged off his jacket. O'Donohue belted on his pistol and collected the keys. As Maloney buttoned up the jacket on himself, Flannagan gagged the guard whose sleep had been so abruptly deepened. When he was ready, Maloney checked his map again and waved the party out of the guard room.

At the cell blocks, the keys were tried until finally the locks answered. When the bolts creaked open, Maloney, the flame of a lighted candle stub shielded in his palm, stepped inside.

'Seamus O'Connor? Patrick Cullen?'

The candle was held high to reveal the stirring, puzzled convicts. One of the convicts spoke, his voice hoarse.

'O'Connor and Cullen are in the cell third along the row. But what . . .?'

At the third cell, Maloney struggled with the bolts, cursing under his breath. Inside he could hear movement and murmurings.

Slowly the door creaked ajar. Two emaciated figures, seemingly more like wild animals than men, crouched on the floor, their eyes ablaze in the candle light.

'O'Connor? Cullen?'

Solomon stood at the cell door while Maloney and his two old comrades embraced fiercely. Then his eyes lit on another figure, lying face down on a plank. In the flickering light of the candle, terrible wounds on his back showed raw and weeping. A wet cloth was draped over his buttocks.

'Out,' Maloney ordered, pushing the two before him. 'Hist! Quietly now.'

Solomon did not move, the pits on his face stark white as he surveyed the remaining figure.

'I'll take that poor thing with me.'

'Ye'll get back to the boat,' Maloney hissed at him. 'Our business is done.'

'I'm taking him aboard,' Solomon answered. 'They've flensed him alive, like a whale for the boiling down. If you've a hope of getting back to the ship, you'll do as Solomon says.'

Eli Stubbs was carried back to the whale boat, barely alive, beyond any comprehension other than that of pain. He lay for days at death's sharp edge, tended by Solomon with balms and soups, as the *Catalpa* made all possible sail across the southern ocean.

'A storm could kill him,' Captain Anthony said, in the mate's quarters where Solomon nursed the man. 'Has he been able to speak?'

'Aye,' Solomon answered, 'if words absent of meaning can be described as speech.' He paused.

'I've thought on it,' he continued. 'You're beholden to me. I neither backed nor tacked from your strange commission. Isn't that the truth, in the log?'

'It's the truth,' the captain said.

'Then you'll make haven, in a shelter free from storms.'

The captain shook his head.

'I can't do that. There could be British ships giving chase. This man is your responsibility, not mine.'

'There's another truth in that,' Solomon admitted. 'Then there's nothing for it but to put us ashore, when the man can stand, with the sealers on Kangaroo Island.'

Eli Stubbs had been six months in the mending at American River. His companion had been injured when a harpooned whale attacked the chaser, Solomon explained to the American sealers.

Young Martin stared at the strange pair, whose stranger history he now shared. Something puzzled him.

'Where was Eli, then,' he asked, 'when you worked in my father's forge?'

'In Ma Ryan's crib,' Solomon answered, 'living like a winkle in its shell, until he could get on the Overland.'

It was quiet now in the staging camp, all camp fires burned away, the cropping horses gone with their bells to forage further afield.

'You see, Martin,' Stubbs said gently, 'the wilderness has offered me a hiding place. In God's good time, shall I not have money enough to try for a passage home from Darwin?'

Thirteen

If old Hannibal Harper had been able to see his twins, as the Overland Telegraph struggled on, he would have had pronouncements to make. Unbeknown to each other, Matthew and Martin had never looked more alike. Martin's romanticism, his earlier introspection, had been sharpened into a different faculty by his ordeal on the Roper River. The terrible truth about Eli Stubbs had further unscaled his eyes. Life could be cruel and barbarous, sharp with many thorns to balance even the smallest blossom won. Every human being was dependent on others, and at the mercy of capricious forces. The existence of men like Ben Barton had made Martin think deeply. His former dreamy expression had all but disappeared from his face.

Meanwhile, the fates had been altering Matthew in the opposite direction. Much that had been gross and selfish on his face had been erased by his experiences; the crushing silence of the centre, the forays into virgin terrain, had brought him to a deeper understanding, almost without process of thought.

As Martin had toughened, Matthew had become more gentle. As Martin's body had hardened and developed with his labours in Solomon's forge, so the rigours of the first Ross expedition had shrunk the surplus meat off Matthew. The fair, blue-eyed Harper twins were becoming replicas of each other, mending the imbalance of their birth.

Todd's latest instructions to Ross had arrived at the Peake, ridden express. That night after the evening meal, Ross scraped his plate, lit his pipe and stood with one foot on a pack saddle, surveying his company.

'Just look at yourselves,' he mocked. 'Sitting there like lairds, and fat as partridges. It's taking your pleasure you've been. Tomorrow we fit to go out again, new orders come direct from Mr Todd.'

Matthew felt his blood quicken, as he stared up at the bearded leader. Billy Hearne halted in the act of lighting his pipe, holding the match until it burned him.

'So it's the centre we're bound for, once again,' he murmured.

'Aye,' Ross answered. 'We're bound for the centre and past the centre. It's all the way, Tom. New orders. All the way to the sea.'

Small whistles and exclamations were forced from the men, who looked at each other, stroked their beards and shifted about on their haunches.

'Tomorrow,' Ross said, 'we start making good the equipment and preparing the meat.' He smiled a little. 'It's rich men you're to be now. Mr Todd has raised wages a shilling a day.'

Tom Crispe whistled again.

'I think I'll buy mesel' a sheep station,' he announced.

The men chuckled. All the same, the news that they were to try and reach the northern sea needed some time to get used to. They laughed in derision at the shilling, too, because they had not gone out for money. They had gone out for the wonder of exploring, the trying of themselves against the unknown. This time, though, if they succeeded, there would be no backtracking. They would be coming home by ship from the sea, rolling down the coast from the northern settlement.

'From tomorrow,' Ross continued, 'it's hard rations in camp. I'll have some of the fat off you before we leave the Peake.'

Bullocks were slaughtered and the meat brought to the Ross camp in drays, then bedded and covered in gum tips. Billy Hearne strung wire for the jerking of the beef and went to work with a butcher's knife, cutting the meat into narrow strips.

In a couple of days, the meat had dried, shrivelled in the sun, and Billy stripped it of its fat and packed it. Other cuts were smoked and dry-salted. Matthew worked with Billy. Tom

Crispe and Alfred Giles repaired and checked hobble straps and reshod the horses.

Next morning parting glasses were drunk and there was a general shaking of hands. The riding horses and the string of pack animals twitched their hides and snorted, as if having a knowledge of their own.

John Ross mounted. The others fell in behind him, each man taking a string of pack animals. They adjusted their rifle buckets and pulled at their hats. Ross turned, pointed forward and gave his horse its head.

An uncertain cheer went up from the spectators as the expedition began to jog off. The riders did not look back.

The first night out the expedition camped at a timbered water-hole. Telegraph poles could be got there, and Ross made a note of it in his diary. Billy Hearne pounded jerky with a tomahawk and boiled up a soup flavoured with leaves of saltbush.

The next day, according to his orders from Todd, Ross bore west for the Finke River, which had been charted by Stuart and named for a supporter of his expedition.

Now, some time out, approaching the river, the party was at war with ants. The country was black with them, in regiments and battalions. When a reasonably uninfested patch of ground was found for a camp, a fire was lit and hot ashes were scattered around for protection.

The following morning Ross went ahead to climb a sandy cliff, taking his field glasses to inspect what lay ahead. As he reached the top he came unexpectedly upon a group of Aborigines, who had been surreptitiously surveying the explorers from above. Ross, unarmed, backed away, and the blacks left behind their spears and waddies to follow him. With this curious entourage, the leader returned to his party.

There had been some contention about blacks between Ross and Tom Crispe on the first expedition. Crispe did not trust them, and tended to become irritable when Ross let them into the camp. Crispe now walked about with his rifle ostentatiously cocked, watching the bush for treachery.

These blacks were low in the forehead and broad in the nose, smaller than the groups nearer the coast. The general camp gear caused them some astonishment. Saddles and packs were touched, as though they might come to life.

'Godamighty,' Billy Hearne said, holding his nose. 'They stink like a boiling-down factory.'

'Get rid of the bastards,' Tom Crispe advised, gripping his loaded rifle.

But the men's swags, still unrolled, had caught the blacks' attention. Humming and dancing small steps, they began to rummage, pulling things about and hiding small objects under their arms and in their elaborate chignons of hair. Ross missed his shotgun, which a wily hunter was trying to hide in the long grass. Alfred Giles chased another for his watch, having suddenly noticed its chain dangling from a black armpit.

The entertainment wearing thin, Ross ordered the camp to be struck, and as the men started for the horses, the blacks made off. The packs were being loaded when they returned. This time they carried their spears and waddies, which they pointed to the group. Tom Crispe swore, then fired his rifle. For an instant the blacks stood still, then turned and ran, melting into the bush.

Matthew could hear Crispe muttering in anger. Ross glared at him, but let the matter pass.

The days becoming hotter when the Finke River was finally reached, Ross declared a spell for the patching of gear and clothing. He carved the word *dig* on a tree and buried a tin with instructions for the construction parties as to where good timber could be found. An old black wandered into the camp, starving and alone. Ross fed him, and even Tom Crispe made no protest.

'Poor old bugger,' he said to Matthew. 'His mob probably left him behind to die.'

On the first expedition north, the days had seemed intolerably hot, but now, as November passed and December wore on, camp by camp towards the centre, the temperature blazed even higher. Harvey sickened with heat stroke, and the men stumbled when they had to dismount from their horses. For a few days the party was limited to one swallow of water a day: the new water bags, sent up from Adelaide for the second expedition, had leaked.

Then, unexpectedly, the country started to alter. Teatrees

appeared on the banks of dry creeks and, a hopeful sign, a few doves, crows, parrots and diamond sparrows in the undergrowth. There had to be water ahead.

A few days before Christmas the explorers entered a great range of hills and mountains, and the men gained new spirit. They began to talk among themselves once more as they travelled, cantering about, pointing to remarkable features of the landscape. Ross named the main range Hart, after the Premier so beleaguered in Adelaide. A great mountain seen to the west was named Mount McLachlan, after a gentleman in Glasgow who had been Harvey's first employer.

On Christmas Day many native tracks were sighted, and a lubra and a girl were seen digging for yams. They crouched down low in the undergrowth as the expedition passed. Ross went ahead and then cantered back to report the presence of more blacks, who had scattered at the sight of him. He brought with him a brace of bronze-wing pigeons for Christmas dinner.

After resting up on Christmas Day, the party began to move on again. They came upon great numbers of wild bees in the hollows, and butterflies in swarms, brilliantly coloured. The butterflies seemed to bother Tom Crispe.

'How would butterflies get to Hell and gone out in these here ranges?' he asked. 'You get butterflies in gardens, now, or in parks, or when an orchard's blooming.'

Alfred Giles was amused. 'How about the bees, Tom?'

'Native bees,' Tom said with derision. 'They're not your civilised bee. Buildin' their bloody hives underground! They can't even sting, the little black buggers. I just want to know how these bloody butterflies got out here where they don't belong.'

The discovery of the ranges had jolted Matthew, and he felt he knew now what had lured the old explorers on. Perhaps this was what it had been like for Captain Cook and Columbus, and the other navigators who had once bored him so in his school days.

He was standing alone at the edge of the camp, unable to get his fill of the mountains, when he felt a hand drop on to his shoulder. Alfred Giles had come up beside him.

'Strange, isn't it, Matthew? All this has waited since the

beginning of time for us to come here and see it. It's as if, after God made this continent, he couldn't make up his mind if he wanted it or not.'

Giles gave the young man's shoulder a squeeze.

'We are privileged, Matthew.'

On that day the Ross expedition was a thousand and two hundred miles into the interior of Australia.

The time in the ranges was more than a privilege, as Alfred Giles had put it to Matthew. It was almost a holiday for the expedition, among the butterflies, bees and blossoms, though Ross and Harvey spent weeks searching and surveying for a feasible route for the poles and wire to follow. The ranges were tumbled about with precipices and peaks, and there was much scouting around before the leaders were satisfied with their maps and bearings.

The blacks stalked the expedition day by day, making Tom Crispe increasingly edgy. Usually a shot was enough to send them off, the reverberations echoing and re-echoing in the mountain chasms. The explosion of powder was terrifying to ears accustomed only to the thunder of storms and voices and the calls of animals and birds.

At last Harvey and Ross folded their maps.

Ross said, 'Tomorrow we make for the Roper River. But it's only a wee bearing we've got, and with niver an idea of what lies between.'

Coming down from the ranges, the party ate well, for the bush was filled with thousands of black kangaroos, taller than a tall man when they reared back on their tails, ears pricked and swivelling, long-lashed eyes questing. They had beaten rock-hard pads everywhere through the bush, on which the shoes of the horses made no imprint. Kangaroo steaks were grilled and stewed. Billy Hearne made a tasty soup of the heads.

Three days after leaving the high country the expedition was still picking its way through gorges, gullies and sudden escarpments of fissured cliffs, from which the string of animals frequently had to be turned back, until the men were wearied by the sight of their own backtracks and the need to seek yet another direction.

Ross called a halt in a deep gorge from which nothing could be seen except the sky burning overhead. The walls of the gorge were as smooth as a plank, and hundreds of feet high. Tom Crispe, Billy Hearne and Matthew were sent to scout ahead. Alfred Giles patched harness while Harvey wrote up his log.

The neck of the gorge finally opened on a desolate vista. A few palm trees bearing small nuts cracked with age straggled up a slope; all else was bare and deserted, empty of life except for a few scrambling lizards. Tom Crispe pulled at his nose, shifting about in the worn saddle.

'Buggered if I know,' Tom said. 'One direction's as good as another. You go off east, Matt. Billy can fork to the west. I'll take a look-see up ahead.'

Tom pulled his nose again, shaking his head.

'Just look at it,' he said with disgust, pointing at the dry creeks, bare outcrops and hills heaped about them. 'Country looks like God smashed it with a bloody great hammer.'

Matthew was no longer afraid to go off alone, as he had been on the first expedition. He had learned to tell the time by the sun, and to take it over a shoulder for direction. He turned to look back over his mount's rump, satisfied by the outline of horsehoes in the dust. He would have no trouble on the backtrack.

He had shaved off the beard he had cultivated for its aura of manhood, tormented by the prickly heat which flourished in its cover. A lick of hair spilled from under the rim of his battered hat, patched black with sweat-stains and brave with an eagle's feather he had stuck in the plaited band.

Hours later, he stopped in a gully to wet his throat from his canteen. He moved the revolver, with which he had practised on targets in camp at the Peake, on his belt for comfort. His eye with carbine and revolver had caused the others some surprise in sporting competitions, although he had never been able to equal John Ross. Ross could put a bullet down the unbroken neck of a flagon at thirty yards and blow out the bottom.

He wiped the sweat off his face, standing in the stirrups, crow's feet of sun squint about his eyes, searching for some order in the disordered landscape. He squinted again, noting a patch of scrub among the arid knolls. The scrub was thick, dotted with tall trees, as incongruous amid the naked erosion as a homestead or a stockyard would have been. Matthew rode towards it, drawn by the very fact of its isolated existence. There were dry creeks to cross, knolls on which the soil crumbled under the weight of horse and man, slipping away beneath them until Matthew had to dismount and lead his floundering horse.

As he drew nearer, Matthew was puzzled at what seemed to be a number of white stones, as big as small melons, spilled on the red earth beneath the treeline. Most of the stones seemed regular in size. He thought it odd that there should be such large white stones at this strange outcropping of scrub. There had been no rocks or stones on his ride, only pulverised pebbles.

He dismounted and peered down. Rounded and half-buried, the stones seemed more like great white eggs now. He kicked one over, then almost cried out at the sight of a vacant-socketed skull, with teeth set in a gruesome grin, as it rolled from its semi-concealement in the soil.

All of the stones were human skulls, or bleached bones, some whole, some broken.

Matthew had never witnessed the ultimate obscenity of death. The triangular holes in the bone, through which breath had once passed, the rounded, empty cavities in which eyes had once laughed and cried, the bared teeth which had grown through baby gums to smile in adulthood were all before him. He wanted to mount and gallop away, but an awful fascination led him on, unmindful of his trembling, or the sweat that was shocked from his face and breast. There were hundreds of skeletons in various stages of decomposition. The jointed bones of legs and arms everywhere, the pitiful frailty of unfleshed hands, bent and clenched into spidery shapes.

He looked up for the relief of the green growth and azure sky, but there was no comfort there for him; the bigger trees were set with platforms, with skeletons poking through wrappings of paperbark or hanging from forked branches. Nothing moved in this scrub of death, no breeze stirred the leaves into life. Matthew again heard his own heart, as he had in the silence of the sand dunes.

He backed out of the burial ground, backing as though from

menace about to engulf him, and a skull shattered under his foot, scattering blackened teeth about his boot. Then he turned and leaped on his horse, sliding it perilously down the creek beds, turning only once to look back at the mocking green, which must have been nourished on the putrefying flesh of the dead, in these badlands where there grew not a blade of grass.

Billy Hearne and Matthew met in the gorge as the sun was setting. Billy's horse was limping.

'Went down on one knee,' Billy said. 'There's no way through to the west. The country looks like waves of earth, all red, hundreds of feet high. Never did see country in such a mess.'

'Same to the east,' Matthew said, his mind still filled with the burial ground.

They went on at a slow pace, Billy walking beside his horse, which stumbled at each step.

'Might have ter put the nag down. If Tom didn't find a way through, we might have ter bloody well put ourselves down. What a hell of a place for a man ter leave his bones.'

Matthew chilled at this chance comment, suddenly seeing his own skeleton, his own skull grinning forever in the scrub.

It was late when they got back to camp, and Tom Crispe was already cooking.

'How'd yer go?' Billy asked apprehensively.

'It was a bit rough,' Crispe answered, 'but we can get through ahead. It's going ter be hard on the horses. It's all gibbers, further on.'

Matthew felt his chest fill. Death had been more a notion than a reality to him, before his experience among the bones in the scrub. Previously when the party might have perished for lack of water, he had endured the pain of thirst, but the prospect of death had been fanciful. Now he couldn't forget the scrub, and his mind protested at this first realisation of his own mortality. He knew now how sweet his own life was to him. He thought of Martin, wondering what he might be doing at home, of all his family, for whom he suddenly felt an overwhelming need.

Two days further on, in hard going, smaller gorges appeared.

Harvey had ridden out in the early morning to take a

bearing, and had not returned. Now it was mid-afternoon.

'He coulda mistaken another gorge for this one,' Billy said worriedly. 'The buggers all look the same.'

Ross was out scouting for timber, and for a route for the Overland wagons. It would be a bitter struggle to get teams and supplies across these barriers of broken country. When the big Scot rode in at sundown, a rock wallaby over the saddle before him, he looked discouraged.

'Here's a stew for you, Billy,' he said as he dumped the carcass and dismounted. 'Where's our Willie?'

'He hasn't come in,' Alfred Giles replied, looking up from his endless harness patching.

Ross stopped unsaddling.

'He's been out all day?'

'Most of it,' Tom Crispe answered.

'Two of you saddle up, then. Ride out into the grass and put up a smoke.'

As Matthew and Crispe went for their horses, Ross rode off at a canter. Alfred Giles continued to work with his punch and needle.

'What's the good of putting up a smoke?' Billy asked, unclasping his knife to skin the wallaby. 'The blacks have been makin' smoke around us for days.'

The wallaby was a female. Billy pushed his hand into the slit of the pouch, feeling for the long, blue-white string of teats.

'This here wallaby had a joey,' Billy said, inspecting his finger. 'This here wallaby is still in milk.'

Billy shared the common bushman's belief that young wallabies and kangaroos were born on the teat. It was an easy mistake to make. At birth the young of the bouncing marsupials, scarcely bigger than grubs, inched their way along tracks of divided fur on the mother's belly to seek the pouch and attach their tiny mouths to the teat, with an instinct and compulsion too complex for simple understanding. If the young embryo was torn off from its attachment to the teat, it bled at the mouth and died.

With the coming of darkness, the men returned. The surveyor had not been found, and now it was too late to search further for his tracks.

There were many shiftings in the bedrolls that night, and periodic stokings of the huge fire kept at full blaze. Matthew stared at the heavens, wondering if the surveyor would be found alive. Will Harvey was a poor bushman; excitable, the least hardy of the party. When he sometimes spoke of his life in Glasgow, it was always with a hint of hauntedness, as though he was unable to comprehend how he could be in this topsy-turvy hemisphere, exploring an ancient continent so far from the gently coloured, soft-leafed forests, the trout and salmon streams and heather hills of his own world, and the crowded streets of the great city in which he had learned his profession. Matthew was afraid for him.

John Ross, the Highlander, had in contrast thrived in the Great South Land, Matthew thought. There was something elemental in Ross, which place and circumstance did not touch. Ross had been born in conflict and adventure, as untamed in his nature as Harvey was tamed in his. He took to new territory as if it were his natural habitat.

At first light the expedition prepared to search again for the surveyor. The sun had risen red-eyed; there would be no mercy in the day. In the string of twenty-two horses there was scarcely a beast fit to travel the gorges and gibbers. The horses limped on tender feet, gaunt ribbed, dull and marbled in the eye. Billy Hearne inspected the string, choosing the likeliest mounts.

With the greatest difficulty, the surveyor was tracked for twelve miles down the range. Harvey had kept a straight course through rocks and precipitous gorges which no experienced bushman would have wanted to attempt. There were no indications of a camp or a cooking fire. Harvey had gone out armed, but he might not have taken matches.

'If he's doin' a starve,' Billy Hearne said, 'at least he's got water.'

The party stayed with Harvey's backtracks until late afternoon. The tracks circled, repassed the camp at a distance, and continued on.

'Godamighty,' Tom Crispe said, 'now he's buggerin' off in the other direction!'

But the tracks soon turned, at a bluff that Harvey must have recognised. When the trackers rode back to camp, Harvey was lying on his pack, snoring. He was revived with coffee, rum, and a tin plate of wallaby stew. In the two days lost among the stones, Harvey's mount had cast every shoe. Blood puddled about its torn hooves and hocks.

Billy Hearne's estimation of the toll taken in the ranges and badlands proved accurate. Harness was falling to pieces, water bags had broken beyond restitching. The horses were almost done in. Once again, there was nothing to do but turn back. There would be no triumphant arrival at the sea, not this time, at any rate. Ross gave the order to turn the horses around.

The retreat of the second Ross expedition to the Finke River became a race with their dwindling supplies. The same impassable rocks that had hindered their approach now barred their return. The weakened party rode grimly on, their pack horses staggering in spite of their lightened loads. Alfred Giles was barefooted in the stirrups, his boots crumbled away entirely. There was no more powder for the carbines, no shells for the shotguns, although tantalisingly plump pigeons perched in the trees. The flour was exhausted. The explorers ate pinches of oatmeal, stirred into boiling water as gruel. After the last of the oatmeal was finished, the only prospect was roots and lizards.

Matthew rode as if in a trance, transported beyond the fear of death that had previously possessed him. He had spoken of the charnel ground in the scrub to nobody. The experience had been too jolting, too intimate; he felt that his mind and body had somehow been broken apart in their pattern and differently repieced. There had been an evil mockery in the litter of gaping skulls and bones, in the lipless grin of rotting teeth. Somehow he felt that he had been beckoned there deliberately, into a silence that had seemed to shriek with message.

Alfred Giles mentioned the change in Matthew to Tom Crispe.

'There's something wrong with young Matt. Something seems to have gone out of him.'

'Boy on a man's errand?' Tom suggested.

'No. He's proven himself as much a man as any of us. It's as if he's seen a ghost.'

Crispe's smile broke a slit in his blackened, cracked lips.

'Take a look at us, Alf. Any self-respecting ghost would flee screamin' at the sight. If I saw somethin' looked like you in civilisation, I'd shit in me breeches.' Crispe pulled at his rags. 'Not that I've got much breeches left ter shit in, or much ter shit out. They say if yer don't eat yer don't shit and if yer don't shit yer die.'

'We'll get through,' Alfred Giles said. 'When we run out of lizards, we've got the horses to eat.'

'What do we ride when we've eaten the horses?'

Alfred Giles considered.

'You'll have to make your own arrangements. I'm going to throw my saddle across Billy Hearne.'

'You bastard,' Tom Crispe said, 'I was savin' up Billy fer meself.'

Even Ross rode uncertainly. He had lost the last of his hat on a thorn-bush and now wore the holed canvas of a water bag to protect his head from the sun. Yet wherever timber good for telegraph poles was encountered, Ross mapped it, and then supported Harvey while the exhausted surveyor took bearings.

The Overland Telegraph had relied upon nothing but the crossing to the Indian Ocean by John McDouall Stuart as evidence that the project was a possibility. John Ross now carried in his saddle-bag, for delivery to Charles Todd, a memento of that historic journey. The expedition had discovered a cairn of stones with a bottle concealed in it, wrapped in oilskin and sealed. The document in the bottle announced the arrival in the centre of Australia by Stuart and his party.

'John McDouall Stuart and party, consisting of two men and himself, arrived from Adelaide on Saturday evening, the twenty-first day of April, 1860, and have built this cairn of stones and raised a flag to commemorate the event, on the top of Mount Stuart. The Centre is about two miles south-south-west, at a small gum creek, where there is a tree marked, facing south – John McDouall Stuart, William Darton Kekwick, Benjamin Heed.'

Now, a little over ten years later, the Ross expedition dragged itself back in defeat to the Finke River.

Fourteen

The northern section of the Overland Telegraph was again on the move south. The central section, halted temporarily by water shortages, was again making progress. In the north Charles Todd was everywhere, planning and replanning and exhorting, 'like', the Leader of the Opposition put it to the House, 'a blue-bummed fly in a bottle'. With good reason.

Old Hannibal Harper's concern about the drain on the Treasury was now being voiced by many. It appeared that the tiny colony had bitten off more than it could chew. The line was still hopelessly behind schedule, and estimates of the forfeits which might have to be paid were the primary topic of conversation on the street and in the clubs. Old Hannibal continued to cry ruin, and repeated to everyone he encountered his vision of the blacks holding corroboree in Government House, cooking goannas in his fireplace and making snake sandwiches in his kitchen.

In the days following Steven Woodrush's abrupt departure with the Milner brothers, her family had found Lucinda's moods and behaviour quite odd and unpredictable. Overriding her daughter's protestations, Mrs Harper had called in the doctor, who diagnosed a nervous condition and prescribed a tonic which, he assured her anxious mother, would soon have her back to her usual cheerful self.

Mrs Harper now had an immediate burden, to add to the others further removed. The two Hannibals had a daily escape in the business. Mrs Harper had no escape from Lucinda. The girl kept to the house, ignoring all invitations, neglecting the Old Bushmen's Home, church affairs, and the choir. She took refuge in nervous outbursts and sudden snappishness that quite outdid Mrs Harper's earlier prostrations.

Three times a day her mother prepared Lucinda's prescription, watching, puzzled, as her daughter contemptuously tossed down the mixture. At the end of the first week Mrs Harper decided that further measures would have to be taken.

'It's choir night, dear. You so much loved the choir. Why not go? Get out of the house and meet your church friends.'

Lucinda stared at her mother. Her hair was disordered, and she was wearing a house gown and slippers. Mrs Harper had to turn away from the furious blaze in her daughter's eyes.

'To hell with the choir. To hell with it all, do you hear?'

Mrs Harper's hand went to her throat at the force of Lucinda's language.

'Is it necessary to use such language? I don't know what has come over you. A few weeks ago you couldn't wait to get to choir.'

Lucinda's fists were clenched. She forced herself to speak more calmly.

'I'm sorry. It's just my nerves – I haven't been sleeping well.'

Shaking her head, her mother hurried off for the medicine. If Lucinda's nerves didn't soon improve she would certainly have to ask for a second medical opinion.

After the shock of Steven's departure Lucinda had spent the first wakeful night on a pendulum between rage and mortification. How could Steven have done such a thing? He had been her conquest, her captive, an objective worked towards over months of planning. She thought she had sealed their relationship in the intimacy of the hired carriage. Had that meant nothing to him?

It was not possible, surely, that a feeling of guilt had driven him away. Guilt was a namby-pamby emotion, something that others let stand between themselves and what they wanted to do. It was absurd to deny oneself for some abstract ideal, or for the sake of others.

She remembered the Bishop's sermon, delivered at Epiphany, concerning sexual immorality and the tides of destruction it caused. How she had smiled behind her fan! The Bishop had failed to make the basic observation that the person causing the waves was the one who could possibly not be touched by them.

Now she narrowed her beautiful eyes in bitter meditation. Had she been caught in the waves of her own making? Why had Steven Woodrush wanted to escape her?

On the morning following her mother's attempt to get her to choir practice, Lucinda opened her eyes and regarded the ceiling intently for a few moments. Then she threw off the coverlet and sat up, swinging her legs over the side of the bed. She would dress and visit Lady Charlotte Bacon. She would throw herself into everything, flirt madly, seek out every distraction. She would waste no more time in grief. Of course there would be those who would take pleasure in what they might choose to see as her humiliation, but they would get no satisfaction from her. Absolutely none. She swung her pretty feet on to the floor, mobilised for action.

On the Milner brothers' drive north, its ultimate destination the head-waters of the Roper River, Steven Woodrush was riding flank.

Ralph Milner, the elder brother, a widower, had not concealed his surprise when Steven had asked to go, unpaid, on the drive.

'The police after you, or some such?' he asked curiously.

Falteringly, Steven had explained himself, while Milner listened. When he had finished, Milner pulled at his beard reflectively.

'I wouldn't let on to the others about training to be a priest, if I were you. They'd either pull your leg or be uncomfortable.'

The seven stockmen hired by the brothers were all in their forties, their faces creased with sun-wrinkles, their hands gnarled, hard men who had lived hard. Among them Woodrush was an oddity, with his white hands and skin like a girl's. But it was bush law to ask no questions of a man, to be and let be. Ralph Milner had taken Woodrush under his wing and that was good enough.

The first month had been hard for Steven, unaccustomed as he was to physical labour, cosseted for most of his life in the bosom of the church. He had become thinner, his soft white hands had become calloused and tanned and his ears inured to the profanities which punctuated the bushmen's speech.

Each day had been doubly new for him; not just because of the alien landscape, but also because of details from which the walls of St Paul's had kept him well protected. He felt dazzled by the new sights and sounds and smells; his body seemed to buzz with a new freedom. At night, in his bedding, when he shut his eyes to pray, he gave thanks for the lessons he was learning.

He had done right, he told himself, to come on the Milners' drive. To have stayed in Adelaide would have meant becoming Lucinda's chattel, her plaything, to be toyed with whenever the fancy took her. In the week after she had pulled him to her in the carriage, he had prayed, closeted in his room, for guidance and strength. But the touch and scent of Lucinda's breasts, the hard-soft sweetness of her nipple, the silken convolvulus which he had entered, so briefly and sweetly, pursued every waking moment and claimed him in turbulent dreams. It was as though previously he had lived with the erotic zone of his brain disconnected, a half man, like someone legless. The spinning, shuddering ecstasy of his first sexual release had blacked out the world, floated his body like a feather. Lucinda had planned for this, and he knew that he could never resist her again.

When he had learned of the Milner brothers' drive north, he experienced a minor revelation. His prayers had been answered.

The caravan of animals and carts spread wide over the open country, the horses in one mob, the sheep in another. The sheep bleated continuously as the men and dogs pushed them forward, the stockmen galloping at groups of stragglers which broke and ran in every direction. There wasn't a stockman in the five colonies who wouldn't agree that sheep were the most stupid creatures on earth.

Following the track beaten by the wagons hauling supplies to the Overlanders, the drive made its laborious way north.

The endless march of poles and wire, sentinel in the emptiness, struck an uneasy chord in Steven. Its stark presence related to nothing about it; its isolation seemed poignant.

After a drive of fifteen miles in warm, moist weather, the expedition made camp for the night. Ralph Milner, tall, stringy and leather-skinned through a lifetime in the sun, sat down next to Steven, clearing his throat noisily before he spoke.

'I've been thinking,' he began. 'You know I lost the missus. She was strong on religion, Jean was. She believed it all. She believed in the hereafter. I'd like to be able to think of her going to some reward. You've studied these things. What do you think about it?'

'I, too, believe it all,' Steven answered. 'It's all in the Bible, the Word of God. The answer to every question is in the Book. There are laws to follow, which we transgress at our peril. There is good in the world and there is evil. Satan crouches on every doorstep.'

Ralph Milner thought, and nodded.

'You have no argument with me on that. But how about the hereafter? I mean, there's no proof, is there?'

'There's no proof that the sun will rise tomorrow, but you believe it will, don't you?'

Milner scratched his neck and viewed the heavens.

'I don't understand you,' he said.

Steven felt an urgent need to explain the lessons he had learnt so well at St Paul's.

'Your belief that the sun will rise is like an act of faith. Your wife's belief in the hereafter was also an act of faith. Jesus died on the Cross and rose again on the third day. That was a miracle. If we have faith in the miracle of Jesus, then everything is possible.'

'Faith?' Milner asked. 'Is that all there is to it?'

'It's the beginning,' Steven said. 'Faith, acceptance, and then the laws. Do unto others as you would have them do unto you. Isn't that simple?'

A great sadness rose in Ralph Milner's eyes.

'I wasn't asking for myself. I was asking more for Jeanie.'

The younger Milner brother's figure loomed out of the shadows.

'Ralph, we've got three horses bogged down at the lagoon. They're in too deep to get at the hobbles.'

'Can we get a girth around them? Pull them out with bullocks?'

'Could be. With a bit of mud diving.'

Ralph Milner got up.

'Come on, I'll take a look.'

The nights turned sharply cold after the heat of the day. Steven lay in his blankets, letting his thoughts stray. He greatly missed St Paul's and the church services. The taking of communion had always been essential to him as a renewal of faith and devotion. He wondered if he had found the right words in his short talk with Ralph Milner. And he wondered again about Lucinda. Had it been cowardly to run as he did? Was he finding the strength to eventually deal with her? There could be no future between them without it.

Lucinda's Christianity had obviously been a sham, a cynical device that had enabled her to get close to him. All her voluntary work had been a spider web with which to snare him. He groaned and tried to pray, but could not still a small voice sounding in his head. That is not true, the voice argued, you are equally responsible, you let it happen out of weakness, or you wanted it to happen. He thought; why do I love her, knowing what I do?

He groaned again, longing for morning, for the clarity of dawn.

When the drive reached the Finke, the river was in full flood, a quarter of a mile wide and up to a man's armpits. The men pressed in hard at the great mob, ordering the dogs in to harass the sheep, whipping the goats into the water to take the lead.

Continually cracking their stockwhips, the sweating drovers forced the seven thousand sheep into the water, to swim for the opposite bank in a current that bore them swiftly downriver. The flock struggled almost in single file, a profusion of woolly heads bobbing in the water while the stockmen laboured to turn them. The sheep had swum a half mile before the leaders scrambled ashore and were hunted up the bank.

Some of the ewes were due to lamb, some of the mares to foal. Ralph Milner decided to camp beyond the Finke and wait out the lambing. It was a hard and uncomfortable camp. A plague of rats arrived, seemingly out of the ground, a manifestation so sudden that it might have been a conjuring trick. Thousands of the big, grey creatures scuttled through the camp, were savaged by the dogs, stamped on by the men. The flour bags were riddled by their attack every night for a week, and Ralph Milner had just decided to move camp when the rats disappeared, as mysteriously as they had arrived.

When Steven Woodrush killed his first rat, he committed his first act of violence. He had taken life from one of God's creatures, a God who marked even the fall of the sparrow. And yet, in the order of nature, most creatures were preying on each other, he realised. The meat-eating human being was such a beast of prey. Steven puzzled at the scheme of things. It was a simple thought to have, yet it had not come to him before.

Old Hannibal Harper opened the pages of his newspaper, and he sipped at his port.

'It has been reported that the Milners' drive is making good progress,' he announced.

Lucinda waited, a little breathless despite herself.

'They're congratulating themselves, no doubt,' her father commented. 'They'll be offering up prayers if ever they reach the centre.'

Lucinda made her voice casual.

'Is Steven mentioned, Father?'

'Who the blazes is Steven?'

Young Hannibal said helpfully, 'Steven Woodrush, from St Paul's.'

'That milksop, why should he be mentioned?'

Old Hannibal continued to read.

'One of the blacks and a gin ran away after leaving the Peake. Typical of the savages. Not to be trusted. I had one steal the hat off my head at Port Lincoln. Didn't know it was gone until my scalp began to burn.'

Old Hannibal refreshed his glass of port.

'There's been another spearing, too. A well-digger on the central line. This is what happens when you let the black man into camp. The black doesn't exist who doesn't take kindness for weakness. I saw proof enough of that in the old days.'

Lucinda was trying to imagine the stock drive. Would Steven be brown and muscular now, like those jaunty Overlanders who shipped back from the north? Would he be thinking of her, as she had been thinking of him?

Steven had escaped her, but it wouldn't be forever. In this matter Lucinda knew herself to be possessed of infinite patience. In the meantime, she had found a new male interest to help her while away the time.

Leaning over the back of her father's chair, she caught sight of herself in the gilt mirror, and felt renewed satisfaction in her reflection.

Charles Todd had pushed his slight body almost to exhaustion. He had travelled the southern and central sections of the line, shipped to the Roper landing and travelled inland to the northern section. He had persuaded the Premier to offer Charles Patterson a bonus of one thousand pounds if he completed the beleaguered northern section on time. A man who could go boating on the flooded Roper River in a bullock wagon would not be easily beaten, he considered.

In Adelaide, opinion was again undergoing a pendulum swing, and renewed support was being expressed for the scheme. The isolation of Australia from Europe had just been practically demonstrated. The Franco-Prussian war had been declared, fought and concluded before a mailboat reached the South Land with news of the deadly struggle. After this event, even old Hannibal began to see Todd's Overland Telegraph in a new light and was drawn into grumbling admissions of how dramatic would be the effect on the colonies when their exile was ended by telegraphic communication with London and Europe.

The *Advertiser* published an editorial eulogising the Overland Telegraph, using Australia's ignorance of the Franco-Prussian war to illustrate the importance of its existence. Pride in the venture again uplifted the optimists and stilled the voices of the critics. The South Australian Premier used the editorial in Parliament as opportunity to gleefully hammer the Opposition.

The optimism, however, was short-lived. Soon the central line could find no more timber for its progress. Poles had to be hauled some two hundred miles while the Overlanders idled in the camps. Estimates of the forfeits to be paid had to be enlarged. The Opposition now hammered again at the Premier.

Old Hannibal, working in his office, looked up as his eldest son rushed in.

'Father, have you heard the news?'

Old Hannibal looked surly.

'I've not heard the news. I don't wish to hear the news. I will read the news tonight.'

Old Hannibal suddenly stopped.

'It's not to do with the twins, is it?'

'I've just come from the port. Everyone's talking about it. The marine cable has broken down between Java and Darwin. It smashed up in a hole on the seabed. They say it might take months to fix.'

'What's that you say? Broken down? Where did you get this information?'

'A ship has just arrived from Java – it was in touch with the cable-layers. Do you see what this means? It's a race now. If Mr Todd can speed the wire, there might be no penalties to pay.'

Old Hannibal clapped his hat to his rosy dome.

'I'm off to the club. By jingo, this will cause a stir.'

Fifteen

When news of the breakdown of the marine cable reached Charles Todd, the deep breath of relief the little visionary took was echoed throughout the colony. It would be a race now between the wire and the cable, just as young Hannibal had told his father. As the news went up and down the line, it fired the Overlanders to greater efforts, and, in the camps, many bets were taken on the outcome.

In the north, the rotten teeth of the Overland Telegraph were about to be permanently pulled, with the arrival at the Roper River depot of the six thousand iron poles ordered by Todd from England.

The replacing of infected poles had been a miserable, everlasting business, each clean pole being condemned to destruction even before the Overlanders moved on.

The arrival of the iron poles greatly cheered the men.

'There,' one Overlander said, patting an iron pole happily, 'get stuck into this, yer little gluttons, I'd like ter have a microscope to see yer teeth busted, yer miserable little buggers.'

In Adelaide, Todd was recruiting a new type of Overlander. Builders, carpenters and stonemasons were now being shipped to Port Darwin, and sent by land up to the Peake, to build the repeater stations that were to boost power on the long wire. At Port Darwin, the north's first substantial claim to civilisation was under construction. The building of the big stone telegraph station, with its two wings to house staff, fascinated the blacks watching from the nearby hill. The white man's tents had borne some resemblance to their own lean-to wurlies, and could be understood as shelters, but this great monument of stone was beyond their comprehension. There were many amazed cries from the black spectators as the building progressed.

At Alice Springs, a repeater station of nine rooms was under construction, as well as another at the Peake. Temporary huts were to be built at Daly Waters, and sites for five others were measured out. The great batteries that would galvanise the wire between the repeater stations were carried up the line from Adelaide and down the line from Darwin. But still to be crossed was the void that was the centre of the continent.

Eli Stubbs had become a different man after his confession to Martin. Having another soul with whom to share his secret seemed to liberate his spirit, and his slow smile was now often to be seen. On the Roper he had had to steal away down the river to wash. Now he could wash in the tent, although he always took his basin to the backing canvas and faced the flaps so that the scored flesh of his back could not be seen. He sometimes talked about his childhood now, of the fox hunts of the privileged through his father's fields of crops. Martin found it hard to conceive of the hunt deliberately riding down the fruits of another man's labours.

'A free man's a free man in these colonies,' Eli said. 'It's not like that at home.'

Martin had often heard talk of 'Home' from his parents and their friends, but the Home they nostalgically evoked over Sunday dinner was certainly very different from the one that Eli described. He wondered at the fates that dealt out such different destinies, as he listened to Eli's stories spellbound. He learned about the hulks used to house prisoners when no more could be crammed into the jails. Eli had himself been imprisoned in one such hulk, a rotting ship on the Thames, before his turn came to be transported.

Sunday was rest day in the camp, a time for washing clothes, patching and mending gear, hunting, playing cards, or creating some other diversion. When there were horses spelling, the men sometimes went for a ride. Martin was itching to ride out and make his own discoveries in the bush.

He could imagine he was Matthew then, out exploring with Ross. There had been many Sundays when Martin had almost asked Ben Barton for a horse.

On this Sunday afternoon, with Solomon gone to play cards, and Eli Stubbs on his bunk reading his Bible, he decided he would ask Barton for a mount. He could only say no. Martin found him in one of the horse yards, treating a hack with an ulcerated hock.

'So you want a ride, girlie?'

Martin decided he would take no offence.

'Yes, Mr. Barton,' he said politely. 'Only for a few hours.'

'I see,' Barton said, a hand on the rump of the horse he had been treating. 'Can yer ride a horse, or should I be on the lookout for a donkey?'

'I can ride most horses.'

'Well, then. Pick out a horse and saddle up. Try a gallop. If I like yer style he's yours until sundown.'

There were saddles and bridles across the toprail. Taking a bridle, Martin moved carefully until he had a young bay mare backed against the rails. The bay obediently dropped her head for the bit. Then Martin led the bay to the saddles. Ben Barton was leaning against the rails, his arms spread out. He smiled and nodded.

'Yer picked a good 'un.'

The compliment pleased Martin. But this change of face was confusing. Perhaps Barton had decided to drop the feud? Martin saddled the bay and had mounted when Barton held up a hand.

'Wait a bit, girlie. Yer girth's a bit loose.'

Barton lifted the saddle flap and Martin felt the girth being loosened and then re-tightened.

'There y'are.' Barton stepped back and opened the gate. 'A gallop now, while I watch yer style.'

The bay mare was tossing her head, anxious to be off. Martin let her have her head, emphasising the direction with his heels, and the canter lengthened into a gallop. Exhilaration seized him. He had only a moment to feel the sideways slip of the saddle, to snatch at the mare's mane, before he saw the ground leap up at him and felt the clout of impact.

When he opened his eyes, trying to focus on the swivelling sun and cotton wool clouds, his head was beating with pain. Something was looking down at him, a blur that slowly began to form itself into Ben Barton's face. The man was holding a saddle.

'Yer came quite a cropper, girlie.'

Martin tried to clear his mind.

'What happened?'

Barton held the girth out from the saddle.

'Looks like it were near enough wore through.' He bared his long teeth in a leer. 'One thing's in yer favour. It's a short walk back ter camp.'

When the sun had ceased its swivelling, Martin got shakily to his feet. Apart from the pain in his head and a few touchy ribs, he had not been damaged in the fall. But the girth had not been worn; it had been sound when he had saddled up, he knew. When Barton had pretended to be tightening the girth, he was in fact, slicing it through to the breaking point. As shaken as he was by the fall, Martin knew that this would have to be kept from Solomon. He would have to make up a story to explain the lump on his head and his limping.

When the report of the breakdown of the marine cable was carried from Adelaide by ship to the Roper River landing and inland to the line by the supply wagons, the men had much fun at the expense of the cable-layers. They barely concealed their pride at what they had endured in the monsoon, and the speed at which the poles and wire were now marching south. The linesmen were everywhere at work on the northern section, repoling with iron from Darwin down, with timber at the line's southern end. The linesmen going up the poles in their çlimbing boots and harness had been an amusement to Solomon.

'To get the proper value of the spectacle,' Solomon advised solemnly, 'you have to stand back a few cable lengths. Then you see it as plainly as a travelling performance. The one where the monkey goes up the stick, for the reward of a banana.'

As the weather again grew hotter, the air clogged with

humidity, laying a greasy scum on the skin. In Solomon's forge, the men had to be rested every hour. The water they ladled from the drinking barrel to gulp by the pint poured out of their skins in sweat and their singlets had to be draped in the sun to dry. Solomon's monkeys-up-a-stick, the hole diggers and the axemen, became casualties of dehydration, sickening in increasing numbers. The salt was going out of their bodies faster than it could be replaced.

No salt had been delivered to Daly Waters in a week, and for days the Overlanders had been on a ration. But there were soda springs with good salt a few days' ride to the west. The depot boss sent two stockmen with pack horses to bring back a supply. All work, except in the early mornings and late afternoons, had been stopped in Solomon's forge. The devil in hell would have been more at ease than the men at the furnace and anvil.

On the return of the stockmen, Martin saw a hushed crowd gathered around them.

'Something's gone aground,' Solomon said to Martin. 'There's nothing on earth, or on the seven seas, that attracts curiosity like a disaster.'

One of the stockmen who had gone for the salt stood with the depot boss.

'We'd filled the packs and camped for the night,' the stockman was saying. 'Jones was as good as gold when we camped. Next morning he couldn't move. The rheumatic fever had got him in the night. I somehow got him inter the saddle and strapped him there. It was mighty slow goin', but I got him back a stage by nightfall. Next mornin' he was in agony. I didn't know what ter do. There were blacks out huntin' and I waited until they moved off. Jones was lyin' on his back groanin'. I built a shade over him and put my revolver and his where he could get them.'

The depot boss interrupted, pointing to a teamster.

'Harness up the express wagon. You others fill it with grass.'

'He got so bad I had to leave him to get help. The pains were shakin' him apart. Several times I'd given him up fer dead and then he'd start in screamin' again.'

'You'll need another hand,' the depot boss said, scanning the faces. 'You'll do, young Martin.'

The driver of the express wagon knew where to go. He whipped up the horses and shouted them on to a pace that had Martin holding on to his seat. All the same, they had to drive for several hours.

'There he is,' the driver shouted, nodding at a rough shelter close to a patch of mulga.

Alfred Jones was stretched stiff, as though in rigor mortis. Ants ran eveywhere on his body, in his eyes and his open mouth. He had not been able to lift a hand to brush them off. The carrion crows, flapping away as the express wagon neared, cawed their disappointment from the mulga tops.

One of the birds lay near the stricken man, one wing only connected to its body by a ligament. Jones must have been able to fire his revolver once as the crows hopped in to try and peck out his eyes.

'By the saints!' the driver said. 'Is he dead or alive, do yer reckon?'

Martin was cleaning the ants away, feeling for the man's pulse.

'He's alive. I think he's had some kind of fit. Help me get him into the wagon.'

Martin sat on the padding of grass, cradling the stockman's head in his arms, trying to protect him from the lurches and bumps. Back in camp, a bed had been prepared, and medicines for rheumatic fever got ready from the medicine chest.

'I wonder will he live?' Martin said that night at the fire. 'He showed no sign of life in the wagon, except for the faint beat of his pulse. He didn't even appear to be breathing.'

'As for that,' Solomon said, 'appearances can be deceiving. I've seen shipmates looking as dead as the dead, until a looking glass was put to their faces. If the glass mists there's life somewhere, deep in the man.'

'It seems too much to expect that he should survive. The soldier ants were eating into his eyelids and mouth.'

'A terrible thing,' Solomon agreed. 'Yet Eli survived the hulks and the transports, and three hundred lashes as icing on the cake.'

'The man will survive if it's God's will,' said Eli. 'We are all in the hands of providence.'

'It was Solomon, not providence, who saved you, Eli.'

'That was providence, lad. God's ways are hard for us sinners to follow.'

Jones died during the night.

The next morning a supply wagon came in from the Roper, with six bags of salt amongst its load. The replacement of the lost body salts immediately cured the weakness and dizziness which had plagued the men. Salt, it appeared, was almost as important as food and drink for survival in the north.

Now another essential for the well-being of the men was about to arrive at the camp. There had been no mail into Daly Waters for months, and when the first shout of 'Mail' went up, every man immediately dropped what he was doing and headed for the hut of the depot boss.

Martin's letters were enclosed in a single package, and he shouted with delight to discover a letter from his twin. The package was like a treasure trove. He read aloud from the letters to Solomon and Eli, putting down one letter for another, going back to Matthew's letter again and again when the others had been read.

Ben Barton, sitting with his back against the horse yard rails, drank from a bottle of rum which had been a bonus on the trade of a good saddle for a rotting one. He looked back over his shoulder at the men reading their mail and heard their guffaws and delighted exclamations. Tipping the bottle again and swallowing, he cursed the camp and all those in it. He had not a relative in the world that he knew about; the stinking blacks had murdered all the family he had ever known. He had no close friend who might have written, because Ben Barton buttered up to nobody. Yet the truth was that even if all the letters in the mailbag had been addressed to him, he would not have been able to read a line. He had had only a little schooling from his mother, and that was soon forgotten after he was orphaned, in the struggle for sheer survival.

He continued to drink, muttering to himself. He'd brought the poxed Yankee's boy a cropper and there had been some satisfaction in that. He'd got one black bastard for sure, out near the swamp. He'd put a bullet into the second one and had put something else into the girl. There was likewise satisfaction in that. And he'd get more of the black bastards before this job was done.

'Go on, read yer bloody mail, yer bastards,' Barton shouted at the horses. 'Yer wife's up the duff and yer daughter's hawkin' her arse down at the port.'

A great rage grew in him as the rum bottle began to empty. His heavy black eyebrows knotted in the ridge between his eyes. He'd be back on the bloody line before long if the Yankee got his way, and the Yankee seemed to get his way more often than not, it seemed. He stung with humiliation at the memory of the fight with Solomon in the forge. The others had smirked to see Ben Barton go down, he who had never before gone down in his life. He tried to remember how the blows had been struck. He had thrashed a dozen men better than the Yankee. Perhaps it had been just a lucky punch, maybe he had slipped. Ben Barton never lost a fight. One time he had taken on three men at once in a grog shanty; two he'd knocked senseless and the third had run like a rabbit for the door.

His brows knotted more deeply in the effort to remember. One of those other bastards might have tripped him. One of the weaklings who couldn't stand up for himself, the way Ben Barton did. Yes, Solomon. No, Solomon. Three bags full, Solomon.

And that English bastard, Stubbs. Too good to mix with anyone other than the Yankee and the girlie. The English were a pack of mongrels, every colonial knew that. Ben Barton could beat Stubbs to a pulp with one arm tied behind his back.

As the rum went down in the bottle, Barton's gorge continued to rise. It must have been a lucky punch, or someone had tripped him. They were all against him in the forge. But in the tent area the ground was hard and flat. Nobody could trip him there. He swilled again and stored the almost emptied bottle in a saddle-bag. He would celebrate with that after he'd flattened the Yankee.

Eli Stubbs carried a water bucket towards the tent, picking up the box he sat on at night. Putting the basin on the box at the back of the tent, he pulled his sweaty flannel singlet over his head. The dark suntan on his face, neck and arms contrasted strangely with the paleness that the singlet had preserved. He began to wash, secure behind the flaps he had let down.

'I'm comin', yer Yankee bastard,' Ben Barton mumbled, already clenching the hammers of his fists. 'There'll be no trippin' Ben this day.'

He weaved a little as he approached the tent, punching at the air.

'No lucky punches this time. Come out and fight, yer bastard.'

He paused at the tent for a moment when he saw the flaps were drawn. Nobody drew tent flaps in weather like this. He cocked his head to consider. Perhaps the Yankee had that boy of his in there. That would be something to put about the camp. That would do for the both of them.

Eli whistled a tune as he bent to pick up the soap which had slipped from his grasp, his back to the tent flaps as Ben Barton pulled them wide. He chilled instantly at the small sound then froze. The hulking figure of Ben Barton stood motionless at the entrance, a silhouette looming in the dazzling light.

Barton shook his head, trying to make a connection in his mind. He opened his mouth to speak, then shut it again. Letting the tent flaps fall, he began to back away. Eli stood for a moment, then sank slowly on to his bunk, his arms about his head.

As Barton edged away from the tent, Solomon appeared. Barton eyed him stupidly for a moment, not moving. Solomon looked from Barton to the tent where he knew Eli had gone to wash. Barton dropped his eyes, unable to endure the savagery in Solomon's face.

'I won't tell. I won't tell,' he whispered.

Solomon spoke only one word but it hissed like a tiger snake.

'Get!'

Barton turned, almost running for the horse yard and the bottle.

Solomon let a few minutes pass before he entered the tent.

Eli was lying on his bed, staring at the canvas walls. The doom in his voice was complete.

'He's seen me,' Eli whispered. 'Barton's seen the back that's on me like a curse. Like the mark of Cain, Solomon. It's all up with me now. God has withdrawn his mercy.'

Solomon sat down and scratched vigorously in his curls.

'Speech is a gift, and there's no gainsaying that. However, we have somethin' of an obligation to make sense when we speak, and what Solomon has just heard with his own ears makes no sense at all.'

'He saw it. He saw it. He saw the brand I must wear until I die.'

'Perhaps Eli has been out too long in the sun,' Solomon suggested to himself. 'As for Ben Barton, haven't I just been talking with the pleasant fellow? Didn't he ask me about the new man washing in the tent? Didn't we agree to forget our small difference, even shaking hands on it?'

'He saw it. He must have seen it.'

'He saw it, he saw it,' Solomon mimicked. 'There's Ben Barton, eyes blinded by the sun, looking into a dark tent and unable to spy Eli Stubbs, thinking him a new man.'

'Is it so? For the sake of pity, is it so?'

'You have my word on it,' Solomon said. 'And if you'd just produce a magistrate, I'm willing to swear to it in proper legal fashion, including signature. But enough of this talk. I came to tell you that you're getting a new dray, Eli. And not before time, with the old one dropping bits of itself everywhere like a cockatoo in the moulting season.'

Solomon went back to the forge and sat down on a bench to think. The nearest police were at Darwin. Barton could pass a letter to them, via a returning teamster. Or he could get it to the Roper, to be carried by ship to the south. He might even invent an excuse to get himself to Darwin.

Back in the horse yard, Barton poured a bucket of water over his head, shaking himself like a dog. His thoughts were racing. Eli Stubbs was an escaped convict, for whose capture there was a standard reward. He couldn't be a ticket-of-leave man, the scars on his back were too new for that. To have deserved such a flogging would have cancelled all the chance of ticket-of-leave anyway.

To get the reward money and take vengeance on the Yankee,

he had to get a message through to Darwin, though it could be risky. If he told a teamster the story to carry back to the police, the man might claim the reward for himself. Barton cursed his lack of book learning.

There was only one sure way. He had to get back to Port Darwin himself.

Eli was sitting outside the tent when Martin returned from a short mission delivering horseshoes down the line. He sat limply, staring at nothing. He gave Martin no welcome, nor asked about the trip.

'Are you all right, Eli?'

'I've got a touch of the fever, lad.'

'Do you want me to go for medicine?'

'No, it's not bad enough for that.'

'Where's Solomon?'

'He's looking at a new dray we've got for the forge, I think.'

Martin was pleased for Eli's sake.

'I hope it has a decent seat and springs. You must be jolted to pieces by now. I'll go and look for Solomon. I'd like to see the new dray myself.'

Passing by the forge, Martin was surprised to hear the hammer ringing, and, stepping inside, he watched unobserved the livid metal that Solomon was beginning to shape.

'What are you making, Solomon?'

Solomon stopped his work, startled.

'A wigwam for a goose's bridle.'

'No, but really?'

'It's a long nose he's got. Be off with you. There are dirty clothes in the tent to be washed.'

Walking back, Martin thought to himself that both Eli and Solomon were acting oddly. Solomon hadn't asked about the delivery either, nor did he mention the new dray. His face had been grim, the pits darkened. What was Solomon making, alone in the forge at this hour?

Solomon continued to hammer and shape, moving between the furnace and the anvil. There were few men in the world who could have identified the glowing objecct. It was becoming the perfect miniature of a New Bedford whaling harpoon head.

Sixteen

After the Milner brothers had crossed the Finke River and camped for the lambing season, they continued onwards in the tracks of the Overlanders, the drive sometimes strung out for miles.

Steven Woodrush had indeed hardened in the image that Lucinda had evoked. His face was masked in sunburn, his thin arms were beginning to enlarge with muscle. Riding in the spring cart with Milner, who was suffering with a swollen and painful knee due to a well-directed kick from a horse, Steven caught sight of a big group of blacks hiding behind the thorn bushes, peering around the foliage.

'I wonder what they think of us?' Steven said, brushing at the flies on his face.

'Who?'

'The Aborigines. They've probably never seen sheep before, or horses and bullocks, let alone white men.'

'They might have come across the Overlanders.'

'Our clothing, our hats, the boots on our feet, how strange they must look to people who have lived naked all their lives.'

Ralph chewed thoughtfully on a piece of straw.

'I've seen them bolt from horses and cattle and camels,' he said, 'but the wild men have a great curiosity about the whites. John and I have often let them into camp, without trouble. They'll steal anything not nailed down, there's no two ways about that, but mostly it's just curiosity. They're like children, really.'

'Dangerous children,' Steven said, remembering the tales of spearings.

'That's their natural tribal instinct. Each tribe has its own territory and knows there'll be a fight if they trespass across its borders. That's probably how they see us, as trespassers. Another tribe, strange to be sure, but trespassers nevertheless. Anyway, most of the trouble in the old days was caused by whites interfering with their women. John says that if you treat them with kindness there's nothing to fear, and he's been out exploring, has brother John.'

Listening to the tales of stockmen, watching them work, each man seemingly able to turn his hand to anything from butchering for the cook and repairing the transport to doctoring both sick animals and each other, had made a deep impression on Steven. He could ride well enough to help with the droving, but he was unreliable with anything else, except perhaps driving a spring cart or dray. He marvelled at the stockmen who took the heavy wagon in turn, in casual, competent command of eighteen bullocks, or eighteen horses when the bullocks were being spelled. He had only recently learned how to harness a horse to a dray.

How many ordained priests, he wondered, knew as little of the world as he did? Priests to whom their parishioners went to ask advice in their troubles? What advice about anything was he equipped to give?

The Bishop of St Paul's had seen a good deal of life, having been an army chaplain in the Crimean war. He had married and brought up children, one of whom had died. He remained a fine figure of a man, even into his late sixties, and there was still a fire quick to light in his eyes at the spectacle of one of his flock going astray. Perhaps his army service accounted for his militant manner. The Bishop believed as much in the devil as he did in the God to whom he was devoted, seeing life in simple terms, as a battlefield on which good and evil contended. Satan was a brilliant general and he never gave up. When a soul was won for God, Satan marked that soul and waited on its moments of weakness. Insidiously, the Bishop had said, the devil would whisper encouragement. Go on, do what you want. Rid yourself of irksome restraints.

How easily the devil had gained a hold on his soul, Steven thought. He was as vulnerable as any other man. If he became a priest, he knew he wanted now to do more than conduct church services. He wanted to go outside the church, to men such as these on the drive. Men who would not come to church until the church came to them. The profanities which had made him wince had become meaningless now. When the men used Christ's name as an expletive, it could be also interpreted as an unknowing prayer. Was not 'For Christ's sake!' a petition of a kind?

When he had fled Adelaide, his one thought had been to escape from Lucinda. He realised now that his escape had provided a testing ground for him. A testing of his devotion and resolution, a testing of the vocation which he had taken for granted, under the Bishop's wing. Each week he thought less about Lucinda, although he could not pretend that he had found the strength to resist her. She had merely been relegated to a lower place in his priorities.

The first priority had become the success of the drive, because its success or failure would be success or failure for each of them. The second priority was the testing of his vocation. He would return to Adelaide either committed to the church, or to the outside world. Lucinda had become the third consideration, relegated not only in priority of attention, but also in importance.

The Overland trail they were following, testament of the men who had made it, and the poles and wire they continually encountered, continued to trouble Steven. Here was man's mark in the wilderness, lonely and stark, without sign or signal of man himself. It was this that gave Steven the sensation that everything he knew had been left behind.

The Finke River now far behind, the drive trailed across a seared landscape. For the last eighty miles, only the working animals and the dogs had been watered from the tank on the dray. Many of the lambs born near the Finke River had lain down and refused to move, despite the prodding of their dams. Steven carried a dray load, as did the other carts and drays. Only the blessing of occasional green feed, sprouted where earlier thunderstorms had struck, saved the flock from extinction. When the drive finally came upon water, the flock could not have kept on their feet much longer. In their first wet camp in many days, Ralph Milner spoke to Steven.

'I don't really know how to say this. We were just about goners back there. If we hadn't struck that green feed, it would have been the end of the flock. Now, I know you're not a priest yet. But you're the nearest thing to it we've got. I'd like you to say a prayer for all of us.'

Steven said, 'You don't have to be a priest to pray, Ralph.'

'I know that. But it might sound better, coming from you.'

Steven offered up a prayer of thanksgiving, to the accompaniment of the bleating of the flock and the jingling of bells on the horses and bullocks.

'Amen to that,' Ralph Milner said, and put his hat back on.

Ross and his party were spelling in one of the expedition's old camps, near the Finke River. There was much activity at the depot, and for miles about it. A party of Overlanders, searching for poling trees, had provided the starving expedition with damper, mutton and tea on its return. It had been a ramshackle party that had met the Overlanders, both men and horses at the end of their tether. While the expedition rested, a report on their condition was carried back to the Peake. The Peake was almost a settlement now, with many camps about the stone buildings which would make it a major repeater station.

In the camps at the Finke, the Overlanders were living a life of ease, waiting on supplies and instructions. Some had slung hammocks between shady trees, lounging in them to read old newspapers and novels, or dozing off in contentment. The more active entertained themselves at target practice with their revolvers, whenever cormorants appeared on the river. Nearly every man had a dog, grown fat and sleek on scraps from the cookhouse. The explorers' camp, as it came to be called, was a poor thing compared to the others. A rough shed of boughs; a dozen pack saddles arranged on a rail; a fire, a bucket and five quart pots for its kitchen.

'Look at them dogs,' Billy said, with resentment. 'Fat enough ter drag their bellies on the ground. I could've done with their scraps, when we were bloody well down to oatmeal.'

After a month in camp, spent shoeing the horses and watching them strengthen, a train of one hundred camels arrived from the Peake, carrying, among other things, supplies for the expedition's third venture north. Ross made a list of the provisions and submitted it to Harvey, as his second-in-command. But Harvey seemed dissatisfied, and he and Ross went off to debate in private.

'I've got a feelin',' said Tom Crispe, 'that our surveyor is goin' ter turn it in.'

Ross soon confirmed Tom's misgivings. William Harvey had declined to go out with such poor supplies. He would take command of a party due to work on the central section.

The news of Harvey's departure struck Matthew like a hammer blow, for in the past couple of days he had come to his own decision. He would return to Adelaide. There would be no shame in it. He had pulled his weight and done his duty. Mr Ross himself had said that he was proud of Matthew. He had gone out twice into country where brave men had perished. He had seen things that no other white man had seen. He had become a man, and had struck up friendships which only death would dissolve. He would greatly miss Mr Ross and his mates. But he would travel with them in spirit, as they thrust again for the Roper River.

William Harvey's decision not to risk himself into the north with dubious supplies now changed all that for Matthew. Although little criticism was voiced by others, it was clear that they were disappointed in Harvey and regarded him as a defector. Matthew could not bring himself to be the second.

But his longing for home and family grew daily more intense, like an ache that would not be soothed. He yearned for the sight of a city street, a civilised house, the gay colours of a woman's dress. Sometimes he shut his eyes in an attempt to conjure up his family. First Martin, then his father and mother, Lucinda next and young Hannibal last. Then he would concentrate on conjuring up the family home and would seat them all for Sunday dinner, with Mr Ross as guest as honour, on his father's right. The talk would be of their explorations, with all the family gazing at Matthew with pride and wonder.

But sometimes the family would not be conjured up, their images blurring as he tried to summon them. Twice he had

had a dream which haunted him for days afterwards. In the dream he could clearly see the surroundings of his father's house, but there was a blank where the house should have been, as if house, garden and family had been spirited into oblivion.

Another camel train came up from the Peake. The camels had a fascination for Matthew; they looked so supercilious, peering down their muzzles, craning their long necks to stare, creating the impression that they only bore their burdens by way of a concession, one which they might revoke at any moment.

Matthew longed to ride one, and after the train had been unloaded and rested, he walked over to the camel camp to ask if he might try. There were three Afghan drivers to the train, with one white camel man in charge. The camel man was a specialist, off a property at Beltana where the camels were bred from imported stock as a general transport for the outback, a transport capable of bearing loads which no pack horse could carry over any terrain.

'Don't see why not,' the camel man said. 'You can try my riding camel if you like. Say, tomorrer afternoon?' He paused. 'Tell me, boy, any idea where the explorer's camp is?'

'Yes,' Matthew answered, surprised. 'I'm one of them.'

The camel man looked startled.

'You?' What I mean is the explorers who go out with Ross.'

'That's right,' Matthew said. 'We only got back from the north a month ago.'

The camel man studied Matthew with new respect.

'If you go out with Ross, young fella, you can have my riding camel any time yer like. Hang on a minute.'

He returned with a large package.

'This'll probably go down well. It's mail for the expedition. Been waitin' at the Peake for months.'

Almost snatching at the package, Matthew made off for the camp.

'Tomorrer afternoon, then,' the man called with amusement, to Matthew's receding figure.

Ross opened the package, shuffling through the mail and calling each man's name. Matthew groaned with impatience.

'Listen ter this, will yer,' Billy Hearne laughed, pointing at his letter. 'Me mate got shikkered at a woolshed dance and walked inter the river gettin' home, the silly bastard.'

The first letter which Matthew opened was from his father. It was the first letter he had ever received from his father, and the unfamiliar style of expression both brought his father closer and moved him further away.

'What?' Matthew cried out, almost in the manner of old Hannibal. 'Will you listen to this? My twin, Martin, the one I told you about, ran away from home and is on the Roper River with the Overland.'

The others made suitable comments and returned to their own reading. Matthew went hurriedly through the other envelopes, looking for the letter which his father had readdressed. It was no trouble to recognise Martin's hand. Matthew had often cribbed homework from Martin's exercise books.

Bug-eyed, he raced through the long letter. Martin expected to leave the Roper for the line when the new crew was shipped in to take over. There he would meet up with Solomon, the American whaler and harpooner. What would such a man have been doing in his father's forge? Martin's description of himself and Eli Stubbs, marooned on racks of pandanus palm in a world turned into muddy water, made Matthew gasp with disbelief. All this time, while he had been visualising Martin at home with the family, even seating him at the Sunday table in his imaginings, his twin had been cut off by the northern floods, had faced starvation and who knew what hazards at the Roper.

He read aloud his twin's account of the northern floods to the other men.

'Godamighty,' Tom Crispe said, 'fancy goin' out on a flooded river in a bloody great bullock wagon. Patterson must've had bats in the belfry.'

Ross said primly, 'He saved the depot. Patterson is a fine man and I'm proud to call him friend.'

Matthew was so full of family that the letters began to run together in his head. His elder brother's letter was dry and dull. Matthew thought, full of the business and how his father worried about him and Martin. His mother's letter conveyed many admonitions, and reminded him about saying his prayers, avoiding bad company, and changing his underwear and socks every day. Lucinda's letter was frivolous, with numerous mentions of her friend, Lady Charlotte Bacon. Old Hannibal's letter was stiff and strained. He had never had to write to a son before, let alone one out in the wilderness.

Over and over, Matthew returned to his twin's letter, picturing everything with disturbing clarity in the light of his own experiences. It was hard for him to believe that Martin had actually run away, harder still to believe that he had seen and suffered so much. Martin had been there, at the Roper landing, which the explorers were still unable to reach – it was almost too much to comprehend.

The Roper landing! Of course! Ross was bound for the Roper River and the northern section. At this minute, Martin was there, somewhere on the northern line. They would get to the Roper next time out, with so much old track to follow. When the expedition reached the northern line it would be easy for him to find his twin. What would Martin look like, after the racks, after having faced starvation? What stories they would have to exchange!

Then he became thoughtful. If it had not been for Will Harvey's refusal to risk himself, he might now be on his way south. His triumphant return to the family would have been miserably blighted, with Martin gone away. He felt a pang, which dwindled quickly as it arose. His solitary glory as an explorer would now have to be shared with a veteran of the Roper marooning. But how good it would be to take Martin by surprise, to walk up and tap him on the shoulder! Matthew blessed Will Harvey and wished that Ross would get a move on. He itched to strike out for the north.

On the expedition's return to the Finke River, the explorers would have encountered the Milner brothers' stock drive instead of the Overlanders, had their approach been a mere few miles to the west.

The Milners were now into good going, with plentiful feed and water, making eight and ten miles each day. The hunting dogs were bringing down numerous kangaroos for the cook, and had greatly alarmed a pair of emus, before the giant birds had outrun them, their sinewy legs flailing the ground, their useless wings partly outstretched, as if in memory of some distant stage in their evolution when they had been able to fly. John Milner thought the pair might have been nesting and poked about in the bush but without success. Two emu eggs would have been more than enough to make an omelette for them all.

Ralph Milner always drove until sunset. When the sun began to dip, it was time to make camp. Routine ordered each man's job, and they went at it methodically. When night began to close in, the animals were settled, the horses hobbled, the bullocks belled, the fire was lit and a meal was cooking.

On the third day of easy travelling, an electrical storm came upon them just as camp was being made. Lightning flashed and zig-zagged in brief and brilliant illuminations. Crashes of thunder sounded around them like a monstrous cannonade. Within the first few minutes every man was soaked, and the horses and bullocks had bolted in fright. There was nothing to be done, the stockmen knew. The round-up of runaway horses and bullocks would have to wait until first light.

The country was open, but patched here and there with saltbush. Some of the horses had run for miles before the storm abated. It was a full morning's work to find them and drive them back.

'All the horses are accounted for,' John Milner told his brother, 'but six of the bullocks are still missing.'

Ralph Milner beckoned to Steven.

'We're six bullocks short. I want to keep pushing the pace while we're still finding green feed. Do you reckon you could go back for the bullocks, without getting lost? They have to be behind us or we'd have found them.'

'Make sure which side of the tracks you're on,' John Milner said. 'You'd better take tucker and water for a night or two – they might take some finding.'

Steven knew that he was being sent back because he could be spared. Yet Ralph Milner trusted him for their finding, and he felt a glow of pride in the importance of the undertaking. The loss of six working bullocks was a serious matter.

Steven found four of the big dappled bullocks in the late afternoon; grazing quietly, they lifted their heads to greet him as if in all innocence of the nuisance they had caused. Belling one of them, Steven scouted for the remaining two in widening circles until nightfall, when he camped for the night in the tracks of the drive, a ribbon of hoofprint and wheelprint across the red earth and the stamped and cropped grass where the moving sheep had snatched at feed. He felt safe and comfortable camped on the tracks which linked him to the drive.

The next afternoon he sighted the two remaining delinquents grazing far out on the plain, and felt a great satisfaction. He would almost be one of them when he rode in, driving the lost stock before him. When he overnighted for the second time, he rationed his corned meat and damper.

Next morning, the bullocks trotted obediently as Steven forced them onwards, snuffling at the track of the drive for familiar associations. He hoped to catch up with the Milners before nightfall; his supply of food was finished and the first pangs of hunger worried his stomach.

His attention was cast no further than the rumps and backs he was driving before him, and the carnage was upon him without warning. The bullocks began to bellow and Steven's horse shied and reared, almost pitching him from the saddle. Everywhere around him, among the small bushes that flourished on the plain, lay the carcasses of sheep, swarming with crows hunting for eyes and tongues. Flies had settled in clusters on the sheep's heads, ants fossicked in their open mouths. Dead sheep, in the grotesque postures of violent death, stretched out to fill all Steven's vision.

The putrid stench of corruption, speeded up by the burning sun, sent the bullocks plunging along the track, rushing at the littered bodies blocking their way, horning and tossing them aside. The bloating carcasses burst as the horns went in, rumbling with an escaping gas that made Steven gag. Tossing and bellowing, the bullocks cleared a path which Steven followed. Once clear of the great scattering of bodies, the bullocks began to stampede, running for more than a mile before they settled.

Steven shook in the saddle. If he had known little of life, he knew nothing of death, life's constant companion. He couldn't remember having seen death in any form. He hurried the now tiring bullocks, in an urgent need to be with the others before the sun began to dip.

Ralph and John Milner were boiling the billy when Steven arrived.

'Didn't you see them dropping?' Steven asked in disbelief.

Ralph Milner shook his head.

'The bushes with the poisonous berries were pretty much at the middle of the mob, when we got them settled for the night.'

'There was nothing to see or hear,' John Milner added. 'We didn't know anything about it until next morning.'

Between sunset that night and sun-up the next day, the Milner brothers had lost two thousand sheep to a poisonous bush which had flourished there for thousands of years, untouched by native animals.

'We saw the bushes right enough, when we camped,' Ralph said. 'There was no way of knowing what they were. This is new country we're travelling through. There's no way of knowing what might come up next.'

Steven's entry into camp with all six bullocks was diminished by the awful loss. But his own pride in his achievement continued to warm him. The sedentary routine in which his life had been spent began to seem unreal. Who knew what he might accomplish in the world outside the church? He was already a part of history, by being on this first stock drive into the far north. The priorities which he had established for himself began to fade away. For the present, he was his first priority. Steven Woodrush, alive and free in the world.

Seventeen

Well over a year had passed since the setting of the first pole and the shovelling of the first earth around that stark and solitary tree, naked of roots and branches, so incongruous among the surrounding forests. The central line was still striving northwards, the northern line still strove south. The southern section had been completed ahead of schedule.

The breakdown of the marine cable south of Java, which had caused so much jubilation in the colony, was again much under discussion. No further news had been brought by the vessels that sailed in those waters. For all that was known, the damage might have been repaired and the cable laying continued. The limbo of suspense tried the nerves of both public and government. It was as though the colony had wagered all its money on one horse in a two-horse race, and the favourite had disappeared.

'Success in sight,' old Hannibal quoted contemptuously casting his newspaper from him in irritation. 'In whose sight, might I ask? In the sight of the *Advertiser*'s editor? Has his sight so miraculously improved that he can see from here to Java? Can he also see underwater? James Richards, who's as blind as a bat without the assistance of his spectacles! Can James Richards assure us that success is in sight, when he can barely see to light the end of his cigar?'

Young Hannibal considered his father's questions rhetorical.

'At least the line is moving, Father. Consider – when everything broke down in the north, most people thought that was the end. When the central line halted for lack of water and the termites were eating the poles, even the Premier almost gave up. You must admit that progress has been made, Father.'

Old Hannibal glared at his son, over the top of his spectacles.

'You'd be glad to say I told you so, no doubt, like that damned J.A. Holden.'

Young Hannibal fidgeted.

'I'm not questioning your judgement, Father. The simple fact is that the impossible seems to have been made possible.'

'I'll give you a simple fact,' old Hannibal glared. 'The simple fact is that nobody knows how soon the marine cable might reach Port Darwin. The simple fact is that nobody knows what penalties might yet have to be paid. There's a simple fact for you. I'd be gladly instructed in how you dodge it.'

All five colonies watched eagerly for news of the race between the Overland Telegraph and the marine cable. The prospect of receiving foreign news, as that news was being made, was a startling concept to colonists accustomed to being years behind the events of the world. Even now, business heads began to plot to exploit the advantages of Charles Todd's extraordinary achievement.

Poling south after the monsoon, the hole-diggers on the northern line had spaded more than earth out of the holes. Gold traces had gleamed in the dirt walls, gold speckled the shovels.

Wild rumours of gold were sped to the south by the ships that travelled the coast. Cunning operators calculated possible gains and organised themselves to exploit the growing gold fever. A fictitious report of quartz reefs, assaying ninety ounces of gold to the ton, convulsed the colony with visions of El Dorado. The sharpest operators booked passages north for their associates, with explicit instructions about the wording of reports to be sent south. Within weeks of their arrival in the north, these fictions were received in Adelaide and posted outside the gold companies' offices.

The magic of the Overland and the lure of the north caused even conservative businessmen to succumb to the fever. A raging contagion seemed to seize the community; scrip was hawked in the streets by men, women and boys; crowds in hundreds jammed the offices of the mining companies, waiting on further news of the bonanza. Many of them invested the last penny they possessed.

Gold prospectors from other colonies fought for ship passage to Darwin. Mining machinery was shipped from Port Adelaide, with great display by its promoters. This material evidence of projects to be worked caused a further scramble for available shares.

Old Hannibal's hard-headed practicality was overwhelmed, as he joined the rush on the brokers. He wrote to Martin, urging him to furnish news about the mines. Having a son in the distant north, who would surely have heard where the richest strikes were being made, appeared to old Hannibal as a blessed event, one which almost made up for the heartache and worry of Martin's running away.

J.A. Holden had new cause to squirm when he met old Hannibal at the stock exchange or the club. Old Hannibal's mighty hints about the privileged information soon to reach him from his son lathered the master saddler in a sweat of envy and frustration.

'Didn't I say there could be gold in the north?' old Hannibal demanded of young Hannibal, having at no time said any such thing.

'No,' young Hannibal answered flatly, much to his father's surprise.

'No? Do you mean to sit there and gainsay me, in the teeth of everything that's happened?'

Young Hannibal avoided the question, being more than a little concerned about the amounts of money his father had invested in the newly fledged mining companies.

'I have no faith in the situation, Father – devil an ounce of the gold have we yet seen.'

'Rot,' old Hannibal insisted. 'The last report from the north has announced that the Royal Standard Gold Company has crushed a parcel of rock for the magnificent return of ninety-nine ounces to the ton. The directors say that the reef is inexhaustible.'

Young Hannibal was stubborn.

'Tubby Baker won't take up a single share.'

'Ha!' Old Hannibal snorted. 'What would Tubby Baker know about it, anyway! The claims have been clearly mapped. If Tubby Baker's brains were dynamite, they wouldn't blow his hat off.'

Young Hannibal retained his composure.

'Tubby owns one of the richest properties in the colony. He might appear easygoing, but he's got a good head for business.'

Old Hannibal held out his brandy balloon and young Hannibal bore it to the decanter. Old Hannibal's brow furrowed. He drummed his fingers on the leather arm of his chair.

'Tubby Baker,' he repeated. 'What would he know about mining?'

'That's my point,' young Hannibal said, returning with the brandy balloon. 'What do any of us know about gold mining! Most of the promoters have come from Melbourne and Sydney. What do we know about the credentials and backgrounds of these men?'

Old Hannibal drummed his fingers harder.

'Do you mean to tell me that you regard these stories of gold strikes as hoaxes?'

'I'm merely exercising caution,' young Hannibal answered. 'It was you who so taught me, Father, was it not?'

But old Hannibal was now deep in thought. He had bought much more scrip than his eldest son suspected, not only investing the cash flow of the business, but drawing deeply on capital. An abrupt realisation of how the gold fever had possessed him left him feeling an icy wind blowing through his veins. There must be gold. There had to be gold. How had he permitted himself to breach his every business rule, every rule that had made him secure, a man of wealth and position? It couldn't be. It must not be.

In the next few weeks, the fervour in the colony was intensified by the arrival of a trading vessel from the Dutch East Indies. A second break in the marine cable had again stalled its progress. The competitors in the two-horse race now appeared to be running neck and neck. Every new pole set in the ground meant more time and distance won.

But the trading in gold shares received the beginning of a setback with the return of the *Omeo* from Darwin. Captain Calder let it be known that the shipments of mining machinery from Adelaide were rusting on the beach where they had been landed, and that a small cutter loaded with a consignment of stampers and boilers had been struck by a squall, and had gone to the bottom, drowning the two men in charge.

On the *Omeo*'s arrival, the hundreds of investors who hurried to the port were greatly surprised by the crew's ignorance of the supposed golden hauls being made by the Royal Standard Gold Company, the Edel Mari and the True Blue Mines. The only satisfaction the crew could give the jostling enquirers was that prospectors from several other colonies had also been arriving in the north, and had gone off into the tropical sun, wheeling barrows loaded with picks, shovels and gold panning dishes, to risk their lives on the supposed gold fields eighty miles to the west. However the *Omeo* also brought some other news.

In trawling for a dray which had slipped from its slings during unloading of the *Omeo*, fine pearl shells had been brought to the surface. Excitement rippled through the crowd. The treasure of pearl shells lay on the bed of Port Darwin, there for the taking.

Old Hannibal sat in his office, staring blank-eyed at his desk. In a return of prudence he had, that day, offered parcels of his shares on the market. The best price he had been able to negotiate would have brought him a loss of more than half the capital he had invested. A fear that he had not felt since the long drought had wiped him out at Port Lincoln, all those years ago, squeezed his insides with panic. In the course of only a few months, his capital had been severely eroded.

He struggled for optimism. The collapse of confidence in the northern gold was only a passing phase. It had to be. It took time to get to the diggings, more time to crush the quartz, more time still to ship the golden metal half-way around the continent.

When the first gold arrived, the mining market would boom. Old Hannibal's losses, on paper, would be transformed into riches. All he had to do was hang on, banish the panic that was quivering in every fibre of his body. He opened the desk drawer in which he had begun to keep the brandy when anxiety about the twins had first driven him to that support, and reached for the glass that topped his water carafe, pouring with a shaking hand. Wasn't he one of the most successful men in the city? Didn't the name Hannibal Harper command universal respect? How could he doubt? It was all there in the reports. Old Hannibal topped the brandy with water, and swallowed it down.

In the following months, shares in the northern gold mines continued to weaken. The promotors brandished their latest reports declaring that more gold had been won, but as young Hannibal had remarked to his father, devil an ounce of it was yet to be seen in the south. Reports of small investors made bankrupt as share values continued to fall caused alarm which even the most recklessly fictionalised prospectus was unable to stay.

Old Hannibal became introspective, his plump frame melting into leanness again, as it had done during the long wait on news of Matthew and Martin's welfare. Mrs Harper's concern for her husband, who had taken to returning home in the evenings flushed in the face and uncertain in his speech, caused such a strain on her nerves that she jumped if a door banged. On those occasions, when she questioned her husband about his strange behaviour, he either dismissed her with a shake of his head, or irritably accused her of nagging.

'It's one thing after another,' Mrs Harper confided to her eldest son. 'It all began when your father allowed Matthew to go out exploring. Martin would never have run away, had it not been for Matthew's example. Then Lucinda fainted at the table and could hardly be talked to for weeks. She at least seems to be her old self again, which is a mercy. But I can't understand what has come over your father. It's really too much to bear.'

Young Hannibal was in no doubt as to what had come over his father. The operating account for the business had been exhausted in the buying of mining shares. Old Hannibal had been required to refinance it, with a cheque on his personal account.

'Father has been having business worries,' young Hannibal said. 'Trade is unsteady at present. And there was a considerable expense in setting up for the Overland Telegraph contracts.'

Mrs Harper hardly heard.

'This was such a united family, before the Overland Telegraph. Everything ran so smoothly. These upsets all come back on to me, you know. It's the women who pay the price.'

With the passing of time, Lucinda's memory of Steven Woodrush had begun to fade. She could still summon him up at will, and sometimes did, but the clarity of his image, the sound of his voice, the touch of his hands, even his uncertain kisses, had become blurred in her recollection.

In any case, she kept herself so busy these days that any reminders of Steven that came to her unbidden she resented as an intrusion into whichever frivolity engaged her at that moment. In the first weeks of Steven's absence, she had gone through her father's newspaper every night, searching for any mention of the drive. But this dedication soon wilted, as did her devotion to St Paul's and the choir. The Bible classes, in which Lucinda had made herself so prominent, were altogether abandoned. When Mrs Harper remarked on her daughter's changed habits, Lucinda excused herself by dismissing the other members of the Church Women's Fellowship as unbearably stuffy and petty-minded.

As the young officer of the 18th Regiment had been dismissed from Lucinda's sentiments before his ship had cleared the bar, only the wound inflicted on her ego by Steven's absurd flight kept him flitting across her mind with an irritating regularity. The physical intimacy that had occurred between them also remained as a bother, and in her cool bedroom at night, she sometimes awoke, flushed and restless, from dreams that surprised her in their frankness.

Marriage began to appear as an inevitability. If she couldn't have Steven Woodrush, and, in any case, she was now unsure of how much she desired him, she could still seek out a practical, comfortable union.

At the writing desk in her bedroom, Lucinda frowned in the same way she did when calculating how much of her monthly allowance remained. She began listing the single men whom she considered eligible for her favours. A prospective husband had to be well-off, with standing in the community. He should be amiable in disposition, educated, but not too much so; intellectual discourse bored Lucinda to tears.

Neither should he have too much character; men with character could prove stubborn over trifling matters. When Lucinda had completed her list, chewing on her pen as she studied it against her requirements, she realised, with some surprise, that her ideal husband would be a cross between Steven Woodrush and Tubby Baker.

Soon after old Hannibal's failure to sell his gold shares without too painful a loss, the collapse of the Royal Standard Gold Company shattered his remaining optimism, of late propped up by frequent recourse to the brandy bottle. The Royal Standard promotors closed their doors and disappeared with all the magic with which they had first manifested themselves. Investors were out on the streets trying to sell Royal Standard scrip for any price they could get. The Edel Mari and True Blue offices were besieged by shareholders demanding proof of the gold which had been so extravagantly advertised.

The final blow was furnished by the return of the first of the prospectors who had set out from Adelaide by ship some months before. Nobody had seen the reefs which the mining experts claimed to be managing, he said. When this information had been passed hurriedly from mouth to mouth, the Edel Mari and True Blue promotions also went into liquidation.

The small colony reeled. Old Hannibal was stupefied. His mind struggled to reject the phantom of ruin which he had brought down on himself. It couldn't be true. How could so many of his peers have been mistaken? Hadn't the Governor himself admitted to having invested? How could his hard-won capital, the accumulation of a lifetime, have melted before his eyes?

In the meantime, young Hannibal had been stiffening his

resolve. After all, the business would one day be his to manage. For some time past, many executive decisions had been left to him; he must know the extent of his father's losses, in order to plan ahead. Yet this assumption of authority, this reversal of roles, was so unnatural to him that a great many cheroots had to be smoked before he could bring himself to act.

Old Hannibal made no attempt to conceal his condition, or the bottle, when his eldest son stood before him.

'You want to know how much I've lost, don't you?'

'I feel that I should be told, Father,' young Hannibal answered, standing almost at attention.

'It's about as bad as it can be. I must have taken leave of my senses. How could such a thing have happened?'

Young Hannibal's voice quavered a little.

'The bank. Surely the bank will help, if we have to raise finance.'

Old Hannibal shook his head, his naked dome appearing almost as desolate as his features.

'The banks have suffered serious losses, made many overdrafts which will never be repaid. I can raise a little, on mortgage, but it will be a tight squeeze.'

Old Hannibal pinched at his nose, and then blew noisily into his handkerchief.

'There's a big bill outstanding right now, for materials purchased locally and from overseas. This must be kept from your mother and sister at all costs.'

There was soon a deeper secret within the Harper family. A secret which, exposed, would have caused a deal more grieving than the loss of the Harper fortune.

Lucinda believed herself to be pregnant.

Eighteen

As darkness fell at Daly Waters, Solomon lit the hurricane lamp that hung from a beam in the roof of the forge. Immediately the walls of the rough canvas and timber shelter became grotesque with leaping shadows that melted and expanded into almost recognisable forms. The furnace seethed with heat.

Perched on his anvil, he watched the harpoon head colouring on the coals. He had shaped it to fit the timber of a long-handled shovel, the big ones used by the hole-sinkers. There would not be weight enough to give him range. Accuracy was more important. A man was a tiny target compared to the streaming back of a sperm whale breaking surface.

He watched the dark shadows flickering their intentions, and let himself dream as he watched, thinking back on his life.

'It's violent you've lived, Solomon,' he told himself in a whisper, 'a violent life in the watery world, there's no denying it. A man's character holds his fate, to be sure. Here you be, beached in the wilderness of the Great South Land, a Yankee curiosity, forging a harpoon head to split the body of a man. There's no knowing what we might come to, and Eli would lay to that.'

He hunched his shoulders, sighing, thinking back on New Bedford, twitching his nostrils to summon up the salt sea, the whale ships laden with spoils of two and three years' hunting. He saw the bustle of ships fitting out for their long exile on the waters of the Atlantic and Pacific, heard the tales in the taverns and the wild, sad songs, felt the hunger of a man for a woman after the long voyage, with money heavy in his pocket and nothing else in the world but his sea-bag.

Suddenly he felt a great need to walk again the streets of New Bedford, to search in the taverns and doss houses for old shipmates, to hear the good or bad news of others. What was he doing here at the bottom of the world, fashioning a harpoon for a man-killing, when he had savings in New Bedford, enough to buy a share in a likely enterprise, to swallow the anchor and settle?

'Solomon is as alone as a wind-blown frigate bird, flapped down on a masthead,' he told himself. 'It's coming and going you've been, since you were a slip of a lad with his eyes filled with wonder at the sight of new things. Now it's grey you've got growing in your hair, and murder growing in your heart. Solomon took Eli's life into his hands, when he found the poor flensed thing. Now it must be the taking of another life, to save Eli's life again. Solomon has taken up his first command, aboard the ship of death.'

Martin and Stubbs sat by the ebbing fire, on which Martin had set a billy to boil to make tea for Solomon's return.

'What can he be doing, Eli? What is Solomon making that keeps him in the forge tonight?'

Eli sat stiffly on his box, almost as removed and solitary as he had been at the Roper River landing.

'Eli?' Martin urged.

'I don't know, lad. Solomon isn't a man to question. I think he has New Bedford on his mind.'

The thought alarmed Martin.

'You don't think he might leave us, do you?'

Eli shook his head.

'Solomon won't leave you, lad, until he sees you safely returned to your family.'

Martin was grateful for the comfort.

'I don't think Solomon will leave you either, until he sees you aboard a ship for home.'

'Home!' Eli echoed heavily. 'There's many a mortal risk between this day and that.'

Martin eyed the bent, grey-haired man who wasn't much older than his brother, Hannibal. Something had changed in Eli while Martin had been down the line. Nor was Solomon acting like himself. Apprehension grew in him.

'Did anything happen while I was away? Something I've not been told about?'

Eli considered his answer, his need to confess to his

awful fear almost overcoming him.

'What would we be keeping from you, lad?'

'I don't know. I've just got a feeling. I feel that something is threatening.'

Eli paled. He had come to believe in Martin's feelings.

'What could be . . . threatening?'

'I don't know. It could be something to do with you.'

Eli turned away, to conceal a sudden uncontrollable trembling.

'There's another thing,' Martin persisted. 'The new dray. Solomon was after it for months. But now that it's arrived, neither of you seem the slightest bit interested in seeing it.'

'Solomon has looked at the dray, lad.'

'No, he hasn't. He hasn't been to the transport section. I know, because I asked. He's been in the forge, making whatever it is he's making.'

'All in good time, lad,' said Eli drearily. 'The dray won't go away.'

Martin bent to see past the fire, as a figure loomed up out of the dark.

Whistling cheerfully, Solomon patted Martin on the shoulder as he made his way towards the water barrel. Dipping water into a dish, he soaped his arms and face, splashing noisily.

'A mug of strong black tea,' he said to the dish, 'strong enough to suspend a spoon in, after it has been twice dipped in sugar – such shouldn't be too much to ask of a young shipmate.'

Martin moved the billy back to the fire's red centre. He looked hard at Solomon.

'A mug of strong black tea isn't too much to ask, for a shipmate who's been dinning this night at something secret in the forge.'

'As to that,' Solomon said, wiping at his arms, 'dinning I was, to be sure. Dinning for the sake of dinning. Such can be a help to thought when a new course has to be set.'

Eli had not taken his eyes off Solomon. He coughed to clear the tension in his throat.

'A new course? I don't take your meaning.'

'You can set a course for this and you can set a course for that. A man's life is told in the setting of courses. In a few weeks from now, this camp is moving south, to the end of the northern line. Solomon has been deliberating on how best to make the move.'

Martin's eyes lit up. The move would surely bring him closer to Matthew. He had heard, down the line, that Ross had been forced to return to the Finke River before striving again for the Roper. Some of the stiffness also went out of Eli Stubbs.

The billy began to bubble. Martin shook in a handful of tea leaves, letting them stew for a minute.

'Strong and black it will be, Solomon. Strong enough to suspend a spoon, after it has been loaded twice with sugar.'

Solomon sat on his box and gave them both his marvellous smile.

Stirring his tea, gazing into the fire, he saw again the figure of Ben Barton, backing away from the tent.

'I won't tell. I won't tell,' Barton had whispered.

Solomon smacked his lips at the tea, reflections from the fire lighting his dark eyes. No, Ben Barton would not tell. His would never be the telling.

Instructed by the overseer, harassed and testy with the business of organising the move south, Ben Barton was at the tack sheds, counting the saddles, bridles, packs and harness in his care. His request for leave, to get his information about Eli Stubbs to Port Darwin, had been peremptorily refused. Every hand would be needed for the effort of shifting camp.

He spat into the dust. The coming move south would be the spoiler of his intentions; it would be almost impossible to get back to Port Darwin from the southern end of the line, since in future all supplies would be short-travelled from the Roper River depot.

If he was going to get his revenge on the poxed Yankee, and see the little English convict where he belonged, he would have to act fast. He sniffed and swallowed, cocking his head to think. He would throw in his hand before the camp moved, get his information to the Port Darwin police, and wait on a ship's passage south.

All the same, he felt a creeping on his skin at the memory of the way the Yankee had crouched before him outside the tent, his eyes almost spitting sparks. He'd be glad when he saw the last of the Yankee. He could even be keeping an eye on him, maybe sending his boy to spy. Barton looked quickly over his shoulder, as though to catch him at it. Then he continued planning.

The overseer had instructed him to put the horses out to graze in the open country near the swamp, while the camp was being struck. Barton sniggered – the boss didn't know how easy he was making his getaway. He'd stow a saddle and bridle in the bush, tether a horse at the last minute, and ride to Port Darwin as the camp moved south.

Getting out his knife to cut a wad of tobacco, he nodded his head in satisfaction. He'd tether the grey gelding, the smartest mount in the mob. Sold in Port Darwin, the grey would put a few more quid in his pocket. With that and the reward, the grog shops and whorehouses of Port Adelaide had better look out – Ben Barton of the Overland was on his way.

In the ground near the anvil, Solomon had buried the miniature harpoon head, stamping the earth with his boots.

He knew the order to move south would force Ben Barton's hand; if the man was to reap the reward of selling Eli to the authorities, he would have to get to Port Darwin before the camp began to move.

He also knew that the horses were to be left out to graze near the swamp, that Barton would have to inspect the mob each morning for strays. On the appropriate morning, he would wait on Barton's riding out from the horse yards to inspect the mob. He calculated, and made a deadly appointment in his head.

The apprehension that Martin had felt after his return from the journey down the line had dissipated with Solomon's news of the coming move and the merriment of his manner. Now, more than ever, Martin was certain that he and Matthew would somehow meet. In the dust he sketched with a stick a map of Australia, marking the course of the Roper River as a wriggling line into the gulf. He tried to guess where the Finke River might be; no matter how often he asked in camp, he had been unable to fix its location. The Overlanders on the northern line, shipped directly to Port Darwin or the Roper River landing, had no knowledge of the interior. A drover believed he'd heard tell of the Finke and passed the opinion that wherever the dratted thing might be at, it had to be north of the Peake.

Squatting, his arms across his knees, he considered the continent, which inconveniently began to disappear as a sudden wind obliterated the shape. He hurried to sketch a line from his imagined Finke River across country to where he had put the Roper River landing, and grimaced in disgust. The track he had drawn for the Ross party came nowhere near the cross which represented his guess at the position of the new camp at the southern end of the northern line. The track he had drawn didn't mean anything.

But still he had his feeling, as strong as ever, that, somehow, he and Matthew were destined to meet.

The shock of having accidentally exposed his back to Ben Barton, the desperation which had slumped Eli on his bed, had only been partly allayed by Solomon's charade. Eli wanted to believe that Barton's eyes had truly been dazzled by the sun, that he had really thought that a new man had been there in the tent. He couldn't disbelieve Solomon's assurance, but the haunt which seldom left him would not be denied. After a week of silent agonising, Eli felt compelled to put himself in Barton's path, in an effort to read what might appear in his face. Barton had merely given him a surly nod and passed on. Eli whispered a prayer of thanks. He never again washed in the tent, without first securely tying the flaps.

Eli's new dray had given pleasure to all Solomon's hands. It proved to be not only new to the forge, but new as few other transports were new on the northern line. The dray had been on a shipment to Port Darwin, driven down the line with a load of wire and insulators. The bright green paint was unmarked, the springs bounced to the hands that tested them, and, best of all, the tailboard was hinged, to be let down and drawn up by a chain. The dray was conspicuous among the work-worn transport. Even Eli's old mare, accustomed to hauling the lumbering, creaking, splay-wheeled wreck, looked back at it, pointing her ears in considerable surprise.

The forge hands were pleased that the quiet 'un was so mounted. They had grown accustomed to his ways. Perhaps he did not join them in their yarns or practical jokes, but he was always polite and considerate. No one begrudged old Eli his treasure, although the men noticed that, characteristically, the attention it brought to him seemed unwelcome.

Bullock wagons had been brought up to the staging camp for the shift, loaned from further down the line. All day the overseer plodded about the camp, harassed and testy, forever licking his pencil to make lists on a sheaf of papers clipped to a square of tin. The staging camp at Daly Waters was in the process of melting away.

On the night before rest day, in the dark of the tent, Solomon lay awake while Martin and Eli, in huddles under the covers, slept. Despite himself, Solomon felt a sorrow for Ben Barton, whom hardly a man in the camp had been able to abide. Something had gone wrong inside Barton, as young Martin had remarked, in his strange and innocent way. But whatever had gone wrong, it was long since too late to repair.

'You've hunted this and you've hunted that,' Solomon thought to himself. 'Many a leviathan's harmless sport in the deep has ended on the bloody bolt of Solomon's harpoon. You've clubbed the helpless seals on the breeding shelves, to steal the fur off their twitching flesh. You near knifed to death a man on Kangaroo Island, when he got out his own knife over the paltry consideration of the whore you'd taken from him. You've cracked heads from New Bedford to the Sunda Straits, and done damage among the heathen.'

He scratched at his chest in the darkness.

'It's violent you've lived and it can't be denied. And now you're fixing to murder a man, as another black mark on your tally. On the day of judgement, Solomon, there won't be much to favour you in the log.'

Eli began to groan and whimper in his sleep, and Solomon turned his thoughts back to Ben Barton. It wasn't likely that his body would be looked for, or found. If so, there would be no bullet hole, only a rent that could have been made by a broad-headed spear, thrown by a black when Barton made his morning inspection of the grazing horses.

'And suppose it's me,' Solomon reminded himself, 'who goes to the bottom, as you might say, here in this far wilderness? A pretty kettle of fish that would make. In the nature of a disaster, not to mention the cost to Solomon. It would be all up with Eli.'

He scratched harder at his chest.

'Not to mention the desertion of young Martin, who only came away from home on Solomon's undertaking.'

'But there's nothing else for it. Solomon has to succeed. All sail is set and Solomon is at the helm.'

He shut his eyes and offered up a prayer.

'Forgive Solomon, Lord of Hosts. Not because he's one of those who know not what they do. The truth is, as you'd be well informed, that Solomon has worked it out shipshape, in his black and sinning mind.'

The men usually lay in on Sunday mornings, enjoying the luxury of not having to answer to the clamouring of the iron triangles which were the camp alarms. When the tent began to lighten, Solomon put his feet on the floor, looking out through the tent flaps.

'The day is as grey as a parson's nose,' he reported. 'Aye, grey and grey it is, to be sure. And who's to say that it isn't fitting?'

Martin glanced at Solomon. Something was noticeably strained in his voice and face.

'I've got clothes to wash and dry. It's not going to rain, is it, Solomon?'

'You should know better than that. It's not time for the rains. We'll be safely settled in the south long before the clouds spill their bellies. Put the billy on, shipmate. Solomon is going for a walk, like a gentleman at his leisure.'

Solomon ate no breakfast. After he had returned and drunk his tea, he went off into the camp again.

'Solomon has something on his mind,' Martin said to Eli.

'He's probably thinking of the sea again. He told me he was parched in the nose for the smell of the salt sea.'

'I suppose it must get like that,' Martin agreed, 'for a man who has spent most of his life in what Solomon calls the watery world.'

A little later, as Martin came back from the wash troughs, carrying his scrubbing brush and soap, Solomon returned to sit on his box outside the tent.

'It comes to me,' Solomon said, 'that I've seen precious little of the country hereabouts. It comes to me to drive out in the comfort of Eli's new and brightly painted dray to take a last look at this and that before we set sail for the south.'

'Do you want me to come with you?' Martin asked eagerly. 'I know where there's a lily pond and a blackwood forest with wild orchids on the trees.'

Solomon shook his head.

'If I should go under instruction, that wouldn't be exploring, would it? I'd be beholden to you, though, if you'd put Eli's old mare in the dray. Solomon would be vexed to know one harness strap from another.'

Eli was reading his Bible, and Solomon was still ruminating on his box, when Martin returned.

'The dray's ready, Solomon. If you get bushed, just give the old mare her head. She'll make for camp in her own way.'

'Bushed?' Solomon stood up, feinting a cuff at Martin's head. 'Solomon bushed? He mightn't have a ticket, but Solomon could make a fist of navigating by the stars before you entered the world.'

Martin laughed, shaking his head and pointing upwards at the leaden clouds.

'It's a fine sky of stars you've got today, to navigate by.'

He watched Solomon walk off and went inside the tent.

'Solomon's gone to have a look at the country, in your new dray.'

'It's restless, he is,' Eli said, and returned to his Bible study.

When he was clear of the camp, Solomon reached under the feed bag behind him and found the harpoon head. The shaft of the long handled shovel lay beside it. He let the mare proceed as he fitted the harpoon head to the wood, knocking them into a tight fit on the floorboards of the dray. Then he dropped the reins over the seat, stepped behind it and stood up. He braced himself, balancing the improvised harpoon, feeling it for weight and balance. Several times he bent his arm, the shovel handle over his shoulder, his body cocked in the whaling harpooner's stance. When he was ready, he looked around for a tree to be his target.

Ahead, the pale bark of a white-box took Solomon's eye. Pale and tender-looking was the tree trunk, as pale and tender as the skin of a white man. For a few seconds he stood still, his shoulder muscles knotting, the bicep bulging in his arm. Then, with slow and deliberate aim, he launched the harpoon at the white tree. The head bit deeply into the trunk, the shovel handle blurring in vibration.

Solomon jumped down from the dray, leading the old mare. He pulled at the shovel handle, weakening its hold on the harpoon head.

'Mother Carey's chickens,' he muttered. 'Sunk deep through the flesh it is, and buried in the bone.'

He got out his seaman's clasp knife and addressed the iron.

'It's digging you out I must be.'

Sap began to ooze from the wound in the tree.

'Taste that,' Solomon advised the harpoon head, as he began the excavation with his knife. 'There will be another taste running on your blade, before the tasting is over.'

Solomon stopped the dray at the edge of the timber. The grassy plain lay before him. At a short distance the hobbled horses grazed contentedly, and there was no sound other than the sudden harsh cry of a cockatoo high in the trees.

There was no sign of Barton. Solomon cursed softly, and stood up, craning his neck for a view of the swamp.

Then the old mare pricked up her ears and lifted her head enquiringly into the wind. From a distance came the sound of crashing in the timber.

A few minutes later, Barton rode out of the scrub, driving a pair of hobbled horses before him. The revolver that he always carried was on his belt, the carbine in its scabbard.

'Get on with yers,' he shouted, freeing a boot to kick at the horses' bellies.

Solomon shook the reins. The old mare began to move forward, head down in patient obedience.

A crowd of cockatoos swept past, their shrieks rending the still air. Following their swooping flight with his eyes, Barton caught sight of the dray, his eyes widening in surprise. He recognised the new paint and licked his lips, considering. What would Eli Stubbs be doing, out in the dray on rest day?

The hunched figure on the seat altered the direction of the dray. Now it was headed straight for him. What could Stubbs want? Had he realised his danger and come to plead with him? The thought pleased Barton. He would like to hear the English convict beg for his life and freedom.

As he watched, the man in the dray shook his horse into an amble, stepped behind the seat and stood up, taking up something from the floor. Barton squinted for clearer vision. Shock hit his guts like a blow. There was no mistaking the stocky figure in the dray, the head of tight black curls.

Barton's breath began wheezing in his nostrils. Panic leant him forward in the saddle. He hadn't fooled the Yankee, not for a second. Solomon was there to get him.

His first instinct was to wheel and ride for the timber. Then he began to steady. Whatever it was that Solomon held, it wasn't a carbine or a shotgun. But the dray was closing in, with only a few hundred yards between them. Spittle dribbled on Barton's lips as he struggled to put his thoughts together. He still had time to ride away from the Yankee, but he knew that if Solomon had come to get him, he wouldn't give up until he had finished his business.

Then his fear dropped away in a sudden shout of rage. He'd give the Yankee a fight, if that was what he was set on. He'd blow the poxed bastard apart. All his bitterness, hate and frustration blinded his mind to rational thought.

He jerked the carbine from its scabbard, pulled round the head of his mount and dug in the spurs. As he galloped towards the dray, Eli's old mare was shocked into a trot. The dray began to rock, like a cradle, on its new springs. Solomon balanced behind the seat and readied himself. The rocking of the dray was not unlike that of a whale chaser riding the waves of the sea, Solomon braced in its bow, hefting the harpoon, the rope in coils at his feet.

Spurts of dust tore off the hardened ground as Barton galloped forward, shouting as he aimed the carbine, firing wildly. Then he threw the carbine from him, pulling at his revolver. Solomon stood as still as a graven image in the dray, the harpoon held over his shoulder. Barton raised the revolver as the distance between them shortened.

The last image in his eyes was the unleashing of Solomon's

body, the last sound an eerie whistling as something sliced through the air towards him. Then the flying New Bedford harpoon head cleaved his chest, travelling easily through the man-bone and flesh as if no resistance was offered there, to emerge from his back, still travelling. He clutched at the shaft, his eyes bulging in their sockets, and fell forward, before slowly toppling from the saddle to hit the ground.

Eli's old mare continued to trot, passing Barton's body with the hat crumpled beneath and the blood begining to froth on his lips. Barton's horse had gone on a little and then stopped, walking back to lower its head and snuffle at the body.

Solomon picked up the reins to turn the old mare. He sat for a long time, his shoulders hunched, staring into the grey-clouded sky.

'A man never knows what he'll come to,' he told the mob of horses, which had temporarily scattered when the carbine was fired. 'Solomon has murdered a man on this grey day. God have mercy on his soul!'

His hand still clenched about the bolt that had gone through him, Barton lay on his back, his body arched over the harpoon shaft whose head pinned him to the earth. His glazing eyes were opened wide, as if in surprise at the terrible thing which had entered his body and abruptly stopped his life. Solomon looked down on the distorted face.

It was done, Eli was safe.

Getting down from the dray, he touched Barton's body with his boot to avoid the blood-drenched singlet, the threadbare coat staining as he watched.

Twisting the shovel handle, he jerked at the harpoon and pulled until he had drawn all its length through the inert body. Then, as Barton had done on that day he found the blacks digging for yams, Solomon looked towards the tongue of swamp intruding into the clearing, and considered.

Taking hold of the booted ankles, as Barton had taken hold of the naked black ankles, he dragged the body towards the swamp. At its edge he stopped, removing his boots and socks, pulling his moleskin trousers up above his knees.

He bent again, backing into the shallows of the slimy, reeded swamp, pulling Barton's body after him. A soft, alien mass squelched under his bare feet, sending a shiver of revulsion through him. Something long and fine tangled in his fingers. He stopped, drawing at the stuff in his hand. It was hair – fine, dark human hair, a wad of it. As he pulled at it, a rotting human face emerged from the water, staring up at him. Water worms squirmed in the nostril cavities and the empty eyes.

Retching, shivering uncontrollably, Solomon gave Barton's body a final heave before splashing out, to snatch at his boots and socks and run for the dray.

Eli's old mare raised her head in greeting. Solomon wrapped his arms about her neck, laid his cheek on the warm, soft coat. Comfort began to fill him. He stayed like that until the stout barrel of his chest ceased its heaving.

On his return to camp, Solomon removed the harpoon head from the shovel handle, and pitched it into a thick run of bushes. Then he snapped the shovel handle across his knees and threw the pieces to the ground.

The grey clouds had dispersed, letting the hot afternoon sun blaze through. Martin and Eli were having a snack of tea and damper when Eli's old mare came plodding past, following her habit of ending her journey at the dismantling forge.

'Where can Solomon be?' Martin asked, concerned.

'He must be in the camp. The old mare probably became impatient.'

Martin got up and hurried towards the main body of tents. He found Solomon playing cards with the drovers. His dark face was deeply flushed, the pits vividly coloured, and he was drinking rum, his bottle already half-emptied.

'Is everything all right?' Martin asked, uneasily. 'The old mare brought back the dray.'

'As to that,' Solomon answered, 'I can't say I'm surprised.' He tipped up the bottle on a long swallow. 'It has come upon Solomon to get drunk with this parcel of rogues. As a farewell to the camp, as you might say. You might get back and unharness Eli's old mare, who has seen some strange sights this day.'

Martin nodded, leaving with some reluctance.

Eli asked, 'Did you find him?'

'He's playing cards and getting drunk with the drovers.'

'It will do him good,' Eli nodded. 'Solomon has been fretting lately.'

Nineteen

The precarious financial balance to which old Hannibal had been brought by the Northern Territory gold hoax had reduced both his robust figure and his robust manner of expressing himself. His admissions to young Hannibal, the transfer of authority between them, had drained the old man of the pride essential to his being. His motivation to work and build had crumbled away, as the northern termites had crumbled Todd's telegraph poles.

Young Hannibal had gone methodically into his father's affairs and had found the situation even worse than he had imagined. There was no escape from the reality of the figures in front of him.

His father, overwhelmed by a melancholia that had made the most simple task or decision beyond his competence, examined young Hannibal's report cursorily. The figures blurred before his eyes. He looked at young Hannibal blankly, hearing nothing but the insistent message of his impending ruin.

At home, he sat in his chair, staring at his boots.

'He's worried about the twins,' young Hannibal told his mother.

'But why should he worry so, now? Your father has always been such a strong man, one whom weaker men have sought out for support. It's as though something – something has broken inside him, like the mainspring of a clock.'

Young Hannibal looked at his mother in surprise. The simile was an imaginative one for Mrs Harper. It exactly expressed his own feelings, for which he had been unable to find a metaphor. Mrs Harper continued, in a rare vein of understanding.

'You also seem altered, Han.'

'In what way, Mother?'

'You've always looked like your father, of course. You even think like him. But, lately, it's almost as if you have become head of the family.'

'Nonsense, Mother. There's only one head of this family. Father will rally. I rather think he might benefit from a tonic.'

Mrs Harper ceased her knitting.

'That is an excellent idea. I will take it up with Dr Thornhill in the morning.'

Young Hannibal wondered at his mother's unexpected insight and considered, with a twinge of bitterness, that she might just once or twice in her life, have applied a little insight to Lucinda.

Mrs Harper could have been reading her son's thoughts.

'Lucinda is as jumpy as a cat on hot bricks.'

Young Hannibal lit a cheroot.

'I hadn't noticed.'

'How could you? You've been working late for weeks. What has been keeping you so much at the business?'

'Stocktaking. Future planning.'

'Your father is putting far too much on your shoulders.'

'He has to retire one day.'

'Retire? Your father retire? Stuff and nonsense. What would he do? Sit on the verandah and stare?'

Mrs Harper took up her knitting needles, clicking away with some violence.

Young Hannibal was well aware of how much things now depended on him. He had been awkward and embarrassed about it, to begin with. Always in his father's substantial shadow, now he found the shadow pale and dwindled. It made him ache, the sight of his father crumpled in his chair. It was truly, as his mother had said, as if something inside him had broken.

Mrs Harper spoke again, as if to herself.

'There should be mail from the twins soon. Perhaps that will make a difference.'

Local spirit had fastened on the race between the longest wire and the marine cable with an irreverence that had begun to ignore the significance of the venture. Bets and odds on the outcome were laid, given and taken, wherever men congregated. The inescapable gamble of pioneering a hard land had entered the blood. Sir James Fergusson had something to say about it.

'I utterly disapprove. The construction of the Overland Telegraph should not be regarded as a steeplechase. This venture could be the making of a nation, a great new nation in the southern hemisphere. Damn these jesting, betting fellows. They lack the imagination of soldiers' lice.'

Meanwhile, Lucinda's new-found equanimity had received a severe jolt. Her menstruation, after her seduction of Steven Woodrush, had, unbelievably, failed to make its appearance. She waited, tensely, into the second week. Like a cat on hot bricks, as her mother remarked.

Her cycle had been punctual, almost to the day, since she had first arrived at puberty. Steven had barely entered her; she had made sure of that. What was happening to her? She damned her ignorance and impetuousness by turn. She needed a trustworthy woman friend, one who had borne children.

Lady Charlotte Bacon, pouring tea in the conservatory and nibbling at a scone, noted with surprise Lucinda's strained expression.

'Your note suggested an urgency, Lucinda. What is worrying that flibbertigibbet head of yours?'

Lucinda's cup shook on its saucer. Lady Charlotte raised an eyebrow.

'You are disturbed,' she murmured. 'That's not like Lucinda.'

'I don't know where to begin,' Lucinda said. 'Oh, Charlotte, I desperately need your help and advice.'

'You are most welcome, Lucinda, to any help I may be able to give. Perhaps you should begin at the beginning. Is this an affair of the heart?'

'It was,' Lucinda answered, her head low, her voice quivering. 'I mean it is . . . Oh, dammit, Charlotte, I don't know that I might not be pregnant.'

Lady Charlotte's composure was shaken. She replaced her cup, dusted crumbs from her fingers with a napkin and blinked rapidly before she spoke.

'I take it this isn't some girlish imagining?'

'I don't know,' Lucinda said, wringing her hands. 'I don't know if it can happen this way.'

'There's only one way it can happen,' Lady Charlotte said, a little coldly. 'I take it we can agree on that?'

'You are so . . . so worldly,' Lucinda implored her. 'You've had children. You even knew Lord Byron.'

Lady Charlotte smiled a little at this.

'I don't see how that fits me to give counsel. Byron fathered children into some of the best families in England. But he usually had the sense to ensure that their mothers were safely married. Are you telling me that you've taken a lover?'

Lucinda became woeful.

'I did. Just the once.'

'Have you missed your monthly periods? Are you usually regular?'

'Always – to the day. And this time I'm late – that's why I need your advice. He . . . he barely entered me, Charlotte – surely I can't be pregnant?'

'I'm afraid you could be, Lucinda. Who is the man? Is he single? Would he marry you, should it prove necessary?'

'He can't,' Lucinda said, wiping at her tears. 'He's driving north with the Milner brothers.'

'I beg your pardon!' Lady Charlotte's composure vanished completely. 'Driving north with the Milners? The stock drive? Heavens above, Lucinda! Are you telling me that you took up with a common stockman?'

Lucinda shook her head.

'Then let us get to the bottom of this,' Lady Charlotte ordered. 'Sit up, for heaven's sake! What manner of man are you involved with? On a stock drive, indeed.'

Lucinda gulped out the story. Once started, she found it hard to stop, and spared no details. When she had no more words, Lady Charlotte left the conservatory and returned with brandy balloons on a tray.

She said, 'I think I need this as much as you do. Steven Woodrush! I can't believe it. I talked to him once, at the Bishop's. An ingratiating nonentity. He almost licked my feet.'

Lucinda recovered a little over the brandy.

'What am I to do?'

'First, you will see my doctor. There could be a hundred reasons why your periods are late.'

'Can he be trusted?'

'It seems clear to me,' Lady Charlotte said, 'that you are the one who is not to be trusted. Don't languish like that. Sit up. All this fuss could well be about nothing.'

She paused.

'I seem to remember now some gossip about you and someone attached to the church.'

'Mother liked him,' Lucinda said defensively.

Lady Charlotte made no answer. She had formed her own opinion about Lucinda's mother.

The financial reverberations of the gold hoax continued to rock the troubled company. Property prices sagged, as bankrupted investors put their freeholdings on the market. Building blocks, bought by old Hannibal as investment, had to be sold by his son at a price much below their original valuation. When young Hannibal approached his father about their sale, old Hannibal, with a trembling hand, had waved his son away.

'Do what you think best, son,' he said mournfully.

'We must not give up the fight, Father,' young Hannibal said, distressed at the spectacle of his father's decline.

'You fight,' his father answered, pouring a brandy. 'I've been fighting all my life. I've fought for myself and I've fought for others. I'm too old to start over. I'm worn out with it all. The only comfort I have left is that I did my best, however misguidedly, for your mother and you children.'

Young Hannibal paced the floor.

'Why don't you talk with the Bishop, Father? Perhaps he could provide you with spiritual comfort. You've always been a man of faith.'

'Perhaps . . . perhaps. But how did all this happen so quickly? I find it too hard to follow. Something in my understanding has failed. My brains have turned into cheese.'

Young Hannibal urged again.

'A talk with the Bishop would perhaps ease your mind. Why not pay him a visit?'

Old Hannibal unexpectedly roused.

'Because I'm a sinner, that's why.'

'You, Father?'

'Me, Father,' old Hannibal declared, smiting the desk with the flat of his hand, 'and my cardinal sin is pride. I'd rather die than be pitied or ridiculed.'

'But, Father . . .' young Hannibal began.

'But, nothing,' old Hannibal said fiercely. 'This is something between me, my conscience and my Maker.'

Young Hannibal left the office, shaken. There were certainly extremes in his father's nature, he thought to himself. But when the limit of this present extreme had been reached, he might well rise up again. Young Hannibal found himself remembering his mother's story of how his father had set fire to a new wagon at Port Lincoln, out of temper with a wheel. He found himself smiling, and trod more vigorously.

News from the southern end of the line was not good. A camel train carrying provisions and wire up from the Peake had been attacked by blacks. Two camels had been speared, while the others had bolted for the timber, tearing their loads apart on the trees. At a staging camp further north, a hundred men were without supplies.

Drovers in the camp saddled up to ride south, hoping to come upon the Milner brothers. They found the drive camped by good water, the men working on pack saddle frames. The Milners accepted a chit drawn against the Overland Telegraph for the sale of one thousand sheep, to be driven hard to the hungry outposts. Success, which the *Advertiser's* editorial had proclaimed to be in sight, still remained precarious for those directly concerned in its achievement.

Lucinda waited, in a limbo of apparent calm, for her appointment with Lady Charlotte's doctor.

His intimate examination, the first in Lucinda's life, was a shock and humiliation. The doctor was in early middle age, well-preserved and handsome. He chatted brightly with Lady

Charlotte's friend, visiting from another colony, as he bent over her body.

He said it was much too early to be sure, of course, but he thought that since Lucinda was a healthy young woman previously regular in her cycles, she was very likely to be early with child. Lady Charlotte had waited outside in her carriage. When the two were seated again in the conservatory, gently lit by the waning autumn sun, Lady Charlotte became businesslike.

'A message must be got to Woodrush,' Lady Charlotte said. 'I might be able to arrange it through Sir James. He would ask no questions, if I were to request it as a favour. He was a good friend to my late husband in England.'

Lucinda shook her head.

'You don't know Steven. He would run like a rabbit.'

'He appears to have already done so. But if you were to write him a letter, if it could somehow be got to the drive . . .'

Lucinda's forehead creased.

'I don't understand it. As I've said he barely entered me. There was no blood, nothing. Shouldn't there be blood, the first time?'

'How long have you been riding?' Lady Charlotte asked.

'Since childhood,' Lucinda answered, surprised.

'Side saddle or astride?'

'Both. I prefer to ride astride, although mother protests.'

'My dear, you probably broke your hymen years ago. Lost your virginity to the saddle, as it were.'

'Can that happen?'

'Of course it can. There's only one recourse, Lucinda. You must marry, and soon. Woodrush must be brought back.'

Lucinda smoothed her dress over her bosom and picked at an invisible thread. There had been no further slumping, or tears. She sat erect, almost tossing her head at Lady Charlotte.

'I don't want to marry Steven. Since he's been gone, I've come to realise that he hasn't got the insides of a gnat. He's a born boot-licker, you said so yourself.'

Lady Charlotte sighed and shook her head. The girl she had first seen as a colonial rose had proved herself thorny on the stem. She made herself stern.

'You have no alternative. Really, Lucinda, it's useless to ask my advice and help, if you reject it when it is given.'

But Lucinda's attention was elsewhere. She was thinking of the list of eligible suitors she had drawn up in her bedroom.

'I could get someone else. Someone with money and standing in the community.'

Lady Charlotte put down her cup in surprise.

'With you almost certainly pregnant? How on earth could you do that?'

'I got Steven Woodrush. Men are fools. I could get any red-blooded man.'

Lady Charlotte became uncertain.

'Do you mean a deliberate seduction? To foist your child on an innocent man?'

'Yes.'

'Good heavens, Lucinda. That would be monstrous.'

Lucinda looked squarely at her friend.

'Why not? It's a matter of survival. Can you think of another way?'

'I really don't know what to think. I have seen and experienced a great deal of life, but sometimes you take my breath away, if I may say so.'

Lucinda sipped at her tea, and helped herself to a slice of fruit cake.

'There's no other way. I have to survive this business somehow with my reputation intact. If I have to pull the wool over everyone's eyes, I will, Charlotte.'

'I won't be a party to any such thing. We shall get Woodrush back. You can make it acceptable to your parents. You said your mother liked him.'

'I'm not worried about Mother. She would support me in almost anything. Why, when we were little, Hannibal once said that if I took to him with an axe, Mother would find a good reason for it.'

'Really, Lucinda!' Lady Charlotte protested. 'You talk like an unbalanced person. We must get Woodrush back.'

'No!' Lucinda was determined. 'I have another idea.'

'I will leave you then,' Lady Charlotte said coldly, 'to your own devices, Lucinda.'

Sitting on the verandah, sipping his brandy and water, old Hannibal was reading a report in the *Advertiser* of the death of one of the hopefuls on the gold fields to the north. Dead of thirst, his rotting body had been found beside his pathetically small pile of belongings. The hawks and crows had eaten away his face and the exposed parts of his arms.

'Picked clean,' old Hannibal muttered, when he had read the report. 'Not the only one, either.'

Young Hannibal had raised what loans he could from the banks, but the interest rates were almost crippling. To add to his difficulties, business at Hannibal Harper and Son had fallen away. Staff had had to be sacked. Young Hannibal often stared at his office wall, while old Hannibal stared at his.

After leaving Lady Charlotte, Lucinda played so loudly at the piano that Mrs Harper had been forced to ask her to stop. Lucinda crashed out a last chord and went off to her room.

'I'm blessed if I know,' Mrs Harper confided to her knitting, 'everything in the family seems to have gone topsy-turvy. I don't know how I bear it.'

Returning home early that evening, young Hannibal was surprised at the warmth of Lucinda's greeting. She kissed him fondly and enquired if he had not been overworking.

'It's a difficult time,' young Hannibal said, eyeing her uneasily. 'Business everywhere is in the doldrums.'

'How is your friend, Tubby Baker?' Lucinda asked.

'Tubby? On top of the world, as always. In fact, I've had a message from him. We are dining together tonight, at the club. Where's Mother? I must let her know.'

'She's down with a headache. Tell me – how long will Tubby be in Adelaide?'

Young Hannibal shrugged.

'He usually makes a week of it. Why do you ask?'

'I thought you might invite him for Sunday lunch. Father hasn't had a guest in ages. In his present mood, it might do him good.'

Young Hannibal was doubtful.

'I'm not sure if Tubby is Father's cup of tea.'

'He's always laughed at Tubby's jokes when you've had him to the house before.'

'Tubby can tell a good joke, that's true. Funny, I've sometimes tried to retell Tubby's jokes, but they always seem to fall as flat as a pancake.'

'It might cheer us all up. Everyone seems so low-spirited.'

'I've never seen you low in spirits, Lucinda. Bad tempered, crotchety, yes.'

Lucinda gave a tinkling little laugh. 'Oh Han! I'm sorry if I'm sometimes a trial to you. But truly – I think it would do us all good to have Tubby's company on Sunday. Why don't you mention it to Father? He's out in the garden.'

'I suppose I could. Then I must wash and change. Will you tell Mother that I'll be dining at the club?'

Old Hannibal was pacing the gravel path, his hands clasped behind him.

'It's getting about that we've had to lay off hands,' he said fretfully. 'That's bad for our reputation.'

'It can't be helped, Father. J.A. Holden has had to let ten men go from the saddlery.'

'He has?' Old Hannibal perked up before succumbing to his better nature. 'It must be hard on the men with families.'

'Tubby Baker is in town. I'm dining with him tonight at the club.'

Old Hannibal approved.

'An evening out will do you good. You need the recreation.'

'I rather thought it might be a good idea to invite him for Sunday dinner.'

'Tubby Baker? Whatever for?'

'He's good company, Father. When he was here last time, even the Bishop laughed at his stories.'

'I don't much feel like laughing,' old Hannibal said.

'Life must go on, Father. And Lucinda finds the prospect of Tubby joining us on Sunday entertaining.'

'Entertaining! That's all your sister thinks about, entertainments! Why the blazes doesn't she find a good man to marry? She's in danger of winding up a spinster.'

'Shall I invite him, then?'

Old Hannibal sighed.

'You know, what sticks in my craw about Baker is that he

has had everything fall into his lap. He knows nothing of the trials his father endured in the early days. All that Tubby Baker has pioneered is fast horses and fast women.'

'That's not fair, Father,' young Hannibal said. 'Tubby has worked hard improving the property he inherited.'

Old Hannibal slapped at a mosquito buzzing around his dome.

'Perhaps I'm wrong in my judgement. I don't seem to have any judgement left. Invite Baker, if you want to.'

Over pre-dinner drinks in the club lounge, Tubby Baker lit a cigar while young Hannibal puffed on his cheroot.

'I hear your father took a tumble in the gold shares. I must say I was tempted for a moment, but I told you, I thought I could smell a rat. I've heard that you've had to lay men off.'

'Extra hands,' young Hannibal said, for cover. 'We needed them while the Overland was being outfitted.'

'Any further news from the twins?'

'Martin is safe in a staging camp at a place called Daly Waters. The American that Father had working in the forge is with him. Matthew was last heard of from the Finke River – Ross had to turn back before he reached the Roper.'

'A spunky pair,' Tubby approved. 'There's good blood in your family, Han. How is the beauteous Lucinda? You certainly did an excellent job on that little sneak, Woodrush. With any luck he might even be speared by the blacks.'

Hannibal became casual, examining the end of his cheroot.

'As a matter of fact, Lucinda was asking after you. She suggested I should invite you for Sunday dinner.'

Tubby ashed his cigar and grinned.

'Did she indeed? I had the distinct feeling that Lucinda didn't like me. Too much the wild man from the bush, you know. I'd be delighted to join you on Sunday, Han. Here, let me refresh your drink.'

Young Hannibal was surprised that it should so please Tubby to be wanted at dinner by his sister. He had been far from flattering about her, during the Woodrush incident.

Twenty

The roundness of Tubby Baker's figure, which had earned him his nickname in school days, was a physical inheritance from his father, rather than an indulgence of fat. Enthusiastic eating and drinking had made additions to his waistline, to be sure, but there was hard muscle on Tubby, and an energy in his shortish frame which often exhausted the sinewy dam-sinkers and fence-stringers when 'the Boss' worked alongside them on his property.

On his arrival at the Harper household for the ritual two drinks before going to table, Tubby's glowing countenance was already brightened by an earlier drink with his horse trainer. He arrived laden with gifts – a bouquet of flowers for Mrs Harper, chocolates for Lucinda and a sample box of imported cigars for old Hannibal. Young Hannibal awkwardly accepted the tributes, his father being in the garden and his mother and sister not yet come downstairs.

'Aren't you overdoing it, Tubby? It's only Sunday dinner, you know.'

He eyed his friend in some surprise. Tubby was more than usually well dressed, especially about the feet, which sported shoes that squeaked with newness. Even at a social function, young Hannibal had never seen Tubby shod in other than his dress-up riding boots.

He was further surprised when Lucinda entered, wearing one of her best gowns and carrying a fan. Smiling radiantly, she told Tubby how delighted she was to see him, enquired after his racehorses, and fussed over the chocolates. Young Hannibal began to feel a certain irritation mixed with his surprise. If Lucinda didn't put away that damned fan . . .

Later, when the soup plates had been removed by Mrs Tom, wife of Tom, the Harpers' general help, and the roast brought forth for old Hannibal's carving, the old man looked down the table to where the twins used to be seated and sighed over the dripping meat. His almost palpable mood of depression had slowed even Tubby's customary chat. Tubby observed the change in old Hannibal, the new burden of grey in his beard, the drooping of the watch chain across the sagging waistcoat. Old Hannibal had been barely courteous when he accepted the gift of cigars.

'You must be doing well,' he had growled.

He made the remark almost an accusation. Tubby decided that the elder Harper must have taken a bad toss over the gold hoax. The stuffing had certainly gone out of him in the few months since they had last exchanged greetings at the club.

Inevitably there was some discussion about the progress of the Overland Telegraph, and Tubby made much of the adventuring twins. He congratulated old Hannibal on having sons who were helping to make history, and suggested to Mrs Harper that she must indeed be proud of Matthew and Martin. This cheered old Hannibal, and he related to Tubby something of what the twins had written in their letters. Mrs Harper, too, decided to be pleased. In her habit of martyrdom it had never occurred to her to be proud of the twins, or of what they might be achieving. Everyone at the table brightened. Old Hannibal refilled his glass and passed the decanter down the table.

Lucinda was bubbling with curiosity about Tubby's country property. Young Hannibal had often holidayed there, and he added his own impressions.

'Mrs Jones is a jolly good cook.'

'Perhaps too much so,' Tubby laughed, patting his stomach.

Lucinda had to know about Mrs Jones.

'My housekeeper. She was with us in my parents' time.'

Young Hannibal asked if the lagoon was in water. He had enjoyed good duck shooting on Tubby's lagoon. Old Hannibal spooned vigorously at his pudding.

'Your father had a head on his shoulders,' he said. 'He advised me strongly against Port Lincoln in the old days. That lagoon was the saving of Gooryanawah in the great drought. Fed by a spring, isn't it?'

'More of a soak,' Tubby said, 'but it certainly does make a useful wet.'

Lucinda had not before heard Tubby's property named. She tried to pronounce the word, failing engagingly, and asked what it meant.

'Home of the wild duck, Lucinda,' he answered. 'That's what the blacks used to call the place.'

'How romantic it sounds. I so often yearn to get out into the country. Adelaide can be so stifling. I am hardly ever out of the city.'

Old Hannibal stabbed at his pudding in irritation.

'You, Lucinda? You wouldn't last five minutes away from your entertainments. That's all she thinks about, you know,' he continued. 'Luncheon parties, dinner parties, gossip, flirtations, showing off to others.'

Mrs Harper protested, flushed with annoyance.

'Really, Hannibal! What a thing to say in company, about your own daughter. Lucinda is much admired. A young woman should enjoy herself while she can.'

Old Hannibal was silenced, surprised by his own outburst and reproaching himself for bad manners. A slight embarrassment settled on the table. Young Hannibal topped up his wine and offered the decanter to Tubby. He did wish that his mother would not be quite so insistent about the importance of Lucinda having fun.

Tubby's colour had deepened. He picked up his glass, put it down, picked it up again and was finally compelled to clear both the impulse and the uncertainty which had lodged in his throat.

'If it causes no offence, I'd be delighted if Lucinda should visit Gooryanawah. She'd be in the good hands of Mrs Jones and the black servants. There's blood stock that Lucinda could ride. Can't promise much excitement. But the country does look well after the autumn rains.'

Young Hannibal stared at his friend in astonishment, as Lucinda recovered the ivory fan from her lap.

'What a lovely idea! I can't think of anything I'd enjoy more.

Mother? Father? Might I accept the invitation?'

For a moment, Mrs Harper considered the house emptied of her daughter's coming and goings. Since she herself now ventured out so seldom, she depended on Lucinda for company and gossip. But, she reminded herself, Lucinda had suffered that fainting spell, had not been herself at all of late. Perhaps a change in the country was the very thing her daughter needed.

'If your father agrees . . .' she said doubtfully.

'Father? Might I?'

'I don't see why not.'

Old Hannibal's preoccupations had diminished his parental concerns. He wouldn't have minded getting out of the city himself. Each time he passed the abandoned offices of the gold companies he felt himself impelled towards flight.

Lucinda's face softened, in the contradictory fashion which always attended her success in any plot. Her pretty features appeared to melt into a gentle repose. Her eyes shone luminously at Tubby. By George, Lucinda really was a smasher, Tubby thought. He'd obviously been all wrong about her. That business with Woodrush – all talk most likely, probably put about by the old cats who worshipped at St Paul's and who had nothing better to do than ruin a young girl's reputation.

He coughed, suddenly aware of young Hannibal's puzzled gaze upon him.

'I'm staying over for the race meeting tomorrow. I expect my stallion to win the cup.'

He addressed himself to old Hannibal.

'You could pick up a bit there, sir. The odds won't be worse than fives.'

'I never gamble,' old Hannibal answered, which was a lifetime truth based on the codes of his upbringing. He stopped, in some confusion, as his recent losses again whirled in his head.

'That is to say, never on racehorses or on cards.'

'Perhaps Lucinda would care to return to Gooryanawah with me. I travel the first leg by rail. One of the hands meets me at end-of-line. It's quite civilised, really. I've a most comfortable small carriage. My father bought it for Ma.'

'I can vouch for that,' young Hannibal said, feeling a need to contribute.

Lucinda clapped her hands.

'Might we make that arrangement, Father?'

Old Hannibal absently repeated himself.

'Don't see why not.'

He tinkled the small brass bell beside him to summon Mrs Tom, looking again down the table to the twins' empty chairs. Martin would be safe enough at the Daly Waters depot. But news had come down the line that Ross was to try again for the Roper River. Where might Matthew be now? What trials might he be enduring?

At the Finke River, soon after Harvey, the surveyor, had declined to again attempt the interior with the expedition's poor supplies, Tom Crispe had gone down with such crippling bouts of fever that only his clammy yellow skin appeared to prevent the exposure of his bones. It was obvious that the bushman would have to be got south. Billy Hearne was greatly upset by the striking down of his mate, spitting angrily into the fire and making his remarks to Matthew.

'It's all bloody well and good for Todd and the bloody government, building this here telegraph line. It wasn't their arses the crocodiles were eating. We've near done a perish twice, for a few shillings a day.'

'But it's been worth all the hardship, hasn't it?' Matthew demurred, 'to join the colonies to the rest of the world – that was Mr Todd's vision.'

'Vision, is it? I'll give yer a bloody vision. How about the vision of Tom whose own mother wouldn't recognise the poor bastard? If I had a brain in me head, I'd tell Ross where to stick his expedition.'

Alfred Giles approached, sucking on his pipe.

'If you did that, Billy, it would damage Tom more than the fever. The best medicine Tom will get is when he learns that we got through to the Roper.'

'The hell with the Roper,' Billy declared, but his voice had quietened and his eyes had lost their anger.

'Ross has engaged a new fellow, Abrahams, to replace Tom. We're to go out in a few days.'

Billy looked up, flaring again.

'What do yer mean go out? Without a bloody surveyor?'

'Ross is confident that he can manage the navigation. We already know some of the country between here and the Roper.'

Billy said, 'There's a hell of a lot of it we know bloody nothing about. How is Ross going to navigate?'

Alfred Giles removed his pipe and poked a finger into the bowl. He looked across the glowing red soil, the scrub and the tall gums that swayed their tops in the wind.

'He has one prismatic compass, a protractor, a tracing of Stuart's map and a carpenter's lead pencil,' he said.

Advancing once again in the tracks of the Overlanders, the third Ross expedition early found itself short of flour. Ross was forced to make camp, while members of the party searched out other camps and depots in an effort to locate further supplies.

The camp, on the banks of a river, proved to be a misery. Small bush flies swarmed in uncountable numbers, blackening the food, swelling the men's eyes with infections, causing a vomiting and diarrhoea so constant and severe that the party became almost entirely invalided. By day the men lay under their mosquito nets, loathing the sight of food, oblivious to everything except their own misery.

And yet the nights were beautiful in this illogical land. As the sun sank below the rim of the land, the flies would miraculously vanish, and the men would drag themselves from the beds to the river bank where they sat enjoying the silence, a silence broken only by the occasional leaping of fish, the strange cry of the curlews, the screeching of night owls and the howls of a distant dingo.

Billy Hearne was disturbed by the haunting cry of the curlews.

'Them there curlews sound like a human in pain. The bloody things could curdle the milk in yer tea. But what buggers me is where them flies go at sundown. What do they live on, anyway? There's nothing out here to feed a million trillion flies. The rotten little buggers must be cannibals.'

Alfred Giles smiled, lighting his pipe.

'If the flies are cannibals, Billy, there'd hardly be a million trillion of them.'

'It just don't make no sense,' Billy concluded. 'The only thing'll make sense for me is when Ross gets us out of 'ere.'

By the next month the Ross expedition was fully equipped, the flour bags filled and weighed. But the men were debilitated by their enforced stay on the river. Even Ross, the ironbark post, had been weakened by the weeks of illness and idleness. As the expedition rode away, Billy Hearne vented his feelings.

'Thank gawd fer that! If we'd been stuck in them flies any longer I think I'd of slit me throat.'

Matthew could barely manage a smile. The feeling that had so haunted him when he had run from the death scrub had returned to him in a rush. As his mount trotted forward, he seemed to see, spread far over the seared landscape, the heaps of knobbled, parched bones, the empty eye sockets, the bleached jaws leering at him; the stillness and hush of the beckoning green scrub seemed to roar in his ears. He rubbed at his head as if to obliterate the vision, and suddenly leaned from the saddle, hawking up a sticky green string of bile.

'Bring it up, Matthew,' Alfred Giles advised. 'It's only the leavings. We're out of the fly country now.'

There were many good camps and bad camps made before the expedition came down once again from the precipices and peaks of the ranges. In the foothills there was mulga scrub and wild orange country where the party feasted, filling the spaces in their saddle-bags with the unexpected bounty of fruit. Claypans, cotton and saltbush led to a well-grassed plain. But Ross was disturbed by the spectacle of poor and stunted timber, which would be useless for telegraph poles.

On the edge of the grassy plain, the country transformed itself with endless stands of porcupine grass. A garbled shouting halted the horsemen, causing the pack animals to bump into each other. Ross had been leading at a fast amble. A big group of blacks stood on the other side of a gum creek, threatening with their spears and boomerangs.

'Move on,' Ross ordered. 'I've a notion that our sable brethren intend to make trouble.'

Fires sprang up behind the expedition. The tribesmen, carrying great torches of porcupine grass, sped to both sides of the party, intent on creating a ring of fire from which they could not escape.

'Keep calm,' Ross shouted over his shoulder, until the bolder blacks torched the saddle-high porcupine grass even within a few yards of the snorting and panicked pack horses.

Ross raised a hand and, drawing his shotgun from the scabbard, galloped at the leading warriors, firing both barrels over their heads, shouting in the broad Scottish accent which often overcame him in moments of emotion. The blacks' intention to burn the expedition was deflected by the blasts of the shotgun and by those pellets of bird shot which found their mark. They dropped their torches and ran.

The party tugged at the pack horse leads, moving the long string of snorting and rearing animals into a trot and then into a canter. When they had left the great blaze behind them, the party halted, each man breathing hard.

'Those bastards skeered me,' Billy Hearne admitted, 'Fell inter a fire once, when I were knee high to a grasshopper. Never have been much good at fires since. Except camp fires, with me mates around. Funny how fires can change.'

'It's funny how each of us can change, if we want to,' Alfred Giles considered, 'although I've known those who should have changed and couldn't. That's like falling into your own fire, Billy.'

Before the expedition had left the Finke River, Matthew had gleaned from reports from the north that the depot at Daly Waters was to be moved to the end of the existing line. His thoughts had been of Martin, then of the likelihood of a meeting between them. But he had not crouched down to sketch a map in the dirt, as Martin had done when the news eventually reached the depot that Ross was to try again for the Roper. Matthew's experience of the country, his sights of the estimates Harvey had made, had left him with a firm impression of where the headwaters of the Roper reached into the interior. If Ross did not get them lost, deprived of a surveyor as they were, Matthew fully expected that the expedition would meet with the northern wire.

As the party progressed into the wilderness, his vision of the death scrub began to recede. Ross, with his prismatic compass and protractor, accurately located some of John McDouall Stuart's old camps. They went without water again, but they were never severely tried as they had been on the earlier expeditions.

As the men rode, the cradling saddles rocking their private thoughts, with no words between them sometimes for hours, Matthew's thoughts were again on home and family. On his father's authoritative figure and manner, which could be touched with such unexpected softening. On how much Hannibal resembled his father, both of them so absorbed in the business. On the heavy gold watch chain which sat so proudly on his father's corpulence. On how much his mother lived for the family, and worried for the family, and doted on Lucinda.

In the last camp, the night had been turbulent with rain and thunder. Now the weather was humid and steamy, which slowed the pack horses. Lathered on flank and neck with a white foam, they looked as if they had been soaped and not washed down.

Considering the tatters in which the expedition had retreated to the Finke River, with Tom Crispe almost naked in a ragged remnant of trousers, Alfred Giles riding barefooted in the stirrups, his boots rotted off his feet, Ross wearing a water bag for a hat, the party looked almost smart now as it followed its leader. Each man except Matthew wore a new hat, only just beginning to stain with sweat. Matthew wore the battered old felt of his first issue, the eagle feather wilted in the band. He was sentimental about that hat and feather, and intended to take them home as a souvenir, when it was all over.

Ross called a midday halt to give the horses a breather, and the men made a meal of tea and damper.

'I wonder how Tom's gettin' on?' wondered Billy, stirring his tea.

'He'll be resting up in Adelaide by now,' Alfred Giles answered.

'The Overland will take good care of Tom.'

'They'd bloody better,' the little stockman said.

Alfred Giles smiled at his own thoughts.

'It will be autumn now in the south. A gentle, sweet-smelling season, and everything soft with sunshine. I used to walk by the Torrens in the autumn.' Billy Hearne paid no attention.

'They'd bloody better,' he repeated. 'That's all I got ter say.'

In the southern autumn so affectionately recalled by Alfred Giles, Lucinda was keeping her mother in a whirl with endless changes of mind about what she would pack for the trip to Gooryanawah. They were still debating the subject when old Hannibal and young Hannibal returned in the evening.

'What's the fuss about?' Old Hannibal demanded. 'I could hear you two clucking like hens before I opened the door.'

'It's Lucinda's packing,' Mrs Harper explained.

'A damned fuss to make about packing. I can pack in an hour to take a ship for Sydney.'

'I nearly forgot my riding habit. I will certainly need that if I'm going out with David,' said Lucinda.

Young Hannibal was puzzled.

'Who's David?'

'Tubby,' Lucinda flared at him. 'Who do you think?'

Young Hannibal had quite forgotten that Tubby's christened name was David. He had been Tubby to everyone as long as could be remembered.

'If you intend addressing Tubby as David, he's not going to know who you're talking to.'

Lucinda stamped a foot.

'Will you stop being so smart? A woman can't address her host . . . her . . . her . . .'

Young Hannibal again felt the irritation which had come over him at Sunday dinner.

'Her . . . her . . .' he repeated, 'her what?'

'Her host. It's different for a man. The nickname would be disrespectful, coming from me.'

'You've always called him Tubby before. Has Tubby ever objected?'

Mrs Harper coloured.

'Will you two stop this ridiculous argument?'

Old Hannibal stomped off to the brandy decanter.

'What the blazes does it matter what she calls him? Why not Lassie, or Rover?'

Lucinda flounced from the room, and Mrs Harper followed.

Young Hannibal pushed a cheroot into his mouth, slapping at his pockets for matches. Old Hannibal sat in his chair and sighed.

'Your sister becomes more vexatious by the day. Why she doesn't find a good man to marry, I'm blessed if I know.'

Young Hannibal lit his cheroot thoughtfully. It had been Lucinda who had suggested inviting Tubby to Sunday dinner. It had been Lucinda who had announced how much she would enjoy a visit to the country. It had been Lucinda who had leapt at Tubby's invitation. Good Lord! he thought suddenly. Was Lucinda on the prowi again? Was Tubby to be another Woodrush?

Twenty-one

The homestead on Gooryanawah was both practical and comfortable and without pretension, other than that of a slate roof which had replaced the original wood shingles. A privet hedge enclosed a small garden, an oasis watered by a bore-well and pump, in which flourished roses, sunflowers and hollyhocks. The kitchen garden was nurtured by a limping old soldier, a taciturn recluse who lived alone in a small shack on the property.

A few hundred yards from the homestead, a row of huts housed the station hands who worked the sheep, castrating and docking tails in the lambing season, and crutching the wool from the hindquarters of the grown sheep with their shears when fly-strike left fat maggots eating the flesh.

The shearing shed was a paddock away, with separate quarters for the itinerants who worked the sheds from property to property, coming from places as far flung as Queensland and New Zealand. Rough, hard men, whose back-breaking labour was rewarded according to the number of sheep they shore.

The horse yards and the lines where the working dogs were chained each evening lay at a distance from the back of the homestead. Only the stables for Tubby's blood stock had an appearance of newness, with smart gate doors, a feed shed and bales of straw for the comfort of the thoroughbreds. Tubby's blood stock had become his ruling passion.

As the carriage entered the property, Lucinda was disappointed by the sight of the straggling bush and barrenness of the first paddocks. The carriage horse trotted along a seemingly endless dusty track.

'Almost a mile from the gate to the house,' Tubby announced with some pride. 'There's three hundred thousand acres of the old place, you know. It's the biggest sheep station in the colony. You feeling all right, Lucinda?'

Lucinda was unsure how she felt. If she did succeed in her intention, and she knew that she must, could she live in this desolation? As the carriage continued through the cheerless landscape, she felt a need for home, for her indulgent mother, for her friends.

'Lucinda? You're not getting carriage-sick, are you?'

'Just a slight headache. Nothing to be concerned about, David.'

Tubby held the carriage strap.

'You know something, Lucinda? I probably sound like a bit of a fool, but I like it when you use my real name. Not that it matters. I've always been called Tubby, except by the old Dad, Ma and Ada.'

'Ada?'

'That's Mrs Jones, the housekeeper.'

Lucinda dimpled.

'David has always been my favourite man's name. It seems to suit you so well.'

'Well, I'll be damned,' Tubby said. 'What I mean to say is . . . ah . . . thank you, Lucinda.'

The horse yards came into sight, the outbuildings and, finally, the homestead.

'Here we are, then. The old homestead,' said Tubby fondly.

The arrival of Tubby with an unexpected female companion sent the servants into an uproar.

Mrs Jones fairly flew to the kitchen to order tea and cakes, rearranging cushions in the big room as she went. Two young Aboriginal house girls were sent running to prepare the best room.

'It used to be the master bedroom,' Mrs Jones confided. 'It opens out on to the garden. Oh dear! I must air the room.'

'Take it easy, Ada,' Tubby said. 'Miss Harper is Hannibal's sister, you know.' He turned to Lucinda, 'Ada has a soft spot for Han.'

'Indeed I do,' Mrs Jones agreed. 'We have such fun at cards

and guessing games when Hannibal comes to visit.'

When Tubby had seated Lucinda comfortably and put a brandy beside her, as a restorative after the journey, he followed Mrs Jones to the kitchen, where she chided him for his thoughtlessness.

'Why couldn't you have advised me in some way? Really, David! There are no flowers in the sitting room. And I must look out the French linen.'

'Don't make such a damned fuss, Ada. Lucinda has a headache. She doesn't need you flying about like a whirlwind.'

Mrs Jones clasped her hands.

'How beautiful she is. Such hair! Such colouring! I had no idea that Hannibal had such a sister. How long will she be staying?'

'About five minutes, the way you're carrying on. I'm telling you, Ada. Let Lucinda rest.'

Lucinda sipped at the brandy and walked around the big old room, cluttered with so many things in themselves strange to her, but familiar in type. The grandfather clock had stopped, as had the one at home, which now existed only as a decoration after its many failures had driven her father into refusing any further attempts to keep the pendulum performing its duty. The windows, with outside shutters against the summer heat, were opened now, their brocade curtains moving slightly in the breeze. Everything seemed to be at once foreign and homely. Lucinda looked and touched, hurrying back to be seated when she heard Tubby's boots clumping along the wooden floorboards of the passage.

'How's the headache, Lucinda?'

'Better now, thank you, David.'

'Ada will be in with tea in a jiff. Do you mind if I smoke a cigar?'

'Of course not. If I did, there'd be no living in Hannibal's company.'

'Yes, Han certainly goes through those cheroots. Now tell me – what do you think of Ada? She's part of the place, you know.'

Lucinda had formed an immediate impression on meeting Mrs Jones. In age and figure, and in some other strange way,

Mrs Jones reminded Lucinda of her mother.

'I think she's a dear.'

Tubby was pleased.

'She's been a good-looker, you know. Lived in Sydney when she was young. Her husband had a commission in the army. Got himself shot dead by some damned fool during rifle practice. Ada came to Adelaide to live with her sister. Ma met her somewhere and brought her back to Gooryanawah to be housekeeper.'

'She must get lonely for female company.'

'The old duck keeps on the move. Reads a lot, that kind of thing. You've got her in a tizzy.'

'Have I put her out, arriving so unexpectedly?'

'Hardly. She reckons you're a beauty. She's going to be at you for female gossip.'

Lucinda became demure.

'What do you think, David?'

'About what?' Tubby asked, who had now added a brandy to his cigar.

'About Mrs Jones's kind compliment.'

'About your looks?'

'It's just curiosity, David.'

'I agree with Ada. I've always thought so, if you must know. But I've always thought that you didn't think much of me.'

Lucinda gave a pretty laugh.

'Isn't that silly? I've always wanted to know you better. I had the impression that you didn't approve of me.'

'Well, I'm damned.' Tubby beamed through the curling cigar smoke.

Mrs Jones entered with a tray.

'You poor dear, you must be dying for a nice hot cup of tea. David, move the side table closer for Miss Harper.'

Lucinda had already planned to make an ally of the housekeeper, who seemed to be almost one of the family.

'I do wish you'd call me Lucinda. I would feel so much more at home.'

'Make it Lucinda and Ada,' Tubby said, feeling a new authority.

'May I?' asked Lucinda.

'I'd be most flattered, dear.'

Tubby said, 'I'll leave you two to have a chat. Must take a look at the blood stock and find out what's been doing while I've been away.'

In Lucinda's absence, Mrs Harper felt the house resoundingly quiet, and when her husband and son put life back into the house the first evening, she let loose with a flood of pent-up emotion.

'I fear we have erred in letting Lucinda go.'

'Rats!' said old Hannibal. 'Do you think she's going to be speared by the blacks?'

Young Hannibal said, 'Mrs Jones will probably be serving her tea and cake by this time. Tubby's place is hardly uncivilised, Mother.'

'You don't understand,' Mrs Harper went on. 'I don't think either of you have understood Lucinda. She's so outgoing, so trusting. She's still a baby in many ways. I don't think we should have let her go.'

Young Hannibal was feeling tired, and burdened with the cares of Hannibal Harper and Son. He poured a sherry and lit a cheroot, feeling an anger that suddenly shook him.

'What damned rot. It's you who have never understood Lucinda. Pampering her in everything. Giving in to her about everything. Being her supporter in everything, no matter what. Lucinda is about as much of a baby as her toffee-nosed friend, Lady Charlotte Bacon. And there are a few stories going round about her career, I can tell you.'

Mrs Harper clasped her throat, unable to believe her ears.

'How can you speak to your mother like that? How can you say such things about your own sister?'

'Because I'm fed up. I could go on with a few other things, but I won't. I just don't want to hear any more of this rot about Lucinda. If you'll excuse me, Mother, I'm off to the club.'

Mrs Harper turned on her husband.

'How can you sit there and not say a word?'

'My dear, what Hannibal says has some truth in it. You've always taken Lucinda's side in everything. Now, please, can we have some peace? I've had a hard day.'

'Everything comes back to me,' said Mrs Harper despairingly, dabbing at her eyes as she left the room.

Old Hannibal continued to sit, staring blankly, after his wife's departure. The inescapable facts of his business dealings rose up again before him like spectres. The interest rates on some of his borrowings were hardly covered by profits. One note was due for repayment in three months. He rubbed his hand hard on his dome as though to massage into stillness the throbbing inside it.

Everyone seemed to be making do with what they had. In the depressed state of the economy of the colony, nobody was buying. The government had tightened the purse strings on the Overland Telegraph; the Overlanders were having to make do with their abused wagons, carts and drays. Tents were being patched and repatched. The gold hoax had either wounded or frightened most people. Only the wool growers continued to grow fat, with their London markets.

The evening had turned cold at Gooryanawah. In the sitting room, pleasantly cosy with a fire blazing in the hearth, Mrs Jones served coffee before discreetly retiring. She had observed Tubby's attention to Lucinda, and felt a twinge of jealousy at what she suspected might be in the air. But she also hoped for it. David should be married. There should be heirs for Gooryanawah.

In the intimacy which had already grown between them, Tubby had begun to realise how much he would miss Lucinda when she returned home. Yet one doubt still nagged at him. He reached again for the bottle of port, the level of which had dropped appreciably during the evening.

There was little diplomacy in Tubby's nature.

'Look here, Lucinda. What was the strength of all that gossip about you and that Woodrush chap?'

Lucinda answered quickly, with engaging frankness.

'Steven was a friend, that's all. We were involved in the choir together. I rode with him once or twice.'

'Han thought there was more than that to it.'

'Hannibal had no right to think anything. I heard about the wagging tongues. Nobody ever said anything to me, nobody gave me the chance to deny such absurd rumours. I don't know why, but I have so often been the innocent target of spiteful gossip.'

'Hannibal went to see the fellow. That's why he took off.'

'Rubbish,' said Lucinda scornfully. 'Why, the Bishop mentioned to father that Steven Woodrush had requested a year's leave of absence in order to gain some experience of the world – outside St Paul's.'

Tubby tried to clear his mind.

'Is that the straight fact of the matter?'

'I'd hardly lie about it, would I? Isn't this a silly discussion? I'd much rather talk about you, and the splendid job you've been doing here at Gooryanawah since you lost your parents.'

Tubby's doubts vanished. Lucinda could not possibly be pretending. Her eyes had been as clear as crystal, looking directly into his own.

'Damn the fellow, anyhow. He was a little sneak by all accounts.'

Tubby became sentimental.

'I was very close to my parents, being the only child. There would have been a sister, but she died soon after birth.'

Lucinda put her hand on Tubby's knee, and he held it for a moment.

'You don't have to talk about it, dear.'

The word 'dear' momentarily stopped Tubby. He hastened to hide its effect.

'The old Dad was thrown from a horse while he was out mustering, hit his head on one of those rocks, down near the lagoon. Later I smashed that rock to bits with a mattock. That was ten years ago. I was twenty at the time.'

'Poor David,' Lucinda murmured, touching his knee again.

'Ma never recovered. Went downhill for two years. Then she had a heart attack in the kitchen. Died in Ada's arms. Dad and Ma are both buried at a spot they loved, near the gum creek on the northern boundary.'

Tubby wiped at his eyes.

'Haven't told anybody all that for a long time. I think I've overdone the port.'

Lucinda said, softly, 'I hope I'm not just anybody, David.

How brave you have been, running this big property since you were twenty.'

'I couldn't make up for the old Dad, but I've tried to do things the way he would have wanted. It's been bloody lonely at times.'

'Why didn't you marry, if you were lonely? A man like you could have his pick.'

'Marry?' Tubby sobered a little. 'Never gave it a thought. Never met anybody I felt about that way.'

'You must have met many girls who would have made you a good wife.'

'Met a few who set their hats at me,' Tubby admitted, 'but that would have been for the money, I suppose. I'm well off, you know.'

'I mean someone who appreciated you for yourself. You have many fine qualities, you know.'

Tubby swallowed his port at a gulp, his round face beaming at Lucinda in the firelight.

'Oh, I don't know about that, Lucinda. But you're right, you know. About the loneliness, I mean. Of course, I've got my blood stock, but I don't suppose that's the same thing.'

'The sport of kings,' Lucinda said dreamily. 'How I used to love a day at the races!'

Tubby was astonished.

'You? I've never seen you at the track, Lucinda.'

'I used to go often, with a girl friend. But Mother didn't approve.'

Lucinda had attended a race meeting once in her life, with the officer from the 18th Regiment, and she had paid a marked lack of attention to the horses. But her face was soft in the light of the fire, and looking at her through the port he had drunk, Tubby thought he had never seen such a beautiful woman.

'I'll tell you something. I've had the occasional wrong idea about you, Lucinda. You really are a smasher. Like one of my thoroughbreds.'

Lucinda rose and made a small curtsy.

'Thank you, kind sir. Now perhaps I should be going to bed, if we're riding early in the morning.'

Tubby hauled himself out of his chair.

'I'll escort you to your room.'

Lucinda giggled skittishly, 'Then you must offer me your arm, if you're going to escort me.'

Tubby bumped against the furniture in his progress. At the bedrom door he attempted a flourish.

'Goodnight, fair lady. Sleep well.'

Lucinda gave Tubby a small kiss on his astonished cheek.

'Goodnight, David. It has been a beautiful evening.'

Tubby tottered back to sit again at the fire.

'What the hell's happening?' he asked the expiring logs.

The room which had been the master bedroom at Gooryanawah was large and graciously furnished. A four-poster bed was canopied in embroidered linen. Wardrobes of polished cedar covered one wall. A couch in fine leather, which was positioned near the French windows, had been a day bed for Mrs Baker; a marble-topped table supported a porcelain basin and jug, both decorated with tiny pink roses. A dressing table and embroidered stool completed the furnishings.

Lucinda removed her gown and sank on to the bed in her underthings. For a moment she lay still, luxuriating in the fresh sweet smell of the pillows, congratulating herself on the progress of the evening. There had been a definite gleam in Tubby's eyes tonight, an emotion that marked his speech and gestures.

And he wasn't a bad old thing, despite the appropriateness of his nickname: those light cotton shirts he wore on the property certainly didn't do very much for his figure. She smiled; he would have made two of Steven.

Then her smile faded and she sat up, her heart beating so hard she could almost hear it. Four weeks since that botched affair in the carriage, four weeks the thing had been growing inside her. If she were not married within the next month, certain disaster awaited her.

There would be no forgiveness from her father; her life in Adelaide society would be finished. Damn Steven Woodrush! A trembling seized her, and she heaved herself up from the bed, hastening towards the mirror as if to find the solution in her own reflection. The sight of her image calmed her a little.

She became thoughtful. Should she try to seduce Tubby and then insist on his obligation to her?

The days passed, making Mrs Jones wonder.

'How long will Lucinda be staying, David?'

'As long as she likes.'

'Haven't you been neglecting your duties a little?'

That was something Tubby didn't want to hear. His foreman had also been dropping hints.

'Look here Ada. I run Gooryanawah. You run the bloody house.'

Later, while Lucinda was taking an afternooon rest, Tubby sat ruminating on a bench in the garden. Life had certainly taken on a new aspect since Lucinda's arrival. It wasn't that his life hadn't been pleasant before – damned pleasant, all things considered. There was the satisfaction of running the property, occasional trips to Adelaide where he'd visit the racecourse, his club and a certain house where the girls – good-lookers, too – really knew how to please a man. But it was true that he sometimes got lonely, especially in the lambing and shearing seasons when he couldn't get away for months.

Suddenly the prospect of that appalled him. It was queer – it had scarcely bothered him before. Having Lucinda around seemed to have turned his thinking upside down.

He didn't want her to leave, it came down to that. He wanted to come back to her at the end of a long day, every day. He wanted to take her to Adelaide and show her off to his chums. It dawned on him. He wanted to make her Mrs Tubby Baker. He corrected himself. Mrs David Baker.

She certainly had a body to her. She had borrowed trousers and a shirt to ride astride. It fairly shook a man to see Lucinda in a shirt and trousers. She'd handled the big roan like a man. How her hair had streamed in the breeze when she put the roan into a gallop!

Tubby decided to give himself a port, although he usually never drank during the day. He filled a pewter mug, taking care not to be seen by Ada, and went back to the bench to think more on it.

It was sunny there, the air sweet with the scents of autumn roses. Tubby knew every inch of the garden, had done so since he was a child. Thinking on that jolted Tubby on his bench. Children! Godamighty! He could have a son for Gooryanawah. More than one. Sisters to go with them. Tubby put down the mug and rushed inside for a cigar. Returning, heady with the aroma of port and cigar, his thoughts tumbled with a speed that he found difficult to follow. What a life that would be! He had the money to give a family everything.

'I'll bloody well have a go,' he told the mug and the cigar.

Lucinda had called him dear. She had let him hold her hand. She had said that a man like him could have his pick. She even adored racing. Han would be his brother-in-law. So would those game twins. He would be marrying into good blood, good breeding stock. Old man Harper and the old Dad had been mates in the early days. The old Dad would have wanted nothing better.

His thoughts took another turn. If Lucinda turned him down, life wouldn't be worth living. He'd pop the question at the first opportunity. There was no point in messing about. He either had a chance or he didn't. He'd ask Lucinda that very night, after Ada had gone to bed.

Lucinda sat at the dressing table, brushing her gleaming hair. She had come to a decision. She would have to seduce him. It would help if he drank too much, as he usually did each evening. When he escorted her to her bedroom door, she would invite him in, on the pretence of helping unbutton her gown. It would have to be this evening. There was no more time to waste.

At dinner, Tubby's mood had altered from a noticeable excitement into little absences of attention that caused Mrs Jones concern. He ate little, drank many glasses of wine, and several times appeared not to hear when Mrs Jones spoke to him directly. He was so altogether unlike himself that Mrs Jones became offended.

His mood remained unchanged when they went to take coffee by the fire, although he made frequent visits to the port bottle. Lucinda was at her brightest, telling stories of society and flattering Tubby with glowing comments about his property, his skill as a horseman, his fine stable of thoroughbreds. Each time Tubby went to the port, she noted it with satisfaction. He continued to be unresponsive to Mrs Jones, and, not a little hurt, she excused herself early.

Lucinda chattered on gaily about their proposed picnic at the lagoon next day. Then she declared that she felt a little overheated, and drew on the bodice of her gown so that the cleavage of her rich breasts could be seen. Tubby got up and walked about, then plumped down again into his chair.

Lucinda asked, 'May I ride the roan again tomorrow, David?'

There were so many thoughts in Tubby's mind, so many rehearsals of approaches, that everything had got into a tangle. He had not intended what finally came out.

'You can have him. Lucinda. Have him to keep. You can have everything I own, as long as I can have you.'

Lucinda stared, in genuine surprise.

'What do you mean?'

'I mean I want to marry you.'

Lucinda's breath shook on a long intake of triumph.

'David, are you proposing?'

'That's what it comes down to. I can't imagine this place without you now. For God's sake tell me. Have I any chance?'

Lucinda waited a respectable time before she answered, while Tubby agonised.

'Why, David, I would be most honoured to become your wife.'

'What? You will?'

Tubby could hardly believe it.

'Just as soon as it can be arranged, my love.'

Tubby went down on his knees, laying his head in Lucinda's lap. She stroked it, smiling over Tubby into the fire. She had done it. There was nothing more to worry about. She would have to get home as soon as possible, to make the announcement and begin making the arrangements.

Tubby stood up.

'I'm the happiest man in the world.'

Lucinda stood for a long embrace.

'When shall we marry, my darling?'

'Now, if it were possible. I can't imagine this place without you now.'

'Perhaps instead of picnicking tomorrow, I should give the news to the family and set an early date?'

'The earlier the better. I can get you to the midday train.' He paused. 'I'd like to see Han's face when he learns about this.'

Lucinda was thinking that she'd like to see Steven Woodrush's face.

'He'll be delighted. Now I think I'd best go to my room.'

Tubby went with her. As she opened the door, she turned back to him.

'Will you come in and help me unbutton my gown?'

She slipped the gown off her shoulders and allowed Tubby to kiss her *déshabillée*. When he had left, almost reeling with delight, Lucinda was already considering how she might hasten the date of the ceremony.

Tubby lit a cigar, pacing before the fire. He had done it. By George, he had done it! He had pulled it off in one go. He'd have something to tell Ada in the morning. He'd throw the biggest stag party Adelaide had ever seen. He'd buy Lucinda the biggest diamond ring in the colony. He'd name the first son after the old Dad. Tubby hurried for the port. He couldn't stop congratulating himself.

Twenty-two

On the Sunday of the last rest before packing up the depot, when the old mare had brought the new dray back alone to the forge, Solomon returned late to the tent, stumbling about and lost in his own thoughts. He sat on his box at the fire, sipping from a bottle, mumbling words that the others could not understand. Martin and Eli had seen Solomon the worse for drink on several occasions. Martin made a guess.

'Did you lose at the cards, Solomon?'

'Lose, is it? Solomon won at the cards.'

Eli shook his head at Martin. The action seemed to suggest that they should be understanding of Solomon's mood.

Martin said, 'The overseer came by, Solomon. He said it was your responsibility to see that everything connected with the forge should be packed up as soon as possible.'

Solomon fixed his small shiny eyes on Martin, the lids puffed by the rum he had drunk. The look was charged with hostility that hurt and frightened Martin.

'As to responsibility, Solomon has had a full cargo. Responsibility can be easy to come by and devilish hard to put down. It can barnacle a man like a ship's hull. When I let you come away with me, wasn't that a responsibility? Solomon has had responsibility enough for this day. The word doesn't ring well in his ears.'

Martin paled.

'I didn't know you thought of me as a burden, Solomon.'

Solomon tipped the bottle. Eli Stubbs put up his hand to Martin in warning.

'We're both beholden to Solomon. I owe him my life and freedom.'

Solomon had quietened, head bent, staring into the fire as though to read something in the flames. He scratched the back of his pitted neck and then drained the bottle.

'Pay no attention to Solomon, lad. No man could wish to bunk with better shipmates. What you heard was the rum talking, using Solomon's tongue. Many's the black devil that's hidden himself in a rum bottle in order to get inside a man and take charge of the helm, so to speak.'

Solomon beamed a shadow of his smile at Martin and Eli.

'I'll be getting to my bunk, before I go aground.'

Within minutes a clamour of snoring signalled Solomon's abrupt laying aside of his responsibilities. Eli filled Martin's pannikin with the tea that had been brewing.

'Don't let it rankle. Solomon holds you high in his affections. Didn't I tell you that he had been fretting about something? Whatever it was, it seems to have come to a head on this day.'

Martin sugared his tea.

'I know he didn't mean anything by it. It wasn't just the words. It was the look he gave me. It was a strange look. As though it came from something secret, deep inside his head.'

'Forget about it, lad. It's a great bustle we'll be in from tomorrow.'

'How long do you think it will take us to get to the end of the wire, Eli?'

'That depends on the wagons. They'll be heavily laden, moving everything at once.'

'Make a guess, Eli.'

'A month, if we don't have any breakdowns. You're thinking about your twin again, aren't you?'

'I can't seem to think of anything else. I wonder how far north Mr Ross has got?'

'There's no speculating on that.'

'I've been missing my family lately, Eli. It's so long between mails. I didn't feel like that at first; all I thought about was the chance of meeting Matthew.'

'Haven't your famous feelings told you that you will? It might be soon now, Martin.'

Martin frowned.

'That hasn't changed, but lately there's been something else. A feeling of danger for Matthew.'

'There's been danger for us all, lad. You and I could have starved to death on the Roper.'

Martin shook his head.

'No. I knew we'd survive. I told you that at the time.'

'The dangers to Mr Ross's explorers would have been on the first expeditions. The Overland has come a long way since then. Didn't we learn months ago that Mr Ross had almost got through to the Roper?'

'I wonder if Matthew looks different now. What experiences he must have had! He's a hero, isn't he, Eli?'

'He's been an explorer in this strange land. He's seen things never before seen by white men. Yes, he's a hero. And will be treated as such when he gets home.'

Martin was wondering where Matthew would be on the seventeenth of next month. On that day they would both turn twenty-one. What a party there would have been at home!

'We must turn Solomon off his back when we go in,' said Eli. 'Otherwise there'll be no sleeping for us this night.'

In the days spent packing up the forge, its equipment and materials, Solomon's crew were engaged from sunrise to sunset. Solomon had returned to his customary cheerfulness. It had got about that Ben Barton had deserted, though his absence was not noticed for some days, since he had spent most of his time at the horse yards, even sleeping in one of the feed storage huts.

The overseer let it be known that Barton had pestered him for leave to go to Darwin. The desertion was remarked on by the men and then forgotten in the hard work of clearing camp. Barton's desire to go to Darwin was of no interest to anyone, except to Solomon and Eli.

Solomon reassured the trembling Eli as best he could. Barton had not recognised him in the gloom of the tent, had not seen his back. Barton had deserted for reasons of his own.

Then one morning, a uniformed policeman appeared in the camp, and Eli's heart almost stopped. But the man had been sent by the government resident at Darwin, with mail for the Overlanders, and showed no interest in him. Eli's anxiety fell away.

'There are good and bad things on the land as there are in the watery world,' Solomon later told himself for instruction and comfort. 'Ben Barton would have been as bad a creature on the sea as he was high and dry on the land. Good and bad is in the nature of creation. You've exchanged a bad for a good,

Solomon. Now put it out of your mind.'

Soon after daybreak the next morning, a breakfast of fried bully beef and porridge was eaten in the mess, the last tent to be struck. The long caravan of wagons, carts, drays, horsemen and stock began the move south. The depot, which had been home for so long to some of the Overlanders, was left behind as a small scar on the landscape, a place of leavings and rubbish, with only the horse yards and the small building which would become a relay station remaining as testament to their occupation.

Solomon and Martin rode in Eli's dray, Martin looking back as they left.

'How sad it looks. Like something rejected and abandoned.'

'Aye,' Solomon said, 'there's more than enough of that in the cruelty and beauty of the world.'

In the contemplation and prayer which Steven gave himself up to each night before sleeping, he had come to see deeper and deeper into himself. There was a weakness in him, he saw now, an essential lack of the manhood obvious in the men with whom he travelled. None had made a friend of him, except Ralph Milner who sometimes talked with him about God and life and death.

His earlier euphoria had vanished as completely as his new-found set of priorities. This rough bush world was not his world, could never be. He began to dread the start of each new day, the ever-increasing miles that distanced him from the serene city he had run from.

He let Lucinda back into his thoughts, feeling the loss of her in a way that he now made efforts to understand. The act of love between them, the shock of his first love-making, did not now seem of great importance. He realised that it was of more significance to him now that her attention, and even that of her mother, had elevated him in the esteem of others, something which he had never managed for himself.

There was something in him that yearned for Lucinda's thrilling dominance of him. He was still her lackey, he told himself disgustedly; but more than that, he knew now he longed to be overwhelmed by her again.

The clarity of these perceptions helped resolve many of his

conflicts. He would not have been able to so understand, had he not ventured into the wilderness. But he could still be safe in the church. He was free to leave the drive whenever he wished and make his way back to Adelaide, travelling south in the tracks of the Overland.

Today there was a threat of storm in the air. Only Steven, a stockman called Yorkey, and John Milner remained in the home camp, the rest of the men having gone out scouting for a suitable camp site further on. In the warm, still air, Steven sat, his back against a tree, dozing.

Then he became aware that a shadow had passed over him. Opening an eye, he saw a solitary young Aboriginal, tall and well built, carrying a club and a boomerang, passing silently by him. There was a sense of purpose in his movements that made Steven suddenly sit up straight.

Yorkey, saddling up his horse, caught sight of the black and reddened in annoyance. He didn't like the Milners' casual attitude to the blacks. He automatically felt for the handle of the duelling pistol in his belt as he shouted to John Milner, busy at the fire.

'One of your black friends has called to take tea. I don't like the looks of him.'

John Milner looked around as the black man approached him.

'He's all right,' he called. 'Leave him be. He's just curious.' He stood up, yawning, as the black continued to move towards him.

It happened in an instant, so quickly that Steven had no time to shout a warning. The black swung his club at Milner's skull, and without a sound, he slumped to the ground.

Steven heard himself screaming, high girlish screams that kept coming and coming until they filled his head.

'Get a rifle, for God's sake!' he heard Yorkey yelling. 'Get a rifle!'

His limbs were frozen. He could not move. A whimpering came out of his throat, and would not stop.

The black was raising his boomerang when Yorkey dashed towards him, both hammers on the duelling pistol cocked. He aimed and fired at his stomach, and the black fell, got up and began to stumble away. Yorkey fired again at his back, as he ran to snatch John Milner's rifle, hanging from a tree. Kneeling, he snapped the trigger three times. Each time the cartridge failed to fire, as the black was swallowed up into the bush.

Steven Woodrush stood shuddering over John Milner's body. The blow had smashed his skull from the ear to the eye. Both eyes had been bolted from his head and now lay on his cheeks like soft marbles. Blood and brains began to ooze from the widening crack in the bone.

'Why didn't yer go fer the black, instead of sittin' there screamin'? Yer snivellin' coward, yer lily-livered swine!'

Almost crying, the stockman clenched his fists and delivered a blow that lifted Steven Woodrush off his feet and sprawled him on the ground. He continued to rage as Steven lay motionless in his misery. Then he calmed a little.

'If I tell the others what yer done they'll tear yer ter bits. When Ralph gits back, you git on south, quick-smart.' He paused. 'Fer the present I need yer ter help hold the mob.'

Steven turned on his stomach, his tears spilling into the dust. The stockman kicked at his ribs.

'Get up. We'll have ter put John in the dray and cover him.'

Late in the morning of the next day, Ralph Milner and his drovers returned. Steven shivered at the sight of the elder Milner, as he and the others swung out of their saddles.

'There's good country ahead,' Ralph Milner announced. 'Plenty of feed and water to keep us going. Where's John and Yorkey?'

He looked critically at Steven.

'You been sick? You look like a ghost.'

'Ralph . . . ' began Steven.

'What's been going on here?' Ralph Milner asked, sensing trouble.

Yorkey galloped into the camp and jumped down from his horse. Ralph Milner's leathery, sun-creased face was questioning, as his hunting dogs sniffed the air.

'Everything all right?'

'Come fer a bit of a walk,' the stockman said, gently touching Ralph Milner's arm. 'I've got something to tell yer, Ralph.'

Woodrush sat and waited, his back against the same tree on which he had leaned when the black began walking towards John Milner, and he had watched.

'What's going on?' one of the other men asked, seeing Ralph

Milner and Yorkey halt at a distance.

Steven shook his head mutely and turned away.

'Somethin's bloody funny.'

The man returned to his mates, who were also beginning to wonder. They looked towards the two figures halted near a thorn bush.

Yorkey returned and went to squat with the stockmen, who instinctively quietened at his approach. Ralph Milner walked further into the scrub.

The wagon and carts, all the familiar inanimate objects in the droving camp, seemed to exude the same hush of shock that Steven Woodrush could feel as a pulse among the squatting, whispering men. When Ralph Milner returned, each man stood up. Milner's face was fixed, his gait stiff. His lips hardly moved when he asked the question.

'Where is he?'

Yorkey pointed to the dray. Ralph Milner lifted the tarpaulin which covered his brother, looked and let it fall.

'Get shovels,' he said quietly. 'We'll bury John under that big tree. I'm going off for a bit.'

One of the men digging spoke to his companion.

'First his wife and now his young brother. Why does it happen to a man like Ralph? He's the salt of the earth, Ralph is.'

As the men with the shovels dug deep into the red earth, others cut timbers to fence the grave. The stockman who doubled as cook hammered a nail at a sheet of tin to be fixed to the tree, pricking out John Milner's name, his birth date, and the cause of death.

When earth had been shovelled over the tarpaulin-wrapped body, dampened from a water bucket and trod hard and even, Ralph Milner stood, his hands clasped before him and spoke his few words.

'We put John into your hands, dear Lord. He didn't get to live long but every year of his life he lived in honesty and decency and courage. No man ever had a better brother. Yours is the resurrection. Amen.'

'Amen,' the stockmen repeated, shuffling and fingering the hats held to their chests. Ralph Milner turned from his brother's grave.

'Pack up camp. We're moving on. We're going to make a night drive.'

As the surprised men went to pack, Yorkey stepped up to Steven Woodrush, his mouth near the other's ear.

'Git! Git now, yer miserable cur.'

All the previous night Steven Woodrush had stared up at the sky, mind and spirit locked in a vice of shame. He had pleaded in prayer for the strength which had always been denied him. He knew he was lying there in the great Australian loneliness because he had let Lucinda Harper use him, because he had permitted himself to become her chattel, and then had run from that. He realised all that now, when it was too late.

'Git!'

The word echoed in his head.

Ralph Milner was checking his equipment as he saddled a fresh mount, his face wooden. Steven went up to him.

'Ralph?'

Milner paused, without turning.

'What is it?'

'I want to go south.'

'Leave the drive?'

'Yes.'

'There's nothing to bind you. Take a horse and food.'

Milner turned then and put out his hand.

'Glad to have met you. Ride west until you strike the Overland. Follow it south.'

In the preparations for the night drive, only one man noticed Steven Woodrush ride away. The stockman Yorkey bared his teeth like a dog for an instant, but said nothing.

Lucinda, who now so embittered Steven's thoughts, was devoting all her energies to the organisation of her wedding. Her unexpected return to Adelaide had taken the family by surprise. They stood in a tableau of three, speechless, when Lucinda arrived in the evening. After her mother's first embrace, Lucinda, aglow with delight, had removed her hat and shawl.

'Mother . . . Father . . . Hannibal . . . I . . . have something important to tell you.'

Mrs Harper immediately became anxious.

'There's nothing wrong, is there?'

'On the contrary, everything's wonderful. I'm going to be married.'

'What's that?' old Hannibal gasped.

'David has proposed. I have accepted.'

Young Hannibal was incredulous.

'Tubby? Tubby proposed?'

'He insists that we be married, just as soon as it can be arranged.'

Mrs Harper slowly sank into her chair.

Young Hannibal said 'I think I need a brandy.'

'I think we all do,' his father agreed.

Mrs Harper began to sniffle.

'Oh, Lucinda! Oh, my baby!'

Young Hannibal was busy with drinks, his head buzzing. Why had Lucinda deliberately gone after Tubby? How on earth had she got him, in no more than a week? He stared at his sister. None of it made sense. Tubby to marry Lucinda! To insist on an early wedding?

'Well I'll be a monkey's uncle,' old Hannibal said, and then to his wife, 'Will you stop that sniffling, woman?'

Mrs Harper burst into tears.

'It's such a surprise. My baby!'

'Give your mother a handkerchief,' old Hannibal ordered his son, 'before she floods the room.'

Lucinda said, 'Mother, we must begin making arrangements tomorrow. Father, you must speak to the Bishop. I would like him to conduct the ceremony. Mother, you and I must make up a list for the reception.'

A sudden realisation shook the glass in old Hannibal's hand. He would be obliged to pay for the reception, as the father of the bride. His wife and daughter would no doubt invite all Adelaide society. In his present straits, how could he finance such an extravaganza?

Above her mother's sniffles Lucinda asked, in a small voice, 'Isn't anyone going to congratulate me?'

'Congratulations,' young Hannibal said, unable to keep an edge from his voice.

'Of course, of course,' old Hannibal said mechanically. 'Congratulations.' Lucinda picked up her hat and shawl.

'I must change. Will you carry up my bags, Hannibal? The coachman put them down on the porch.'

In her room, Lucinda poured cold water into the basin, pulling back her hair in a clasp before splashing her face. The birth would simply appear to be premature. If her mother became suspicious and asked questions, she would simply tell her that she had previously been with Tubby. Her mother would accept that, as she accepted everything that Lucinda did. Ada would also have her suspicions, but Ada would assume the same thing. She knew what Lady Charlotte Bacon would think. Lady Charlotte Bacon could think what she liked.

On the first night after leaving the drive, Steven rode in the moonlight until he almost fell from the saddle. Again and again he heard his thin scream, the whimper of which seemed to fill his head. The wild bush passed him by, as his horse plodded on, like a figment of his imagination, the unreal finishing of a dream which had no meaning.

At last he tethered the horse and lay on the ground, pressing his back into the stones that prodded him, his eyes blind to the moon and stars, his body immune to the creeping cold, the wind biting through his clothing. The stockhorse tried to crop, still burdened by the saddle, the tight girth, the rolled blankets and saddle-bags. Only in the early morning, when the cold suddenly began to penetrate him, did Steven force himself up, unfasten the blanket roll and unsaddle the weary mare, who blew out her belly in long-awaited relief and tried to scratch herself on the bush which was her tether.

He wrapped the blankets about him and lay down again on the stones, in the piercing cold that regularly preceded the heat of day. He wondered if a man could freeze to death if he unclothed himself. If he lay out until the cold reached his heart? He was dreaming a little when the sky began to colour with sunrise. The faces of the Bishop and Yorkey, the stockman, loomed over him. Together they were chanting:

'Yer miserable, lily-livered swine.'

Twenty-three

In the week after Lucinda had returned home to reveal the news of her forthcoming marriage to her astounded parents, Tubby arrived in Adelaide to present himself as their future son-in-law. The occasion was confused by solemnity on the part of old Hannibal, awkwardness on the part of young Hannibal, and further tears from Mrs Harper. Tubby took Lucinda into the garden to bestow upon her the clustered diamond engagement ring which had been burning a hole in his pocket all day. In the house, Mrs Harper once again took up her refrain.

'Lucinda has swept me off my feet this week past. I don't know whether I'm coming or going. Why does he insist on such an early marriage? An engagement period should be at least of six months. I simply don't understand it.'

Old Hannibal sipped at his champagne, from a magnum which Tubby had brought for the occasion. He had visibly aged and weakened in past weeks. The twins were much on his mind again, and the thought of their next birthday, their twenty-first, caused his eyes to wet.

'What have they got to come back to?' he had asked young Hannibal in his office. 'I had thought to see you all settled for life. What will happen when that promissory note becomes due?'

'We shall have to mortgage the house, Father.'

Old Hannibal straightened momentarily before sagging again.

'Mortgage the house? The family home? How can you suggest such a thing?'

Young Hannibal answered gently. 'It may be necessary, Father.'

'Don't speak of it,' old Hannibal cried.

Young Hannibal, too, was thinning with worry. But the

authority which his mother had previously noticed had grown with his father's decline.

'The drink isn't helping you any, Father.'

Old Hannibal accepted the chiding, which would have been unthinkable before his losses.

'You can't begin to understand how it feels to see everything that you've built crumble before your eyes. I'm too old to start again. The brandy helps me sleep. Helps me to stop thinking.'

He grasped young Hannibal's arm.

'You're a wonderful son, Han. You've always been a wonderful son.'

'Why don't you lunch at the club? Have a chat with your old friends?'

'I'm afraid of my circumstances becoming known. That's my pride again. Hannibal Harper's sin of pride.'

'We'll pull through, Father. At least Lucinda will be settled.'

'Yes. That is certainly something. But have you considered what this marriage is going to cost us? Your mother is right. What's all the hurry about?'

Young Hannibal was to dine at the club that night with Tubby, who had been busily arranging his stag party and fittings for his wedding suit. It was the first opportunity they had had to talk together since Lucinda had made her announcement. Tubby's beaming face shone like a beacon in the club lounge, as Hannibal shook his hand.

'Well, Han. What do you think? Did you get a surprise?'

'You could have knocked me down with a feather. How did it happen? You had never shown any interest in Lucinda before. In fact, you've been damned critical on occasions.'

'You mean that Woodrush business? That was a lot of rot. Lucinda hardly knew the fellow. You were wide of the mark there, Han.'

'Is that what she told you?'

'I got a bit tight and mentioned it. A lot of rot. She told me so, to my face. And as for the other stories – well, a beautiful girl like Lucinda is always a target for spiteful gossip.'

Hannibal thought of all the things his sister had told him to his face. He took out his cheroots and lit one.

'Why the big hurry about the wedding?'

'Lucinda wanted it, and that suited me.'

Young Hannibal coughed smoke.

'Lucinda wanted it?'

Tubby poured more champagne.

'What does it matter? Isn't it great, Han? I'm going to be your brother-in-law. Who'd have thought it, old boy?'

Tubby examined his friend more closely.

'You've lost weight, Han. The old hair is disappearing. I don't mind telling you that I was surprised at the change in your dad, too. You're both looking seedy. What's the trouble?'

Young Hannibal didn't know how to answer. He thought of his father, the need to mortgage the house. Tubby pressed him, suddenly aware that there must be real trouble at Harper and Son.

'Come clean, Han. I'm almost a member of the family.'

Suddenly young Hannibal felt a great urge to unburden himself.

'We're just about broke, Tubby,' he said slowly. 'Father lost a great deal of money in the gold hoax. Business everywhere is almost at a standstill. We've had to borrow at exorbitant interest. One of the notes is due for repayment next month. Father and I have kept it from Mother and Lucinda.'

Tubby poured more champagne and signalled for another bottle. He considered his bubbling glass, his round face serious.

'Look here, Han. We can't have this. Do you have a figure in mind that would get you out of trouble?'

'Not in my head. I've got it all in the office, with estimates of the running costs we have to bear until the economy improves. But that won't happen unless the Overland Telegraph is completed in time.'

Tubby hesitated.

'You know that I've got plenty, Han. I'll make you an offer. I'll take over all of Harper and Son's debts, interest free, with enough to see you through until business improves. How's that? Shall we drink to it?'

Young Hannibal swallowed in a sudden rush of emotion. He had to turn away in the big club chair. Tubby, with rare tactfulness, was asking a steward to fetch him a cigar. He let Hannibal take his time. It would feel satisfying to be able to help Lucinda's family.

'I don't know what to say, Tubby.'

Young Hannibal had never considered approaching Tubby for financial help. Such an offer, he realised, could mean everything. Put his father back on his feet. Banish the burden which had so sapped him. Would his father's pride permit him to accept such an offer? There was no longer room for his father's pride, he thought suddenly. Harper and Son was on the brink of ruin.

'All you have to say is yes,' Tubby was saying. 'We can fix it up with your bank tomorrow.'

Hannibal, after a moment, nodded mutely.

Tubby raised his glass.

'Would it crack your face to give a smile, Han? Here's to the future. I'm bloody well looking forward to mine.'

When young Hannibal awoke next morning he was aware first of a headache. He blinked his eyes at the ceiling, trying to recall last night. Then he shot upright, tumbling the bedding, still wearing the shirt that he'd been unable to unbutton. Tubby's offer! No wonder he had celebrated.

Mrs Harper was disapproving when young Hannibal got himself downstairs.

'Really, Hannibal! You woke up the whole house when you came in last night. How ever did you get yourself in such a condition? It's late – your father has been gone for an hour.'

'I was celebrating.'

'Celebrating – Lucinda's wedding?'

'In a way. I'll make myself ready and be off.'

'Your beard needs trimming,' Mrs Harper observed crossly, 'and so does your father's. You've both been neglecting your appearance lately.'

Old Hannibal was going through the books when his eldest son entered.

'Good afternoon,' he said, sarcastically. 'Are you aware that you awoke the house when you came in last night?'

'I had something to celebrate.'

Old Hannibal dipped his pen in the inkwell.

'Celebrate,' he muttered. 'Good God, what is there to celebrate?'

'What would you say, Father, if our debts were to be taken over, free of all interest, plus we were given a sum of operating capital, also interest free, until such time as Harper and Son gets back on its feet again?'

Old Hannibal looked at his son sourly.

'I'd say that you'd lost your wits at the bottom of a bottle last night. Now will you let me get on with my calcuiations?'

'It's true, Father. Tubby has made such an offer. I'm to meet him today and fix it up at his bank.'

Old Hannibal dropped his pen.

'What's that?' he shouted, almost with his old vehemence.

'Tubby has offered to take over our debts, until Harper and Son is back on its feet. He said that he would feel privileged, as a member of the family.'

'He'll do no such thing, son-in-law or not. How dare you betray our business position to an outsider?'

Young Hannibal found, with surprise, how firm he could now be with his father.

'This is no time for useless pride,' he replied. 'Just think on it – the twins will have something to return to. Doesn't that give you good enough reason to accept his offer?'

Old Hannibal was scrubbing his dome with both hands, unable to digest Hannibal's startling news.

'I don't know what to say.'

'That's exactly what I said to Tubby. All you have to say is yes. That's all Tubby wants to hear.'

Old Hannibal got up, walked a few yards and returned to his chair.

'Everything, Father. Including the note due so soon. Nobody need know. Tubby said he wouldn't even tell Lucinda.'

Young Hannibal had to wait on his father's internal struggle. The old man was in his chair and out of his chair. He drummed his fingers on the slats of the roll-top desk.

'He will have to have a paper. A paper on the entire business, until he is fully repaid.'

'I will arrange that. Now I must go and take out the figures.'

Old Hannibal paced the floor, long after his son had gone. Young Hannibal was right. This was no time for pride. He blew one last sigh for the past, and then squared his shoulders. He would lunch this day at the club. He could face his successful friends. He had Harper and Son to rebuild.

* * *

As the Ross expedition continued to map the way north, Matthew's thoughts, in the daydreaming private to each man during the long silences in the saddle, continued almost exclusively of home and family. Soon he and Martin would attain their majorities. He wondered how Martin would celebrate the date. The thought overcame Matthew with loneliness. He so much wanted to be with his twin on the seventeenth of the month.

His father had given Hannibal a fine party on his twenty-first birthday. The house had been crowded; Lucinda had played on the piano for hours and Tubby Baker had made a game of musical chairs in which even his mother had taken part. He and Martin had been schoolboys then, sixteen years of age. They had both been permitted a sherry to toast Hannibal's twenty-first birthday.

The trials of the third Ross expedition had not been severe. The men and horses had suffered the usual shortages of water, with plagues of mosquitos and a lack of flour, which had become so infested by weevils that the bags were tossed away for the blacks. Many of the hobbles were broken beyond repair. Only ten horses could be hobbled at night and much time was wasted each morning in searching out and rounding up the strays. After the expedition's escape from the ring of fire, there had been a continuing feeling of danger from hostile tribesmen, whose fires at night kept the men anxious. The fires made Billy Hearne particularly jumpy, and he swore loud and long at their distant light.

There was much to be wondered at in the new country through which the expedition was travelling. It was unlike anything they had previously seen, and the now the party hoped to be done permanently with sandhills and porcupine grass. There were new kinds of trees, shrubs and grasses. Flights of geese, gulls and waterfowl passed overhead at night, beating on their routes of migration. Fat bush turkeys fell before John Ross's shotgun, a delight and a healthy supplement to the rough and meagre rations.

For days the party journeyed through undulations of heavily-timbered country which kept them all talking and pointing. Some of the trees looked like fig, others like apple, plum or pear, luxurious in foliage and casting dense shade. But the trees bore no fruit. Otherwise, as Alfred Giles said, they might have been riding through an enormous orchard. Billy Hearne shook his head at it all.

'This must be the most up-jumped land God ever made. Yer never know what ter expect.'

Glimpses of blacks, many painted in ochre and ash, were had each day as they trailed the explorers. Ross was certain that the tribesmen would not attack, but Alfred Giles insisted that he should order guard-shifts at night. The blacks' fires, lit ever closer now to the camps of the explorers, shortened vision by murking the darkness with smoke. Alfred Giles feared that the blacks would attack, using the smoke as cover.

Matthew's nerves began to trouble him again. He dreamed of the death scrub, waking in a running sweat despite the cold of the night. A feeling of foreboding seized him. It came and went, without definition. He seemed to witness the spectacle of his own bones in that stark, silent and terrible place. The slightest noise alarmed him when he stood guard, with carbine cradled, his revolver loosened in his holster.

Camped for the night between two great paperbark trees, Giles took the first watch. He judged that the blacks' fear of horses would keep them away from their feeding ground, and concentrated his attention to the west, straining his eyes at the misting smoke. The others had eaten and gone to rest on their blankets, smoking their bedtime pipes.

Giles began to puzzle at what appeared to be a black stump between the giant paperbark trees, silhouetted against the night sky. He could not remember seeing a stump when the camp was being made. Giles tried harder to see clearly. As the smoke thinned on a puff of breeze, two more stumps appeared to have joined the first. Suddenly the gap between the trees filled with black stumps. Giles buckled on his cartridge belt and shouted. The explorers tossed aside their blankets, reaching for their weapons.

'An attack!' Giles shouted. 'Between the paperbarks. Fire in volley.'

The startled explorers aimed into the darkness and smoke, firing their carbines and revolvers. The reports made great crashes in the night. The black stumps rose up silently, and disappeared into the smoke.

'Follow them!' Ross ordered.

Some of the men grabbed for flaming sticks from the fire, crouching and dodging as they ran toward the paperbarks. But the area was deserted. Bundles of spears had been abandoned, some ten feet long, with a variety of killing heads: barbed, double-pronged, shovel-nosed and stone-pointed, each sharpened like a razor for the attack. The spears were collected to be burned in the camp fire. It was an uneasy night, the remainder of it. John Ross doubled the watch. In the early morning spears fell on the camp, thrown from a distance and spent on arrival.

Billy said, 'They're an angry lot of bastards hereabouts. They'd better keep their distance from me. The first bugger shakes a spear at me again is goin' ter get a bullet up his arse.'

John Ross had become grave. He had been mistaken about the tribesmen. Had Alfred Giles not persuaded him into setting watches, the party would have been murdered in their blankets.

'They'll noo be any more fraternising,' the Scot said, and then pointed at Billy, 'but there'll noo be shooting at the savages either.'

Next morning there was no sign of the tribesmen. Billy Hearne scouted for blood. He could find no evidence that the volley had found human targets.

The failure of the attack somehow settled Matthew's nerves. That must have been the danger he had sensed, he concluded, the premonition which had caused him to dream of the death scrub. His thoughts again leapt forward to the chance of meeting Martin. To reaching Port Darwin and taking a ship for home. Perhaps Martin might even ship out with him. Matthew tipped the battered brim of his eagle-feathered hat and smiled at Alfred Giles' back, jogging along in front of him. The Overland was catching up with its time schedule. All Adelaide would be festive on the day of its completion. As a veteran who had ventured into the unknown with Ross, path-breaking for others to follow, Matthew would be a celebrity. He certainly would cut a figure among the Adelaide girls!

Alfred Giles turned to inspect the pack horses. The long journey had begun to exhaust them. The local feed appeared to be lacking in nourishment. Many of the animals weren't much more than bags of bones. He squinted at Matthew, puffing on his habitual pipe.

'What are you smiling at, Matt?'

'Just my thoughts, Alfred.'

'Are you thinking about getting home?'

'Something like that.'

Alfred Giles nodded.

'Your family is going to be proud of you. There'll not be another young man like you in all the colony.'

Matthew was glad of the beard he had regrown. He could feel all his face blushing with pleasure.

The explorers had come to agree with Billy Hearne that Australia must be the most up-jumped land God ever made. They had crossed gibber plains, stunted, tormented-looking scrub country, oceans of sandhills, forest, great ranges that had waited for aeons to disclose their secrets to civilised men; deserts and oases of springs and palm trees. They had been starved of water over hundreds of miles, and then drunk deeply at sweet lakes that spread like inland seas. But now, far into the north of the continent, it was like being transported into another country altogether.

The new man, Abrahams, said, 'I've heard tell of jungle from old soldiers that had served in India. Never in me born days did I think to see the like of this in Australia.'

The rainforest was dense, with palms, flowering creepers and lush ferns. Mulga trees grew so straight and tall that their tops could not be seen. Parrots of dazzling plumage picked at berries and buds high above the heads of the men. In this stunning exuberance of nature, forward vision was reduced to about fifty yards. Ross tacked about for days, trying for more open country. They came out at last to easier travel, grassed and sandy, though still bountiful with much growth which, however, they could thread a way through. But again the men and horses suffered for want of water. Billy, Matthew and Abrahams each separated to make a search while the others rested.

A few miles into the more open country Matthew found a native well, a narrow hole some three feet deep. He lay and slopped the sweet water into his burning mouth and throat.

He could feel the restoring joy of it running in his stomach. Stronger, he fired his revolver as a signal of success. Then again at intervals of fifteen minutes, entertaining himself at the same time with target practice at a growth on a white gum. After the explorers had arrived and pitched themselves down to drink, the water bags were filled.

'Look,' Alfred Giles said, 'this is a soak. The well is refilling itself.'

He dug at the narrow walls with his sheath knife, clearing the earth away by handfuls.

'We can water the horses, one at a time. It will be enough to get them through. Some of them have already got the staggers.'

All that night and into the middle of the next morning, the twenty-five horses were watered. The walls of the well, which Alfred Giles widened, were now far enough apart for a horse to get its muzzle into the water. Again the expedition was able to proceed.

Ross was well out, leading, when he stopped and made a signal. He had cut across a pad of horse and bullock tracks, which caused no little remark and conjecture. It was a shock to come so unexpectedly on the traces of other white men.

Billy Hearne was the expert tracker now that Tom Crispe had been sent south.

'These are months old. We must be gettin' close ter the northern Overland camps.'

Each man felt a great excitement. They had waited long for this far appointment in the furthest reaches of the continent. Billy rode ahead.

'The tracks turn east,' said John Ross, pointing. The party swung gladly into line behind him.

Matthew got out his pipe, with which he still remained clumsy. He had had to ration himself in the use of matches because of his trouble in keeping it burning. They were close at last to the northern line! That meant he must be close to Martin. Matthew tingled with anticipation, trying to light the old tobacco in the bowl. He wanted to give a shout of hurrah. What if he and Martin were to meet on their birthday?

The next afternoon the Ross expedition struck the northern line. The poles were bare. There was neither wire nor insulators.

The stumps of the trees felled for poles were sprouting with new, green growth. There was no indication of horses or transport having recently passed on the track cleared beside the poles.

'They've been poling well ahead of the wire,' Alfred Giles commented optimistically.

Ross cut a stake, which he drove into the track, fixing a piece of board to it. On it he wrote:

'The Adelaide Overland Telegraph Exploring Expedition struck the telegraph road this day.'

He added the date and signed it, 'John Ross, Leader'.

Ross got out a bottle of rum from a pack and the men drank to the occasion, and to the memories of their hardship. It was easy going, following the track, like riding down King William Street, said Alfred Giles, compared to what they had already experienced. Their destination now seemed secure. It was a strange feeling after so many months of endeavour and challenge. The rum led Billy Hearne to take out his harmonica, which he played as they rode along.

'It's noo the bagpipes,' Ross called back, 'but keep playing, Billy.'

Three more camps were made beside the bare poles, with the usual morning troubles with the unhobbled horses. In the early morning of the fourth camp, Alfred Giles rode back from the mustering after a long delay.

'I can't find Gazelle.'

The mare was not given to wandering, as were most of the horses chosen to be hobbled.

'I saw a few blacks back there, but they scurried off. They didn't seem to be hostile. There's a bit of broken country to the west. Gazelle might have lost herself in it.'

Matthew jumped up. The prospect of meeting with Martin had made him restless. He couldn't sit still for more than a few minutes at a time.

'I'll go and look for Gazelle,' he volunteered.

'She's come a long way with us,' Alfred Giles said. 'We wouldn't want to lose her now.'

John Ross nodded. Matthew hurried to saddle his mount.

'Don't let no blacks walk up ter yer,' Billy Hearne called, 'friendly or not, the buggers.'

Twenty-four

In the long journey from the old depot at Daly Waters to the new location at the end of the wire, two of the Overlanders' bullock wagons had broken down. The great wheels splayed, the spokes jutted, and the timbers on both sides were gone, spilling the great coils of wire they carried on the ground. Until unloaded wagons could be sent back from the relocated depot, the drivers were left with them to protect the cargo from marauding blacks.

The track, cut through the bush for the line of poles, was often rough and hard going. Solomon, Martin and Eli were the envy of the others, riding in the new, sprung dray.

At the end of the wire, wells had been sunk into sweet water. A camp site had been cleared by the axemen who now greeted the arrival of the caravan with satisfaction. They had long been short of tea, sugar and tobacco. The new faces were also welcome, and the first night was given to the trading of adventures, facts and rumours. Martin's first enquiry was for news of Ross, but the men at the new camp had no information as to his whereabouts.

The hard work involved in packing up the old depot was now repeated in setting up the new, and Solomon's crew laboured at re-establishing the forge.

Then a delivery of mail temporarily halted work in the camp. There were some names which were not called, and those men turned aside to conceal the bitterness of their disappointment.

Martin's package was bulky, with letters from all his family back in Adelaide. Curiously, he opened the fat envelope addressed to him in Lucinda's handwriting. A bundle of newspaper clippings fell out, with a scribble from Lucinda in the margins.

'Lucinda has been married! My sister has married! It's all here in the newspapers. A society wedding at St Paul's, the ceremony conducted by the Bishop. How extraordinary! A man named David Baker.'

Solomon said, 'Well, now. And isn't it in the nature of women to marry? Taking it by the long and the short, that's what keeps the population going. Although I've known this one and that one to make contributions, absentminded, like, about the churching.'

Martin continued to read from the clippings.

'Who can he be? Good God! David Baker, of Gooryanawah. It's Tubby! Lucinda has married Tubby Baker. He's my brother Hannibal's best friend.'

'Being a provident man by nature,' Solomon said, 'I've kept a bottle of rum in the sea-bag. On such an occasion, might we not drink a tot to your sister's churching?'

The policeman who had delivered the mail also had news of the progress on the central line. To the cheers of the Overlanders, he announced that the Overland Telegraph was holding its own in the race with the marine cable.

The Overlanders were given half a day's rest to answer their mail, and Martin was busy all afternoon, almost filling a pad with his pencil. His father's letter had sounded more cheerful than his last, he thought. Old Hannibal had written that the twins' twenty-first birthday would be celebrated when they got home, whatever the date. Now that the two ends of the wire were nearing each other, business had already improved.

His father also wrote of Lucinda's wedding. Everyone in Adelaide society had attended the lavish reception. But nothing further had been heard from Matthew since his last letter from the Finke, when Ross had been refitting to again attempt the north.

In his letter to Martin, old Hannibal made no mention of the raised eyebrows and the curious stares that had followed his daughter's progress down the aisle. What, indeed, was all the hurry about, the appraising eyes seemed to ask? But relieved, seemingly miraculously, of the financial burdens that had been threatening to crush him, old Hannibal was immune to the undercurrents that coursed through the gathering. And Tubby – Tubby was so sublimely, so blissfully happy, that no undercurrent was even remotely apparent to him.

So Lucinda settled into Gooryanawah, soon firmly ensconcing herself as its mistress. The homestead she had previously thought of as pleasant and comfortable she now saw as somewhat shabby, and, she confided to Tubby, 'needing a woman's touch'. Tubby scratched at his chin and was glad that Ada was not within earshot. She had soon explored every niche of the house, even Ada's room when the housekeeper was out in the garden, noting with satisfaction the odd piece of furniture or china. This is mine, she thought, all mine now.

Five weeks from her wedding night, she planned to announce that she thought herself to be pregnant. She had stiffened herself for the first matrimonial love-making. Tubby had been initially tender, and then wild in his passion, astonishing Lucinda with his virility and experience. She began to enjoy his attentions beyond the necessities of her plot. She thought only once of Steven Woodrush, and then with contempt.

Five weeks later, to the day, Tubby and Lucinda arrived in Adelaide for a short stay at one of the city's finest hotels. Lucinda wasted no time in hurrying off to the doctor, and that evening Tubby was the delighted recipient of the startling news that his wife was, indeed, very likely pregnant.

'I must tell Mother and Father,' Lucinda said, when Tubby put her down from whirling her about the room.

'Of course you must. When shall we go?'

'I'd rather go alone, David.'

'Of course you would, my pet, I'll send a message to Han to meet me at the club. Why don't we have a little family dinner tonight? Invite your parents. I'll arrange something special with the manager of the hotel.'

Tubby was in the bar when young Hannibal arrived. He clutched his brother-in-law's elbow and hurried him into the lounge.

'What do you think, Han?'

'Think about what? Why are you and Lucinda back in town so soon?'

Tubby ordered drinks and cigars. Young Hannibal said that he preferred his cheroots.

'Not this time. Cigars are in order.'

'But I don't like the damned things.'

'You'll smoke this one, Han.'

Tubby's evident excitement puzzled young Hannibal.

'What's going on, Tubby? Where's Lucinda?'

'She's gone to see your mother. We're going to have a family dinner tonight, at my hotel.'

Young Hannibal became rebellious.

'I don't want a cigar. I want to know what's got you so up in the air.'

Tubby laughed, shaking his head.

'How'd you like to be an uncle, Han?'

'A what?'

'An uncle, you nitwit. I'm going to be a father. How's that for first past the post?'

Young Hannibal gasped.

'But you've only . . . I mean . . .'

Tubby thumped his friend's knee.

'That's right, old boy. I might even have set a track record.'

The excitement of having reached the poling of the northern line still beat hard in Matthew as he set off to search for the lost mare, Gazelle. It could not be much longer before the expedition met with an Overland camp. He tried not to torment himself with the hope that Martin might be in it. As his horse trotted forward, Matthew's feelings swung like a pendulum; the great adventure was almost over and soon he would be returning home. He should be glad. But in some ways the time before Ross had become scant and shadowy. He had come to love the men with whom he had shared so much, was already regarding with nostalgia the thousands of miles through which he and his companions had endured the violent, beautiful, unpredictable continent. Somehow the time with Ross had become more a part of his being than anything which had gone before.

Kangaroos bounded away before him, through the mixed growth in which he could still find no sign of the mare. The broken country reported by Alfred Giles must be further to the west. He put his mount into a canter, wiping at his neck with a sweat rag. The morning was beginning to heat up; a warm breeze dimpled the leaves on the trees.

The broken country appeared abruptly, an ancient geological scar, fissured with defiles. If Gazelle had ventured there, she could easily have lost herself. It was anybody's guess which gorge she had entered. Entering a narrow gully, the walls of red earth smooth and bare above him, Matthew leaned back from the saddle, hoping for tracks.

The four blacks who had been noiselessly following Matthew's progress from a distance, concealing themselves in the undergrowth as they went, pointed silently with their chins, and began to clamber to the top of the gully. They carried no weapons, only their digging sticks, as they crept ahead of the rider below, his head down as he searched for tracks.

The floor of the gully was carpeted in small stones. Even Tom Crispe or Billy Hearne would have difficulty tracking here, Matthew thought.

High above, the blacks were collecting small boulders, which they poised on the edge of the steep red wall, at a turn in the gully. Then they waited, watching the horse and rider picking their way towards them.

When Matthew reached the turn he rode forward a little and stopped. Ahead, the gully suddenly terminated in a sheer face of red earth. Cursing, he was turning his horse when the blacks pushed the first boulder down on top of him. It smashed into his shoulder and forearm, knocking him forward in the saddle. A smaller boulder glanced off the side of his head, felling him to the ground.

His startled horse galloped to the end of the gully, reared to wheel back over the stones, neighing as it slipped among them, saddle-bags flapping, its reins caught in its mane.

The blacks dropped on their bellies to stare curiously down at the unconscious man. Matthew lay on the stones, his smashed arm soaking blood on to the ground, his head dripping dark blood down his neck.

When the sun began to fill the chasm with light, the flies came. It was not long before they found the boy.

John Ross looked up at the sun and pulled worriedly at his thick beard.

'The laddie's been gone three hours.'

Billy Hearne chewed his lip.

'Matt's too good a bushman ter git 'imself lost.'

'We'll mount for a search anyway,' said the leader tersely.

All that day the explorers searched, Billy Hearne swearing over the tracks of the unhobbled horses.

'There no telling one from the other. I can't pick Matt's tracks among them.'

In the broken country, the explorers found the mare, Gazelle. She had indeed lost herself in the fissures, as Alfred Giles had suspected. The walls there were low, with cropping on the sides. Gazelle was finding what food she could, and waiting patiently to be taken back to camp.

Only a short distance away, Matthew lay on his back on the sharp stones. He could not account for the pain racking him, could read no meaning in the blank red wall of earth rearing above him. He scrabbled amongst the warm stones with his good hand, and fingered the rim of his old eagle-feathered hat beside him. Why was it lying there amongst the stones?

The flies buzzed.

In the late afternoon the explorers regrouped.

The new man, Abrahams, said, 'There's no sign of his horse. That has to be a good sign, at least.'

In the sunset, blazing the skyline with streaks of colour, the defeated explorers returned to camp. There they found Matthew's horse cropping with the hobbled animals, tripping on its reins as it stepped. Billy Hearne hurried forward.

'No sign 'er blood. But his canteen's on the saddle. Matt's got no water, wherever he is. That does it. I'm goin' fer the Overlanders.' John Ross nodded agreeement.

The little stockman saddled up a fresh horse. Alfred Giles, bringing him damper and jerky, enquired if Billy had any matches.

'I'm lightin' no bloody fires. When I leave that saddle, it'll be when I hit the Overland camp.'

All night Billy Hearne rode, except when he dismounted to walk and rest the big bay, following the naked poles which were his pale guidance in the almost moonless dark. At sunrise he ate and drank in the saddle, pushing the big bay onward. There might not be an Overland camp in hundreds of miles, he thought bitterly. He could be on a wild goose chase, while Matt lay dying. The tent and hutments of the new depot came, miraculously, into view at mid-morning. Billy grunted with relief.

The men who saw the lone rider galloping in from the south stopped in their tracks.

'Where the hell are you from?' one asked.

'I'm with Ross. He's down the line. Who's the boss here?'

'I'll get 'im,' another answered.

Billy dismounted, leaning against his saddle. The big bay dropped its head, breathing hard.

The explorers in whose track the line from the south had been strung had become legendary among the Overlanders. To have one of Ross's explorers in camp aroused great curiosity. The men stared at Billy while the overseer was being fetched.

News of the arrival of one of Ross's men took a little longer to reach Solomon's forge. Martin was feeding the furnace when an Overlander came in, rolling a hubless wagon wheel before him. He spoke laconically.

'One 'er Ross's explorers just came in from the south. He's with the boss in his tent.'

Martin turned, his eyes sparking in the light of the spitting red furnace.

'Did you say one of Ross's men? One of the explorers?'

'That's right, young 'un. A rough-lookin' little bastard, too.'

Dropping his log, Martin raced from the forge. Solomon looked quizzically over his anvil at the Overlander.

'What's put young Martin into bending his sails?'

'Don't know,' the wagon man answered. 'Might be somethin' to do with one of Ross's men being in the depot.'

Solomon wiped away his sweat.

'Hell's fire and Mother Carey's chickens! At last! It's long that Martin has been waiting on this meeting.'

Inside the overseer's tent, Billy Hearne broke off at the sound of racing footsteps. Then the tent flap lifted and Billy went white, the pannikin dropping from his hand.

'Matt . . . ?'

'I'm Martin, Matthew's twin. Where are the rest of you?'

Billy opened his mouth to speak. But no sound came.

The overseer shook his head, and, standing up slowly, he put a gentle arm around Martin's shoulders.

'Step outside with me a moment, young Martin.'

Trembling, Martin listened as the overseer haltingly explained.

'I'm getting a search party together. Don't take on. Our men will help the explorers find your brother.'

Martin tried to control his voice. This explained the premonition of danger he had felt for Matthew. It rose again inside him now, almost choking him.

'I must go with the men, Mr Evans.'

'I know. Take Eli's dray and two strong horses. The dray will be needed to carry water.'

Returning to his tent, the overseer took a bottle of rum from his trunk, and poured from it liberally into Billy's pannikin.

'You can do with this, if you're riding back without sleep.'

'Thanks. You know, I've been hearin' tell of Matt's twin brother since we first went out with Ross. Seein' 'im like that, I didn't know if I weren't seein' a ghost. It fair shook me up.'

'Here's a pipe and tobacco. Get what rest you can. I'll round up my best bushmen.'

Martin ran back to the forge, where Eli was unloading timber. Solomon ceased hammering when he saw Martin's face, recognising that something was badly wrong.

'It's Matthew,' Martin told him. 'He's lost. The explorer came in for help. I'm to take Eli's dray.'

'As to that,' Solomon said, 'Eli and Solomon will sign on with you.'

'You'd be of no use, Solomon. The boss is only sending bushmen.'

When Martin had run again from the forge, Solomon went to a bench and sat down. His crew stood around, uncomfortable and silent. Solomon leaned his pox-pitted face on the heel of his hand.

'The cruelty and beauty of the world,' he said. 'I've seen both of them. But it has long come to Solomon that there's a great lack of balance between the two. Old Nick is captain of the ship. And there is more than enough misfortune to lend him every assistance.'

In the gully there was a slight mercy in the cold of the night, for it helped to freeze the pain in his arm. In his infrequent returns to sense, bright pictures flashed across his mind, glimpses of lagoons and mountain ranges, of sandhills and porcupine grass, of Martin and the little attic room they used to share in their father's house.

An uncertain clarity returned to him with the warmth of the morning sun. He put out his hands to push himself up, toppling sideways on his useless arm. The pain that speared through him brought up a vomit which stuck to his mouth and chin. Again he tried to sit, using the good arm to prop himself up. The sickening throb in his head blurred his sight, as he leaned forward and squinted at the bloody mess of his arm, trying to understand.

The veils of darkness in his mind began to lift. He remembered now. He had gone out to search for the missing mare, Gazelle. Something had struck him. Something had struck him again.

He touched the wound on his head and looked up at the sun. It hadn't moved much, he thought. He couldn't have been there for long.

Then he became aware of his thirst: every cell in his body seemed parched. His arm trembled with weakness as he strove to unbuckle his belt, looping it around the smashed arm above the elbow, pulling it tight. With a great effort, he swayed to his feet, leaning against the wall of the gully, closing his eyes against the dizziness. Haltingly, he began to move towards the entrance of the gorge.

Then, abruptly, the colour faded from the glowing red walls, and the gorge became dark again.

* * *

There were a great many gullies and defiles in the badlands, some running for miles before intersecting others. The explorers rode them all that day on their used-up horses, until the animals failed for lack of water. When the men returned to camp on the second day, there were few words spoken between them.

Alfred Giles said, 'Unless Billy finds an Overland camp nearby, help will arrive too late for Matthew.'

The Overlanders detailed by the overseer followed Billy Hearne back to the camp on their well-fed, well-watered horses. Billy was on a mount exchanged for the bay. The little stockman had been in the saddle on the first day's search for Matthew, and all that night and into the morning. And now he was in the saddle again, riding into the lengthening day.

Miles behind, Martin followed in Eli's dray. Two barrels of water were tied down securely behind him, with blankets and a medical kit; a horse was tied to the tailboard, to rest the animal in the shafts. A bullock driver sat beside Martin, to rest him also when the time came.

In the widely-shot colours of the setting sun, which appeared to lodge in the tops of the trees, the bullock driver nudged the silent and tensed figure at his side.

'We'll change horses now, young 'un. I'll drive the dray. You can take a spell on the blankets.'

Martin, knowing he had to save his strength, nodded wordlessly.

At the depot, Martin's unoccupied box by the fire drew the eyes of his two friends.

'I've prayed,' Eli said. 'I've prayed for Martin and the other.'

Solomon nodded.

'It's also prayer, as you might say, that Solomon has made. But Solomon has black and more black in his log, Eli. I doubt if Solomon will be much heard by the Almighty.'

When the mounted Overlanders reached the explorers' camp in the early hours of the morning, Alfred Giles was up, heaping wood on the fire that served as a beacon. The others were soon out of their blankets, putting cans of water on the fire to boil.

Billy Hearne's face was haggard.

'Yer found nothin'? No sign?'

Alfred Giles shook his head.

'The further we went into that broken country the more and the worse it got.'

The Overlanders were awkward in their awe of the explorers, particularly of the tall and gaunt Ross.

'Matt's twin were in the depot,' Billy Hearne told Ross. 'He's comin' in on a dray. The first sight I took fair shook me. For a minute there I thought I were lookin' at Matt.'

In the early morning, before first light, the dray arrived. For a few moments Ross and his party stared at Martin, silently.

Then Ross put out his hand.

'It's much we've heard of you, laddie, in all this long time.'

'I came on the Overland in the hope of meeting Matthew,' said Martin. 'And we were so close. What do you think has happened to him?'

'We dinna ken, laddie. Take your rest. It's early we'll be riding.'

Martin lay in his blankets, his eyes opened to the stars. He could feel the presence of his brother, could sense he was close and in pain. A refrain repeated endlessly in his head.

'I'll find you. I'll find you. I'll find you, Matthew.'

Twenty-five

When Steven Woodrush rode away from the drive, after the clubbing of John Milner, he followed the central line south. He was occasionally provisioned by the Overland camps that he passed. He rode close to the poles, in great fear of the blacks and often hungry, being unarmed and unable to hunt. His fear of the wild country was so multiplied by his solitude that sobs sometimes shook him as he rode. Once in the safe proximity of the camps he would sometimes lie idle for days, too listless to do much more than doze in the shade.

Steven was cautious of speaking to the men he met. He had made up a story to explain himself. Until recently he had been with the Milners, but now Ralph Milner had sent him back to Adelaide with messages. The Overlanders thought that this unmanly-looking stranger was an odd one for the Milners to hire, on a great stock drive across the continent, but they kept their silence.

The understandings of himself which had come to Steven dissipated with his courage. He desperately needed someone to lean on, someone who would direct him, as Lucinda had done. His idea of being an evangelist to bushmen misted away in his misery. So did the safety of the church. With Lucinda, he decided he could be someone, even as her chattel. With Lucinda as his wife, he under her protective wing, Steven could grow again in his own esteem.

He had to get back to her. In the dazed muddle of his thoughts, he rode south with an idea that had become an obsession.

He wanted to get out of the hellish bush as fast as he could. He could almost see and feel Lucinda, her body, her whispered words, the certainty of her character. Let Lucinda use him as she wished. She would be his meaning and salvation. The Harpers were wealthy. Lucinda and her mother would see that he was found a place in the business. He would eventually wear down young Hannibal's hostility. Somewhere ahead there would be peace and safety and security.

On Gooryanawah, at shearing time, Lucinda quickly tired of Ada's company. Tubby was gone from the homestead long before she left the bed, and when she awoke, her heart sank at the prospect of another endless day. She took to bullying the young black housegirls, picking at them for faults.

Ada observed how restless the mistress of Gooryanawah had become. At first she had feared that Lucinda might take over the running of things, but Lucinda had shown little interest. She had also become a little careless about her hair and dress. Ada thought that Lucinda might have a reason.

'Do you feel unwell in the mornings, dear?'

'Unwell? Why should I?'

'There is such a thing as morning sickness, in your condition.'

'I've never heard of it. Whatever it is, I don't have it.'

Lucinda was petulant. She missed the entertainment and distractions of her life in Adelaide. There was no company on Gooryanawah in which to flirt and display herself.

'Must you be gone all day, David?' she complained to her husband. 'I'd like to go on a picnic.'

'You know it's the shearing season, my pet. There's all the property to muster. The shearing shed has to be bossed. I've got all kinds of tallies to keep, decisions to make. The shearers always find something to complain about. Burred wool, the food, the pay, the wash-house, their hutments. It's the same every year. I've got to be everywhere at once. I had trouble with the wool-classer – doesn't know his job. It's too late to get another.'

Lucinda pouted. She did not see that the sheep could not be left to their own devices.

'Before we were married you took me riding. We had picnics at the lagoon, champagne lunches. Why can't we go riding now?'

Tubby was startled.

'Riding? In your condition? You can get that out of your head, Lucinda. Right out of your head. Any time you want, I'll have the stable boy prepare the pony and trap for you and Ada.'

'I see Ada every day, all day. Why can't you come with me? You've got a manager. Let him manage.'

'Bertie Chivers is as much up to his ears as I am. And his bad knee is giving him trouble. Can't you understand, my pet?'

'Very well. Ada and I shall take the pony and trap and inspect your wretched shearing shed.'

Now Tubby was really aghast.

'For God's sake! I'd have a strike on my hands – the shearers think it's bad luck to have a woman around the shed.' He paused, calculating. 'In six weeks, or two months, we can spend some time in Adelaide.'

Tubby put down the brandy he habitually poured when he came in from the paddocks. He knocked dust wearily from his soiled and sweated shirt.

'I'll wash and change. Then we can take a drink in the garden before dinner.'

He leaned and kissed Lucinda on the lobe of her ear.

'I don't know what I'd do without you, pet.'

When Lucinda appeared for breakfast next morning there was even more petulance in her manner.

Ada asked mildly, 'Would you like to borrow a book, my dear? I've quite a library in my room.'

'I don't read books. They give me an ache in the head. Have you any fashion magazines?'

'My time for fashion magazines is long past. Why don't you ask David to have them sent up from Adelaide?'

Lucinda decided that indeed she would. There was something else she had in mind. She would ask David for a piano. A truly good one. Lucinda missed her hours of fantasy at the piano.

As the sun rose, the explorers and Overlanders made a quick breakfast while Alfred Giles mustered the horses. John Ross held a short conference, drawing maps in the dirt to instruct the Overlanders, attempting to identify the upheavals and troughs which the explorers had already searched. Because of the possibility that Matthew had been attacked by blacks, Ross advised the new men to look to their weapons and be on guard.

Alfred Giles became anxious when he saw Martin saddling one of the horses.

'The lad's no bushman, John. We don't want to lose both Harpers.'

Billy Hearne was standing beside Ross.

'Yer can't leave 'im in camp. He'd fret clear away. I'll ride with the boy. That way there won't be no worry.'

John Ross nodded.

'Tell him, Billy.'

The men rode in a group through the bush country, now much patterned by horse tracks. When the broken country appeared, Ross halted the searchers to deliver his final instructions. The men wheeled on their mounts to take the directions which John Ross assigned them. The explorers knew that if Matthew were to be found alive, it had to be on this day or never. Otherwise, unless by a miracle he had found water, he would die of thirst, if nothing else, baked and withered away, choking on his own cracked and swollen tongue.

Billy Hearne and Martin had been given a wide circle to ride before entering the badlands. Martin was cramped with tension. Billy could see it in the muscles of the bare forearms, in the way he sat the saddle, in the strained ligaments of his neck.

'Yer surely look like 'im. Only younger.'

'I was never as big as Matthew.'

Billy Hearne was thinking that Martin would be bigger and stronger than his twin on this day. He said nothing. They rode for an hour in silence.

'It's a wide scout,' Billy said. 'We'd better get these nags moving.'

Billy put his horse into a fast canter, weaving through the timber in stockman's fashion, ducking the low branches.

Martin rode well, Billy had observed. He would be able to follow. It was some time before Billy looked back. When he did, there was no rider behind him.

The little stockman reined in, cursing. Where the blazes was Matt's twin? How had he lost him? He waited, looking back. Nothing moved among the trees. Billy cursed again, cantering to where he had last spoken to the boy. He tracked about and found Martin's trail. It went off at a right angle, west, directly towards the broken country. Billy pulled off his hat and banged it on the saddle.

'Godamighty! Is he loony, or what?'

The bush, as always, remained mute. Billy jammed his hat on and began tracking Matthew's twin.

In the gully, Matthew pulled at his belt to tighten the tourniquet. There were maggots now in the exposed flesh of his arm. He couldn't feel them feeding. Matthew knew from a story Tom Crispe had told that maggots could be useful in a wound, eating the flesh before it poisoned. The maggots had lengthened and fattened from when he had first observed them.

Matthew had passed beyond thirst. His swelling tongue could barely move around the pebble he had put in his mouth to suck. He had no strength to move further, it was useless to try. As useless as the matches in his pocket. There was nothing in the cutting that would burn, nothing that could put up smoke. At times Matthew fell into a doze, a lantern slide of images flickering intermittently in his mind. The death scrub often appeared. Matthew could see himself running from it, as clearly as if he were another person, looking down from a height. He knew now why the death scrub had haunted him.

Sometimes these flashes of lucidity were painful to bear. He could see Martin, as if his twin stood before him. See his father, mother, Lucinda, Hannibal, gathered at the family table. Why had he not been found? Had Ross deserted him in this, his own arid scrub of death? This stony, red-walled place in which his bones would bleach and crumble, as had those in that green outcrop in the desert where no other trees grew, nourished on dead flesh and dried blood?

He closed his eyes, passing into oblivion.

Just as Billy Hearne had put his horse into a canter to weave and duck through the trees, Martin had seemed to hear himself being called by Matthew. The voice was clear as it beckoned Martin towards it. Martin had turned towards this summons as though in a trance, forgetful of Billy Hearne, forgetful of everything. The summons became louder, more urgent. Martin felt his stomach pitch and crawl as he kicked his horse into a gallop, blind to the trees which the horse narrowly avoided, insensate to the growth that whipped at his chest and face.

Billy Hearne was following in Martin's tracks.

'Godamighty! He must've gone like a bat outa hell,' he said to himself.

The tracks did not deviate in their line to the west, except in the skirting of obstacles. Billy gave up tracking and cantered in the same direction. The broken country stopped him, confronting him with a labyrinth of ravines like the fingers of a hand spread wide. Matt's twin had vanished. Billy began to doubt his own sanity. He took off his hat to scratch his perplexed head. Why had he volunteered to nursemaid a loony? Bily began tracking again, scouting the entrances to the ravines. When he cut across the first faint tracks the breath went out of his lungs. When he cut across the new tracks, not far away, the little stockman was too thunderstruck to do more than gape at them.

'Godamighty!' he whispered.

He rode into the deep, narrow gully floored with round, smooth stones, following where the old and the new tracks had entered. Billy shook his head in disbelief. How could such a thing be? How could Matt's twin have known? Billy hurried his horse over the stones, feeling goose-pimples on his skin. What would Martin have found? Would Matt be alive? Then the little stockman had to rein in for an instant, at the shock of what he saw ahead. One boy held another cradled in his arms, held a canteen of water to the other's lips. Two brothers, mirror images of each other, their heads of fair hair close together, oblivious to everything else.

Twenty-six

At the end of the shearing season, with the flocks on Gooryanawah spilling back naked into the paddocks, white and skinny, unburdened of their weathered fleece, Tubby again took Lucinda to Adelaide. Lucinda fairly flew about, calling on her friends and family. Tubby spent much time at the track, watching his two thoroughbreds working and holding long discussions at the stables with his trainer, as well as lunching with his chums and playing cards at the club. He had Lucinda's family to dinner at his hotel and entertained Lucinda's friends when she asked that he should. They had already gone together to order a piano. It pleased Tubby to see Lucinda so happy.

'She's having a great time,' he told young Hannibal, 'just like the old Lucinda. It's a bit lonely for her at home. Lucinda will settle in when the baby comes, though. That will be the day, eh, Han?'

Lady Charlotte Bacon had declined to attend Lucinda's reception, or the wedding ceremony, on the pretext of being unwell. Lucinda decided to face down her friend's disapproval. The meeting was not a success. Lady Charlotte had been courteous but formal. Lucinda cut short her visit.

On the Sunday Tubby and Lucinda attended the morning service at St Paul's with the family. Following the service, Tubby returned with the ladies to the Harper home for Sunday dinner.

Old Hannibal and young Hannibal walked by the Torres, as had been their habit. Old Hannibal had taken it up again. He had stopped the Sunday walks after the gold hoax, when so much that was habitual had been disrupted. But now with the recovery of the family business his watch chain no longer sagged on him as it had done.

'There's talk of building more rail,' old Hannibal ruminated. 'The government is getting cocky, now that the Overland is near completion. The overseas business of all the colonies will be passed along that wire. There will be money in the coffers. Lots of money, Hannibal. I confess I was wrong at first about the Overland.'

He pointed his walking stick at the river.

'The city should get rid of those weeds. The pesky things are spreading. They rot, and make mess and slime.'

'Transport will be required to build the new rail, Father,' young Hannibal remarked. 'Charles Todd has just about everything on wheels working on the Overland. Harper and Son could build the transport for the new rail. I've already made an initial approach for the contract.'

Old Hannibal stopped.

'What's that you say?'

'I've already made an approach for the contract.'

'Why didn't you mention it?'

'It was only a feeler, at first.'

'At first? And now? Speak up, won't you?'

'I think we can depend on it.'

'Depend on it?'

'I think so, Father.'

Old Hannibal whipped at the grass with his stick.

'Well I'll be damned! You think we can depend on it? You really think that?'

'I have a final appointment with the government contractor tomorrow evening at the club.'

'Where's Tom with the damned carriage?' old Hannibal demanded. 'I've got an appetite today.'

The family had received no news of Matthew in many months. He had dated a letter from the Finke on the day before Ross was to try again for the north. Harvey, the surveyor, had resigned, Matthew had written. This news worried old Hannibal. But young Hannibal had reassured him – of course Ross would replace Harvey with another surveyor. He would hardly go north by compass.

Martin's letters, as usual, had been full of anecdote and description. Mrs Harper kept them in her bureau, adding to them one by one, tying them with a ribbon. She intended to have them bound in leather when Martin came home. Mrs Harper felt that she almost knew the quiet Englishman, Eli Stubbs, and the American with the strange name, the whaler, had become almost a romantic figure to her.

While the two Hannibals waited on the carriage, old Hannibal went into reflection.

'In a few months, Han, everything could be back to normal. Martin's safe, and Ross must be in the north by now. There have been times when I never thought to see the day. Can you imagine it? The twins at home, the business prospering, Tubby repaid?'

Old Hannibal frowned at himself.

'Lucinda has expressly asked that we should refer to Tubby as David. I utterly forgot, at the church.'

'Tubby has been Tubby to me since we were at school. He'd think me a damned fool if I started calling him David. Lucinda can jump in the Torrens.'

'I must try to remember,' old Hannibal said. 'After all, we owe a great deal to Tubby's generosity.'

He paused, and then banged the ground with his stick.

'Dammit! You see? There I go again, calling him Tubby.'

When the Bakers returned to Gooryanawah, Tubby made extra opportunities to be with his wife. Lucinda had begun to swell, a development which Tubby thought to be early.

'When does it usually begin to show?' he asked Ada, in the kitchen. 'Pregnancy, I mean. Lucinda seems to be well away.'

Ada was busy baking.

'There are no rules, David. It depends on the way the mother is built. I had a friend in New South Wales who showed practically nothing, as late as seven months. Lucinda must be of the other type.'

Tubby nodded. He had once had a brood mare like that. You could see that she was carrying a foal almost before the stallion got off her.

Lucinda had made calculations on her writing pad, estimating her time carefully. Well before that date, she would insist on a visit to her parents. She would stay there until the baby was born, seemingly prematurely. Lucinda checked her notes against the calendar. Then she tore the page into tiny pieces.

As Steven Woodrush neared the Peake, the urgency driving him towards Lucinda had become a compulsion that jangled his mind and nerves. Nothing else in the world held significance. The horse he rode had become a ribby wreck, saddle sore for lack of attention, poor from the little feed if could find at the end of the long reins which Steven had cut to tie into a tether at night. He would have to get a new horse at the Peake. His own provisioning had not been much better than that of his mount, and he trembled with weakness when he walked.

There was much news at the Peake when, finally, he arrived. The impossible had almost been achieved. The race between the longest wire and the marine cable would now almost certainly be won by the wire. Charles Todd and an assistant had been up and down the line, driving in a sulky, locating the positions for the telegraph relay stations and seeing to their building. There was to be a big complex in the centre at Alice Springs.

The supply camp at the Peake had shrunk as the central line advanced to Alice Springs and across the ranges. The Overlanders there were cheery with achievement and the prospect of returning soon to their homes. Steven Woodrush, repeating his story that he was carrying messages south for Ralph Milner, was made welcome. He was fed in the mess tent on stew and fresh damper, eating as a man famished. His clothing was threadbare and rent.

'Funny bugger,' one Overlander remarked. 'There's something wrong there. Wild in the eye, he is. Educated, though. But he's no stockman, that's for sure.'

Steven slept for hours after eating, finding some shade and using his saddle for a pillow. With the consideration common to bushmen, a drover approached him when the young man awoke.

'Could yer do with a bit o' terbacca, mate?'

'I don't smoke,' Steven answered, propping himself up on an elbow.

'That nag you've got is done in. I'll hobble him to feed if yer like.'

'Thank you.'

'Here's a newspaper. It's an oldie. We don't get many. Yer might like ter have a read.'

'Thank you,' Steven said again.

The drover unbridled Steven's horse and led it away by the mane.

Steven lay back for a moment, his head on the saddle, the ancient, much-thumbed copy of the Adelaide *Advertiser* in his hand. He spoke Lucinda's name aloud. His need of her was like a pain in his body. She would be his refuge. He would be esteemed by all, with Lucinda Harper as his wife. Her father might set them up in a house. There had been a small legacy from the mother he had never known which the Bishop had been managing for him since Steven first became a church ward. He would keep that matter a secret, until he knew what Lucinda might have, or expect.

When these thoughts ran out, Steven sat up again and tried to read the newspaper. But he found it hard to concentrate, and almost missed the account of Lucinda Harper's society wedding at St Paul's, to David Baker of Gooryanawah.

The tattered margins of the old newspaper shook in his hands as though windblown. The type shimmered and jumped into a meaningless mass. The same whimpering which had filled his head when the Aboriginal stepped towards John Milner with his club loudened into a scream. Woodrush held his head, rocking his body. He felt that his brains were bursting, that his heart and body were bursting.

'No . . . no . . . no . . .'

The anguished cry was repeated.

'No . . . no . . . no . . .'

In the last light before darkness an Overlander, who had been out hunting, hurried, ashen-faced, into camp. He called urgently to his companions.

'That bloke from the Milners' drive! He's back there in the timber, hangin' from a tree. He done himself in with his own reins. Get the boss. I didn't know whether ter touch him or not. He's dead, though, right enough. Stone dead.'

As the child continued to grow inside her, Lucinda became more careless of herself. She bitterly resented this burden that she carried, the backaches, the loose gowns it became necessary for her to wear. Tubby's patient consideration increased as Lucinda's discontent mounted, and he stoically endured the frequent crashings on the piano which appeared to be her only interest. There was little affection between them. Lucinda had become chilly. She retired early on most nights, to leaf through piles of fashion magazines in bed. Tubby sat up alone, pensively drinking port. Ada sometimes suggested a game of cribbage or draughts, which Tubby played without interest.

'I thought pregnant women were supposed to be happy. Glowing, or something. Lucinda's about as happy as a bloody bear in a barrel. You've heard her on the piano. She plays as though she'd like to destroy it. I'm thinking of pulling the loud pedal off the bloody thing.'

'I think Lucinda's playing goes with her moods. You must be patient, dear. Pregnancy affects each woman differently.'

'How would you know? You've not had children.'

Tubby stopped, appalled at what he had said, but it was too late. Ada dropped her head in sadness.

'Crissake, Ada,' he said miserably, 'forgive me, will you? I must be a right rotter to say a thing like that.'

'It's just that you're upset and concerned. Lucinda might be frightened. It's not easy, giving birth.'

Tubby scratched his round chin.

'Never thought of that. I see what you mean. If Lucinda is frightened, she's never let on. Why didn't I think of that?'

'Be patient, dear.'

'Never thought of that. I've probably been around animals too long.'

When the date Lucinda had chosen began to draw near, she

again made herself amiable to her husband. Tubby was delighted by this change in her and remarked on it to Ada. Lucinda chose her moment, the habitual drink before dinner in the garden.

Tubby frowned as he passed Lucinda her drink.

'I really don't know if you should be drinking. You're well on the way. The thing is, I don't know anything about this business. All I know is brood mares and sheep.'

Lucinda skilfully changed the subject.

'David, I've been missing my mother so much. I'd like to go home for a few weeks. You wouldn't mind, would you?'

'I'd mind, sure enough. I'd miss you like hell.'

Tubby remembered his conversation with Ada.

'Are you perhaps a bit frightened, my pet? is that why you'd like to go home?'

'Frightened?'

'You know. Giving birth and all that.'

Lucinda seized the opportunity.

'Perhaps I am,' she said. 'It would be a comfort to talk to Mother about it. To know what to expect.'

Ada had been right, Tubby thought. Lucinda had been plain frightened. That explained her moods. And all the time she had kept it to herself. Tubby felt such a shaft of love and pride for his wife for a moment that he could not speak.

'When would you like to go?'

'Would the end of the week be suitable?'

'Very well, pet. But I'll miss you like hell.'

Looking ahead, a few weeks became a long time to Tubby.

'Wouldn't a week do?'

'A week passes so quickly. Do you realise that I've not yet bought baby clothes, although Mother has been sewing and knitting for weeks? We haven't even thought about a cradle or a pram.'

Tubby slapped his forehead.

'I'm a great father, aren't I? I bought new horse blankets for the blood stock when we were in Adelaide. I never gave a thought to what my own child might need. I don't know how you put up with me. I'm a bloody great nitwit. A man's own child, coming into the world naked.'

Lucinda had to laugh.

'You don't expect it to be fully clothed, do you?'

Tubby looked blank for a moment, and then laughed with Lucinda.

'A nitwit. A bloody great nitwit. That's what you've got for a husband, pet.'

The stirrings and kickings which Lucinda had been feeling had much increased, but in the celibacy which Lucinda had declared, she was able to keep this from her husband. She wore a light bodice to bed and a heavy petticoat under her nightgown. She knew that her time was soon coming and could hardly wait to get the wretched business over and done with.

The stable boy took a note to the railhead, announcing Lucinda's imminent arrival to the family.

Mrs Harper so cosseted Lucinda that her daughter began to feel stifled.

'Don't fuss so, Mother. I'm perfectly well. I just needed a little break from Gooryanawah.'

'I know exactly how you feel, dear. Sometimes, in the early days at Port Lincoln, I felt that I could scream. You can't imagine what the colony was like all those years ago. And me from a good English home, put down in a pioneer's hut.'

Lucinda, in the light of her own experience, tried to imagine how it must have been for her mother. She had never considered it before. Two weeks passed. In the beginning of the third week an anxious letter arrived from Tubby. Why had Lucinda not yet given him a date of return? Lucinda decided not to answer the letter. If she pretended to be unwell as the excuse of her protracted stay, David would be on the next train to Adelaide. The stirrings inside her had become extreme. She prayed that the baby would come soon. Whatever happened, she had to stay on in Adelaide.

Old Hannibal had returned to his evening commentaries on the news, as he had returned to his Sunday walks by the Torrens. He had made only one remark on Lucinda's extended stay. He didn't think it fair to Tubby.

'David,' Lucinda reminded him.

At the end of the third week Lucinda was reading constantly in the big book, *Family Doctor*, which was present in almost every colonial household. Getting about had become slow and laborious. The slightest thing caused her to quiver with nerves. She was carrying in a tray of cocoa from the kitchen when she heard her father's exclamation.

'Good Lord! Do you remember that chap from St Paul's? Woodrush? The one that went off with the Milners?'

The name temporarily opened the doors in Mrs Harper's ears, which had closed automatically when her husband began his comments on the press. She paused in her knitting of a baby blanket.

'What is it?'

'The fellow went and hanged himself, at the Peake. He was travelling south from the drive.'

A great sound filled Lucinda's ears, like a rush of wind. For an instant she staggered, while the sitting room spun and darkened, then fell forward in a deep faint, the spilled tray of cups and saucers, the sugar bowl and silver pot beneath her. Mrs Harper screamed. The two Hannibals jumped from their chairs.

Lucinda did not stir as the men were getting her upstairs. Mrs Harper sponged at the cocoa-soaked gown, brought cologne to bathe her daughter's forehead. She had become calm, almost forceful, her voice level and steady. She addressed her son.

'Hannibal? Hurry for Doctor Thornhill. I think Lucinda is in labour. It could be a premature birth.'

Old Hannibal wiped at his forehead and scalp, his waistcoat quivering on his churning stomach.

'What are we to do, woman?'

'There's nothing that you can do. Go downstairs. I will care for Lucinda until Doctor Thornhill arrives.' She paused. 'Off you go, Hannibal,' she repeated, as her husband stood still.

Downstairs, old Hannibal poured himself a shaky brandy. There was a risk in any birth, let alone one premature. He collected the broken china, set the spilled pot upright and took the tray to the kitchen, little aware of what he was doing. Suppose that Tom Thornhill was out? It was his grandchild – his first grandchild. Old Hannibal wiped at his forehead and eyes, blew into his handkerchief. Suppose that Lucinda had injured herself, falling like that? It didn't bear thinking about. Old Hannibal hurried up the stairs again. He opened the door and looked in.

'How is she?'

Mrs Harper had Lucinda in a nightgown. She turned her head when she heard her father's voice. Her own was thin and weak.

'Don't worry, Daddy.'

The childish 'Daddy' was too much for old Hannibal. He had to get out his handkerchief and wipe at his eyes.

'Go downstairs,' said Mrs Harper gently. 'There's nothing that you can do.'

Old Hannibal blundered down the stairs, leaning heavily on the railing.

'He hanged himself,' Lucinda whispered. 'He hanged himself, Mother.'

'Don't think about that. We have other things to do. When the pains come, push with your feet at the bed end.'

Old Hannibal waited in his chair, starting at every outside sound. He heard his wife's voice again, taking control upstairs. She had been like that in the old days. What a wife she had been to him then! He rose, hearing the clatter of Doctor Thornhill's trap, and opened the door for the doctor, midwife and young Hannibal.

The baby, a boy, was born before midnight. When it was all over, Doctor Thornhill stood with the brandy that old Hannibal had pressed on him. Mrs Harper took him aside.

'He's a fine little fellow, considering that he's premature,' she said firmly. 'Don't you think so, Doctor Thornhill?'

Thornhill removed his glasses, polished them and reclipped them to his nose.

'Indeed he is, Mrs Harper. Considering that he's premature. Where is Lucinda's husband?'

'He's on his property. Lucinda was paying a visit. She fainted and fell. That must have been what brought it on.'

'Indeed, indeed. Well, well. I must be going. I feel somewhat tired.'

Old Hannibal escorted Thornhill to the door.

'I can't thank you enough, Tom. Can't thank you enough. Both mother and baby are well, you say?'

'There's nothing to worry about, Hannibal. The midwife will take care of things tonight. I'll be back in the morning.'

In the sitting room young Hannibal lit a cheroot.

'Wait until Tubby hears. He'll go through the roof. What a night this has been.'

Mrs Harper said, 'I have to make up a bed for the midwife, in the twins' room.'

Old Hannibal looked up the stairs, cocking his head to listen.

'Shouldn't the baby be crying? You bawled your head off, Han.'

Young Hannibal decided to ignore this.

'I'll get a message off to Tubby, first thing in the morning. He's going to come in like a cyclone. An heir for Gooryanawah! You'd better prepare yourself, Father.'

'I'm prepared for anything now,' old Hannibal stated. 'A grandson, Han. Can you believe it?'

It had been arranged that the midwife would stay on for a few days, as nurse to Lucinda and her baby. Mrs Harper took fresh linen to the twins' room. The cups Matthew had won at sports were arranged on the mantel. Martin's old cricket bat and his shelf of books stood beside his bed. There were many other reminders of the twins in the attic. It had been for that reason that Mrs Harper had for so long avoided the room. Now she sat on Matthew's bed, her hands clasped in her lap. How extraordinary that Lucinda had called for Steven Woodrush in her labour. She must have been reacting to the impact of hearing her father remark on the tragedy. They had been friends. Why would a young man do a thing like that? A student for the clergy as well. Wasn't suicide a sin?

The other matter on Mrs Harper's mind had to be confronted. Lucinda's child was not premature. It was a lusty, well developed infant. There was only one possible conclusion to reach. It was hard to believe it of Lucinda, but it did explain David's insistence on such a hasty marriage. Mrs Harper sat deliberating and came to a decision. Least said, soonest mended, she thought to herself. No comment would ever pass her lips.

The two Hannibals, being men, would never even notice.

Lucinda was almost recovered by next evening, sitting up prettily in bed to receive visits from the family. Doctor Thornhill looked in, to check on mother and child.

'Lucinda?' he answered, to Mrs Harper's question. 'It's going to be hard to keep her in bed. Lucinda is as strong as a horse.'

Lucinda was unaware that she had called on Steven Woodrush during her labour. All she could remember was the excruciating pain tearing at her insides. But it was done. All done. She lay back and tried to feel something. Something substantial and enduring. Some thread of continuity on to which she could hold. Nothing came. What she could feel seemed to whizz past her without touching, like the trees she had watched from the train. Why had Steven hanged himself? She felt differently towards him now, with his son asleep beside her. She felt a tenderness for the baby, but no love for it had come with its birth. She must forget Steven Woodrush, put everything about him out of her mind. It could be dangerous, otherwise. She could not afford any indulgence in sentiment. The baby had been fathered by her husband. That was what she must remember, only that. Lucinda nodded at a new thought. That Steven Woodrush could never return to claim his son would simplify things for her.

Tubby had not come in like a cyclone, as young Hannibal had predicted. He had arrived travel-stained and almost speechless, stuttering his greetings before Mrs Harper led him upstairs. It was a long time before he rejoined the family. He had been down on his knees beside Lucinda's bed. Young Hannibal decided to get Tubby out of the house, into the more familiar surroundings of his club. Tubby improved after a few drinks, which he swallowed like water.

'I didn't know it would be like this, Han. I'm shaken to the soles of my boots. How beautiful Lucinda looks. She almost looks like something holy.'

'She looks well, if that's what you mean.'

'I was out in the paddocks when one of the hands arrived with your message. I don't mind telling you, I bloody near fell out of the saddle. Your mother says that Thornhill told her it won't matter that the baby was premature. He's well made and strong. What would he have been like had he gone all the way? He'd have been a whopper. I'm going to name him Harold, after the old Dad.'

Tubby had come to Adelaide straight from the paddocks, in his work clothes, and was oblivious to the disapproving stares from club members and staff.

'Harold Hannibal Baker. How does that sound?'

'Father will appreciate it.'

'I'm going to have a bloody great christening party. Harold Hannibal Baker . . . I don't think he much looks like me. I'm gingery. He's dark. A bit of a throwback perhaps. You can see Lucinda in him, though.'

A steward whispered in Tubby's ear.

'I'd forgotten how I'm dressed, Han. I'll have to get hold of some decent clothes. Come with me. I'll get flowers for Lucinda. I'll fill the bloody room. I tell you, I still don't know if I'm on my head or my feet.

The midwife had taken Lucinda's baby to bathe it in Mrs Harper's bedroom, where it made considerable noise. The first breast feedings had hurt Lucinda's nipples. When Lucinda contemplated having to do this for perhaps a year, she began to fill with anger and despair.

She arranged herself on the pillows. She would put off the return to Gooryanawah by every day she could. Tubby would want more children. She would be stuck there on Gooryanawah. Stuck for as far into the future as she could see. A brood mare for her husband, in the midst of hundreds of thousands of sheep. His life and her life riveted to their seasons of lambing, marking, crutching, shearing, living and dying. And every day, all day, Ada. Wallowing in the children, being unfailing in her understanding and consideration. How many more children would she be forced to take to her breast, after this one?

It had all been her own doing. Lucinda could smell retribution as she could smell the milky, sickening sweetness of herself and the child. A darkening as distinct as a cloud covering the sun appeared on Lucinda's face.

'Dammit! Dammit! Dammit!' she cried. 'Damn everything to hell.'